RHYTHM OF THE ROAD

(Lost Kings MC #16)

AUTUMN JONES LAKE

COPYRIGHT

Rhythm of the Road (Lost Kings MC #16)
Copyright 2020 Autumn Jones Lake
Cover Photographer: Wander Aguiar Photography
Cover Designer: Lori Jackson Design
Model: Jeff Button
Edited by Creating Ink
Digital ISBN#: 978-1-943950-47-8
Print ISBN#: 978-1-943950-48-5

ALSO BY AUTUMN JONES LAKE

THE LOST KINGS MC SERIES

Slow Burn (Lost Kings MC #1)

Corrupting Cinderella (Lost Kings MC #2)

Three Kings, One Night (Lost Kings MC #2.5)

Strength From Loyalty (Lost Kings MC #3)

Tattered on My Sleeve (Lost Kings MC #4)

White Heat (Lost Kings MC #5)

Between Embers (Lost Kings MC #5.5)

More Than Miles (Lost Kings MC #6)

White Knuckles (Lost Kings MC #7)

Beyond Reckless (Lost Kings MC #8)

Beyond Reason (Lost Kings MC #9)

One Empire Night (Lost Kings MC #9.5)

After Burn (Lost Kings MC #10)

After Glow (Lost Kings MC #11)

Zero Hour (Lost Kings MC #11.5)

Zero Tolerance (Lost Kings MC #12)

Zero Regret (Lost Kings MC #13)

Zero Apologies (Lost Kings MC #14)

White Lies (Lost Kings MC #15)

Swagger and Sass (A Lost Kings MC Novella)

Rhythm of the Road (Lost Kings MC #16)

Lyrics on the Wind (Lost Kings MC #17)

Crown of Ghosts (Lost Kings MC #18)

Standalones in the Lost Kings MC World

Bullets & Bonfires

Warnings & Wildfires

Cards of Love: Knight of Swords

The Hollywood Demons Series

Kickstart My Heart

Blow My Fuse

Wheels of Fire

<u>Paranormal Romance</u>

Catnip & Cauldrons

Onyx Night

Onyx Shadows

Feral Escape

The open road has owned my heart for as long as I can remember.
Until a certain sassy little singer stole it.
Hookups don't lead to happily ever after.
A couple nights together. Nothing more.
We made no promises.
Our worlds couldn't be more opposite.
She's sweet lyrics and sunshine.
I'm danger and destruction.
She's miles away, but all I see when I close my eyes.
The rhythm of the road is what I need to settle my mind.
Problem is, it's taking me straight to her and away from everything else.

GLOSSARY

The Lost Kings MC™ World
© Autumn Jones Lake
Glossary of Characters and Terminology.

The series has had a few shakeups in the last few books. I've updated the glossary to reflect this. *It may contain spoilers* if you are not caught up on the series or have skipped books! If you're brand new to the series—welcome! This guide might be handy. If you've been part of the LOKI family for a while—welcome back! This might help refresh your memory.

Please note, this glossary only pertains to *my* romantic fictionalized motorcycle club world. It should not be construed as applicable to any other fictional club or real life club.

THE LOST KINGS MC: UPSTATE, NY

President: Rochlan "Rock" North. Leader of the Upstate NY charter of the Lost Kings MC.
Sergeant-at-Arms: Wyatt "Wrath" Ramsey.
Vice President: Blake "Murphy" O'Callaghan. Murphy was the road captain up until White Lies (Lost Kings MC #15)
Treasurer: Marcel "Teller" Whelan.
Road Captain: Dixon "Dex" Watts (newly appointed to the position.)

THE LOST KINGS MC: DOWNSTATE, NY

President: Angus "Zero" or "Z" Frazier, as of Zero Apologies

(Lost Kings MC #14) Z is the president of the Downstate, NY charter of the Lost Kings MC.
Vice President: Logan "Rooster" Randall
Sergeant-at-Arms: Steer
Treasurer: Hustler
Road Captain: Jensen "Jigsaw" Kilgore

OTHER LOST KINGS MC MEMBERS

Grinder: Rock's mentor. Grinder is an older member who we met briefly in *Corrupting Cinderella*. He's been incarcerated since before Rock took over the Lost Kings.

Cronin "Sparky" Petek: Sparky is the mad genius behind the Lost Kings MC's pot-growing business. He is rarely seen outside of the basement, as he prefers the company of his plants.

Elias "Bricks" Serrano: We have seen Bricks and his girlfriend Winter throughout the series. One of the few members who does not live at the clubhouse.

Sam "Stash" Black: Lives in the basement with Sparky and helps with the plants.

Thomas "Ravage" Kane: We've gotten to know Rav and his snarky humor a little bit better in each book. Ravage is a general member who helps out wherever he is needed.

Sway: Former president of the downstate charter of the Lost Kings MC. We've seen Sway and his wife Tawny off and on since *Strength From Loyalty*.

Hoot: We've seen glimpses of him since *Slow Burn* when he was a lowly prospect. He finally got his full patch, but still gets a lot of the grunt work.

Birch: Recently voted as a full-patch member.

Priest: The Lost Kings MC National President. We first met him and his wife, Valentina in *After Burn*.

Malik: Soon-to-be prospect for the Lost Kings MC.

T-Bone: Member of the Virginia charter of the Lost Kings MC

New characters are introduced in this book that we have not met yet, so I won't name them here.

THE LADIES OF THE LOST KINGS MC

Hope Kendall North, Esq.: Nicknamed *First Lady* by Murphy in *Corrupting Cinderella (Lost Kings MC #2)*, Hope is the object of Rock's love and obsession. Their daughter is named Grace.

Trinity Hurst Ramsey: Wrath's angel. Former caretaker of the club. She now has her own photography and graphic design business. She is married to Wrath, fiercely loyal to the club and best friends with Hope.

Heidi "Little Hammer" O'Callaghan: Murphy's wife and Teller's little sister. Heidi just graduated from college and works at Empire Med. Murphy officially adopted her daughter Alexa Jade.

Charlotte Clark, Esq: Teller's sunshine. Often credited with taming the brooding treasurer of the Lost Kings, Teller.

Lilly Frazier: Z's brave and devoted siren. The new queen of the Lost Kings MC downstate charter. One of Hope's best friends. Z and Lilly's son is Chance.

Shelby Morgan: First introduced in Swagger and Sass. Country music singer from Texas. Rooster's love interest.

Swan: Lost Kings MC club girl and dancer at Crystal Ball.

Willow: Bartender at Crystal Ball. But once or twice we've caught her sneaking into or out of the basement with Sparky.

Serena: Former downstate clubgirl still a little broken-hearted over Murphy. Abused by Shadow, the former VP of the downstate charter. We have not seen her since *Zero Regret*.

Tawny: Sway's ol' lady. The former "Queen B" of the downstate charter of the Lost Kings MC.

Stella: Pornographic film actress. The downstate charter is the sole investor in her production company. Ex-girlfriend of Z. Current...*something* of Sway. Her *Sex in Every City* series sometimes requires members of LOKI to work as bouncers on her film sets.

OTHER RECURRING CHARACTERS RELEVANT TO THIS STORY

Russell "Chaser" Adams: President of the Devil Demons MC in Western NY. (The Hollywood Demons series is his story.)

Mallory "Little Dove" DeLova-Adams: Chaser's wife. Daughter of mafia boss, Anatoly DeLova.

Linden "Stump" Adams: Chaser's father. Former president of the Devil Demons MC.

Carter Clark: Charlotte's goofy, often inappropriate younger brother.

Remington "Ruthless" Holt: Owns "the Castle" with his best friend Griff. It's an underground fighting ring Murphy used to participate in. We've seen him most recently in White Lies. Caretaker of his younger sister Molly. Considering forming a support club to the Lost Kings MC with Griff, Eraser, and Vapor.

Griffin "Stonewall" Royal: Remy's best friend and business partner.

Eraser: Owns Zips. A racetrack near the Lost Kings MC territory. Married to Ella.

Roman "Vapor" Hawkins: The book *Cards of Love: Knight of Swords* is his story. We've seen him and his wife Juliet in the series since *After Burn*.

Jake Wallace: One of Wrath's business partners in Furious Fitness. Jake has appeared off and on throughout the series.

Sullivan Wallace: Jake's brother. Owner of Strike Back Fitness. He's a significant character in *Bullets and Bonfires* and his own book *Warnings and Wildfires*.

OTHER MCS

Friendly Clubs:

Devil Demons MC: Based in Western NY. Long-time friend of the Lost Kings MC. Their clubs are intertwined and share a lot of history.

Wolf Knights MC: Mostly an ally of the Lost Kings. Run Slater county but have had a number of shake-ups in the last few years. Whisper is their current president.

Iron Bulls MC: (From the Iron Bulls MC series by Phoenyx Slaughter) Southwestern outlaw club. Meet up and do business with LOKI once in a while.

Savage Dragons MC (From the Iron Bulls MC series by Phoenyx Slaughter): Texas outlaw club.

ENEMY CLUBS:

Vipers MC: Used to run Ironworks until Lost Kings took over that territory. Still active in other parts of the country.
South of Satan MC: Vermont MC who has stirred up trouble for LOKI in the past.

LOST KINGS MC TERMINOLOGY

LOKI: Short for LOst KIngs
Crystal Ball: The strip club owned by the Lost Kings MC and one of their legitimate businesses. They often refer to it as "CB."
Furious Fitness: The gym Wrath owns. Often just referred to as "Furious."
War Room: Where the Lost Kings hold "church."
Property Patch: When a member takes a woman as his Old Lady (wife status), he gives her a vest with a property patch. In my series, the vest has a "Property of Lost Kings MC" patch and the member's road name on the back. The officers also place their patches on the ol' lady's vest as a sign that they always have her back. Her man's patch or club symbol is placed over the heart. Rock's patch is a crown. Wrath's a star. Murphy's a four-leaf clover. Teller's a dollar sign. Z, the letter Z. Rooster's is a rooster wearing a crown. As a joke, Wrath gave Rock and Hope a "product of" patch for baby Grace. Maybe it will catch on as more kids are born into the club.

PLACES IN THE LOST KINGS MC WORLD

I use a mix of real and imaginary names to describe the places in my series. Again, I bend and shape geography to my needs as this is a fictional world that I created.

Empire, NY: The territory run by the Lost Kings MC upstate charter. This is a fictional version of Albany, NY, the capital of New York State. Many of the Lost Kings MC's businesses are located in Empire.

Slater, NY: based on Schenectady County. Until recently it was run by the Wolf Knights MC.

Ironworks, NY: based on Rennselaer County (Troy, NY) In the beginning of the series it was run by the Vipers MC. It is now the territory of the Lost Kings MC.

Union, NY: A fictional area two hours south of Empire, NY where the "downstate" charter is located.

Johnson County/Johnsonville: Fictional area where Heidi grew up. About an hour west of Empire. Where Strike Back Gym, The Castle and Zips are located.

Zips: Racetrack owned by Eraser where all the illegal gambling/racing happens.

The Castle: The building that houses the underground fighting ring run by Remy and Griff. Murphy used to fight here. Formerly a juvenile detention center. Located in the middle of nowhere NY, it once-upon-a-time housed Griff, Vapor, and possibly Teller during their "troubled youth" days.

Kodack, NY: Another fictional NY area located in Western New York. Somewhere near Buffalo, perhaps. This territory is run by the Devil Demons, MC.

Empire Medical Center: Local hospital where all the Kings receive medical treatment. Heidi also works there now.

OTHER MC TERMINOLOGY

Most terminology was obtained through research. However, I have also used some artistic license in applying these terms to my romanticized, fictional version of an Outlaw Motorcycle Club. This is not an exhaustive list.

Cage: A car, truck, van, basically anything other than a motorcycle.

Church: Club meetings all full patch members must attend. Led by the president of the club, but officers will update the members on the areas they oversee.

Citizen: Anyone not a hardcore biker or belonging to an outlaw club. "Citizen Wife" would refer to a spouse kept entirely separate from the club.

Cut: Leather vest worn by outlaw bikers. Adorned with patches and artwork displaying the club's unique colors. The Lost Kings' colors are blue and gray. Their logo is a skull with a crown. The *Respect Few, Fear None* patch is earned by doing time for the club without snitching. Brother's Keeper patches are earned by killing for the club. *Loyal Brother*: A brother with more than five years with the club.

Colors: The "uniform" of an outlaw motorcycle gang. A leather vest, with the three-piece club patch on the back, and various other patches relating to their role in the club.

Fly Colors: To ride on a motorcycle wearing colors.

Muffler Bunny or "bunnies": Club girl who hangs around to provide sexual favors to members.

Nomad: A club member who does not belong to any specific charter, yet has privileges in all charters.

Old Lady/Ol' Lady: Wife or steady girlfriend of a club member.

Patched In: When a new member is approved for full membership.

Patch Holder: A member who has been vetted through performing duties for the club as a prospect or probate and has earned his three-piece patch.

Road Name: Nickname. Usually given by the other members.

Run: A club-sanctioned outing, sometimes with other chapters and/or clubs. Can also refer to a club business run.

I'm sure I'm forgetting something! But that should get you started!

CHAPTER ONE

ROOSTER

Certain people who come into your life change you in ways you can't fathom at the time.

For me, one of those people is Shelby Morgan.

Whether she's changed me for the good or bad remains to be seen.

Haven't laid eyes on her since earlier this summer.

But not a day's gone by when she hasn't been on my mind.

Then, there are other people in your life. The ones who are hell-bent on annoying the shit out of you. That honor goes to my Lost Kings MC brother and road captain at the moment.

"Oooh, Shelby, I *loooove* you." Jigsaw hugs himself and kisses the air in front of him, earning laughs from the rest of the guys.

"Shut the fuck up." I cross my arms over my chest and stare at the road straight ahead, determined not to punch Jiggy this afternoon. No matter how much he's begging for it.

Where the fuck are they?

I pull out my phone. No text from Murphy. No response to the last text I sent Shelby either. Not that I'm worried or anything.

"You want to head up without 'em?" Jigsaw gestures toward the road. "I'll tell Murphy you got tired of waiting."

"We all ride together." Exasperation colors my refusal. The bond of brotherhood is the whole point of both charters riding to the country music festival together. Taking off on my own sends the wrong message.

The rhythmic thrum of a half-dozen Harleys punctures the suburban quiet. I lift my head and slip my phone in my pocket. *Finally.*

We have plenty of time to kill before Shelby goes onstage but I'm still itching to get on the road.

A few minutes later, Murphy and Dex thunder into the parking lot with several other brothers and the club's plain, black cargo van trailing behind them. They execute a lazy but loud circle around the building. Murphy pulls in near us and shuts down his bike. A few seconds later, he swaggers his big, ginger ass my way.

"What's up, brother?" he greets, tapping my knuckles and lifting his chin. He shakes a few hands and accepts quick back slaps from everyone else before returning to me.

His wife, Heidi, bounces over and gives me a quick hug. "Are you excited to see Shelby?"

I'm not touching her question. "How you been, little hammer?"

Her lips curve into a sly smile at the new nickname she earned by being a badass ol' lady. "Behaving myself."

"I doubt that." I reach into my back pocket and pull out an envelope. "This is from Z and me."

She tilts her head and slowly takes it.

Murphy raises an eyebrow while he waits for her to take a peek inside.

"Oh my God!" Heidi squeals and flails her hands in the air. The envelope floats to the ground and I lean down to grab it.

2

"Will you add it to your vest?" I ask. She's not wearing her 'Property of Murphy' patch tonight—a civilian event like the outdoor music festival we're attending just isn't the place for it.

"You bet I will." She grins at the small rectangular patch embroidered with three symbols: a four-leaf clover, a crown, and a hammer. "Murphy's queen carries a hammer."

"Yup. Swings it well, too." I hand the envelope to her again. "You missed one."

"Rooster?" She pulls out my patch of a rooster wearing a crown. The king of cocky bastards. "You're giving me *your* patch?"

"I know you're an upstate old lady and the officers there already gave you their patches a long time ago." I glance at Murphy. "But the loyalty you've shown the club and the way you're always there for your man—the world should know I'll have your back if they fuck with you."

"Rooster, that's so sweet." She reaches up on tiptoes and gives me another quick hug. "Thank you."

Murphy holds out his hand. "Thanks, brother."

"Thanks for making the rest of us look like assholes," Jigsaw says, joining us to inspect Heidi's new patches.

"You don't need my help to do that."

Heidi frets for so long about where to put the patches so she doesn't lose them tonight, I almost regret not giving them to her later. Murphy ends up stashing them in the pocket inside his cut.

"I wish Z was coming with us too," she says.

"I don't think he's a country music fan."

"He was an admirer of fine ladies in denim cut-offs," Ravage says, joining our group. "Until he settled down with Lilly."

Heidi rolls her eyes at him. "I'm pretty sure Lilly will wear whatever he wants."

"More hotties for us!" Ravage and Jigsaw high-five each other.

Murphy and I share an eyeroll.

"Ready?" I ask.

"Let's do it."

"Wait!" Sparky runs up and passes out homemade brownies wrapped in clear plastic to everyone.

3

Jigsaw studies the treat. "Why now?"

"Eat 'em in the parking lot before we go in." He shrugs as if the answer should've been obvious. "They'll get all mashed up on the way there if I hang onto 'em."

Stash shoves half of his brownie in his mouth and chews loudly. "Tastes like ass."

"You would know," Ravage zings back.

I don't want to offend our club's official stoner mascot, so I thank Sparky and stuff the brownie in my pocket.

"Everyone have their tickets?" You'd think I wouldn't have to ask a group of grown men that question.

"Fuck," Sparky moans. "They're on my dresser."

"I have them right here," Willow announces, patting her hip.

Murphy lets out a long-suffering sigh that makes me chuckle. Guess it's been like this all morning. No wonder they were late.

Since our two charters are riding to Wellspring together, we switch up the formation. Murphy and I, as vice presidents, take the lead. Jigsaw and Dex fall behind us, then everyone else.

We take it easy, pulling out of the parking lot and onto the Northway.

The eager-to-see-her sensation rolling around in the pit of my stomach is a first for me. I'd love to blame it on Sparky's pre-concert edibles but since I didn't partake, I can't.

I twist the throttle, increasing my speed and to my left, Murphy does the same.

Part of me wishes I'd come alone so when I finally get my hands on Shelby, I have her all to myself. Or maybe so there are no witnesses in case our reunion goes south.

I'm keeping my expectations for tonight low. She's on tour. She'll be busy. While she's aware I'm coming to the show, I don't expect her to drop everything to cater to me. There's a chance I won't even be able to see her before her performance.

In our daily text exchanges and frequent phone calls, she still sounds like the same sweet, sassy girl I left in Texas. Still doesn't mean we'll click the same way we did when we first met.

We're still twenty minutes from the outdoor venue where the

4

concert's being held when a blur to the right catches my attention.

A bunch of people standing around, staring at the back tire of an older Ford Super Duty van.

I slow the bike.

One figure in particular catches my attention.

Short, curvy, ass to die for, long legs encased in tight blue jeans, and plump thighs I've been dreaming about having wrapped around me for months. Long blond curls pulled into a high ponytail.

Like I conjured her up straight out of my fantasies.

Shelby.

Can't tell if anyone else recognizes her.

That *was* Shelby, right? She's on my damn mind so much, maybe I'm having hallucinations.

Fuck it. Either way, someone's broken down on the side of the road and could use our help. I signal to Murphy that I'm pulling over and guide the bike to a stop on the shoulder, leaving enough room for my brothers to pull in behind me.

I barely have my helmet off when someone shouts my name over the crunch of gravel. I swing my leg over my bike and turn.

Yep, that's my girl.

"Rooster!" she shouts again.

I only have a few seconds to open my arms before she flings herself against me, knocking me backwards a step.

"What are you doing here?" she asks.

She tips her head back and that's all it takes. One look in her sparkling eyes and I slam my lips against hers without answering the question. She's as soft as I remember. Tastes sweet and lemony too. I curl my arms around her plush body, dragging her against me while our mouths tangle. The hot summer sun beats down on us but it's nothing compared to the heat and desire sparking between our bodies—ready to combust into white-hot flames.

She angles her head, deepening our kiss, and I dive in. I've been starving for this woman for months and now that she's finally in my arms, I plan to gorge myself.

Unfortunately, we're not alone.

Nope, we're on the side of a busy highway with a bunch of my club brothers and her entire band here to witness our reunion. Can't speak for her band but my asshole brothers waste no time hooting and whistling at our ravenous greeting.

It doesn't stop me from kissing the fuck out of Shelby.

Not even a little.

CHAPTER TWO

People cross paths for a reason. I firmly believe that. Rooster and I were destined to meet. I believe that too. Whether he's part of my future or will become part of my history, I'm not sure yet.

What I *do* know is that he's on my mind a lot more often than is probably healthy. This is the worst possible time in my life to be head over boots for a man, as my mother gently reminded me before I left home for my first national tour.

This is a huge opportunity for me to grow my audience, connect with existing fans, and prove to people that I'm more than the cute blonde singer with the big tits who didn't even win the lame reality show that made her famous.

So, my mama has a point. It's a terrible time to pine for a man.

But Rooster's not any man. Right now, with his tongue stroking mine and heat searing my skin, it seems like the perfect time to be caught up with *this* man. Which is why the second he pulled over, I raced over like a lunatic hell-bent on monkey-climbing his hard body as if it was my favorite banana tree.

We part for a second and I blink up at him. "What are you doing here?"

Ignoring my breathless question, he wraps his big arms around me even tighter, anchoring my body to his, and silences me with another sizzling kiss.

The familiar tickle of his beard only makes me lean in closer. I can't get enough. I've missed him so much. Threading one hand in my hair, he slides the other one over my ass, his fingers firmly and possessively digging in, claiming me in front of everyone.

The long, loud honk of a tractor trailer horn tears us apart.

"I'm so happy to see you," I whisper, daring to peek up into his dark eyes.

Applause erupts around us. Heat crawls over my cheeks. How'd I forget we're surrounded by a bunch of his club brothers as well as my band?

"Nine-point-five, brother. Shoulda used more tongue." Jigsaw claps loudly, ramping up the embarrassment factor.

Without shifting his gaze, Rooster answers with his middle finger.

"Why are you out here on the side of the road?" He sets me down gently, still ignoring everyone else. "What happened?"

I take a second to stare at him, running my gaze over all the familiar details. Neatly trimmed beard. Navy blue T-shirt, sleeves stretched over his rolling terrain of tattooed, muscled arms. Ink peeking from the neck of his shirt. His easy, casual stance and manner exudes masculine energy, reminding me the only attention my girly bits have had lately is of the battery-operated-boyfriend variety.

"The stupid van broke down." I finally stick my tongue back in my mouth and find some words. "I'm going to miss soundcheck if I don't get to the venue soon." Being late won't exactly endear me to the biggest country singer on the planet. Dawson Roads was kind enough to take me out on tour this summer; I don't want to disappoint him.

"Hey, Shelby." Heidi rushes over and envelops me in a hug. "How've you been?"

Warmth seeps into my chest as she squeezes me tight. I don't have many girlfriends. Heidi and I had gotten along well when we met in Texas. I haven't kept in touch with her as much as I've been in touch with Rooster, but I've been looking forward to seeing her.

"Been better." I flip my hand toward the van. "Overall, I can't complain. Thanks for coming."

"I wouldn't miss it. Trinity and Charlotte will be up later too."

I bite my lip, feeling shitty about my lack of perks as the opening act. I'd managed to wrangle exactly two tickets and two backstage passes. "I'm sorry I couldn't get more tickets—"

Heidi waves off my apology. "Hope's bought me tickets to Country Fest for Christmas for the last couple years. The other guys have lawn seats. They wouldn't want to be caged in anyway. It's all good."

My gaze skips to Rooster's brothers. A solid, protective wall of hard-faced men. I recognize most of them but can't remember everyone's name. I can't believe they all came with Rooster. To see me or to support him?

Or just to have a good time. Not everything's about you, Shelby.

"Hey, Shelby," Jigsaw says, sliding up to Rooster's side. "You're looking as fine as ever." With a playful smirk stretched across his lips, he opens his arms wide and takes a step closer.

Rooster stops him with an arm across his chest. "Don't," he warns in a low tone.

My heart does another little annoying two-step at Rooster's possessive display.

Jigsaw's as mischievous as I remember and not offended in the least by Rooster's implied threat. Hug thwarted, he grins and winks at me instead.

Rooster slings his arm around my shoulders and steers me toward the van. "What's going on here?"

"Back tire blew."

He slowly turns to me with a raised eyebrow. "And?"

My cheeks flame hot again, and I give him a sheepish shrug. "None of us know how to change a tire."

He chuckles then tips his head toward his brothers. One of them yells, "On it."

"You don't have to," I protest. "Triple A is on the way..." Who am I kidding? Rescuing me is Rooster's thing. It's how our relationship started. Reuniting this way almost feels like destiny.

Besides, I need to move my ass.

"You could be here all afternoon, waitin' on them," he points out.

"I *do* have to get to soundcheck."

"Let's go." He gestures toward his bike and my feet automatically move in that direction.

"Wait, Shelby, what are you doing?" Trent calls out. "You can't leave."

Rooster growls so low, I'm not even sure he did it on purpose. More like an instinctual stay-away-from-my-woman noise. While the sound probably didn't carry, the deep scowl and scary gaze Rooster shoots at Trent can't be missed.

Trent holds up his hands and backs away.

I better defuse this fast.

CHAPTER THREE

Rooster

Shelby's band can't stop staring at us with their totally freaked out eyes and open mouths. But it's one of the guys I recognize from the show I caught in San Antonio—Brent, Bret. I can't remember—who's five seconds from having a size-thirteen boot up his ass. I didn't like the way he looked at Shelby then, and I don't care for it now.

"Shelby, are you sure this is a good idea?" He tosses me a cool look.

Other than trying to stare a hole through his face, I don't react.

Shelby sighs. "I can't show up late, Trent."

Trent. Whatever. Close enough.

Shelby tips her head back, shines her sunshine smile at me and adds, "Besides, Rooster and I have lots of catching up to do."

It's her sweet face, not Trent's horrified expression and gaping jaw, that lures me to bend down and press a quick kiss against her cheek. "Yeah, we do," I say against her ear.

Heidi jogs over to the club's van and pulls out a backpack, rifling through it and returning with a dark blue hoodie that she hands Shelby. "I don't have an extra leather jacket but take this."

"Thanks." Shelby slips it on and gives Heidi a quick hug.

My gaze slides over the sweatshirt, admiring the way our Lost

11

Kings MC skull and crown logo lands perfectly over Shelby's ample chest. Damn, she wears my club's colors well.

"Ready?" I hand her the extra helmet I brought because I planned to take her to upstate's clubhouse after the concert tonight. She's supposed to have tomorrow off and spending time with her is the only item on my to-do list.

"All set."

She waits for me to mount the bike before resting her hand on my shoulder and lifting herself into the space behind me. Damn, I forgot how good it feels to have her back there. Haven't had another passenger since her.

Shelby hasn't forgotten how to ride, either. She snuggles up against me, the heat of her body soaking into my soul. To compensate for the extra weight on the machine, I start off slower than normal, easing our way back into traffic. Murphy and Heidi come up on my right.

We don't get far before we're forced to slow down by miles of backed up traffic. Since I still don't listen to a lot of country songs—other than Shelby's—I hadn't fully appreciated Heidi's warning that this festival's one of the bigger events to come to the Capital Region every summer. Murphy signals for me to follow him, and together we weave in through the line of bumper-to-tailgate vehicles—jacked up trucks, cars, and jeeps, their radios blaring one form of twangy shit or another.

Shelby squeezes me tighter and I chuckle. Do any of these drones in their cages realize one of the stars of tonight's show is whizzing past them?

While I'm familiar with the performing arts center, I've never been to the backstage area where the artists' buses park. Once we're inside the huge public park, Murphy and I pull into a small, circular patch of dirt off the road.

"Where are we headed?" I ask.

Shelby tugs and jiggles her phone out of her pocket. "Hang on." She finally finds what she needs and recites a set of directions.

"I think that's straight ahead and to the left." Murphy points to the forked road in front of us.

"Look at you." I smirk at him. "Almost like you used to be a road captain or something."

He rolls his eyes and sweeps his arm out in front of him. "Lead the way, smartass."

This time, I fall into the front position. We take left after left until the narrow, paved, unlined roads turn into dirt and gravel. Finally, the road opens into a wider space with a few scattered wooden barricades indicating it's a private area.

A lone "security" guard walks up to greet us. Maybe he'll be stricter as the night goes on, but for now, he takes Shelby's word for it that she's supposed to be there and waves us through.

Three massive tour buses are lined up near a loading dock attached to the back of the large amphitheater. Dawson Roads' face is splashed all over two of the buses. The name of another band I don't recognize decorates the third. Must be where Shelby's expected to show up.

The piece of shit Shelby's been traveling in could fit in the storage compartment of Dawson's bus.

I back the bike into a spot near the loading dock and shut it down. Murphy glides in next to me.

"Shelby?" a guy calls out as he jogs over to us.

"Hey, Greg." She braces herself on my shoulders and hops off. "I'm here."

He slows his steps. "Where's the van?" His curious gaze slides over me, then Murphy and Heidi. "Who are your friends?"

She makes the introductions, but it doesn't seem to lessen Greg's suspicions. If I thought it was because he was actually worried about her I wouldn't care, but that's not the vibe he's projecting.

"Hey, Greg." I tip my head to him instead of offering to shake his hand. "Heard a lot about you." Nothing good, but now's not the best time to antagonize her manager.

"Thanks for picking her up. Well, they're ready for you, Shelby." He glances at me again. "You can come watch."

As if I was planning to leave.

"Shelby," Greg says, drawing her closer. "I got a call from some lady with the local Dream Makers organization. I explained you don't have room in your schedule—"

"No." Shelby stops in her tracks and whirls on Greg. "Call her back and tell her I'll be there."

Murphy and Heidi slide matching what-the-fuck faces my way and I shrug.

"Come on, Shelby," Greg grumbles, yanking out his phone. "It's *one* kid. And you never let me send a photographer to make it worth the trouble."

"I don't care. Where is it?"

He scrolls through his phone. "Empire Med. She sent an email too."

"Forward it to me. I have tomorrow off."

"Yes, but it's not that close. How are you planning to get there?"

"I'll take you," I offer, touching Shelby's shoulder. I don't even know what I'm agreeing to do but it's obviously important to Shelby.

"Thank you." She blows out a breath. "I'm spending my day off with Rooster anyway."

Greg narrows his eyes at me. "She needs to be four hours west of here by Friday morning."

This motherfucker doesn't understand who he's dealing with. "I've got plenty of road experience. I'll get her wherever she needs to go."

His gaze slips to my VP patch and his eyes narrow. *Huh.* Maybe he's not a motorcycle enthusiast.

"I'm sorry," Shelby whispers while Greg answers a call and walks away.

"What's Dream Makers?" I ask.

"It's. . ." Shelby drops her gaze and shakes her head.

"It's a children's charity." Heidi gently touches Shelby's arm. "Right? They grant wishes for sick children?"

Shelby nods. "I started working with them when I was on *Redneck Roadhouse*. If someone asks for me, I *always* go if I can line up my schedule."

How did I not know this about Shelby?

"Empire Med has a very dedicated team in the Children's Hospital," Heidi says. "They'll appreciate your visit."

"I'll get you there tomorrow. Put it out of your head and focus on what you need to do tonight."

She bites her lip and glances toward the loading area. "Are you sure you don't mind taking me tomorrow?"

"Not at all." My only plan was to soak up as much time with Shelby as possible. Doesn't matter where.

Now that we've settled Shelby's transportation issues, her shoulders relax, and a hint of a smile returns to her pretty face.

Fuck if I'm not doing whatever it takes to make this woman happy every second of the short amount of time we'll be together.

CHAPTER FOUR

Shelby

Heat stings my cheeks, but I flash a quick smile and I pray no one asks me for more details about Dream Makers. It's not something I can talk about before a show or I'll never walk out onstage tonight.

"Alexa and I made these little craft kits I was going to drop off at the children's hospital. Do you want to take them with you?" Heidi asks. "I work there so I try to bring stuff when I can..."

Tears sting my eyes, emotions bubbling way too close to the surface for me to handle. "That's so sweet. Thank you."

"You don't have to. I just..."

I hate that Heidi seems nervous around me today. I'm still the same person who went boot shopping with her in Texas. Nothing's changed. I glance around the concert venue—a far cry from the Tipsy Saddle, the sketchy little honkytonk I was performing at the first time we met. So, maybe a few things have changed. I reach out and squeeze her hand. "That sounds perfect. I usually try to bring something with me. Thank you."

"Well, you better go get ready." She shoos me toward the tour buses and loading dock bustling with roadies moving equipment. "I'll be dead-center, screaming the loudest for you."

Gosh, I go onstage so early, some nights hardly anyone's even in their seats yet. It'll be nice to have at least one person I know out there in the audience. "Thank you."

Murphy nods and wishes me luck before curling his arm around Heidi's shoulders and steering her toward his bike.

Then Rooster and I are alone, and I'm not quite sure what to say.

I scuff the toe of my boot over crumbling asphalt, drawing Rooster's attention to my feet. "You're not wearing your electric teal boots?" he teases.

"I—they're special. I only wear them onstage."

He blinks and also seems at a loss for words. "Guess we need to get you another pair. Day boots. Stage boots."

"I don't need a pair of boots to keep you on my mind, Rooster." My whispered words are almost swept up in the breeze and rustle of leaves.

He curls his fingers around mine. "Show me around?"

"You forget, I haven't been here myself yet."

"Shit, that's right." He glances toward his bike. "Do you need me to go so you can get ready?"

He doesn't say it with much conviction. That makes it easier to tug him toward the loading dock. "No way. You're my guest for the night." I stop. "Shoot. I have another pass if Heidi wants it."

"Nah, Murphy ain't lettin' her out of his sight." Rooster sweeps his gaze over me. "And I'm not letting you out of mine."

My eager heart pounds even faster, ready to burst out of my chest and into Rooster's hands. Taking a calming breath, I wrap my arms around his waist and rest my chin on his chest. "Did I mention that I'm really happy to see you?"

A half-smile teases at the corner of his mouth as he watches me, like he's pretending to consider the question. "I don't think so."

Longing for him almost brings me to my knees. I'm completely addicted to the heat of his stare. Trembling, I lean up on tiptoes, teasing my nails over the back of his neck into his hair. "Your hair's longer."

His eyes close and he gives me a sleepy smile. "Haven't had time to get it cut."

What's keeping him so busy? A desire to probe into every last detail of his life threatens to turn me into a dang fool. "I can cut it for you."

His eyes pop open. "I think you have more important things to do than shear me."

"Rooster?"

He quirks an eyebrow. "Yeah?"

"Please kiss me again."

Instead of a cocky comeback, he edges closer. Tall, he's so damn tall. Roughly beautiful. Strong. My whole world fills with him. His scent—crisp summer grass, leather with a touch of motor oil. His warmth. His touch. Gently, he teases his fingers through my hair and tugs my head back.

He pins me with a stare that sends shivers of anticipation down my spine. Slowly, he dips down and brushes his mouth against mine. His beard grazes my chin but I press my hands against his cheeks, tugging him closer.

His arms tighten, lifting me again so we're at the right height. This time, no one's close enough to interrupt, so I wrap my legs around him, holding on. Everything about him entices me.

He flicks his tongue against my lips and tingles of sensation race down my spine. The gentleness is sweet but I'm ravenous and I've missed him.

I squeeze closer, clinging to him, and he seems to snap. His soft kisses turn demanding. Rough fingers tease under the edge of my shirt, tickling my skin. My heart pounds in my ears. His breathing quickens. This inescapable attraction between us still burns lightning-rod hot.

The crunch of gravel invades our moment. I draw back and peer over his shoulder. My van rolls into the parking lot. "Well, shoot. The band's here."

Rooster's mouth twitches and he kisses the tip of my nose before setting me down. My gaze drops to the bulge in his jeans, and I slick my tongue over my lip.

He groans. "Don't. I'm trying hard not to fuck up your night."

I tip my head to the side, meeting his burning stare. "What?"

"Shelby." He leans down and brushes his lips against my ear. "It's taking all my control not to bend you over my bike, yank your jeans down, and—"

"Shelby!"

Dammit, Trent!

Rooster's eyes turn hard as he twists around to see who dared interrupt us.

"Rooster." I grip his chin and turn him to face me again. Curling one finger, I beckon him closer. "You owe me new panties."

Curiosity erases his murderous expression. "How's that?"

I wiggle my hips and he groans. "These are *soaked* because of you."

The scrape and crunch of several pairs of boots puts an end to my teasing. Rooster's not finished, though. He leans down again, whispering, "I'll require proof later."

"Shelby?" Trent stops next to us and I straighten, dropping my arms to my sides. Rooster keeps me close, his hand curled over my hip, our bodies pressed tight. "Did you check things out yet?"

"No, we just got here." I wince at the shaky wobble to my voice. Trent's disapproving big brother face shouldn't have any effect on me. "I spoke to Greg, though."

Trent grunts and gestures toward the loading dock. "I'll grab someone to help us unload." He sends a dismissive glance Rooster's way. "Let you get ready."

"Thanks."

Rooster glances at the van. "You need help?"

"We've got it." Trent rejects Rooster's offer with a quick shake of his head.

Rooster's eyes narrow, and I tug on his hand. "You're with *me*."

The usual nerves that leave my stomach fluttering before a show seem to have taken a vacation with Rooster here. Hand in hand, we stroll toward the loading dock and climb the stairs to the backstage area. A gentle breeze blowing through the open structure keeps the summer heat bearable.

"I want to do whatever I can to help you out," Rooster says.

"You already are." I nudge him with my shoulder. "You can play bodyguard if it makes you feel better."

His protective, growly expression returns. "Do you *need* a bodyguard?"

Am I going to tell him about the guys who get too handsy night after night? Nope. He already had a taste of that mayhem in Texas and ended up getting into a brawl over it. "I'm fine."

"That didn't really answer my question."

His concern wraps around me like a warm security blanket. More often than not I've felt like a petal tossed in the wind on this tour. My emotions twist and tangle. Should I share some of my fears and doubts with Rooster? Or pretend it's all roses?

"Everything's perfectly peachy." I smile up at him. There's no reason to dwell on negative things he can't help me fix.

Because one thing I know for sure.

Our time together always has an expiration date.

CHAPTER FIVE

Rooster

I've never been a master at keeping my hands to myself. With Shelby so close, it's damn near impossible. But I didn't show up today to distract her or jack up her pre-show anxiety.

After her concert? Game on.

"Shelby! You ready for soundcheck?" Someone calls out.

"Yup! Coming." She jogs down the long corridor toward the stage, hair bouncing around her shoulders and down her back. I have to quit gawking at her and pick up the pace, she's moving so fast.

"Here." Greg stops me with a hand on my chest—a hand he's dangerously close to losing. I open my mouth to issue a warning, when he offers a shiny laminated rectangle with the name of the festival and *VIP: All Access* in big black letters across the bottom, strung on a black lanyard. "You need to wear this so no one hassles you backstage."

Well, now I almost feel bad for wanting to break his arms. "Thanks." I sling it around my neck and search the area for Shelby.

"She'll be out onstage." Greg points to a stack of amps a few feet away, near what looks like an entrance to the stage. "You can watch from there."

"Okay." I wander over to the spot. My gaze lands on Shelby

standing in the center of the scuffed stage testing her earpiece and mumbling a few things into a microphone. She taps it with her palm a few times. "Where's my rhythm section?" she hollers.

A few guys I recognize as her band members, as well as a few I don't recognize, push past me. They carefully set up their gear and play a few experimental notes.

"Y'all wanna do 'Big Lies?'" Shelby waves her hand out toward the rows and rows of currently empty seats and the rolling lawns outside the pavilion.

Instead of answering, the guy on the drums taps the cymbals a few times. They start up with a melody I recognize. For the last few months it's been playing roughly every ninety minutes on the satellite country music station I listen to for the sole purpose of catching one of Shelby's songs or the rare after-concert interview.

It's an upbeat song. Heidi calls this one a boot-stomper—and yeah, she's caught me tapping my toes along to it more times than I care to admit.

My heart burns,
> *From the lies you tell me*
> *Your tongue twists,*
> *Empty words you feed me*

THE SPEAKERS LET OUT AN EAR-SPLITTING SCREECH. SHELBY STOPS singing and waves her arms in the air.

"Try it again, Shelby!" someone calls out from the upper-level balcony of the pavilion.

The band starts but Shelby waits, listening for a few seconds before jumping into the song.

Big lies
> *Small truths*
> *Fake promises*

Her mouth twists in frustration as she stops to send another round of hand signals to the other guy working the soundboard in the middle of the venue.

CRYING EMPTY TEARS,
   From the lies you tell me
   Your lips move,
   Empty words you feed me

"AGAIN!" THE GUY IN THE BALCONY CLAPS HIS HANDS.

BIG LIES
   Small truths
   Fake promises

SHELBY'S MOUTH TWISTS WITH FRUSTRATION. I SEARCH THE AREA for Greg. Shouldn't he do something to fix whatever's wrong?

Finally, she makes it through the chorus without stopping and flashes a thumbs-up. As the song winds down, people from the lawn cheer and wave. With a big grin stretched across her face, Shelby waves back. "How y'all doing?" she says into the microphone.

They scream declarations of love but can't get past the locked gate or grouchy security guards.

Shelby's pretty face is a mask of tension as she walks off the stage toward me. "How'd that sound?" she asks.

"Fantastic. I'm not an expert, but it sounds much better than it did at the Tipsy Saddle."

She gives me a thin smile in return. "Trent said it's a little tinny. But I don't know if we can do much to fix it." Her nervous gaze darts to the side. "And we're out of time, anyway."

"I didn't notice." I cock my head. "Your fans seemed to love it."

A more genuine expression of happiness flashes over her flushed cheeks. "Do you know where Greg ran off to?"

I tap the pass around my neck. "He gave me this and told me where to stand but I haven't seen him since."

"I need to find my dressing room." She waves me along, and I fall into step beside her.

We're not walking down the wide, straight hallway long before we find a white door with a poster of her face and her name tacked on it.

Greg flies up to her and opens the door. "You're in here." He flicks his gaze my way. "Dawson wants to come by to talk to you in a bit. And Cindy got tied up, but she'll be down to do your hair later."

I guess that's his way of saying "don't fuck in here" or something.

"Your stuff's already unloaded," Greg says, following us inside.

It's a small room. Clean and neat. A large mirror and long white counter take up most of one wall. A nubby green couch sits across from the door—I'm already starting to feel about as useful as a cactus in a rainforest, so I'm planning to park my ass on the couch to stay out of her way.

"Wear your flowered dress to the meet and greet," Greg says. "Keep it simple."

Who knew he acted as Shelby's wardrobe adviser too?

"Save the peacock dress for the show." He presses his palms against her cheeks. "Okay?"

The vibe of the gesture is more fatherly than flirtatious, so I don't fantasize about beating him to death—not too much, anyway.

"Did my trunk make it?" she asks, searching the room. By the frantic look in her eyes, it must be important. Again, I'm struck with the urge to do *something* to help her out. But what?

Before Greg has a chance to answer, her gaze lands on a huge black and brass trunk resting on the floor at the foot of the couch. She rushes over and squats down. With two crisp snaps, she flips open the locks. "Perfect!"

"I'll be back to check on you later," Greg promises, throwing me another dirty scowl.

"Yup," Shelby mutters, barely acknowledging Greg's departure as she tosses clothes out of the trunk and onto the couch.

Awkward isn't something I'm used to experiencing or ever allow to dictate my actions. But now that we're alone again, a distance between us that I'm not sure how to close creeps into the room.

"Do you want me to go, Shelby?" I offer, even though it's the last thing I want to do. "I don't want to be in your way. Or make you nervous."

She stops her frantic searching and peers up at me. "Not at all." The corner of her mouth twists downward. "Are you bored, though? Do you want to hang—"

"No. I'm just happy being around you. Do your thing. I'll keep my big ass out of the way."

"You don't have a big ass." A bit of tension melts from her expression. She lifts her chin. "Is that a bathroom behind you?"

I reach over and tug the door open. "Looks like it."

Her nose wrinkles. "Is it clean?"

"Mostly."

She growls this cute little annoyed noise as she hurries past me with an armful of clothes.

"You know I've seen you naked, right?" I call after her.

She pauses outside the bathroom. "Trust me, I remember." She nods to the door leading to the concert venue. "But I never know who's going to pop in to check up on me."

"I can always stand guard."

"Nah." She leaves the bathroom door open, and naturally, I can't help watching her strip her sweatshirt off and shimmy out of her jeans. "I hope Heidi doesn't mind me keeping this for later," she says, tossing the sweatshirt my way.

"Doubt it." I catch the sweatshirt in my outstretched hand and can't resist a quick, furtive sniff of Shelby's scent. Fuck, this woman's reduced me to a damn foxhound.

I glance at the clock above the door. "Do you need me to grab you something to eat or drink?"

She returns, dressed in tight little yoga shorts and a tank top. "I can't eat before a show. Or after."

"You need to eat sometime."

"I ate breakfast." Her lashes flutter as she peers up at me. "I'm really happy you're here. Sorry if I'm all over the place."

"Shelby." I curl my hand over her hip—almost forgot how perfectly she fits in my grip. "I get how important all of this is. Told you, I don't want to be in your way or make you lose focus."

"You're not. I usually hang out by myself for as long as I can. I'll meditate. Do some stretches. A few vocal exercises. Hair and makeup. When there's a meet and greet set up, I do that. Right before I go onstage, I slip into my dress of the night and huddle with the band."

Her lips quirk as she casts a look over her shoulder at the trunk. "I'm not big enough for costume changes yet. So, I try to make the one dress count."

Laughing, I push a stray piece of hair off her face. "You don't need costume changes. You're already stunning."

"Thank you," she whispers.

"'Big Lies' sounded good."

Both eyebrows crawl up her forehead. "You recognized it?"

"Hell yeah. I told you, they've been playing it on the radio constantly. And every time I've been to Southwest Steakhouse lately it's been on."

She narrows her eyes. "How often do you go there?"

I shrug, not getting the change in her demeanor. "We've been using it as a meeting point between the two clubs. Told you we had Heidi's graduation party there too."

"So, you're not stopping by to pick up pretty waitresses?" Soft laughter follows her question, but the tense lines around her mouth remain.

That's what she's worried about? How adorable. The club has plenty of girls prowling around on a nightly basis. No need to troll for waitresses if I want female company.

Saying that out loud probably won't take this conversation in a pleasant direction. And I don't want to do anything to upset her before she goes onstage tonight. "No waitresses, Shelby."

She flicks a bit of hair out of her eyes. "I'm just messing with you."

Sure she is. Her spark of jealousy sends an inexplicable thrill singing in my veins and eases the awkwardness between us.

She moves to her trunk and pulls out a small tube from a shiny purple bag. Flipping it away from her, she unrolls a small, thin mat and gracefully kneels down. She slides an elastic off her wrist and gathers her hair into a ponytail. "I won't have a chance to do this later."

With that, she kneels down, and sits on her heels for a second before inching her knees apart. Slowly, she folds her body forward, extending her arms in front of her, palms down, resting her forehead on the mat.

Is she trying to drive me insane?

It's way too easy to visualize myself directly behind her, gripping her by the hips, sliding her back a few inches...

She shifts her body up and forward, until she's on hands and knees.

The fuck, Shelby?

Slowly, she arches her back, pushing her tits up and out before rounding her back, pulling her stomach up and hanging her head.

It's taking all my control not to mount her like a wild grizzly bear.

But I'm a grown-ass man. I can watch a woman...stretch her arms in front of her and raise her ass high in the air while keeping her palms on the mat...and not whip out my dick.

Pretty sure each of these poses can double as a sex position. Her routine is excruciating to watch and I'm panting by the time she returns to the first position with her forehead on the mat.

Damn, she's making it difficult to honor my promise to keep my hands to myself.

CHAPTER SIX

Shelby

The weight of Rooster's gaze settles over me as I attempt to center and ground myself. I work through a few of the yoga poses and stretches I do every night before a show. The other rituals, I'll probably skip. It feels too pretentious to sit and meditate in front of Rooster. Besides, the negative energy from my anxiety could make things worse.

That's not superstition. It's caution. Caring for the energy around me that I'll take onto the stage later. Every night is a new chance to impress a new audience. I can't afford an "off" performance on this tour. There are no second chances.

I can't find words to explain any of that to Rooster. Instead, I remain in extended child's pose—butt resting on my heels, arms stretched in front of me, and forehead to the mat, rolling my head from side to side, hoping to stimulate my third eye for a creative energy boost.

Rooster clears his throat. "I promised myself I would keep my hands off you until after your show, but you're making that...*difficult*."

I turn and peer at him under my arm. "No one said you couldn't touch me."

"I want to do a hell of a lot more than *touch*, Shelby," he rasps, so low the words move right through me.

I shift onto all fours and go through a few other movements without answering, keenly aware he's still watching. After I've finished, I carefully roll my mat and tuck it into its slim, satin bag.

"Come here." He curls his finger and pats his leg.

As I move closer, my leg brushes against his knee. He sits forward and grips my thigh, pulling me closer until I lose my balance and fall into his lap.

"Hey!" My protest is swallowed up and negated by my laughter.

He shifts me to the side and pulls my legs up, draping them over him while keeping a firm hold on my outer thigh.

"That's better." He leans in and brushes a kiss over my cheek, his beard lightly tickling my skin.

"This is nice," I murmur, resting my head on his shoulder.

He curls his other arm around my body, hugging me to him. It's a sweet, quiet moment that does more to settle my nervous heart and mind than any of my pre-show rituals.

"I could get used to this," I mutter.

"Yeah?" he rumbles.

Dang, I need to glue my mouth shut. He's going to think I'm begging him to come out on the road with me.

Someone knocks on the door, and I shoot straight up. There's no time to scoot out of Rooster's lap, though. Cindy enters and holds up her makeup case. "Ready for me, Shelby?"

Her steps falter as her gaze lands on Rooster.

I scramble to sit upright, bracing my hand on Rooster's incredibly firm chest.

"I'll give you a minute, hon." She backs out the door. "I forgot my curling iron."

I open my mouth to stop her but she's gone.

"Fun's about to start." I turn to face Rooster. His neutral expression gives nothing away. "How do you want me to introduce you to people? Do you want me to use your road name with non-bikers? Should I?"

He tilts his head and reaches up to tug on the end of my ponytail. "Logan's fine."

"I should've asked you that sooner, huh?" I rub my palm over his bristly cheek.

"You have enough to worry about." His eyes close and he leans into my touch. "I'm fine either way."

A rush of emotion floods through me, and I wrap my arms around him tight for one last squeeze before scooting off his lap.

He hooks his fingers around mine, loosely tugging. "You okay?"

"I think so. Sure you won't be bored watching me get all dolled up?"

"Nope."

"I'm back!" Cindy thrusts her curling iron in the air with a triumphant smile as she pushes into the room.

"Oh, Cindy, this is my friend Logan." I squeeze Rooster's hand quickly before letting go and moving to the makeup chair. "Logan, this is Cindy. She's a magical artist."

Cindy scoffs. "You don't even need makeup. Nice to meet you, Logan."

I can't remember anyone besides my mother, Greg, Trent, or someone from the band watching me get ready before. Certainly not a boyfriend.

Not that Rooster's my boyfriend, of course.

I cast a furtive glance his way, expecting to find him on his phone. But no, his gaze is strictly fixed on me. My cheeks heat and I face straight ahead, staring into the mirror.

"What are we doing tonight?" Cindy asks as she loosens my ponytail. "Up or down?"

"Down, maybe? I'm wearing the strapless blue dress. I think I'll feel too naked with my hair up. Or like it's prom."

Cindy chuckles and leans over to plug in the curling iron. She pauses at my tank top. "Do you want to change into a button-up?"

"Nah, I'll be careful."

She clips a short cape around my shoulders and starts dotting primer over my face.

"The hospitality room's all set up next door, Logan," Cindy says, "if you're bored."

"I'm fine." He sits forward, coming into view in the mirror. "You need water or something, Shelby?"

My cheeks heat again. This request will make me sound like such a precious little princess. "They should have room temperature water. And tea. Decaf and a slice of lemon. If there's a packet of honey, can you grab that too? Just don't put it in the tea."

He stands. "Room temp water. Decaf tea, lemon slice, honey packet. Got it." He gently squeezes my shoulder as he passes. "Cindy?"

"I'm good. Thank you."

In the mirror, I catch her eyes following him. As soon as the door closes, she blinks rapidly and grasps my shoulders. "Quick! Tell me all about him. Is he your boyfriend? This the guy you've been texting?"

The corners of my mouth twitch up and I drop my gaze to my hands in my lap. "That's him."

"Good lord, he's hot, Shelby."

"I know."

Her gaze slides to the door again. "So polite for a biker too."

Something about the comment rubs me wrong. Sure, they look rough around the edges, but Rooster's biker brothers have always been kind to me. "Bikers are nice. One of his brothers gave me the shirt off his back when I almost drowned."

While she bends and preps the set of false eyelashes she's about to apply, I tell her the story of how Rooster and I met.

"So romantic. Oh my God!" she yelps. "'White Knight!' That's about him?"

I chuckle. "Yeah, kinda."

The door clicks open, cutting off our conversation. Rooster pushes into the room, casting a smile our way. Resourceful as I remember, he seems to have fashioned a tray out of a cardboard box. Carefully, he sets my drinks on the counter in front of me. "Brought you water too, Cindy." He sets the extra bottle next to everything else.

"Thank you."

"Greg insisted I bring a sandwich back. Are you sure you won't eat something?" he asks.

"I can't." I rub my fingers over my throat. "Besides being too nervous. It's not good for my vocal cords."

"You won't mind if I do?" He lifts the box in one hand.

"Nope." Honestly, I'm happy he has a distraction. Something about having him watch me get made up—false lashes and all—feels awfully intimate.

"What color is your dress tonight?" Cindy asks.

"The royal blue one with the teal and blue ruffles."

She stares at her eyeshadow palette. "Gold. Let's go with a smoky gold. Maybe a little teal liner on your lower lashes for some pop."

"Go for it." I close my eyes.

She's slow and methodical, no longer ruffled by Rooster's presence once she starts working.

"Lash time," she announces minutes later.

I open my eyes, staring at the little packet in her hand.

"What do you think? Not too dramatic."

Only a portion of Rooster's long legs are visible to me in the mirror, so I can't tell what he's up to or if he's even listening to us. I study the long, feathery lashes for a second. "They're okay."

She sets the packet on the counter and peels one off its backer, slowly flexing it between her fingers.

"Sit still, Shelby. Look right here." Cindy points to a spot over her shoulder. The same ritual we go through every night. You'd think I'd be an expert by now, but I still flinch as the tweezers holding one of the lashes comes at my eye. "Close."

She gently presses it down and then we repeat it with my right eye. When Cindy's satisfied with my face and eyes, she steps back and studies her work. "Good. Go ahead and drink your tea while I start on your hair. We'll do your lips last."

"Thanks."

While she works on brushing my hair, I sit forward and tear open the packet of honey and suck it down in one shot.

"Not for your tea?" Rooster rumbles.

My face heats enough to melt the foundation off my forehead. "A straight shot of it works better for me than diluting it in my tea."

From the corner of my eye, I catch him nodding.

Even more nervous now that I know he's paying such close attention, I sit forward and squeeze the slice of lemon into the paper cup of tea. Before taking a sip, I dip my finger in to check the temperature and take the tea bag out, setting it on a few tissues.

Rooster scoops it out of the way.

"You don't have to—"

"Might as well be useful."

I sip most of the tea down before I start warming up. Some nights, I'll vocalize out loud. Other nights, I'll hum some scales and concentrate on breathing exercises. Tonight feels like a humming night. Cindy's careful tug, brush, and curl of my hair soothes me. I close my eyes, humming my favorite scales, concentrating on the show ahead of me.

Don't trip. Don't croak. Don't flash butt.

Nope, too negative. Concentrate on more positive mantras.

You'll project the voice of an angel.

The sound will be great, not tinny.

Someone knocks, startling me out of my trance. Disoriented, I stare into the mirror, assessing Cindy's handiwork while she leans over to open the door.

"Oh, Mr. Roads." Her voice wobbles.

My heart stops.

"Hey, Cindy. Shelby." He greets me with what my mama would call a thick East Tennessee brogue. Thumbs hooked into his belt loops, he strolls into the room. His gaze lands on Rooster and he tips his head. "Shelby's guest."

"Oh!" I spin around in the chair so fast I almost knock Cindy over. "Mr. Roads—"

"Dawson," he corrects.

"Dawson, this is my friend, Logan. He lives nearby and came to see the show tonight."

Rooster stands and the two men perform a slow assessment of each other. Dawson's older than Rooster by at least ten years. In height they're almost evenly matched but Rooster's a lot bulkier muscle-wise.

"Good to meet you," Rooster finally says.

"Shelby doesn't have guests. So, this is nice. Welcome." Dawson dips his chin, then returns his attention to me. "Shelby, how do you feel about coming out onstage with me for 'Let the Night Go?'"

I blink. My mouth opens but no words or sounds make it past my lips. Maybe I fell asleep while Cindy was working on my hair and now I'm dreaming?

"Huh?" I grunt like a cowgirl who just took a mule kick to the head. "I mean, are you sure? That's, uh, I mean, that's your song with…" The dark expression on his face forces me to swallow down the name of his ex.

"You know it?" he asks.

"Every word." That might be an exaggeration, but I've always been a fake-it-'til-ya-make-it girl.

"Great." He claps his hands like the matter's settled. My inner fangirl threatens to break loose and embarrass the tar outta me, but I manage to remain calm and professional.

Until Dawson swaggers out the door.

Cindy presses her hand to her chest. "Mother of sin, Shelby. Did he really just ask you to—"

"I think so." My gaze lands on Rooster. "Did he say what I think he said?"

"Seems so," he answers in a neutral tone. "First time he's asked you to come onstage with him?"

"Yes." I yank my cell phone out of my pocket. "I need to text my mama."

"Go ahead, honey." Cindy places a few small barrettes in my hair, pulling it off my face. "I'm almost done here. Then we'll get to your lips."

I tap out the quick text and receive an answer right away.

Please send video.

Chuckling, I turn to show Rooster her request.

"I'll record it and send it to her," he promises.

Not expecting that, I blink a few times before answering, "Thank you."

I relay the message and her next text has me doubling over with laughter.

"What?" Rooster asks.

"Nothing." I shake my head, too embarrassed to repeat her request.

"What?" He slips my phone out of my hand and chuckles when he scans the message.

Rooster's there? Send me a picture of that fine-looking man, please.

"Oh, Lynn." A smile flirts with the corners of his mouth and he shakes his head. He holds the phone out to Cindy. "Will you take a picture of us?"

"Sure."

Rooster wraps his arms around me, and I angle my head back, to stare at him for a brief second before Cindy asks us to smile.

She hands the phone back to Rooster and finishes my makeup.

"What are you doing?" I mumble, barely moving my lips while Cindy outlines them.

"Sending her a picture," Rooster answers.

In the mirror, I catch Cindy's swoon. "*Marry him*," she mouths to me.

I'd elbow her if I didn't love her so much.

I'm sure marriage is the last thing on Rooster's mind.

It's definitely way, way down on my bucket list.

Or at least it always has been.

CHAPTER SEVEN

Rooster

I'm trying hard to be the better man and not storm out of here to hunt down Dawson Roads. Shelby's clearly enamored with the guy who just casually asked her to hop onstage and sing what I assume is some 'let's fuck' ballad with him tonight.

It's only a performance. Something that could really help her career.

Must not kick Dawson's ass.

Instead, I concentrate on the pictures Cindy captured of Shelby and me. The first one's us facing the camera, but it's the second one—us looking at each other—that seizes my lungs. I send the first to Shelby's mom and the second to myself before handing the phone back to Shelby.

"All right!" Cindy squeezes Shelby's shoulders. "Perfect."

"Thank you, Cindy."

"You need help getting into your dress?"

"Nah." Shelby checks the clock. "It's almost time to run down to the meet-and-greet room."

"All right." Cindy gives me a quick wave. "Nice to meet you."

I nod at her, then focus on Shelby. "You need anything?"

"What do you think?" She spins around in her chair to face me, tilting her head at a seductive angle.

Honestly, with the layers of shit spackled on, she's barely recognizable. Cindy transformed my girl into some red-carpet-walking pageant queen version of herself. "You're beautiful no matter what."

"I sense a *but*."

"No buts." I shrug. "You look like Shelby Morgan, country superstar."

"Hmm, I guess that's a compliment." She slides out of the chair and walks over to her trunk. "Shoot. I should've hung these up earlier." She pulls out two balls of colorful fabric and some contraption that looks like a tan lace cage.

She shakes out the dresses and tosses a bright blue one over the back of the couch before stepping inside the small bathroom. Again, I watch her all creeper-style while she carefully strips off her top to avoid messing her hair. "Can you help me?"

"Putting clothes *on* you isn't really my thing." But it's not like I'm going to say *no* to touching Shelby.

Reaching behind her, she unhooks the bra she's wearing and slowly slips it off, baring the creamy expanse of her shoulders and back.

That's it. My steps quicken and in seconds I'm close enough to trace my finger down her spine.

She shivers from the contact. "Cindy will kill me if you smudge my makeup."

"I can work around that." I hug her against my chest. "Mmm." I pepper kisses from her neck to her shoulder and cup her breasts. "Fill my hands nice. Just like I remember."

She gasps and grinds her ass against me as I flick my thumbs over her nipples. "Rooster?"

"What?" I move us in front of the small mirror over the sink. We're an interesting picture. Beauty about to be devoured by the beast. "Look how pretty you are," I whisper against her ear.

She moans and wriggles against me. I plunge my hand down the front of her shorts, wedging my fingers between her thighs. "You're soaked."

"It's hot," she whispers.

I slide one finger through her slit and she gasps.

"I want to make you come."

In the mirror, our eyes meet, but my expression doesn't change. I'm dead serious. I press my hand more firmly between her thighs. "These need to come off, right?"

She licks her dark red lips and inches her feet apart instead of answering with words.

Works for me.

I yank her shorts and underwear down her legs, stopping to kiss the small of her back before helping her out of them.

These last few months, I've found myself wondering if my mind exaggerated how gorgeous Shelby is. Her hips couldn't possibly curve in such a perfect way to fit my big hands, could they? *Yup, they do.* Her plush thighs and ass are as gorgeous as I remember too. None of that thigh gap nonsense I've overheard some of the club girls bragging about. Not on my Shelby. She's got smooth legs, toned from years of hard work as a waitress and now the discipline she uses in her performances. "You're beautiful everywhere. You know that?"

"No," she whispers.

"Guess you need me around to remind you more often." Now that she's bare, I pull her against me again.

"This seems unfair. I'm naked. You're fully dressed."

"We'll even up later."

"I'm nervous someone will walk in..."

Without moving my eyes from the mirror, I reach back and slam the door shut. "Don't worry about anything else. I'll take care of you."

She has a point, though. We don't have the luxury of time on our side. I nip her earlobe. "I want to thoroughly lick your pussy and fuck you for hours, Shelby. This is only a preview."

I skate my hand over her stomach, straight between her legs, pressing the pad of one finger over her clit.

"Oh!" She jolts against me.

"Spread your legs."

She inches her feet apart and I bend to get a better angle, gently sliding one finger inside her.

"Oh God," she whines.

I add another finger, slowly stretching and opening her. My lips find their way to her neck, sucking at her skin. My other hand cups her breast, pinching her nipple until she squirms.

"Pretty, Shelby." I grind the heel of my hand against her clit, slowly working my fingers in and out of her. "So tight."

She arches her back and writhes against me. A silent scream parts her lips.

"That's it," I encourage.

I can't help the dirty smirk on my mouth as she grinds herself against my hand, carelessly chasing her pleasure. A few tiny whimpers pass her lips. Sweat mists her skin. I slow my thrusting fingers but don't stop until she drops her head. Her ragged breathing and trembling limbs are the only movement between us.

"Oh my God." She wraps her hand around my wrist, and tugs. "Too much."

Her little body jumps as I withdraw my fingers. Not sure she can hold herself upright, I keep one arm around her. "I can't move," she whispers.

Beating on my chest would probably ruin the moment, but damn if I'm not tempted. I lean over and kiss her bare shoulder instead.

"Let's get you dressed."

"What about you?" She reaches back and strokes my painfully hard dick through my jeans.

"No." I shift away from her touch before I come in my pants. "Later." I brush my thumb over her carefully painted red lips. "When I can properly smear this."

When she finally opens her eyes, they're practically glowing. A deep sense of satisfaction hammers through my blood. She nips the end of my thumb and I groan. "Careful, Shelby," I warn. "I'm short on restraint at the moment."

She pouts but takes a step back. I lean forward and flick the faucet on, quickly washing my hands and wetting a paper towel to dab the sweat off her chest and arousal from her thighs.

"Still need my help?"

A serene smile ghosts over her lips. "The orgasm was more than helpful." She picks up the cage-like contraption from the edge of the sink and arranges her tits into the lacy cups. "But I could use your assistance with this."

Fastening the long line of hooks down her back is a tricky job. Big fingers and tiny metal hooks don't mix. But something worse occurs to me as I work each closure. "Who usually helps you?"

She chuckles softly and shimmies to adjust her tits again. "I'll usually hook it in front and twist it around, but it's a pain in the ass." She shrugs. "I don't feel comfortable asking Cindy."

Her simple admission wraps around my heart and squeezes. Too shy to ask anyone else to help her with something so simple but intimate. I don't know what to think about that. Actually, I suspect I *do* know—I just can't afford to let the feelings form and take hold when she'll be two states away by the beginning of next week.

"There." I pat her ass, enjoying the bounce of her flesh against my palm.

She bends over to pick up her shorts and I groan. It would be so easy to have her grip the edge of the sink, arch her back, and—

But a quick fuck in the bathroom isn't enough. I want to twist my fingers in her mess of blond curls, kiss her until that lipstick's smeared down her chin, and make her come so hard mascara-tinged tears run down her cheeks.

"I'm almost out of underwear." She peeks up at me. "Don't suppose I can do laundry at your place tonight?"

Laughing, I snatch the soaked garments out of her hand. "I had other activities in mind, but yeah, there's a laundry room at the clubhouse."

"Help me into the dress?" She unzips it and holds it up off the ground, demonstrating what she needs me to do.

Balancing on my shoulders, she steps into the dress and I help her pull it in place, finally tugging the zipper to the top.

"Perfect." Her eyes soften and she touches my cheek. "Thank you."

"No problem."

I follow her into the other room and reclaim my spot on the couch while she searches through her trunk, finally digging out a cute pair of the short-shorts I remember she likes to wear under her dresses when she's onstage. Next, she wraps her fingers around a pair of socks and her brown, fringed cowboy boots.

I groan while she shimmies the shorts up under her dress. Finally, she steps into her boots and spins to face me, placing her hands on her hips.

"What do you think?"

My gaze roams over her for a few seconds. "You look like a cowgirl about to conquer the world."

Her features soften. "Rooster."

I hold out my hands and she moves closer, curling her fingers around mine and leaning over to kiss my cheek. "Thank you for *that*." She tilts her head toward the bathroom. "I intend to repay the favor."

"And I intend to collect, lil' chickadee." My gaze drops to the ample cleavage about five inches from my face. "Keep leaning over like that, and I'm gonna bury my face between your tits."

"Oh." She presses her hand to her chest and stands up straight. Laughter flows past her lips. "I better watch how I lean at the meet and greet."

"Yeah, I'd hate to gouge out any eyes," I growl.

Ignoring my comment, she holds out her hand. "Come on."

Time's brought a lot more people backstage. People stand around doing nothing but blocking people trying to do their jobs. Technicians push equipment; people wearing red T-shirts with STAFF in big white letters carry overloaded boxes of drinks; photographers hold their cameras up and out of harm's way.

"Is it always this busy?"

"Worse, usually."

Fans have been corralled against one wall of the hallway by a line of black rope and black metal poles. Some call out to Shelby. Sweet as always, she shines a sunny smile their way and waves.

Greg meets us and gives her a nod of approval. "You only have an hour. I'll be back in a bit."

She gives him a questioning look before ducking inside a room to our left.

He holds out his hand, stopping me from following Shelby inside. I turn the full power of my don't-fuck-with-me glare on him, but he doesn't back off.

"You sticking with Shelby?" he asks.

"Yeah. You're kinda in my way."

His mouth twitches. "Listen, some of these guys get overzealous. Give 'em two minutes apiece. Let 'em snap a picture, ask her a question, sign an autograph, then move 'em along. Anyone puts their hands on her, eject them immediately."

I wasn't aware I was serving as a bouncer tonight. "Who looks after her when I'm not here?"

"I do." He turns and searches the area. "Or Trent. But I need to be in Dawson's room and Trent's taking care of something else. Since you're here, can you help out?"

"Yeah," I growl.

"Keep things orderly." He looks me up and down. "But these are her fans who paid good money to meet her, so don't terrorize them."

"Thin line, Greg." I slap his back and brush past him into the room.

Shelby's smile falters when I walk into the room alone. She focuses on the open door and hallway beyond. "Where the heck's he off to?"

"Said he needs to help Dawson." I shrug. "I'm supposed to keep order tonight."

"Darn it." She gathers the skirt of her dress in her hand and actually stomps her foot like she's about to charge after her manager.

"Easy, chickadee." I touch her elbow. "Might as well put my big, growly ass to good use tonight."

"You're my guest, not free labor. I'm so sorry."

I curl one hand over her shoulder and brush my fingers under her chin, tipping her head back. "I'm more worried about who looks out for you when I'm not here."

"Greg. Or Trent. Sometimes one of Dawson's guys. Or security for the venue. Whoever's around."

In other words, no one makes sure Shelby's safety is their top priority. If I'd known, I probably would've asked Jigsaw to join us. If that scary son of a bitch doesn't scare people, no one will.

"It'll be fine," she assures me. "I'm not that big of a deal to have people here to watch me. We usually have a few kids. Some radio station winners. Everyone's super nice." She shrugs. "But once in a while…"

"I'll be right here." I nod to the fans being let into the room by a local security guard in a black and yellow T-shirt. "Don't worry about anything."

"Thank you."

I stand next to the banner with Shelby's name and image splashed over it, where I can watch her but not be in the way.

A little girl runs up and throws her arms around Shelby's legs, chattering a mile a minute. Shelby squats so she's eye level with the tyke and scrawls her signature over a poster. After a quick photo, the girl's mother nudges her along.

Not that I expected her to be anything but sweet and kind to everyone but the more I watch her, the more that foreign L word keeps pulsing in my chest.

CHAPTER EIGHT

Shelby

Having Rooster at my back gives me a certain amount of peace I don't want to get too comfortable with. Normally, Greg or Trent stand guard, but I can't count on them to stay focused on me one hundred percent of the time. With Rooster, I'm confident he's concentrating on me. I'm completely safe under his watchful eyes.

Security manages the line of people at the door, only allowing a few fans into the room at a time.

"Hi, Shelby!" Another little girl screams and throws her arms around my legs.

"Is this your first concert?" I ask.

"Yes! You're my fav-o-rite." I lean over to hug her, listening to her excited high-pitched chatter with a smile stretched across my face.

Her mother nervously chuckles. "She's a big fan." In a lower voice, she adds, "*I'm* here for Dawson Roads."

Gee, thanks, lady.

I smile thinly and return my attention to the girl, signing her poster and ticket stub. "Have an awesome time tonight."

After that, it's a blur of people. A couple who just got engaged. A girl who won tickets off the local radio show. A little boy who's too tongue-tied to say anything, no matter how hard I try to play it cool and normal.

I smile for so many pictures, my cheeks ache. The last group the guard allows into the room appear to be college-aged guys.

"Hello, Miss Morgan." One of them holds out his hand. He's shy and polite. Cute too, with freckles and an intense farmer's tan. His two rowdier buddies obviously and openly stare at my tits without saying a word. But I'm used to that and my tits are pretty fabulous, so I try to ignore their stares.

The four of us turn to face the camera for a picture. Someone's hand strays to my ass, squeezing hard enough to make me yelp.

A short scream barely passes my lips.

The offender drops to his knees next to me, howling in pain.

"Hands to yourself, motherfucker," Rooster growls, bending the guy's arm back at an unnatural angle. "Apologize. Right fucking now."

"S...sorry, Shelby."

Two security guards bumble over and Rooster releases the ass-grabber with a hard shove.

Grabby hands is escorted away from me.

One of the guards reaches for Rooster next.

Oh hell no. I slap my hand on the guy's chest, stopping him. "Whatdaya think you're doin'? He's with *me*. Maybe pay better attention next time."

The guard's eyes go wide. "Sorry, Miss Morgan."

I turn to thank Rooster, but his steely gaze is trained on the three guys as security pushes them out the door.

"Hey." I tap his arm. "Thank you."

"That happen often?"

"Not really."

He growls an unhappy noise and wraps an arm around my waist. "What's next?"

I flick my gaze at the clock. My heart thunders. Time's ticking down. I gulp in some air and try to settle my nerves.

"Shelby?" he questions.

"T-minus thirty. I need to get ready."

He walks me back to my small dressing room.

Once we're inside, I strip off my dress and shake out the blue one. Rooster presses his back to the door so at least I don't have to worry about anyone popping in for a free peep show.

What's left of my cup of tea has long gone cold, but I take a quick sip anyway.

"Do you want me to get you a fresh one?" Rooster asks.

"Nah, I don't want to have to pee when I'm on stage."

He chuckles. "Okay."

Embarrassed I blurted that out, I duck into the bathroom to empty my bladder. My nerves are already so jangled, I'll be peeing twenty times tonight.

When I return to the dressing room, Rooster's waiting patiently by the door. "Need help with the dress?"

"If you don't mind."

He holds it out for me, and I step into it the same way I did with the earlier outfit. "Careful, or I'm going to hire you. . .as soon as I have money for a personal assistant."

"I'd never take your money, Shelby," he answers in a low, serious tone that makes my belly quiver. He slides the zipper into place and after adjusting the girls in my long-line strapless bra, I turn to face him.

He runs his finger over the tops of my breasts, following the bodice of the dress. "This is pretty on you. Did your mom make it?"

I slide my hands over the smooth royal blue leather top and adjust the layers of teal, blue, purple, and green ruffles that end right above my knees. "Yes." I kick out my feet in the electric teal boots Rooster bought me in San Antonio. "She made it to match these."

A smile flickers over his mouth.

"Hey." I reach up and grab a fistful of his T-shirt. "I didn't thank you properly."

He raises one eyebrow. "For?"

I tug him a little closer and whisper against his ear. "The earlier orgasm."

We're so close, his beard tickles my cheek when he smiles. "Pleasure was mine."

"Well, I plan to repay the favor later."

Heat races across my skin as his gaze roams over my bare shoulders. He reaches out and tucks a wild sprig of hair behind my ear. "Looking forward to it."

I glance down. "And rescuing me. Again." I tilt my head toward the hallway. "Thank you for reacting so quick."

The line of his jaw tightens. "What would you have done if I wasn't there?"

"Slapped him? Yelled for security?" I shrug and force a smile on my face. "I'm going to dedicate 'White Knight' to you tonight." I tickle my fingers through his beard. "You won't be embarrassed, will you?"

His serious expression doesn't change. "Not at all."

Someone knocks and before I answer, Greg pushes inside. "How're you feeling, Shelby?"

I clutch my stomach, willing the flock of two-stepping butterflies to settle down. "About to puke."

Sympathy shines in his eyes. "You've got this. I saw you put 'Empty Room' back on the set list?"

My shoulders jerk up. Greg knows the origin of "Empty Room." I don't understand why I'm so uncomfortable discussing the song in front of Rooster.

"You sure?" he asks.

"I think so."

"Hey, Shelbs." Trent pokes his head inside the room. "Let's go knock 'em on their asses." He lifts his chin at Rooster. "Thanks for having her back in the meet-n-greet."

Guess word spread.

Greg turns his questioning gaze on Rooster. "What happened?"

"Some dude-bro thought he'd grab a handful of my ass," I answer before Rooster has a chance.

"Fuck all." Greg stabs his fingers through his hair. "I'm sorry, honey. I shouldn't—" His gaze flicks to Rooster. "Thank you."

"No problem."

"Dawson spoke to you?" Greg asks me. "You know the lyrics?"

"Not now, Greg." I flap my hands in the air. "Let me survive my own show, first."

He chuckles and holds up his hands in surrender.

Before I know it, my band and our crew circle around me. Together, we walk down the long corridor to the entrance for the stage. Instinctively, I reach for Rooster's hand and he squeezes me back. Having him as part of my posse tonight reassures me more than anything else.

Don't get used to it.

Day after tomorrow, I'll be on my own again.

CHAPTER NINE

Rooster

Even my cynical nature can't ignore the current of excitement in the air as we walk Shelby to the stage.

It's still daylight so the flashing lights don't have the same effect they would have if it was dark out. But the announcer loudly welcoming Shelby to the stage can't be ignored.

A much-needed breeze blows through the hallway, cooling the air.

Shelby huddles with her band and they share a few quick words, chant some upbeat lines, then pile their hands together, whooping as they break.

Two guys swarm around her. One hands her a microphone before rigging a small wireless box to the belt of her dress. Someone else hands her a smaller piece for her ear.

The band swaggers out onto the stage first.

Shelby stands a few feet from the entrance, eyes closed, back against a stack of equipment. One hand's in a white-knuckled death-grip around her mic and the other is balled into a fist at her side. I want to wish her luck, kiss her, or do something to encourage her but I don't want to take her out of whatever headspace she's trying to achieve.

Finally, she opens her eyes, staring straight at me. She takes a few steps closer, goes up on tiptoes, and plants a quick kiss on my cheek before darting away.

"Good evening, Wellspring, New York!" she shouts as she struts onto the stage, one hand in the air, waving to the audience. She's completely confident—regal almost. No one would ever guess minutes ago she claimed to be jittery and ready to hurl.

"Y'all ready to have a good time?" she shouts.

The crowd's reaction is weak at best. They're still not quite paying attention. One excited voice and a shrill whistle stands out, though. I move closer, peering into the crowd, laughing when I see Heidi, arms up, hooting for Shelby. Right next to her, Murphy's standing and whistling. Out on the lawn, the rest of the club makes even more noise. People waiting in line at the food stands turn and look. More people roam over the grass, slowly wandering closer, curiously staring at the stage.

That's right, assholes. Best part of the show's about to start.

The band launches into "Big Lies" and by the time they're finished and headed into the second song, the inside seats have filled with more people.

"That one always draws them in," Greg shouts near my ear.

"I see that."

"She's really got something special. Dawson's been fantastic exposure for her, but I need to get her a tour with a later time slot."

Unsure why he's bothering to explain any of this to me, I nod along.

After three songs, Shelby slows things down. Someone brings her an acoustic guitar and slips it over her head. She turns away, plucking a few strings and signaling to her drummer, then Trent, before turning back to the microphone.

"This song's real special to me." Her husky voice comes through the speakers tinged with sadness. "I wrote it about my baby sister. It's called 'Empty Room.'"

She closes her eyes for a moment.

Sister?

Shelby's never mentioned a sister. I've spent time at the house she shares with her mom outside San Antonio. Never saw any indication anyone aside from the two of them lived there. Hell, no one else could *fit* in that place.

Front and center on the stage, she strums a chord or two. A few seconds later, her voice pours from her soul, firm and heartbreakingly clear.

"Everyone says remember the good times,
Hold them in your heart
Bright memories,
Funny days,
The good times.

But all I see is solitude,
The broken hearts,
Your empty room."

A brick of understanding lands in my gut.
Oh, Shelby. Why didn't you ever tell me?

"All that's left is an echo,
Of a little girl's laughter
Dry your tears in the sun,
Hold the family tighter"

Every word pierces what little soul I have left.

"But all I see is solitude,
The broken hearts
Your empty room."
When she finishes, she closes her eyes and drops her head for a

moment. The hush over the crowd only lasts a minute. People whistle and demand more.

Someone shouts "White Knight!" which wipes the sadness off her face. She smiles and turns her head my way. The cute eyebrow wiggle she sends me lifts the heavy cloud that settled over the stage during "Empty Room." I can't help laughing.

Greg's face screws up. "*You're* the one she wrote this about?"

"Apparently," I growl, hoping he'll shut up so I can concentrate on Shelby.

"Y'all wanna hear 'White Knight?'" she shouts.

The audience responds with a loud and enthusiastic, "Yes!"

"All right." She nods and strums her guitar a few times. "It's a good time to play it. The person who inspired this song is here with me tonight. My very own white knight."

"Sometimes your white knight rides a Harley,
And he doesn't need an army,
To save you from drowning,
In three feet of water..."

Her clear, emotional voice throws me right back to the day we met. The soggy jeans and boots clinging to my skin as I fished her out of the San Antonio River. Shelby's mom catching us in the shower and wondering if I was about to get a shotgun blast to the chest...all of it.

She's embellished the song, added to it since the first time she played it in Texas. It's much more polished now. Again, I'm in awe of this woman. Her talent, sweetness, and beauty smack me in the face every time I'm around her.

"This is already tearing up the charts," Greg says. "We stopped and recorded it in Tennessee. I was able to get special placement on a few of the streaming services."

"That's good." *Now, shut up, Greg.*

Uncomfortable, since she's singing about me and I'm the farthest thing from a white knight, I focus on the audience. The seats aren't filled yet but the people who *are* here appear to be huge Shelby Morgan fans. She keeps saying she's just the opening act, downplaying her role on this tour. Or maybe it's hard for Shelby to see it from the inside. But she's a *way* bigger deal than she realizes.

My gaze strays to a guy hanging over the balcony with a huge, "Will you marry me, Shelby Morgan?" sign.

No, she won't, asshole.

She's mine.

At least for the next two days.

I don't want to think about what happens after we have to say goodbye.

CHAPTER TEN

Shelby

"Phew!" I hurry off the stage and grab the towel Greg hands me, quickly dabbing beads of sweat from my forehead. All the stage makeup feels heavier than ever and I wish I could wash it off now instead of sitting through the next band's set while I wait to go onstage with Dawson.

Holy shit, I'm going to sing with Dawson Roads!

I turn, scanning the area for Rooster. The man must be my good-luck charm. This is the first night of the tour Dawson's asked me to sing with him. And Rooster's here to see one of the biggest moments of my life.

Lordy, I better not screw it up.

My heart skips when I find him leaning against the wall, arms crossed over his chest.

Did I freak him out by playing "White Knight?" I didn't mention him by name, but he knows the song is about him. Is he mad I played it since his club brothers are out in the audience tonight? Will they razz him about it later? Maybe he's embarrassed that some silly girl wrote a corny country song about him.

As I'm spiraling into my freak-out, he pushes away from the wall and through the crush of people around us. "You were phenomenal."

Before I have a chance to answer, he picks me up and plants a kiss on my lips.

Manager, band—heck, everything around us is forgotten the second our mouths meet. I keep my eyes open, staring straight into his. I'm consumed by the taste and feel of him. Reckless, I close my eyes and deepen our kiss, unconcerned that we're making out backstage where lots of spectators are sure to get an eyeful.

People will talk. Pictures could be taken.

Next to us, someone clears their throat.

I fight my way through a fog of lust back to hard reality.

When I pull away, Rooster's face is fierce, hot, and primal, reflecting the desires at war inside me.

He sets me down gently but keeps an arm around my waist.

Greg's disapproving manager face is a bucket of ice water down my dress.

"Shelby, you need to get ready for the duet with Dawson." Although he doesn't scold me for the public display of affection, his stern tone conveys the gist of his feelings on the matter.

"I have plenty of time. Gonna take at least thirty minutes before Thundersmoke goes onstage. Their set's about forty-five minutes. Another half hour to set up for Dawson..."

"Don't blow this, Shelby."

"I won't," I insist, annoyed he thinks I'd squander the opportunity.

Rooster remains surprisingly quiet during our exchange. Once I've made it clear to Greg that I have plans, I tug on Rooster's hand and lead him back to my dressing room.

"I'm so sorry. I originally wanted to leave with you after my set. I never expected..."

"It's fine, Shelby." He settles his hands on my hips and presses my back against the door.

I peer up at him. "Were you mad?"

"Mad?" He frowns, his gaze darting from side to side. "About what?"

"'White Knight?' What I said? Your brothers—"

"I couldn't give a fuck what they think." He strokes his knuckles over my cheek. "You were *sunshine* lighting up that stage. I'm so impressed with how much you've changed since the Tipsy Saddle."

"You think I've changed?"

"Only in the best ways."

"Thank you," I whisper.

"What do you need to do to get ready for this duet?" His voice remains neutral, so I can't tell how he feels about me getting up and singing a love song with another man. Not just any man either, but country music's biggest sex symbol—not that Rooster would know that.

"Uh, well, first, I'd really like to check out the festival."

He draws back, forehead wrinkled. "Can you do that?"

"I've never tried before. But I figure if I change my outfit and slap on a hat, no one will notice me."

"I don't think it works that way, Shelby." He twirls a finger through my curls. "You're extremely noticeable."

"Please? I never get to see the crowd from the other side." I clap my hand over my mouth. "Shoot. I need to bring my guitar with me for the hospital visit. How am I—"

He's already slipping his cell phone out of his pocket and texting someone. "Birch drove the van. I'll have him meet us in the back lot. We can load up whatever you need."

"Really? But...?" I don't even want to ask how he's going to get me to the show the day after tomorrow because that's where we'll part ways, and I can't even think about saying goodbye when we've barely said hello.

He flashes another don't-worry-about-it grin. "I'll scrounge up a vehicle one way or another. I got you, Shelby." He gently turns me around and tugs the zipper of my dress all the way down. "Change. I don't think we have too long before your ass needs to be back here to get ready."

I shimmy out of the dress, toss it on the couch, and run into the bathroom to check out my makeup. Everything's more or less in place. My hair's a little wild but nothing I can't fix later. I race out of the bathroom, grabbing the jeans I'd worn earlier, a tank top with a pair of kissing flamingos on the front, and a pair of red and pink Converse sneakers. "There. No one will recognize me." I hold out my arms for Rooster to inspect my "disguise."

He smirks at the flamingos. "If you say so. Hat?"

I have a ratty red ball cap I brought on tour for bad hair days. *Country Strong* is embroidered across the front in worn white thread. I gather my hair into a loose ponytail and pull the cap into place.

"Better?"

"I guess we'll see." He jerks his chin at my trunk. "What else do you need?"

I grab my bag of dirty laundry, praying he wasn't kidding about the washing machine at the clubhouse. A few clean items, a gift pack for my Dream Makers visit, and other assorted things I like to have with me get shoved into a plain tote. "Anything else, I'll stuff in my backpack."

Rooster picks up my guitar case before opening the door.

I stare down at my sad little bags. "I feel like a vagabond."

He slips his hand around mine, guiding me through the crowded backstage corridor leading to the loading dock. "Why?"

I hold up my laundry bag, which actually has "laundry" printed on the side, and the other plain bag. "Not exactly fine luggage."

"You really don't need it where we're going."

No one stops us on the way out. My pass is firmly around my neck and my cell phone's in my pocket. Still, the feeling that I'm a naughty kid sneaking out after curfew clings to me all the way to the parking lot.

Rooster checks his phone again. "He's here."

A plain black, windowless van idles next to one of Dawson's tour buses. As we approach, a husky man with the same Lost Kings MC cut Rooster's wearing steps out.

"Hey," he greets Rooster with a handshake, and lifts his chin in my direction.

"Thanks, brother." Rooster nods to me. "Shelby, this is Birch; Birch, Shelby. I don't think you two met before."

"Hey, Birch."

"Good show, Shelby."

"Thanks."

They arrange my stuff in the back of the van. A twinge of fear has me checking on my guitar twice before they shut the doors. I don't like to be too far away from it.

Rooster seems to sense my dilemma. "Birch won't let anything happen to it," he assures me. Simple as that. No teasing or telling me I'm silly.

"Promise," Birch swears.

We say goodbye and Rooster searches the grassy knoll around the parking area. "I think this leads to the lawn seating area if we follow it to the right. Then we should be able to get back into the pavilion. That okay?"

"I'm just excited to be out with you instead of cooped up in the dressing room."

He takes my hand again as we hike up a gentle slope to reach the small dirt path curving to the right. "What do you usually do after your show?"

"Chill in my dressing room. Sometimes Dawson invites us to hang out on one of his buses." I lower my voice because you just never know when big ears are listening. "Thundersmoke kinda keeps to themselves. We never really see them unless they're onstage."

"That's...weird."

I shrug. It had seemed odd at first, but I haven't given it much thought lately.

We come to an eight-foot high chain-link fence and stop. Farther down, there's a gate and Rooster leads us toward it. One flash of our passes and the guard lets us through. We hit a sidewalk that leads to a semi-circle of tents selling everything from thirteen-dollar cans of beer to cotton candy.

"You sure you're not hungry?" he asks.

"Nope."

To our right, a couple of booths are set up selling merchandise for the bands. Dawson's is obviously the biggest and busiest tent. But mine has a longer line than I expected stretched in front.

Rooster squeezes my hand. "Think they sell a Shelby Morgan T-shirt big enough to fit me?"

I giggle at the thought of him in one of the pale pink T-shirts. "Probably not. Maybe I'll have some input on the next batch and they won't be girly pink." I point to the flamingos on my shirt. "I want to design one with a flamingo in cowgirl boots."

He throws his head back and laughs. "Cute. Maybe it should have a little guitar too."

"I like it." And I *really* like how he embraces my idea instead of mocking it like other people have.

He pulls out his phone again and sends a quick text. A few seconds later, he searches the lawn where the "seats" are made up of blankets and chairs people brought from home. Greg said the inside tickets sold out the first day they went on sale. Lawn seats were still available until a week ago, and now I see why. Every available square inch of grass is claimed by someone or something.

"They're to the left." Rooster points.

Even though the lawn's crowded, somehow the bikers have managed to maintain a wide swath of grass between them and everyone else.

Rooster presses his finger to his lips as we creep closer. Murphy laughs when he spots our approach but that doesn't provide Jigsaw with enough warning before Rooster jumps on his back, tackling him to the grass.

"Motherfucker!" Jigsaw shouts, pushing Rooster off him.

Rooster rolls to the side, laughing. "That was too easy."

Heidi shakes her head as she approaches me. "Are you supposed to be out here?" she whispers.

I shrug. No one seems to be paying me any mind. "So far, so good."

"You were great."

"Thanks."

Trinity joins us and gives me a big hug. Her husband, Wrath, nods at me.

Heidi reintroduces me to her brother, Teller, and his fiancée, Charlotte. Rooster points out everyone else. Sparky gives me a bleary-eyed smile when I lean down to hug him.

"Best concert I've ever been to," he whispers in my ear.

"Aw, thanks."

Everyone's so careful not to say my name, I wonder if Rooster warned them ahead of time not to blow my cover.

Trinity takes Rooster aside for a few quick words. He nods and glances at me, then calls Heidi over.

Teller taps the cooler next to him. "You want anything?"

"I'm good."

Rooster takes my hand again. "We need to get you ready."

"We'll walk with you," Murphy says. "We're going back to our seats anyway."

"I see how it is. Too good for us," Ravage calls out.

Ignoring them, Murphy takes Heidi's hand and leads her up the hill to the sidewalk.

"You're coming to the clubhouse later, right?" Heidi asks Rooster.

"Yeah. Trinity said we can take Z's old room."

Heidi wrinkles her nose. "Well, if you want to stay at our place, you're more than welcome. Either way, we'll catch up while the guys are in church," Heidi promises. "Hope and Lilly are excited to see you again too."

My heart kicks up. While I haven't wanted to acknowledge it, I've been homesick. Remembering how welcoming the ol' ladies of Rooster's club were last time leaves a warm feeling in my chest. I'm looking forward to seeing everyone tomorrow.

First, I have to survive this duet with Dawson Roads.

CHAPTER ELEVEN

Rooster

Taking a video of my girl singing a duet of what's apparently a 'let's fuck all night' song is not on the list of things I wanted to do. Ever.

Yet here I am, standing to the side of the stage, preparing to do just that.

I must like Lynn.

And I must *really* like Shelby.

Jigsaw elbows me and leans in close. "You feel like a *cuck*, getting ready to film her singing with some other dude?"

Little bit, honestly. "You've been watching too much porn, asshole. I'm not a cuckold. They're *singing*, not fuckin' in front of me."

"Yeah, but what if they get all hot and bothered—"

"Keep runnin' your mouth, I'm gonna end you," I growl. Why the fuck did I give this bonehead the extra pass Greg slipped me earlier?

"Be serious. You think she's banging him?" Jigsaw lifts his chin toward the jumbo screens lit up with Dawson's pretty-boy face. "I mean, they're out on the road together. They're lonely. Things get a little hot—"

"No. Stop running your mouth, dickface." *Fuck, I hope not.* "Her mom wants to see the duet."

"Her mom's hot, right?"

"Would you shut up?" I gesture to my phone. "I don't need your stupid commentary in the background."

He pulls a fake zipper over his lips but continues laughing.

Dick.

I move closer to the edge of the stage to capture the best angle. I've also asked Heidi to record it since she and Murphy have tickets smack in the middle only a few rows back. Lynn will get the backstage and front-and-center experiences.

Dawson finally ends his eye-rolling bro anthem dedicated to tailgates, tan lines, and tiny cut-off shorts—not that I don't enjoy all three things myself, but to devote an entire song to them? Christ. People really pay money to listen to this shit?

"Now, I got somethin' special for y'all." Dawson wipes sweat off his brow and squints out into the crowd. "I've been lucky enough to have this little lady on tour with me for the last couple months. Tonight, I asked if she'd help me sing a certain song." He pauses and the crowd screams their enthusiasm. "Give a big, warm welcome to Miss Shelby Morgan!"

I hit record, expecting Shelby to enter from the other side of the stage like she did earlier. But the giant silver platform that raised Dawson from under the floor earlier rises again. A cloud of smoke billows through the air. As it clears, Shelby's standing at the top of the platform, so tiny, but looking ready to kick some ass. She slowly struts down the ramp, one arm raised in the air, waving at the crowd. "How y'all doing?"

Dawson meets her at the end of the ramp, taking her hand like he's escorting her to a fucking ball.

I'm white-knuckle gripping my phone but keep on recording.

The lights dim, and Dawson's band slides into a slow, seductive melody. Dawson releases Shelby and starts crooning about a one-night stand he doesn't want to end.

I refuse to acknowledge the parallel between his lyrics and my own relationship with Shelby.

Jigsaw side-eyes me with this pitying expression I want to punch off his face. I shove him to the side instead.

Shelby belts out her part of the song, staring at Dawson with a doe-eyed expression that I have to remind myself is all part of the performance.

When the song finally, mercifully ends, I take a breath.

"Shelby Morgan, everyone!" Dawson yanks her close and kisses her cheek. "Thank you, darlin'."

I press stop on the recording.

Jigsaw slaps my shoulder. "Good luck with that, brother."

"Fuck off. It's for the show."

His mouth twists into a devilish smile. I brace myself for whatever's about to come out of his foolish mouth. "Well, look at it this way. She can't ever give you shit for working with Stella's company."

Fuck, I hadn't given the club's budding porn empire a lot of thought lately. Since marrying Lilly, Z's shifted most of the responsibility for running it to me. Which is fine. I don't have the same history with Stella he has, and I certainly have no interest in developing one.

"I'm not worried about it."

He searches the stage again. "This whole tour's one big ol' sausage fest. Shelby's the only chick?"

I nod toward Dawson, who's moved on to a song about bonfires, boots, and big trucks. "He's got backup singers." I tug on Jigsaw's pass. "Maybe this should've gone to Heidi."

"Nah., I got your back."

I snort at that. "You obviously haven't seen Heidi swinging her hammer." I wave at him over my shoulder. "Come on."

The security guard recognizes me from earlier but gives Jigsaw a longer inspection than required. Guy must not enjoy his good health.

Shelby's signing things for a group of fans. Half of them are men with worshipful expressions on their faces. I swear to God, one of them is a grown-ass man with a plushy-looking brown bunny backpack slung over his shoulder. Now I've seen everything.

I place my hand on Jiggy's arm, stopping him.

"Behave," I warn.

We park our asses against the wall across from Shelby. She glances up and smiles at us.

"Shit, she's cute." Jigsaw rubs his hand over his chin while giving my girl a long, slow eye fondle. "I get why you're so—"

"Don't," I warn.

When she finishes with the fans, she bounces over to us, a happy smile lighting up her face. "What'd you think?"

"You were the best part of Dawson's whole show," Jigsaw answers with his hand in the air like he's swearing an oath.

I flash my phone at her. "Sent the video to your mom. Waiting for Heidi to send me hers and I'll forward it too."

"Oh my gosh!" She jumps up, looping her arms around my neck. "Thank you! I was so nervous, I forgot."

"No problem." I lean down and wrap my myself around her, tucking my fingers into the back pockets of her jeans. "Jiggy's right. You *were* the best part of the show," I add in a lower voice.

"Stop." She ducks her head. "I was so shaking so bad, I flubbed a couple lines."

"Couldn't tell."

She tips her head back and yawns, covering her mouth at the last minute. "Sorry."

"You must be exhausted. Ready to leave?" I'm not sure if she's supposed to stick around but I'm dying to be alone with her.

"Yes." She unwraps herself from me and steps back. "Let me check with Greg. You guys can hang out in the hospitality room if you want."

We follow her down the hall. Her dressing room's been cleared out. Looks like most of her band's gear is gone as well. "They pack up already?"

"Yup. We always do as soon as we're finished." She flashes me a quick smile. "No time to waste. The rhythm of the road keeps on rolling."

CHAPTER TWELVE

Shelby

Heart still racing from the unexpected extra performance, I follow Rooster to his bike. He hands me my helmet but before I strap it on, I reach up and touch his cheek. "Thank you so much for everything tonight."

"I didn't do anything."

"Sure you did. It was real nice having you here."

He slides hands around my waist, dipping down to gently knead my butt. "Looking forward to spending time with you."

"I'm sorry I scheduled that thing—"

He stops me with a finger against my lips. "It's not a problem." His gaze darts to the side and he opens his mouth as if he has more to add but then shakes his head. "Let's go."

I tighten the helmet on my own, but he checks to make sure it's secure before throwing his leg over the bike in one fluid movement.

"Come on," he urges.

I rest my palm on his shoulder and slide into place behind him.

Loud, rumbling pipes shake the ground around us, vibrating against my legs and butt. He leans and lifts the kickstand, and my heart jumps. My arms tighten around his middle.

Hanging on tight, I press into his back as he steers us down the bumpy lane. Where the gravel meets the pavement, we run into Murphy. He and Rooster signal to each other before rolling onto the next road. The chaos gathering in my heart and mind settles. The usual fretting I indulge in after a show is forgotten. Rooster's firm presence and expert way he handles the bike ratchets up my desire again.

Since the show isn't over yet, we're able to slip out of the park faster than we came in. No line of cars block our exit.

We meet up with the rest of the club, although I don't know exactly how many came up and if we're all leaving at the same time. We remain at the front of the pack with Murphy and Heidi on our left.

We take the first exit onto the main highway and increase speed. Acutely aware of the wind in my face and pavement under the wheels, I squeeze Rooster tighter. He and Murphy seem to be in tune with each other, easily passing slower vehicles and adjusting to the traffic. After a while, I lose track of the exits and roads they take, leading us farther away from my tour. The chains of responsibility tug at me, guilt for ditching my band. But I deserve a little fun. Haven't taken a day "off" yet. Rooster won't let me miss my show. He understands how important this is to me. I trust him.

When he slows the bike to a crawl and finally stops, I open my eyes. Red light. We're idling in front of a shopping center in a well-to-do suburban area.

The light changes and the guys hit the throttle. Murphy moves ahead, leading us over slower, one-lane roads.

After a few miles, suburbia gives way to country. The houses are farther and farther apart. We climb higher into the mountains. Thick walls of pine trees line the sides of the road. Every now and then there's a break in the trees and a driveway or mailbox whizzes by.

We're so far out in the woods, I start to question where the heck Rooster's taking me. Ahead of us, Murphy signals to the left and the bikes slow. It's bumpy and choppy for a minute but after we clear a high gate, the tires roll onto smooth blacktop.

Rooster guides the bike near a garage and shuts it down. Murphy backs in next to us. I jump off the bike first, stopping to stretch and rubbing my hands over my slightly numb legs.

Once Rooster's taken my helmet, he slips my backpack off my shoulders and slings it over his.

Swoony-swoon-swoon. My mama always told me it's the little gestures that count the most. And tonight, Rooster's made so many little gestures, they've added up to big, big feelings.

The irregular thump of music, distant chatter, and light all pour out of the clubhouse windows and front door into the gravel lot where we're standing.

"Welcome to upstate." Heidi spreads her arms wide and tips her head back, breathing deeply while staring up at the inky night sky.

I glance between Murphy and Rooster, remembering the bottom rockers on the back of their leather cuts. "Upstate. This is *your* home club, Murphy, right?"

"Yup." He slaps Rooster on the back. "We let him visit once in a while."

I tilt my head back, staring at the stars. "It's so pretty up here."

Heidi points to the woods beyond the parking lot. Through the trees, there's a clear path lined with tiny dots of bright, white light. "Our house is out that way. I can show you tomorrow."

"I'd like that."

Rooster clasps Murphy's shoulder. "You at least coming in for a minute or do you need to run home?"

"Yeah, I want to say hi to whoever's here."

The four of us clomp over the gravel to the front steps. Murphy opens the screen door and waves us inside.

The scents of weed and sweat hang heavy in the air. The cloud of smoke hits me so hard at first, I hold my breath rather than risk inhaling. This amount of smoke is liable to do a number on my throat.

Bikers and girls are everywhere. Rooster tugs on my hand, drawing me deeper into the room. No wonder he says he doesn't go out to bars and stuff often. Who needs to go barhopping when he has unfettered access to his own decadent nightclub whenever he wants? The women gracing every square foot are beautiful, and for the most part, barely dressed. I glance down at my sweatshirt, jeans, and boots, then over at Heidi. Except for her tight-fitting leather jacket, Heidi's dressed similarly to me, helping me feel less out of place.

Tucked in the corner, two long couches form an L-shape and that's where Murphy heads.

"Look who showed up!" Murphy leans over and slaps the outstretched hand of the dark-haired man I remember from Texas. Z—the president of Rooster's charter.

Z jumps up and the two men bear-hug each other while trading some good-natured insults.

Rooster butts in and slaps his president's hand, pulling him in close. "Didn't expect to see you until tomorrow, Prez."

"Thought it would be weird to let myself into Murphy's house while he was out."

"As if that would stop you," another man I remember meeting in Texas says in a wry tone. Upstate's president.

"Hey, Rock." Rooster leans over and shakes his hand.

"Good to see you, Rooster." He nods at me. "Shelby."

Surprised he remembered my name, I nod a quiet hello.

"Wrath come back with you?" Z asks.

"He should be here shortly," Rooster answers in a wary tone.

Z seems to sense Rooster's mood. "Go on. No club business tonight." He nods at me. "Hey, Shelby."

"Hi."

Rooster picks up my hand and leads me over to the bar. A girl with short brown curly hair and a tight pink halter top smiles at both of us.

"You want a drink?" Rooster asks me.

"A coke."

The girl behind the bar slides a can of Coca-Cola my way. Right. Coke in the northeast is cola. "Thank you," I chirp.

I sip it slowly, savoring the cool bubbles against my tired throat while I take in the room around us. Two girls work their way through the crowd picking up the sea of party debris, keeping things neat and orderly despite the amount of people.

Two younger guys without leather cuts swagger our way. They stop in front of us and Rooster knocks knuckles with both of them.

"Where you been?" the one with darker hair asks.

"Aw, you been waitin' on me, Remy?" Rooster reaches out and slaps the guy's cheek a few times. "Country Fest, ya nosy little prick."

Maybe he's not as bulky as Rooster, but Remy's certainly not what I'd call "little." Seems more like Rooster's way of putting this non-patch holder in his place for questioning him.

Remy doesn't seem bothered by the treatment. "Feelin' unloved by my *mentors*, that's all." He jerks his chin in Murphy's direction.

"You talk to Z?"

"Yes, sir." Remy smirks. "Spoke to Rock too."

"Good boy." Rooster sneers.

While Remy and Rooster verbally spar with each other, the guy at Remy's side runs his gaze over me. Recognition flickers in his dark eyes but he doesn't say anything.

Rooster slips his arm around my shoulders. "Remy, Griff, this is Shelby."

The corners of Griff's mouth curl up, like he's happy his guess about my identity was confirmed. "Nice to meet you, Shelby."

Remy just nods at me.

They talk in low tones for a few more minutes while I study the party and sip my drink.

"I'll catch you two later." Rooster takes my hand and leads me toward the staircase. He moves through the crowd easily—stops to shake a few hands or say hello but otherwise keeps moving.

Excitement bubbles up inside me. All night long I've wanted to be alone with Rooster. Truly alone. Who am I kidding? *All night* is a big fat lie. I've wanted to be with him since we parted ways in Texas months ago.

The fact that we've kept in touch, that he wanted to see me tonight, made the effort when he clearly doesn't need to go far to be surrounded by beautiful women makes my foolish heart pitter-patter way harder than it should.

CHAPTER THIRTEEN

Rooster

Some of the noise from the party retreats as we climb the steps to the second floor of the clubhouse. The heels of Shelby's boots make a *click-thump* over the shiny hardwood floor as I lead her to the end of the hallway.

The night's young. Even the "free" rooms are mostly unoccupied. We pass a few couples who haven't quite made it to a bedroom. At least nothing has seemed to shock Shelby yet. While she saw plenty of this when we spent time together in Texas, the place I was staying down there belonged to a different MC. The atmosphere is a notch tamer tonight, but it's still wild if you're a sweet southern lass who's not used to club life.

"This place is something else." Shelby stares at each door we pass.

"Upstate's done well." Too bad she won't be as impressed with downstate's clubhouse, if I have a chance to take her there. Our last president, Sway, spent too much time and money fucking around instead of investing into the club he claimed to care about so much. While a lot of that's changed under Z's leadership and I'm committed to helping him build something like this for our charter, our clubhouse is nowhere near the setup Rock's crew have built for themselves.

I stop at the last door on the left side before the president's suite at the end of the hallway. This used to be Z's room. I guess technically it should be Murphy's now, but he has his own house, so tonight, it's mine—or ours.

Trinity assured me someone had cleaned it up since Z was here last. I open the door and flip on the light and take a sniff. The room's free of condom wrappers and strange smells, so that's promising.

Shelby yawns and stretches once she's inside.

"Are you tired?" I had a lot of plans in mind for us tonight. Sleeping was way, way down on the list.

"A little," she admits. A playful smile curves her lips and she presses her palm against my chest, lightly pushing. Her soft touch couldn't move a sprig of grass, but I rest my back against the door anyway.

I stare at her fingers as she trails them down the front of my T-shirt. "But I'm not ready to sleep yet."

"No?" I reach out and tug on her slightly windblown ponytail. "What'd you have in mind?"

"Repaying favors." She sneaks her hands under my shirt and teases my belt buckle.

"You don't owe me anything." I close my eyes and my head hits the back of the door as she slides her hand over my zipper.

"What if I want to suck your cock?"

I crack open one eye. "Be my guest."

"Hmmm." She works my belt. "You plannin' to help me?"

Chuckling, I unbuckle and unbutton my jeans but leave the rest up to her.

She steps back and slips her sweatshirt over her head, folding it neatly and dropping it at my feet. Her T-shirt comes off next. Licking her bottom lip, she sinks to the floor in front of me, staring up with wide eyes.

"Fuck," I mumble. "Been thinking about this for a long time."

"Me too." She draws in a deep breath like she needs strength for the next part or maybe she's just remembered how big I am. But there's no hesitation as she tugs my zipper down.

Careful not to yank on any knots, I pull the elastic from her hair, sinking my fingers into her pretty blond curls like I've been fantasizing about doing all night.

I groan as she slides her hands over my hips, working my pants down. My cock springs out harder than motherfucking stone. She wraps her hand around it, pumping up and down a few times before opening her mouth and moving closer. She stares up at me as her hot breath ghosts over my sensitive skin. I'm completely trapped, held hostage by her eyes, anticipating her next move.

Finally, the warmth of her mouth surrounds me, and I suck in a stuttered breath. "That's good."

She sucks, hard, but takes her sweet time sliding down before drawing away and swirling her tongue around the tip of my cock.

"Fuck," I groan. "Do that again."

She flattens her tongue against the underside and does it even slower this time—sending a million pleasurable tingles straight to my balls. My fingers twist in her hair, pulling it up, pushing her head down while pumping my hips forward.

"Mmm," she encourages me, bobbing her head while working the rest of my cock with her tight little fist. She sneaks her other hand between my legs to cup my balls, gently squeezing and massaging.

"Fuck." I can't stop watching her—she's so intent on pleasing me. She flicks her gaze up again. With her red-stained lips stretched around my cock, she smiles, and I almost lose it. "Holy fuck, Shelby."

This isn't quite how I pictured our night once I got her alone but I'm sure as fuck not grumpy about it. I also can't last much longer.

"Shelby," I gasp.

"Mm-hmm." She rests her hands against my thighs. She opens her mouth wider, giving me permission to drive inside at my pace. Not quite wide enough to take all of me, though.

"Open," I demand. "Wider."

As soon as she does, I grip her hair harder, thrusting inside her hot, wet little mouth.

Still staring up at me, she hums a desperate noise. Her hands cup her tits, lifting them up in her pretty white, lacy bra.

"You want me to come on your tits?" I rasp.

She nods quickly and makes another excited noise.

Works for me. I'm already picturing painting her in my cum. It's enough to trigger my climax.

Brushing her hands away, I wrap my hand around my dick, pumping faster. I barely pull back in time. Her chest heaves from all her heavy breathing and that's where I aim, shooting cum all over the plump swell of her breasts and the lacy white cups of her bra.

"Oh, fuck," I groan. White lights burst behind my eyelids.

When I can finally see straight, I almost come again at the sight of her. Just as I'd pictured earlier. Red lipstick smeared all over her lips and chin, mascara streaks around her eyes, and thoroughly mussed hair.

"Come here." I reach down and help her up, quickly kissing her forehead. "Thank you."

SHELBY

My heart's still racing as Rooster helps me stand. Satisfaction rushes through me. That was even better than I'd imagined. Leaving a rough, hard man like Rooster shaking with pleasure is a huge turn-on.

"Your turn." He stares down at me with dark, glittering eyes and curls his hands over my shoulders.

I swipe at the corner of my mouth. "I'm a bit of a mess. Can I clean up first?"

"I like you messy."

I blink up at him and the feral glint in his eyes shifts to concern. "Yeah. Come here." He takes my hand, turning us toward the bathroom. "I'm not sure what's stocked in here, but I can grab whatever you need from downstairs."

I snag my backpack on the way to the bathroom.

He glances at me. "You need your other stuff?"

"Kind of."

He leans in and kisses my forehead again. "I'll go see where the van is."

"Thanks."

He closes the door behind him, and I strip off the rest of my clothes, dropping my bra in the sink. I probably should've taken it off before asking Rooster to come all over my tits. I'm traveling with a limited amount of lingerie and don't exactly have time to pop into Wal-Mart for new stuff.

I glance around the small, but neat and clean bathroom, and locate a few towels that smell fresh. I dig my travel cosmetic bag from my backpack. The large bottle of face wash Cindy insists I use to clean off the heavy stage makeup is in a different compartment, and I pull that out as well. Carefully, I peel the false eyelashes off and toss them.

Stripping out of the rest of my clothes, I twist the taps on in the shower and wait for it to warm up before closing myself inside. My hair's a mess of snarls. After thoroughly wetting it, I carefully shampoo all the sticky hairspray out, then slowly work conditioner through, using extra on the ends.

"Hey, I wanted to do that." The door opens and Rooster steps into the shower behind me.

I turn to face him, and he cups my cheeks, staring down at me with such intensity, my gaze flits away. Stripped of makeup and clothes, a sense of naked vulnerability washes over me.

He grazes my chin with his knuckles and tips my head back. "Much better."

"What?"

"Now I can see your pretty face."

My lips twitch into a half-smile. "You really hate the makeup, huh?"

"No, I just like the girl underneath more." He brushes wet strands of hair off my cheek. "You wrecked me out there, you know?"

"I've been waiting all night to give you one hundred percent of my attention."

Instead of answering, he leans down and presses his lips to mine, gentle at first. With a sweet reverence, he deepens the kiss, sinking his fingers into my hair and angling my head. Our bodies mold together under the streaming water, slick and hot. His hands move from my face, sliding up and down my back, pulling me against him. He's all hard, solid muscle and warm, wet skin.

"Shelby," he groans against my neck, kissing his way to my shoulder. "Are you done? I want my mouth on every part of you."

Delighted shivers race over my skin, tightening my nipples to hard points that Rooster dips down to kiss.

"Uh…" I can barely think.

He smirks up at me. "Yes?"

He rests his hands on my shoulders and turns me to face the water, gently rubbing his big hands through my hair. "Good?" he asks.

"I think so."

That's enough of an answer for him to reach forward and slap the water off. Holding onto my hand, he steps out and I follow. He reaches for a towel and crouches down, rubbing the fluffy terry cloth over my damp skin.

I grab another towel and flip my hair, twisting it into a turban.

"Cute." He taps the tip of my nose with his finger and wraps a towel around his hips. I cover myself with the other towel, knotting it over my breasts.

"Are you sure you're not hungry?" he asks, melting my heart with his concern. "You haven't eaten all day and did an awful lot."

"I'm a little bit now. But I don't want to eat this late." I run my hands over my hips. "Trust me, I'll eat like a horse tomorrow."

"Good." He twists one hand in my towel and yanks me forward. "Can't have those sweet curves disappearing."

I snort-laugh. "Trust me, they run in the family. They're not going anywhere."

"I don't think you're understanding how wild you make me."

"Well then, show me."

Rooster

Finally, finally, I have Shelby all to myself.

Wet, naked, and squeaky clean so I can dirty her up again.

I sweep her up and carry her into the bedroom, then gently set her down on the bed. She reclines against the pillows and I follow, trailing kisses down her neck. She arches her back and threads her fingers in my hair.

"Rooster?"

The heaviness in her voice stops my exploration. I shift my gaze to her face and wait for her to continue.

"We never really…but, uh, have you…you know…?"

By the little crinkles on her forehead and anxiety in her voice, I don't need her to finish the question.

Part of me wants to lie because she won't believe me anyway.

"Have I what?" I force some lightness into my tone. "Given anyone else a ride on my beard?"

She doesn't laugh.

I shift my weight forward so I'm staring straight into her eyes when I give her the truth. "No."

Relief flickers over her face, followed by, just as I'd guessed, disbelief.

Can't blame her. If someone had told me five years—hell *one* year ago—I'd be turning down free pussy because I was inside-out over a chick who lived two thousand miles away, I would've laughed my ass off. Loyalty and brotherhood are the main reasons I joined the MC, but I'd be a fuckin' liar if I said tapping as much club ass as possible wasn't also on my list back then.

"Really?" Her brow wrinkles again. "I saw the party downstairs. It must be like that all the time."

Worse, actually. Upstate's tame compared to downstate. Although, Z has cleaned up our downstate clubhouse a lot since he took over. Still, some nights you could film a movie on the decline of the Roman Empire in our clubhouse.

"I've been busy." I lean down and kiss the tip of her nose. "Besides, every time I close my eyes, I only see one girl."

"Who?"

She really needs to ask? "You."

You'd think she'd look happier after that declaration.

Shit, maybe there's a reason she's not turning cartwheels. "I don't expect you to say the same thing." I barely force the lie past my lips. I'm ready to hunt down any motherfucker who's touched Shelby and—

"I haven't either."

"Why?"

"Well..." She reaches up and strokes my beard. "I've been pretty busy myself."

"I saw the line of fans dying to meet you tonight. Saw the guys with their marriage proposals. Never figured there were *male* groupies."

"Oh, yeah," she drawls. "Some of 'em are super sweet. Bring all sorts of presents with 'em. Then they're too scared to talk to me."

I growl. Why didn't it occur to *me* to bring her anything tonight except my hard cock and a handful of 'wanna ride my beard' jokes?

"Others offer to take me to hotels, or ask me to invite them onto the bus, or into my dressing room."

Another low growl I can't control rumbles out of me. "And?"

"I haven't met anyone else with such a kick-ass beard." Her big eyes and tilted lips are at odds with her teasing words.

"That a requirement for you?"

"It is now."

"So, you've got guys handing out marriage proposals every night, Ms. Morgan?"

"It's *Miss* Morgan." She wiggles her brows at me. "Ms. Morgan if you're nasty."

I snort with laughter. "Please, you weren't even *born* when that song came out."

"Neither were you!" She taps the side of her head. "A good musician knows music from *every* genre and decade."

That doesn't surprise me. Maybe I'm biased but watching her performance and then Dawson Roads' show were two different experiences. Everything about Shelby's music is genuine and from her heart. She's so fucking talented, I'm not sure the world deserves her. Then again, neither do I.

Keep giving her the truth. "I haven't been with anyone since you."

"How is that possible?" She runs her fingers down my chest.

I hold one hand up in front her face, wiggling my fingers. "I renamed this one Shelby and the other Morgan. They work fine."

She snort-giggles, rolling toward me until her head's resting on my chin.

I draw back, staring down at her. "What do we do about this situation, Shelby?" Jesus Christ, am I really the one initiating this conversation? Right now? Tonight? My dick's ready to go feral if I don't get it inside her soon. That stellar blow job wasn't nearly enough to satisfy me.

Her body stiffens. "What do you mean?"

My inner commitment-phobe recognizes where her fear's coming from. "I'm not asking you to leave your tour or stop what you're doing. I'm not even asking you to move up here after your tour's over." Not yet anyway.

Underneath all her sassy, southern charm, I've always sensed Shelby's skittish when it comes to...whatever the hell I'm proposing here. I haven't been interested in being in a relationship since high school myself, so I don't hold it against her.

She blows out a long breath. "Thank you."

I twist my index finger around a wet, blond wave. "I want to see you more often, though."

"You do?"

"Hell yeah." *Honesty. Just be honest.* "These last couple months have been hell."

Her eyes shine. "Really?"

"Can't you tell from all those needy texts I send you?"

"They're not needy, Rooster," she whispers. "I love...every one of your messages."

"I'd rather give you more in person."

Her gaze slips away. "I'm on the road until almost Thanksgiving."

"I'm a biker who lives for the open road, baby."

Shocked eyes rush to meet mine again. "You'd really come visit me?"

"Fuck yeah." Now we're getting somewhere.

"But that'll be expensive. I only have a handful of dates kinda close to here."

I roll to the side, propping myself up on one elbow. "Have I given you the impression I'm some sort of bum?"

"No. You've never really told me *what* you do."

"I do fine." I just got her to understand that I haven't fucked any other women, no reason to bring up the porn company now.

"I don't want you to waste your money on me."

"It's not a waste." I stop myself. Maybe she's looking for excuses to keep me away. "If you don't want me to visit you on the road, say so, Shelby." I hate the hard edge creeping into my voice but can't help it. "You won't hurt my feelings."

No, it will annihilate me but I'm sure as fuck not giving any woman that kind of ammunition.

"I do," she whispers.

"What?" I cup my hand over my ear. "I can't hear you."

"I'm afraid to say it."

"Say what?"

"That I *want* you to visit me. I want to see you. I loved having you there tonight. So much." She squeezes her eyes shut and rolls onto her back. "All these amazing things have happened over the last couple months, but I still miss you all the time. I'm always wondering, 'What's Rooster up to right now? I wish Rooster was here so I could tell him about this. Who's Rooster with?'"

The smile slides off my face. "Sounds like this Rooster asshole is ruining what should be a good time in your life, Shelby."

She pounds both fists into the mattress. "That's not what I'm saying at all."

"What are you saying?"

Her mouth's twisted into a frustrated pout when she turns and glares at me. "I miss your face." She blows out an annoyed breath. "I don't know why. You're probably a troll under that big ol' beard."

"Troll, huh?"

Her pissy expression softens. "I feel selfish asking you to take time away from your life to come visit me. You have your own things to do."

I study her downcast eyes and pink cheeks. Her admission's genuine. She's not trying to keep me away. Who's let her down so much that she's too afraid to ask anyone for anything?

"Some things are more important."

Wide eyes blink up at me. "What are we, Rooster?" She touches my shoulder, trailing her fingers over my ink instead of meeting my eyes. "I mean, this was a hookup back home. What does... What are we if you're, you know, visiting me when I'm out on the road on a regular basis?"

Fuck, do I like how *visiting her on a regular basis* sounds coming out of her mouth. I lean down and brush a kiss over her forehead, then her cheeks, the tip of her nose and finally her lips. "You need to call it something?"

"I don't *need*—"

"You're my girl." Oh, fuck that feels good to say out loud. Way better than I ever expected it to. "I'm your man."

"My man, huh? That sounds serious." She narrows her eyes. "I'm hardly a girl."

"*You're my woman* sounded like I ought to thump my chest while sayin' it but that works for me too."

The corners of her mouth twitch. "You're more Viking than Tarzan."

I cock my head and pretend to think it over. "True."

"Can we really do this, Logan?"

"What do we have to lose?"

"Our hearts?"

I trace my thumb over her bottom lip. "Told you once before, I don't want to break your heart. I'd rather hurt myself than ever hurt you."

She tilts her head, rubbing her cheek against my knuckles. "I don't want to hurt you either."

"Give us a chance, Shelby."

Her eyes glitter with hope or happiness as she stares up at me. "It's boring on the road most of the time."

Fuck, yes. "As long as I'm with you it doesn't matter." I open my mouth to say the club gives me plenty of excitement, then stop myself.

What the fuck am I doing?

Forget breaking her heart. Shelby's all sunshine and sweetness. I've *killed* for my club and I have no doubt I'll do it again. My life, the choices I've made, could *ruin* the career she's trying to build. She's so damn talented. I want her to accomplish everything her heart desires. I don't think she understands the risk she's taking being with me and I'm a selfish bastard for not explaining. It's not just her heart I could break. It's her whole world.

It's one truth I don't say out loud.

Instead, I lean down and brush another kiss over her lips, promising myself I'll do everything in my power to protect her heart.

CHAPTER FOURTEEN

Shelby

My foolish heart won't stop racing. Even though I didn't want to admit it to myself, I'd dreamed about this moment happening when we finally saw each other again. The physical spark remains, no question. But the emotional connection—that burns hot too.

This is the worst possible time to be falling for a guy.

A relationship, love, anything that might tie me down right now is such a bad idea.

But Rooster's not trying to tie me down. He didn't hesitate to say he'd visit me on the road. It means the world to me that he understands and respects this crazy dream I'm chasing.

Previous boyfriends told me how ridiculous I was, or my odds were so little, I should just give up. Worse, some bitched like babies when music took my attention off them.

That's why they got kicked to the curb.

Teachers, so-called friends, almost everyone except my mother have mocked my dreams. I'm hell-bent on proving them all wrong. While I'm at it, I'll force the music industry to take me seriously too.

I can't afford to get sidetracked. Not even by this sexy biker who says all the right things.

Is it possible to have both?

Rooster's slow, soft kisses melt into deeper ones that steal my breath. My body reacts instantly, and I arch my back. I reach up and run my fingers through his hair, over his broad shoulders, his arms, down his sides to the edge of his towel, teasing my fingers underneath.

"Beautiful Shelby," he rasps. "Fuckin' love having you under me again."

"You sure could have your pick of pretty women downstairs."

He stops cold and stares down at me. "I don't want *pretty women.* I want *you.* Did you miss what I said?"

"No," I whisper.

"If I wanted a random fuck, I could do that anytime."

"Gee, thanks."

"I want more than a fuck," he continues as if I hadn't said a word. "I like being with you. Listening to you." He easily undoes the knot and flicks my towel out of his way, kissing a path down my neck. "Staring at your beautiful body. Been waiting to do this all night."

"You had a taste," I tease, running my fingers through his hair.

"Not enough." He kisses one breast and then the other. "Never enough."

"Oh," I sigh. "You promised to put your mouth all over me, remember?"

"Still plannin' to. Give me time to do this right, chickadee."

The anticipation threatens to kill me. But I trust Rooster to make this good. He'll make it worth the wait.

His mouth surrounds my nipple and he sucks hard. My back bows off the bed, the sensation shooting south. He buries his head between my breasts. "You smell good."

"I used whatever was in there."

"No, it's you. Missed your scent." He continues kissing his way down my stomach. "Missed your taste." He dips his tongue in my belly button and my stomach quivers with laughter.

"That tickles."

He lightly sweeps his beard over my belly, the sensation sending jolts of electricity over my skin. "Still tickles."

He moves lower, planting a kiss on my bare mound. His devilish smile returns as he peers up at me. "Let me know if this tickles too."

Pushing my knees wide, he dives closer, kissing my exposed center. I grab a fistful of his thick hair and twist.

My heels dig into the comforter and my back arches off the bed even higher. He keeps kissing in between murmuring sweet and dirty words. A low moan builds in me.

"What are you doing?" I whisper.

"If you need to ask…" He traces one long, slow stroke of his tongue against my lips, stopping at my clit. He keeps up the teasing licks and kisses until I buck my hips against his face. Finally, he focuses all his attention where I need it most. A delicious tremble starts in my hips, an electric current flowing down my legs until my toes curl. He makes a growly humming noise of encouragement and slowly thrusts two fingers inside me.

"Uh." My entire body convulses, my legs shaking uncontrollably. I moan even louder. The orgasm building, breaking, crashing through me. I'm overwhelmed with mind-numbing, breath-stealing pleasure.

"That's it." He presses feathery kisses to my inner thighs while still working his fingers in and out. "So good."

"Ugh," I mumble, not sure my lips can form words. My legs won't stop shaking with aftershocks. "So much better than my DIY ones."

Shoot, did I say that out loud?

Rooster's staring down at me with a smirk on his shiny lips, so yeah, I guess I *did* say that out loud. "That right?"

A hot flush of embarrassment works over my cheeks and I turn away. "I even have this little bullet vibrator, but I haven't been able to use because it's so dang loud."

Oh, yeah, that was less embarrassing. It's like the man tongued me stupid.

He squeezes his eyes shut and shakes with laughter.

"I'm serious." I'd smack one of his granite-hard arms but my hands barely feel connected to my body. What did he do to me?

Done laughing, he leans in and kisses my cheek. "Happy to help anytime you need me." He reaches down and covers my pussy with one big hand. Still sensitive, I jump from the contact. "What's wrong? Too much?" he whispers with a devious smile.

"Mmm." My eyes drift shut. This is why it was easy to turn down any guy who's shown me a hint of interest over the last few months.

It would've been a waste of time.

No man would ever match Rooster's savage yet somehow gentle way of claiming me.

CHAPTER FIFTEEN

Rooster

The sun's barely touched the edges of the curtains when some fucker's knocking at the door. I jump out of bed, hoping to stop whoever it is before they wake Shelby.

Z grins at me when I swing the door a quarter of the way open. "Morning."

I yawn, and in an effort to be as disgusting as possible, hoping it'll chase Z away, dip my hand under the waistband of my shorts and take a long, slow scratch of my balls. "Why are you waking me up at this hour?"

"Why do you think?"

Guess the ball scratch won't get rid of him. "You missed me?"

"Close." He reaches out and slaps my cheek a few times. "Church this morning."

I cock my head, listening to the still-silent clubhouse. "You trying to win a 'first one there' medal or something?"

"No, smartass. I wanted to talk to you before we all sit down."

I glance back at Shelby, who's thankfully still asleep. "Can you give me a few minutes?"

"The girls will be over in a few." Leave it to Z to know exactly what was on my mind. "Shelby can hang with them."

"Thanks." I stop and grin. "So, how was it at Heidi and Murphy's last night?"

"Great." Z's quick, snappy answer seems sincere. "Woke up this morning to the kids singing along to Sesame Street."

"*Yeaaaah?*" I draw out the word like I'm talking to his three-year-old son instead of my club president. "You learn anything new, lil' buddy?"

He slaps my cheek harder this time. "Yeah, C is for cock-suckin' VP better get his ass downstairs."

I frown and run my hand over my beard. "That doesn't seem suitable for children."

He points at my bare torso. "S is for put on a damn shirt—no one wants to see that first thing in the morning."

I open the door wider, spreading my arms. "Take a good look, Prez. You're the one who woke me up, remember?"

"H is for hurry the fuck up." He chuckles as he backs away.

Shaking my head, I close the door as quietly as possible. Still, when I turn around, Shelby's sitting, knees to her chest, arms wrapped around the sheet covering her legs and body, a soft smile playing over her lips. "He's wrong, you know."

"About what?"

"I definitely want to see you without a shirt first thing in the morning."

"This is your lucky morning then, chickadee." I reach under the comforter and wrap my hand around one of her ankles, tugging her toward the end of the bed.

She giggles and digs her other heel into the mattress, trying to scramble away. "I like waking up with you."

"Good, now let's say good morning properly."

She stops her mad squirming and I slide her to the edge of the bed, resting her feet against my chest.

"I like waking up with you too." I kiss the top of one foot and then the other. "How are even your feet so cute?"

"You got a foot fetish, Rooster?"

"Nope." I lean over and grab a condom off the nightstand. "Got a dick-in-Shelby fetish though."

She covers her mouth and laughs softly. "Sounds intense."

"It will be."

"Is it wise to keep your president waiting?"

"He'll understand." Grasping her ankles, I spread her open and bend down to line myself up with her. "Put your feet on my shoulders and lift your butt for me."

"So bossy," she murmurs, doing exactly as I asked.

"You just noticed?"

"Oh." Her eyes roll back as I slowly push inside.

I reach over, grab a few pillows and stuff them under her hips. "That better?"

"It's so good." She lifts her hips higher, angling her body so I press into her in all the right places.

I don't want this to end. Not just this particular moment.

Every moment with her.

CHAPTER SIXTEEN

Rooster

"I'm really not in the mood to get shot this morning."

"No one's getting shot," Z assures me with a smirk. "Rock loves when I show up for breakfast."

Yeah, right.

Even if that's true—which I highly doubt—our upstate prez is known for ruthlessly guarding his family and privacy. Rock and Z have been friends for decades. His tolerance for Z barging into his home unannounced might not extend to me.

As we stomp through the woods, Z glances over at me, gaze lingering on my T-shirt. "Took you that long to get dressed and that's what you came up with?"

"Since when are you, of all people, the fashion police?"

"It was really more of a way to express my displeasure at you taking so damn long."

I smirk at him. "I had things to attend to."

"Poor Shelby. The girl gonna be able to walk?"

I ignore the question as I follow him onto the path leading around the side of Rock's house. "Uh, shouldn't we knock on the front door?"

Z lightly steps onto the back deck of Rock's custom-designed log cabin. "Nah, it's fine," he whispers, creeping over the porch to the back door.

"If Rock loves you popping in on him so much, what's with the stealth act?"

"Where's the fun in announcing my arrival?"

"Jesus Christ," I mutter, following him. Who knew I'd need to wear a Kevlar vest before breakfast?

As he lifts his hand to knock against the glass, Hope calls out, "It's open, Z!"

I chuckle under my breath.

"Why you leaving your door unlocked?" Z asks, shouldering through the opening.

"You can come in too, Rooster." Hope waves her hand at me, inviting me inside.

"Thanks, Hope. For the record, this wasn't my idea. I said we should use the front door like normal people."

"Aw, but then I wouldn't know it was Z stopping by." Hope wraps one arm around him and leans up to kiss his cheek. "Where's Lilly?"

"Still over at Murphy and Heidi's." His eyes widen and he grins down at baby Grace. "Morning, Gracie-baby."

She giggles and coos as Z picks her up and carries her around, babbling nonsense at her.

Hope watches them together for a minute before turning my way. "How was Shelby's show last night?"

Pride—that I'm probably not entitled to, since I didn't do a damn thing—ricochets through me. "Great. I mean, I'm not an expert but I think she blew the other two acts away."

"And you're not biased, either." Her mouth curves into a teasing smile. "Right?"

"Nope. Not at all." I grin at her. "Seriously, it was wild. She had guys hanging over the railing with banners begging her to marry them."

"She's getting more popular. That's good."

Now I kind of feel like an asshole. Hadn't meant to sound jealous. "It is. Dawson Roads asked her to sing a duet with him. I guess it's a big deal. First time he's had her do that on the tour."

Z stops baby-talking to Grace and lifts his gaze to me. "Was that some sort of 'fuck you' to you?"

"What?" The thought had never occurred to me. "No, I don't think so. Her manager works with Dawson too. I think he's trying to get her more exposure. Even if it was, it only helps Shelby, so I really don't care."

Hope rests her hand on my forearm and squeezes. "You're so sweet."

"Well, I didn't particularly enjoy them singing their 'let's fuck all weekend' ballad but, you know..." I shrug.

Hope taps her chin. "'Let Go the Night?' He recorded that with his ex-wife or ex-girlfriend if I remember right." She shakes her head. "Clearly, I spend way too much time scrolling through social media when I'm up with Grace."

I shrug. "I don't know anything about him other than he's got roughly fifty songs about beer, bars, and brawling in his set list."

She chuckles. "Some of his older stuff was really good, but yeah, lately it's all the same good-ol'-boy, party anthem stuff." She slaps her hand over her mouth. "Don't tell Shelby I said that."

"I'm sure she's aware," I tease. "Her songs, though." I press my fist against my gut. "Hits you here."

"Yeah, I heard she sang a song just for youuuuu." Z's high-pitched songbird voice makes baby Grace screw her little face up and start bawling.

"Aww, I'm sorry, baby G," Z coos. "We make fun of Uncle Rooster, that's what we do. Yes, it is."

Hope chuckles and shakes her head.

"Asshole," I grumble. "Uh, Z, I'm supposed to take Shelby down to Empire Med today for a thing. We got a lot to discuss at the table?"

"Church won't take long," Z says without looking at me. "Family breakfast isn't optional, either."

"What sort of thing?" Hope asks me.

"I didn't get a lot of details." I shrug, feeling stupid now that I didn't ask more questions. Not like I had all night or anything. "The children's hospital. I guess a patient asked to meet her or something."

"Oh." Hope bites her lip and darts a quick look at her baby

daughter. "That's a really sweet thing for her to do with her limited free time."

Yup, one more reason Shelby's taking up all the free space in my heart.

Rock pounds down the stairs and groans when he sees us. "Morning." He nods at me but turns his annoyed president glare on Z before taking his daughter in his arms. "Is there a reason you're in my house at this hour? Infringing on my family time?"

"I told him it was inappropriate, Rock." I slap Z's back, harder than necessary.

Z pulls a seriously offended face. "I'm family." His trouble-making eyes land on Hope. "Right, Hope?"

"Yup. You're the big brother I never knew I wanted."

"See?" Z grins. "That's better than Wrath. He's the big brother you *never* wanted."

She snickers but doesn't agree with him.

Grace fusses and wiggles in her dad's arms until Hope finally takes her from him. "I'm going to feed her." She leans up, kisses Rock's cheek and whispers something in his ear.

Rock keeps his eyes on his wife as she disappears down the hallway.

"Now that they moved out, you turn Alexa's room into a downstairs nursery for Grace?" Z asks.

Slowly, Rock turns his head. "Yeah. Left Heidi and Murphy's room for guests, though." He holds up a hand. "For Alexa or Chance—not you. Just so we're clear."

"I'm wounded." Z presses his hand to his chest.

"Z's welcome too!" Hope shouts from the other room.

Z grins at Rock. "Hope loves me."

I snort. "I think she feels sorry for you."

"Fuck off." Z punches my shoulder.

Once the fucking around is out of his system, Z settles down and finally gets to the reason he dragged me out here this morning. "A certain phone call woke me early this morning."

"I thought Sesame Street woke you?"

Rock side-eyes me.

"That was after the phone call," Z says.

"So, what? You decided to spread the cheer?" I ask.

Rock pads into the kitchen and starts a pot of coffee. "Do I even want to know?" he asks over his shoulder.

"Priest." Z glances between us.

"Fuck. What now?" Rock grumbles. "And thank fuck he's calling you instead of me."

"Yeah, it was a real thrill for me too." Z rolls his eyes.

"What's he want now?" Rock asks.

Z pulls out one of the dining table chairs, sits, and leans back. Stretching out his big body, he tips the chair onto its back legs and tucks his hands behind his head. "Washington's still a clusterfuck."

"And that's your problem, why?" Rock asks.

"Well, it turns out, since I'm so amazing—"

"For fuck's sake," Rock mutters.

"For the way I turned downstate around..." Z lifts his chin at me. "No offense."

I'll always give credit where it's due, and Z's accomplished a lot since he took over. He shook all of us out of our complacency. Weeded out the bad apples in our charter. Brought everyone closer together. As much as I love to fuck around and give him shit, he will always have my loyalty, respect, and full support. "None taken."

He holds one finger up. "Hold that thought."

"I'm listening."

"He wants someone more responsible to check up on Washington and a few other charters."

Rock turns to face Z, leaning back against the counter. "Let me guess. He wants that someone to be you?"

"Correct." Z focuses on me. "I was, of course, obligated to explain that change did not come to downstate without the help of my loyal brothers, especially my VP." His serious expression doesn't change.

"Appreciate that." I grunt.

"I didn't say it to get out of a road trip, brother."

"What then?" I work to keep my voice on the respectful side and dial back the suspicious tone.

He glances at Rock. "We need to put together a small, casual team of brothers we trust to visit Priest's 'problem children' over the next couple months. It's the only way to get Priest off our backs."

Rock stares at the ceiling for a few seconds before speaking. "Fuck. We're short-handed enough."

"I thought you wanted me helping Murphy with the support club, Prez?" Expanding and securing our existing territory was also high on Priest's list last time I checked.

"I do. I also want to avoid more six a.m. phone calls from Priest." His mouth twists into an annoyed smirk. "He lovingly reminded me he'd like to see our charter kicking up more money."

"Fuck me." I run my hands through my hair.

"Washington's bleeding the coffers dry with their never-ending legal fees and fines," Rock says, staring into his coffee.

"They gotta get out of guns for good this time. Not the half-assed shit Pony's been doing since he took over. It's gonna end up bringing the entire organization down." Z points at me and then taps his own cut. "We all wear the same patch. Feds could decide every charter deserves a one-way ticket to the Graybar Hotel."

"How exactly do you expect to convince them of a career switch this late in the game?" I ask.

"I don't."

"We should go in low-key and see who's receptive to a change," Rock says. "Build on those relationships. Push out the die-hards."

"That was my thought," Z agrees. "I impressed upon Priest that it can't be you or me."

Rock raises an eyebrow.

"You're welcome." Z smirks.

Rock grunts at him.

Z shrugs. "You're seen as Priest's golden boy."

"Thanks," Rock says slowly, not sounding at all thankful.

"I'm just saying. If Rochlan North comes riding in, brothers are gonna piss themselves." He touches his chest. "I can't go, either. Another charter sees me coming, they'll assume I'm there to clean house."

"That leaves my favorite *motherclucker*." Z settles his gaze on me.

"Rooster. You're in a position to commiserate with them on how mean ol' Z came in and stole your charter—"

"Except you made me your VP, so they ain't gonna trust me either," I point out.

"Flip their worldview, brother. Show them how much more money they could be making with porn instead of guns. Pony will be receptive to change, but he needs some hand-holding."

"Great choice for a president." Rock lifts his gaze to the ceiling.

I chuckle at Rock's observation before commenting on Z's suggestion. "Setting them up could take forever. And Stella won't take a trip out there to help me recruit."

"You don't need her." He waves off the mention of his ex. "I know a girl out there."

"Of course, you do," I mutter.

Rock stops pouring coffee and turns a slow glare Z's way.

Z holds up his hands. "Not who you're thinking. Ease up, Rock."

"So, what do you want, Z? Want me to go out there and see if the brothers are eager to be porn kings?" I ask. "I don't anticipate any of them saying *no*."

"I'd rather you find out if they're a good fit. If they're a bunch of dicks who are gonna wag their tongues instead of providing protection—"

Rock snorts.

Z slides his gaze Rock's way. "You trying to say something?"

"Not at all." Rock takes a sip of his coffee and leans against the counter. "You're the epitome of professionalism."

"Protection? This girl plannin' to steal Stella's fuck-a-stranger-in-every-city schtick?"

"She's got a different angle, but similar idea. I need someone technical enough to set it up and assess the situation." He sets all four feet of the chair down with a *thud*. "Washington's gonna be tough. Virginia is where I think you need to start."

"More film-making?"

"See? You're smarter than you look."

"What exactly are we trying to accomplish here?" I ask. "One giant amateur porn network?"

"Ice has expressed an interest." Z shrugs. "Help 'em out."

"It's still regulated to some degree. They up for that?"

"Not this amateur shit. That's why I need you to set it up so it looks like the girls own everything themselves, but we still have access to the back end."

"Regulated or not, it won't bring the same heat other shit brings," Rock says.

"I suppose you know a girl down there too?" I ask Z.

"Not anyone specific. Ice says a few of his club girls might be interested."

"Bro, there's a big difference between a girl fucking her way through the clubhouse and fucking on camera for the whole world to see. I'm not settin' up shit if they're forcing girls into it. That's not cool."

Z's expression turns hard. "You think I'd ask you to do that?"

No, I really don't. "Then what's the plan?"

"Same thing. Feel the situation out. If you get a bad vibe, make up an excuse for why it won't work."

"They'll figure it out with or without me. Any asshole can throw some videos on PornHub."

"You know by now there's a lot more work involved. And money to be made for quality content."

"And I gotta spend half my days sending notices to take down illegal shit people post everywhere."

"So, hire a company to do that." Z jerks his thumb over his shoulder. "Hell, Hope can do it."

"Hope has enough to do," Rock says, cutting that idea off.

"What mindless, legal drudgery are you trying to sign me up for, Z?" Hope asks, carrying Grace over to Rock.

"Takedown notices," I answer. "People are constantly pirating Stella's videos."

"Can't a lot of that be automated?"

"Rooster's very hands on with our content," Z explains with a dickish smirk.

I shrug. "The shit's expensive to produce."

Hope lets out a long, sarcastic sigh. "Well, as much as I'd enjoy surfing for pornography and drafting notices all day long—"

I hold up a hand. "I'm not asking you to, Hope. That was all Z."

Z grins up at her.

The corners of Hope's mouth twitch with amusement. "Are you worried that I'm bored, Z?"

"Nope. Just trying to keep work in the family."

"I have a company in mind," I say. "They're fuckin' expensive though."

"Take it out of Stella's end," Z says.

"Yeah, that sounds more like a conversation *you* should have with her."

"Let Sway handle it. They're tight these days." Rock smirks into his coffee cup.

"You got a timeframe for when you want me to run down to Virginia?" I ask Z.

"Soon. T-Bone's been bitching about us not coming to visit for a while now."

"I'll work it out. Probably gonna take Jiggy with me."

"I figured." Z drums his fingers against the table for a second. "Here's what I'm thinking. Get Virginia set up and profitable. Then we have something solid to convince Washington to move in the same direction. Two successful charters. Not a fluke."

"All right. That makes sense."

"While your early morning visit has been delightful..." Rock's dry tone makes it clear our visit was anything but. "...why don't we finish this at the table?"

My feet are already moving toward the front door.

Outside, I wait for Z. Once we're closer to the clubhouse, I stop him with a hand to his chest. "Hold up."

He raises an eyebrow and glances down at my hand.

"For the record, I never felt like you came in and 'stole' our charter from Sway. You know that, Z. Right?"

"Fuck yeah, I do."

"If anything, I feel like we stole *you* away from your home." I glance at the woods around us, painfully aware Z had been planning to build a house on this property for his family.

"It's worked out," he answers, sidestepping the conversation. He slaps my shoulder. "Come on. Lots to discuss this morning."

"I'm gonna run up and check on Shelby first." I glance back at Rock's house. No sign of him yet.

"Yeah, go ahead." He follows my line of sight and smirks. "He'll be a while. No doubt."

CHAPTER SEVENTEEN

Shelby

After Rooster leaves, I finish my laundry. It's early so no one's awake yet.

I return to the room, locking the door behind me as Rooster asked.

One thing I didn't get to do last night because I was too embarrassed—a reading.

First, I need to put myself in the right frame of mind. I make the bed, smoothing the comforter out and stacking all the pillows at the top. I can't find any candles but I switch off the overhead light and pull the blinds up. Morning sunlight streams into the bedroom, a sliver of it landing over the bed.

That'll do.

I grab a towel from the bathroom, spread it on the throw rug and kneel, touching my big toes together, widening my knees and sinking back into extended child's pose for a few breaths. From there, I do a few spinal flexes and move into downward dog, then warrior one. When I'm feeling calm and centered, I end with my hands at my heart.

After tugging my backpack open, I pull my dark green velvet pouch from the bottom and climb into the center of the bed. One by one, I unpack the contents of the pouch—colorful square cloth, notebook, pen, amethyst crystal, and my favorite deck of tarot cards.

I pull the cards from their magnetic box and hold them in my hands, closing my eyes in an attempt to connect with them and form my question in my mind.

Last night, Rooster and I...what we discussed was huge. Trying to turn this into a relationship. There's a giddiness in my stomach but fear lingers in my heart.

Where is this relationship headed? Will it mess with my career? Can I be in a relationship? Am I cut out for a long-distance relationship? Can career and love co-exist?

Nope. Too many questions for a simple read.

Where is this relationship headed?

I focus on that question while shuffling the deck. My skills are weaker than a baby bird's wingspan. I haven't been seriously reading cards as long as my momma but I sort through them until I'm satisfied, then lay them out. One, two, three. Past, present, future.

First, the past. Today it feels like I should reflect on where we've been to understand where we're going.

Ten of Pentacles.

Hmm. I haven't gotten that one often. I need to look it up.

I flip over the middle card—the present—next.

The Lovers.

Wow, obvious, much, universe? My lips can't help but curve up.

Finally, I turn over the last card—what the future holds.

The World.

I sit back and study the cards, attempting to create a story from the pictures in front of me before I pull out my guide and read their meanings.

Past, where we started. That's easy. A one-night hookup that turned into two, three, four nights, and now, here we are. I pick up the book that came with the deck and flip through it.

Ten of Pentacles. Strong bonds and opportunities in a relationship.

Well, Rooster and I definitely had a spark and connection in the beginning.

The Lovers. A unique bond between two people. Mutual trust and respect. An authentic and deep connection.

The sex is hot for sure. We connect well in that area. But there's more. I've felt it from the beginning. Obviously, Rooster feels it too.

The World. This is always a positive card for me. I've never had it come up in a love reading before—not that I've done one in a long time. It *has* come up in career readings, something I've always taken as a sign that my dreams will come true if I work hard and don't lose faith.

Maybe my questions were too jumbled up in my mind.

My galloping heart doesn't want to slow.

Or maybe Rooster and I are meant to be. I can have both.

If anyone can help me get clarity on the cards, it would be the one who taught me to read in the first place.

I reach over and pluck my cell phone off the nightstand. I forgot to plug it in last night but still have enough charge to call my mom.

"Shelby!" she answers. "Where are you?"

"At Rooster's clubhouse."

"Oh."

For someone who asked for a picture of him yesterday, she doesn't sound all that excited. "I had a day off. He's taking me to the hospital later for a Dream Maker connection."

"That's mighty sweet of him."

I hesitate for a moment. "I played 'Empty Room' last night."

"Shelby," she sighs.

Sure, she doesn't want to talk about Hayley. I get it. I probably shouldn't even remind her when I'm so far away.

"I got the video of you singing with Dawson Roads," Mom says in a brighter tone. "What was it like being on stage with him?"

It already seems like a dream. Day before yesterday, I would've still been going over every second of the performance this morning. But something about last night with Rooster has pushed everything else out of my foolish brain.

"It was incredible. I made my entrance using the riser. Had me nervous as a kitty-cat in a room full of rocking chairs. Worried I'd trip and roll my way onto the stage."

She laughs softly. "I couldn't tell. You looked fabulous, honey. I'm so proud."

"I flubbed a line or two but kept right on going." *Just like you taught me.*

"Good job, Shelbs."

While she goes on about showing the video to everyone at the restaurant we both wait tables at back home, I nibble on my thumbnail debating whether I should ask her opinion on the cards or not.

"So..." I pick up the Lovers card and tap it against my notebook a few times before setting it off to the side. "I did a reading this morning..."

"Do tell."

That eagerness in her voice won't last long. "I, uh..."

It was a good reading. Rooster and I have a shot. That's the only way to interpret the cards that makes any sense. Why am I'm struggling to follow my own intuition? Why am I seeking my mother's approval when I know she'll never give it?

"Shelby?" she prompts.

I relay the cards and their positions.

Momma's silence on the other end tells me all I need to know about her interpretation of the cards and her opinion. "*What* were you asking, Shelby?"

"Rooster and I talked last night. We were makin' plans...I wanted to be sure..."

She sighs. "Now isn't the time."

"That's kinda what I was asking. Where is this relationship headed?"

"Shelby," she says in a more forceful tone, "I like Rooster. He's lovely to look at—"

"He's more than that, Momma." A spark of anger fires me up. "Yesterday you seemed happy I was gonna see him."

"Sure. Thought you'd shake the sheets, have some fun, not plan a future with him."

"We're not planning a future." Not really. "We talked about him coming to visit me on the road more. He understands how important this is to me."

"He'll say that now, but next thing you know, you'll be gettin' knocked up—"

"Jesus, Momma," I snap. "I know how birth control works."

"Sometimes that don't matter."

I squeeze my eyes shut and rub my throbbing temple. "You should've seen how sweet he was yesterday, helping me out, lookin' after me at the meet-and-greet when some grabby-handed jerk decided to help himself to an ass squeeze, recordin' that video and sending it to you—"

"How'd he feel 'bout you singing with Dawson? Can't imagine that went over well."

"He was fine with it. Hells bells, Dawson's old enough to be my dad."

She scoffs. "Not quite."

"Rooster understood it was a big deal for me."

"This ain't the time to be off wool gatherin'. You lose your heart to some bossy biker, you'll be giving up everything you've worked for your whole life."

Too late. I lost the battle for my heart the day Rooster fished me out of the San Antonio River.

"A man like that won't tolerate his woman running all over the country for months at a time," she continues. "And how're you gonna trust him not to screw around behind your back while you're on the road? You don't need the distraction right now, Shelby."

"Love's not a choice, Momma," I whisper. "I can't make it happen when it's convenient."

"Baby, there are plenty of men out there. You're young, beautiful, talented. You'll fall in love when it's the right time." She completely ignores what I said. "You got an itch, scratch it with some of those nice boys showin' up with flowers after your shows. What about Trent? He's been cow eyed forever over ya."

"'Cause I can't get knocked up tearin' up the sheets with every guy who looks at me sideways? You're not making sense."

"I get it. You're young. Full of hormones."

"Dammit, Momma! I'm not some cat in heat who can't control herself."

She's silent on the other end.

"I've sacrificed so much for you, Shelby. Your whole life. Gave up everything for you. And your *father*." She spits out the last word. "You want to end up like me? A forty-year-old waitress?"

"There's nothin' wrong with honest work. And you could still sing if—"

"Those days are gone for me. Don't make my same mistakes."

"I'm not." It sure gets old having her refer to me as a *mistake*.

"You're so stubborn. Always have been."

"That's not true."

"Use that stubbornness to make your dreams come true, Shelby. Not to fight me."

"I'm on this tour, aren't I?"

"Good. Now, I love you. When's your next show?"

There's no point fighting. She's made up her mind and expects me to fall in line. "Tomorrow night."

"Rooster's taking you?"

"Yup," I answer with a note of defiance.

"Is it your last show in New York?"

"Yes, why?"

"Then when you're finished, say goodbye and be done with him before your hearts get any more entangled."

My burst of defiance gives way to defeat. "Sure."

"Love you, Shelby. Let me know how the next show goes."

"Bye, Momma." I almost choke on the lump in my throat. "Love you too."

"I'm sorry if I seem harsh, Shelby. But trust me on this. You can't depend on anyone but yourself. Rooster will say all sorts of things now. Heck, he'll probably mean every word. But men can't change their nature. You don't need a man to be happy."

"I never said I did." I don't *need* Rooster to make me happy, but I sure do crave his smooth, mellow voice at the end of a long, grueling day. He always listens and offers words of encouragement—something I seem to require more than usual these days.

"Use him for what he's good for and be on your way," she says.

Maybe she'll never believe me, but Rooster's good for more than sex. These last few months, it's been nice to have someone—besides my mother—to share good stuff with. Like, the deal I landed that put two of my songs in heavy rotation in every single Southwest Steakhouse in the country. Rooster had been so stoked when he saw my picture in his local restaurant, he called me right away.

I don't need years of experience to know men like Rooster are rare.

Arguing with her when she's wound up on this topic is pointless. "Sure."

"You need to invest your time and energy into yourself, not a relationship."

Tears well up in my eyes. I'm so done with this conversation. "You're right," I answer in a calm, even voice. "I'll end it tomorrow."

I hang up, only feeling a little guilty for lying to my momma.

CHAPTER EIGHTEEN

Shelby

Something scratches against the lock and a few seconds later the door swings open.

Rooster. Even better-looking than he was when he left.

I swipe a stray tear or two off my cheeks, swallow down the lump in my throat, and force a bright smile.

He's not fooled.

"Who were you talking to?" He steps into the room, closing the door behind him. He's all menacing scowl, as if he wants to hunt down whoever has upset me.

"My mom."

His frown gives way to a smile. "How is Lynn? She get the videos?"

"Oh, yeah. She wanted all the details."

His gaze drops to the tarot cards spread out in front of me.

I lean forward and hurry to scoop them up—not that he would be able to interpret the cards any better than I did. No, I bet a logical, practical man like Rooster would think I was ridiculous for dabbling in this stuff.

"What's that?" One corner of his mouth twitches.

"Nothing."

"You trying to talk to spirits or ghosts or somethin'?" He flashes a grin.

I roll my eyes. "You're thinking of a Ouija board. Not the same thing. At all."

He moves closer to the bed. Concern darkens his features. "What's wrong? You look upset. Is your mom okay?"

Bet he wouldn't give a damn if he knew how adamant she was that we shouldn't be more than fuck buddies.

I sniffle, annoyed with myself for letting my momma rattle my cage. I'm twenty-two years old. But her dang guilt trips do me in every time. I'm tired of feeling responsible for ruining her life.

"She's fine." I let out a sad laugh and shake my head. "Opinionated as ever."

"Was she happy about your duet?"

"Oh yeah."

He drops down on the edge of the bed and I reach over, placing my hand over his. Gosh, he's big. "Be honest—did it bother you? Me singing with Dawson?"

His mouth twists and he glances away.

My heart sinks.

Momma was right.

"Hey." He places a finger under my chin and lifts my head. "*Bother* isn't the right word. I can't lie, though. I want to beat any man who gets too close to you half to death." His lips quirk. "But I *can* control myself." He half shrugs. "Most of the time."

His teasing finally pulls a chuckle from me. "Great. Feeling much better now."

"I'm not dumb, Shelby." His mouth flattens into a serious line. "I get how important last night was for you. You need the visibility. I hope every one of his fans went home and bought your album. Don't ever think you have to turn down an opportunity like that because it's going to make me jealous."

Shoot, if all these sweet words keep flowing past his lips, I'll never stop falling for him. I push forward onto my knees and shuffle closer, wrapping my arms around his neck. "Thank you for saying that. It means a lot to me."

He kisses the tip of my nose. "Now, if he touches you *off*stage, or says something inappropriate, all bets are off. I *will* fuck him up."

I shake with laughter. "That's fair."

"I meant what I said. I want to be by your side, not stand in your way."

My silly heart sprouts wings and threatens to fly out of my chest. Too bad I'm about to open my big mouth and risk slapping it down. "Yeah?" I tease, feeling shitty for what I'm about to say. "The big, bossy biker won't eventually demand I put down some roots? Be home to cook dinner?"

"Is that how you see me?" He cocks his head. Shoot, maybe I hurt his feelings. "Some meathead asshole who thinks your career is a cute little hobby?"

"No, Rooster. It's not." *It's how my momma sees you.* And now her words are messin' with my head.

He studies my face for a few seconds before leaning away to touch the tarot cards.

Embarrassment washes over me. "Don't."

"If you're not talking to spirits, what are you doing? Fortune telling?"

I gather the cards up, stuffing them in their case so fast I probably wrinkle their pretty holographic edges. "None of that. It's a way to connect to your inner wisdom." I place my hand over my chest. "Or guide you to understand a situation and determine what path to take based on what you already know."

He narrows his eyes, as if he's trying to follow along with my explanation.

"Too woo-woo for you?" I ask.

"A little." He shrugs and glances at the cards again. "What'd you learn?"

I follow his line of sight. In my hurry to pick up the cards, I'd forgotten that I'd set the Lovers card aside when I was on the phone. He reaches over and plucks it off the bed, a teasing smile playing over his lips. "This a good one?"

I snap it out of his hand. "Don't make fun of me."

His playful expression disappears. "I'm not."

"Yes, it's a good one." I shift to the middle of the bed again to fold my cloth, pick up my crystal, and shove everything back into the little velvet pouch.

Rooster places his hand over mine. "I'm sorry. I didn't mean to make fun of something that's important to you."

"It's not a big deal."

Rooster's phone buzzes. He pulls it out to check the text while I hurry to shove my pouch to the bottom of my backpack.

Between my mother's lecture and Rooster catching me, I'll need to track down some sage and a selenite crystal to wash the negative energy off my dang cards.

Lordy, I hope burnin' a little sage is enough to erase these doubts.

CHAPTER NINETEEN

Rooster

Regret clings to me as I scan the text from Z demanding I get my ass downstairs. Stuff like tarot cards seems about as reasonable to me as climbing up on the roof, flapping your arms, and claiming you can fly. Never expected Shelby to be into that.

But the hurt in her expression made me wish I'd kept my damn mouth shut.

I'm well aware of the reputation many bikers have, so her assumption I'd turn into some demanding caveman doesn't bother me. The more time she spends around the ol' ladies in my club, the more she'll understand those stereotypes don't always apply. Besides, all I need to do is keep showing her that I support her—what better way to do that than visiting her on the road?

"Do you need to go?" she asks.

"Yeah. Want me to walk you downstairs? I think the girls are hanging out in the dining room."

"I need to grab my laundry and then I'll meet up with them." She glances toward the window. "If that's okay."

I hesitate before answering, "Yeah, that's fine." No one's up here now except the brothers—who will all be in church—and the girls.

"Anyone unfamiliar approaches you, just let 'em know you're Rooster's girl."

She tilts her head. "Is that something I need to worry about?"

"Not really. Just in case."

"Okay."

Really wanting to apologize for teasing her but not sure how, I nod to her backpack. "So, that Lovers card, does it mean you're gonna get lucky?"

Her laughter's slow to come. "My mom didn't think it was a good sign."

Shit, her mom's into it too? Now I feel even worse for teasing Shelby.

My phone buzzes again. Without checking the text—who else would it be besides Z?—I lean in and kiss Shelby's cheek. "I can't check my phone during church, but text Heidi if you need something, okay?"

"Will do."

I jog downstairs and find half the brothers milling around. Z's waiting by the war room with his bossy prez expression firmly in place.

"The fuck took you so long?" he grumbles.

"You're gettin' a little clingy, Prez. Calm down."

Murphy chuckles and leans down to kiss Heidi's forehead. "See you in a bit."

I glance over at Z. "Give me a sec."

Before she darts away, I call out to Heidi. She turns, lifting her eyebrows.

Not wanting to be overheard by everyone, I motion her toward the bar. "Think you can check on Shelby?" I ask. "For some reason, she seems shy about coming downstairs to hang with everyone."

"Yeah. Sure. Of course." She flicks her gaze toward the staircase. "Right now?"

"Maybe give her a few minutes."

"You got it, Rooster." She pats my shoulder. "I need to do a few things. Then I'll go upstairs, okay?"

"Thanks."

Murphy's waiting for me by the war room doors. "Everything all right?"

"Yeah, I just asked her to check up on Shelby for me." Do I feel like explaining that I poked fun at Shelby's hobby? Not really.

I stop at Z next. "What are you so antsy about?"

"Nothing. Just don't want to take all fuckin' day to get our asses to the table." He cocks his head. "Weren't you the one bitching you had places to be this afternoon?"

I roll my eyes and he shoves me into the war room. He nudges me in Murphy's direction on the other side of the table. We haven't really come up with formal seating arrangements for when the two charters hold church together. Otherwise, we've adapted well.

"You mind if I take this one?" I ask Murphy, pointing to the chair closest to Rock. I'm not fond of sitting between Murphy and Teller. Feels too much like breaking up conjoined twins or something. They'll spend half the meeting reaching over to smack or poke each other anyway.

"Nope." He drops into the chair on my left.

Jigsaw swaggers into the room and as soon as his demonic eyes land on me, I brace myself for the choke hold that's coming.

"Why you so far away from me, buddy?" he asks, wrapping his arm around my neck and kissing my cheek.

"Stop slobbering on me." I reach up and dislodge him. "Whaddya wanna do? Sit in my damn lap?"

"Since you're offering." He attempts to squeeze his big ass in between me and the old, scarred table.

"Get the fuck outta here." I shove him to the side, and he shakes with laughter.

Teller eyes Jigsaw warily and leans forward to catch my attention. "You wanna switch with me so you two can hold hands?"

"You're one to talk."

Murphy slaps him.

The rest of our brothers are just as obnoxious, but it's all good-natured ribbing and shoving. Sparky ends up on one of the couches in the back of the room with some of the younger brothers, giving up his regular chair to one of downstate's members. Stash razzes him a little but eventually joins him.

After Wrath drops his heavy frame into the chair on the other side of the table from me, Rock prowls in and surveys the room. He gives everyone a few seconds to shut their mouths before taking his seat and slamming his gavel against the table.

Z remains standing even though a chair has been added especially for him at the opposite end. Not sure if he's got some extra energy to work off or if someone's getting their ass kicked this morning.

"Welcome to our downstate brothers." Rock nods at Z, then Steer and the rest of us. "Always good to have everyone here at the table, and we always appreciate you making the trip up."

Murmurs of thanks go around the room.

"First order of business: the new clubhouse in Empire is almost finished. Z and I are riding down to take a look if anyone wants to join us later."

A lot of hands go up. While it's nice upstate will have a clubhouse that isn't so far out in the middle of nowhere to entertain out-of-town guests, it's not high on my list of concerns. The proximity to Crystal Ball probably has something to do with my lack of interest. I grew out of my fascination with strippers years ago. Whatever interest remained has been thoroughly snuffed out by working on our porn production company.

"Slater county—what have we heard from our Wolf Knight friends?" Rock turns toward Teller, so I guess he's got the answer.

"Whisper's still local. I'm working out the deal to buy the drive-in from him but I think he's trying to milk all the summer profits out of the place before signing the paperwork."

"Sounds about right," Wrath says.

"Let's continue to stay clear of Slater for now," Z says. "Give them time to wrap things up and go before we move in."

"Vermont?" Rock asks.

"No word from South of Satan," Murphy answers.

"They been out hassling your boys?" Wrath asks with a hint of his usual dickish smirk.

"Remy and Griff are not *my boys*." Murphy sneers. "And no, they haven't seen anyone suspicious coming to the fights at the Castle. Eraser says no one out of place has been to Zips for weeks."

"Good." Rock nods. "Stay on top of it though. They make a move in our territory, we need to know about it. Loco's got eyes in Ironworks so if I hear something, I'll let you know so you can warn them."

Murphy nods. "Thanks, Prez."

I raise my hand. "I'm riding out that way tomorrow. I can stop and pay a visit on my way back."

"How far west you going?" Z asks.

"The fairgrounds outside Kodack."

"As a sign of respect, call Chaser before you head out." While Z says it in a neutral tone, it's an order not a suggestion.

"Yeah, no problem." I cock my head. "You realize I didn't slip this cut on for the first time yesterday, right?" I'm well aware of the etiquette requiring me to let another club know when I'll be in their territory. Especially if I'm planning to wear my colors.

"Don't get your boxers in a knot." Z drills me with a more serious stare than usual. "Feel him out. Make sure he's not pissed we turned down those jobs for his father-in-law. Smooth things over if he is."

Is Z serious? "And how would you like me to accomplish that?"

"You're smart. Use that winning personality of yours." Z's gaze bounces around the table. "You taking anyone with you?"

"Wasn't planning to. I gotta get my hands on a cage or something anyway. Can't strap Shelby's guitar to—"

"You can take my old truck," Murphy offers. "I haven't sold it yet." His gaze lands on Rock. "Thinkin' I'll just keep it. Grinder's gonna need something if he's gettin' out in the winter."

Rock nods at him. "Thank you."

"Thanks, bro." I slap Murphy's shoulder. "Appreciate it."

"You going with him?" Rock asks Murphy.

Murphy's gaze shoots to me. "Uh, I didn't think Rooster needed a chaperone..."

Jigsaw raises his hand so fast he practically falls out of his seat. "I'll go."

"Thought you said demonic forces invented country music to prepare people for an eternity in hell?" Z asks.

Jigsaw shrugs. "Yeah, but the girls at those shows are worth the suffering."

"Did I do something to anger you, Prez?" I glare at Z. "Why you punishing me?"

Jiggy reaches behind Teller and Murphy's chairs and flicks my shoulder. "You love me."

"Fine." I snort. "This time you're gonna make yourself useful."

"What's wrong?" Z asks.

"Nothing. Shelby has to do these meet-and-greet things and some asshole got grabby with her. Be nice to have an extra set of hands to scare the shit out of these fuckers."

"Fuck yeah." Jigsaw pumps his fist in the air.

Rock's steely glare settles on Jigsaw. "Take it easy. We don't need attention drawn to the club. Don't start trouble in Chaser's territory."

"I'll be on my best behavior," Jigsaw promises.

"Fantastic," I mutter.

Rock smirks at me before settling his presidential stare farther down the table. "Dex, why don't you go with them." It's an order, not a request.

"No problem, Prez."

I nod in appreciation. "At least Dex is an adult and won't embarrass me."

"Feeling the love, brother," Jigsaw says.

Dex rumbles with laughter. "This is gonna be a fun trip."

Rock and Z share a look. "Two RCs and a VP. Respectful but not threatening," Z says.

I point between the two of them. "Might as well bring a fourth. Make it an even number." I fight the smirk threatening to form. "President is the ultimate show of respect."

They both give me *fuck no* glares in return.

Laughing, I settle back into my chair.

As we're winding down, Wrath reminds us there's a bonfire tonight. Everyone's invited to stay. As if anyone would say no.

Fuck knows, Shelby needs to have some fun.

Here I've just been handed a bunch of responsibilities for the club. But the thing that matters the most to me is making Shelby happy.

CHAPTER TWENTY

Shelby

Even though Rooster reminded me several times that Heidi and some of the other girls would be downstairs, for some reason I find myself dragging my feet.

Maybe it's the weirdness clinging to me from the reading, or my momma's phone call, or talking to Rooster. I'm not sure.

I check my phone and read the email from the Dream Makers liaison.

After shooting her a response confirming the time, I set my phone down and sort through the small pile of clean clothes I brought with me.

I slip on a loose mint-green tank top with an image of a meditating flamingo on the front, a denim skirt and pair of sandals. While I'm finishing brushing out my hair, someone knocks.

Hesitant, I stare at the door for a minute before reaching over and opening it.

Heidi waves at me. "Morning! I hope you don't mind. I wanted to see if you needed anything."

"No, I was just on my way downstairs." I toss my brush on the bed.

"Oh, cool. I can show you where the dining room is then. The layout is simple, but the clubhouse is pretty big."

"Thanks." I glance at the room once more before closing the door behind me.

"Some of the girls do yoga in the mornings if you're into that." She glances down at my skirt. "Well, maybe not today."

"No, I would love that. Maybe later. Like, y'all have a class or something?"

"One of the girls is a teacher and she leads classes for Hope, Trinity, and whoever else wants to join them."

"Dang, I'm impressed."

"Yeah, Swan does a modified mommy-and-me version for Lilly and me and our little guys too sometimes. It's fun."

With Heidi's longer legs, I have to hurry to keep up with her as we jog downstairs. The living room's empty this morning. The large wooden double doors opposite the staircase are firmly closed.

Heidi notices me staring at the doors. "That's the war room. Members only."

"Okay." I mean, I wasn't plannin' on barging in to hunt Rooster down, but it's kinda cute how she's so protective over the guys' space.

We make a wide right turn and I'm faced with another long hallway. It's probably a good thing she came and fetched me after all.

"Bathroom." She snickers as we walk past another closed door. "That used to be the guys' champagne room but Hope, Trinity, and Charlotte sort of took it over and turned it into their yoga studio."

"Champagne...oh, I get it."

"There's a gym and another laundry room down that way." Heidi waves at a hallway to our right.

She stops at a wide set of swinging doors and pushes inside. "Our dining room."

Two long, rectangular tables are set up in the middle of the room with a bunch of circular tables scattered to the side. Almost looks like the kind of cafeteria you'd expect in a fancy-pants private high school. Not that I'd know anything about such places.

"We eat family-style on Thursday nights and weekend mornings," Heidi explains, gesturing to the tables.

To our right, there's a larger bar than the one out in the living room. A huge Lost Kings MC mural covers the wall behind it. "Impressive."

She shrugs as she navigates through the dining room. "Kitchen's back here."

Our whole house could fit inside the industrial kitchen. There's lots of counter space, and double ovens, sinks, and a massive silver refrigerator. "Wow."

"Bikers eat. A lot." Heidi laughs.

"She's not wrong," Trinity says. "Morning, Shelby."

Busy gawking at the dream-house kitchen, I didn't even notice the other people in here. "Morning. Heidi just gave me the grand tour."

"Good. Hope that means we'll see you up here more often with Rooster."

"I keep forgetting this isn't his clubhouse, right? He seems so at home here."

"Well." Heidi and Trinity share a look before Trinity continues, "Every brother should feel at home at every charter. But upstate and downstate have gotten especially close recently."

It's a vague answer and I know better than to ask follow-up questions.

The girl who'd served me the Coke last night waves from the refrigerator.

"Shelby, this is Swan," Trinity introduces. "I don't know if you met last night?"

"We did, sort of." I guess I'd been a little rude not saying hi to her last night. "Mornin'."

"Welcome," Swan says.

"You're the yoga guru too? Heidi told me you teach classes?"

Pink spreads over her cheeks and she drops her gaze. "Yup. I help out around here too."

Trinity wraps her arm around Swan's shoulders. "Helps out is a massive understatement."

A taller, slender dark-haired girl pushes open the kitchen door, nervously glancing at our little group before joining us. "What do you need me to do?"

"Lala," Trinity says, "This is Rooster's girl, Shelby. Shelby, Lala's a friend of the club."

"Oh!" Lala blinks rapidly. "Hey. You're the singer, right?"

"She's *the best* country singer right now," Heidi gushes.

"It's true," Trinity insists. She taps her finger against her jaw for a second. "I'd say you're like a twenty-something mash-up of Dolly Parton, Etta James, and Taylor Swift."

My heart's ready to burst from the compliment. "I might love you forever for comparing me to three of my favorite artists."

Lala blinks at us. "I don't know those first two, but you sure do have a Taylor Swift thing going on." She drops her gaze to my feet. "Minus the gazelle legs."

Sacrilege! Who doesn't know who Dolly Parton is? I smile to hide my surprise. *Wait a second, did she just call me short?*

"Anyway, what do you need me to do?" Lala asks Trinity.

Swan takes her aside, helping her with cartons of orange juice and other drinks for the tables.

Trinity watches them for a few seconds before leaning on the counter. She glances at my shirt. "Cute." She narrows her eyes and gives me a playful smile. "You have a thing for flamingos, Shelby?" She touches her chest. "You were wearing flamingos last night, weren't you?"

"Sure was." Rooster hadn't made fun of my idea and the girls have been nothing but nice so far. Maybe it's safe to share my kooky idea with them. "I don't know if you saw those god-awful shirts they sell at my merch booth last night?"

Trinity's lips twitch. "I noticed them." Clearly, she doesn't want to insult me.

"They're cute," Heidi insists.

"Well, no one consulted me about them. The whole me-sitting-in-a-patch-of-wildflowers concept is so not my style. Plus, I'm not all that fond of pink."

"Amen." Trinity raises her hands.

Heidi snickers. "I tried giving Alexa all gender-neutral stuff from the day she was born. So of course, now *all* she likes is pink."

"Well, *choosing* it is different than having it forced on you," I point out.

"True. And boy did she choose it." Trinity laughs and gently shoves Heidi.

Mild jealously bubbles up inside me at how close they seem to be. Singing and working didn't leave me a lot of time for making friends growing up.

Don't get too attached. Who knows when I'll be back to visit?

"You okay, Shelby?" Trinity asks, concern darkening her amber eyes.

"I'm peachy." I force a sunny smile.

"Your shirts?" Heidi prompts.

"Oh. Right." I flap my hands in the air, losing my nerve. "It's a dumb idea."

"There are no dumb ideas," Heidi says.

Trinity side-eyes her. "There are *plenty* of dumb ideas in the world." She winks at me. "I doubt yours is one of them. Spill."

"I want to have shirts made up with a flamingo in cowgirl boots," I blurt out.

"Oh. My. God," Heidi squeals. "I *love* that!"

Spurred by her positive reaction, I continue, "I want to call my next album 'Flocking Fabulous' and have the flamingo with boots on the cover."

"That's freakin' adorable," Trinity says.

"Greg doesn't think the label will let me do it." I wobble my hand in the air. "Country leans a little conservative."

Both of them roll their eyes, much like I've done many times myself.

"I kind of had a whole bunch of shirts in mind with flamingo puns. *Flocking fabulous. For flock's sake. What the flock?* Silly stuff like that."

"Who gives a flying flock?" Trinity picks up where I left off.

Heidi snaps her fingers. "No flocks given!"

"Party like a flock star," Trinity shoots back.

"Sassy as flock," I add.

The three of us burst into giggles.

"Girls," Swan interrupts in her soft voice. "Calm the flock down."

"Yes!" Heidi shouts, jumping around in a circle.

"Now I wish I had my notebook," I mutter, patting my pockets.

Trinity taps the side of her head. "We got you. Don't worry."

"Hey." Heidi settles down and touches my shoulder. "Maybe if the record company won't let you use that title, you can like, start your own label and call it Flocking Fabulous?"

"Or have a side hustle selling your Fancy as Flock T-shirts," Trinity adds. "A lot of musicians do stuff on the side, right?"

"Oh yeah. They have to since they're not making money off their music."

Heidi's mouth twists down. "That sucks."

I shrug.

"Well, Hope helped me set up the legal end of my photography and graphic design business, so if you ever want help with it, let her know." Trinity slaps her hand over her mouth. "Shoot. She's only licensed in New York. You probably want to set up in Texas. But I'm sure she could still give you some pointers or whatever."

After having so much fun laughing and goofing around with the girls, the reminder that I don't belong here stings.

Maybe the disappointment shows on my face. Trinity's quick to reach out and touch my arm. "You think you'd move to New York?"

Somehow, I don't think we're talking about a T-shirt business anymore. Feels like they want to assess my relationship with Rooster. I shrug. "Maybe. My mom's in Texas, though." I hate to admit to them that except for a trip to Disneyland when I was a kid, I'd never traveled outside of Texas until I was picked for *Redneck Roadhouse* and now this tour.

The two girls share a sneaky look. "So, are you planning to keep things long distance with Rooster?" Heidi asks.

"Wow, y'all going right for it, huh?" I smile to cover the annoyance that crept into my tone.

"Just curious."

"I like him." I swallow hard. "A lot. We're going to...I think he might visit me on the road."

Heidi squeals and bounces on her toes again. "So romantic. I can totally see Rooster doing that."

"I feel bad. But he offered..."

"Don't feel bad." Trinity gestures toward the rest of the clubhouse. "These guys don't do *anything* they don't want to do. And they live for a nice, long road trip."

Trinity's words calm the uncertainty that had been creeping up on me since last night. I glance over at Swan who returned to cooking after her *calm the flock down* contribution. "What can I do to help out?"

"We could use a batch of sweet tea, if you don't mind," Trinity says.

"Sure. I can do that. Hope you've got lots of sugar." I glance at the clock. "It might not be totally done in time for breakfast but the longer it's chillin' the better it gets. We can pour in some bourbon for dinner."

"Perfect." Trinity touches my shoulder. "I'm glad you're sticking around."

So am I.

ROOSTER

"You staying for breakfast?" Wrath asks, clapping one of the bear paws he calls hands on my shoulder.

"I think so." I glance at my phone. "Taking Shelby to a thing. Still have to ask her what time she needs to be there."

"She's probably doing yoga with the girls," Ravage says. "Do you know the ol' ladies stole our champagne room?" He waves his hand at Wrath and then Rock. "And *they* allowed it."

One corner of Wrath's mouth slides up. "You can thank us later," he says to me before shoving Ravage sideways. "Fuck off. You guys still use it at night."

"No, we don't. Your wife put a lock on the door."

"Oops." Wrath smirks.

"Aren't you guys building an entire clubhouse of sin down in Empire?" I ask Ravage.

"Yeah, that's *why* we had to build it."

"Build it and we will come. All over the place," Stash adds.

I groan at the lame joke. "How are we the same age?"

Jigsaw joins them to discuss a trip down to Crystal Ball. Wrath nudges Sparky. "You might want to warn Willow there's going to be a full house tonight."

"Me?" Sparky's voice climbs several octaves. "Why would *I* warn her?"

"I'm sorry." Wrath scratches his chin and feigns confusion. "Was Willow sneaking out of the basement every Sunday morning supposed to be a secret?"

Muttering and cursing to himself, Sparky heads back down to the basement. Stash follows a few seconds later.

"You're such a dick," Ravage says to Wrath.

"The biggest," Wrath agrees.

"Let's go!" Z calls. "Girls are waiting. Food is ready."

I follow the rest of the herd down the hallway, hoping Shelby's downstairs by now.

The dining room is loud and boisterous. There are so many of us that the room has been arranged into two long rectangular tables side-by-side to accommodate everyone and their families.

This is one of my favorite things about weekends upstate. And today's even better because I have someone who's with me. I've been picturing Shelby by my side for Saturday morning breakfast for months —and now she's finally here.

There she is. By the kitchen door, talking to Trinity. Yeah, I definitely like Shelby getting cozy with Wrath's wife. Trinity's opinion means something to the guys. Not that Wrath would be one of the officers to vote Shelby in—should I ever want to patch her. I just like how she easily fits in with my club's ol' ladies.

Trinity's gaze lands on all of us crowding into the dining room. She nudges Shelby. A few seconds later, they approach us.

"How's it going?" I ask Shelby.

"Good. I helped Trinity make a big ol' batch of sweet tea."

Wrath sort of scowls at Trinity. "I can't drink that."

"It's not for you." She pokes his side. "Beast."

He snarls and picks her up. Trinity's laughter rings out over the rest of the noise as he carries her to the table. Shelby watches them with an amused smile.

I don't have a chance to ask her anything else. Heidi's daughter runs over and smacks into my legs. "Ooster!"

"Hey, pumpkin." I glance down at her. "You planning to play football?"

"Sorry," Heidi says. "Shelby, this is my daughter, Alexa. Alexa, can you say hi to Shelby?"

While she was nice enough to the kids at the show last night, I have no idea how Shelby feels about them in her free time. She squats down so she's almost eye level with Alexa. "Well, aren't you cuter than a sack full of puppies?"

Alexa squints at her, then up at her mom. Guess she doesn't find Shelby's Texas-isms as fucking adorable as I do.

Shelby winks at Heidi. "I am *living* for these pink camo overalls."

"I told you." Heidi shakes her head and the two of them share a laugh. "Come on. Let's go clean up before breakfast." Heidi grabs Alexa before she scurries away.

Something slams into my other leg. I glance down, already knowing who it is. "You two trying to cripple me today?"

Z's son flashes a toothless grin before running over to see Hope. "That one's Z's," I explain to Shelby. "Chance."

"I didn't expect it to be so...family-friendly at a motorcycle club." Shelby stares at the scene in front of us. The couples and a good portion of upstate's members situate themselves around the first table while the rest of the guys grab a seat at the next one.

I wrap my arm around Shelby's shoulders and lead her around to the other side. Murphy points at the three chairs next to him. "Heidi's sitting there if you want to sit next to her, Shelby."

I lift my chin, a quick thanks for trying to help Shelby feel included and pull out her chair. Jigsaw pulls a chair over to the corner right next to me.

"You plannin' to eat off my damn plate?" I ask.

"Only if you ask nicely."

Swan and Lala bring out platters of food for both tables, with Birch and Stitch helping them carry the heavier loads.

"What time do you need to be down at Empire Med?" I ask Shelby.

"One."

"Okay. We've got time."

Heidi's got tons of questions for Shelby and they end up talking through most of breakfast. I rest my hand on her knee, absently running my fingers over her soft skin. Never thought I'd enjoy having someone with me at the club this much.

It doesn't take long for a bunch of bikers to demolish a breakfast. Shelby pushes her chair away from the table. "I'm stuffed."

Little Alexa toddles over and hands Shelby a broken ponytail holder. "Fix it."

Murphy stretches his arm and taps her shoulder.

"Please," she adds.

Poor Shelby does a quick scan of the room for Heidi. She even throws a pleading look Murphy's way, but he's busy talking to Charlotte now.

"Okay, sure. Come here." She sets Alexa in her lap and reaches into her back pocket. "Aha. I've always got an elastic on me. Okay, what're we working with here? Your momma do these pretty braids?"

"No, Daddy."

Jigsaw leans over the table. "Murphy, your kid's ratting you out."

"What?" Murphy turns.

"You braid hair?" Jigsaw draws out the question, like he's hoping to embarrass Murphy.

Dex punches Jigsaw's arm. "Real men actually know how to take care of their children."

"Teller," Jigsaw shouts. "You braid hair too?"

"I'm not coordinated enough." He wiggles his fingers in our direction, ending with a middle finger aimed at Jiggy.

Alexa giggles and beams at Shelby.

While I think Alexa, Chance, and Grace are adorable, and I don't mind spending time with them in small doses, I've never really thought about what it might be like to have kids of my *own*. Never met a woman I'd want to share that responsibility with.

But Shelby, sitting right next to me, being all cute and snuggly with a kid she barely knows and working so hard to fix her little braids just right? Well, fuck if that doesn't sock me right in the gut.

"Aw, look at Rooster giving Shelby the baby-making eyes," Ravage coos. "Ain't that sweet?"

I shoot a glare at him. "What?"

"Yeah, what was that?" Shelby finishes Alexa's hair and sets her down, laughing as the tyke runs over to hug Chance. "You're barking up the wrong tree."

"Careful, Shelby, or you'll end up the oldest mom in your birthing class," Hope calls down.

"That's fine by me." Shelby lifts her hands in the air like she's praising the baby gods. "Don't want any until I'm at *least* thirty-five."

The guys have a good laugh at that. For some idiotic reason, Jiggy elbows me in the side. When everyone goes back to their conversations, I lean down toward Shelby. "You don't want kids?"

Her eyes snap to mine. "You do?"

"Not now. Not anytime soon, even. Just...curious."

She blows out a breath. "Momma's been drilling it into my head not to get pregnant since I was like fourteen. She had me at seventeen. Had to marry my dad and give up singing."

"Your mom was a singer too?"

"Oh, heck yeah. I think that's how they met."

Huh. That was a lot of information. I run my hand over her leg.

"Sorry, was that more family history than you wanted?"

Sure, that was a lot to take in. But learning something new about this woman every second I'm with her is high on my list of priorities. "Not at all. I want to discover every last detail about you, Shelby."

CHAPTER TWENTY-ONE

Rooster

After breakfast, Shelby jogs upstairs to grab her guitar while I walk outside to inspect Murphy's truck.

"You sure you don't mind me borrowing it?" I ask.

"It's just sitting here. I'll run it down to Lowe's every now and then but you might as well use it this weekend if you need it."

"Appreciate it, brother."

"No problem."

"You cool meeting up at Eraser's place Monday?"

"Yeah, just text me when you're on your way back."

Shelby's squeezing through the front door with her guitar case and I go over to help her. "Ready?"

"Sure am."

We say goodbye to Murphy and a few of the other brothers before hopping in the truck and heading out.

"Wow, it's so much prettier during the day," she says, staring out the window. "And now I know what you meant about Texas having hills not mountains."

"Glad I could show you around a little."

"That's one of my favorite things about being on tour. Seeing so many new places."

"Yeah?"

"Well, I don't have enough time to stop and appreciate any of them, but I've been trying to make notes of where I want to go back and visit one day."

"What cities made the list?"

"Honestly?" She laughs. "Everywhere."

"You might be singing a different tune come winter."

"No doubt." She stares out the window again. "I'd love to see snow, though. Like real snow. Not that slush-mush we sometimes get."

"We get plenty of snow up here."

She glances over. "Sorry, I wasn't trying to—"

"Trying to what?"

"I can't leave my momma alone around the holidays," she answers quickly.

Okay, I kinda understand. Although, Shelby's twenty-two. It's not unreasonable that she'd spend the holidays somewhere else. I'd say Lynn's invited too, but something about Shelby's mood seems to have shifted.

Maybe she's nervous about the visit we're about to make?

Ever since I listened to her sing "Empty Room" last night, I haven't been sure how to bring up the topic of Shelby's sister. I'll leave it to her to decide when she's comfortable talking about it. Her participation with Dream Makers could be related. Maybe that's a safer topic of conversation.

"So, you do a lot of these visits?"

She turns to look at me. "I wouldn't say a lot."

Not much of an answer. We're a few more miles down the road before I attempt another approach. "Are you nervous?"

"Not really." She glances at the clock. "How far is the mall from here?"

"A little out of the way but not too bad. Why?"

"Can we swing by? I want to pick up a couple things."

"Okay."

Good thing she mentioned it when she did. I hang a quick left and slow my speed on the rolling country roads that eventually lead to the Stonewell Mall.

"You can drop me off and I'll just run in." She points to the big box electronics store at one end of the mall.

"Hell no." I'm offended she thinks I'd let her run around a strange place she's never been before by herself. All she needs is some dickhead from last night recognizing and harassing her while I'm sitting in the truck with my thumb up my ass. Not happening.

I back Murphy's truck into a spot and help her down. "You know what you want?"

"I have an idea."

The electronics store has seen better days. Guess most people order shit online now. But it doesn't seem to faze Shelby. She heads to the middle of the store and picks up an MP3 player and a gift card. For a second she stands there, biting her thumbnail, her gaze roaming over the aisles.

"What else do you need?" I ask.

"I'm not sure."

She ends up grabbing a pair of pink headphones before hurrying up to the register. When I offer the clerk my card, Shelby pushes my hand away. "This stuff isn't for me."

The girl's barely making any money from this tour but she's buying shit for a kid she doesn't even know?

"I got it," I assure her, shoving my card into the machine's slot when the clerk gives me the okay.

"Rooster," she sighs.

"We can argue about it later. We're running late." I grab the bag and take Shelby's hand, hustling her out of the store.

"Thank you."

"No problem."

Thank fuck Heidi gave us specific directions. Empire Med is huge. And although I recently spent a lot of time here when Murphy was in the hospital, I don't think I would've found my way to the children's wing easily. It has its own separate entrance a few blocks away from the main building.

I pull into a parking spot and hop out. While I'm unloading

Shelby's guitar and bags, I catch her still sitting in the passenger seat with her eyes closed.

By the time I make it to her side of the truck, she's jumping down onto the pavement.

"I can take something." She reaches for the guitar case but I shift sideways.

"I've got it." I lift my chin toward the front of the building. "Go on. I'm right behind you."

Inside is more homey than hospital-y but it's still a sterile environment. Splashes of color and cartoon-filled posters attempt to make it kid-friendly but somehow it just makes the place more depressing.

A slender woman with chestnut hair wearing a green-print wraparound dress meets us by the front desk.

"Shelby Morgan, right? I'm Elaine." She holds out her hand. "I can't thank you enough for making time today."

"No problem." Shelby's soft voice doesn't carry far.

The woman's confused gaze darts between Shelby and me.

Shelby touches my arm. "This is my friend, Logan. He offered me a ride today."

I've offered you a lot more than a ride. But this isn't really the time or place for off-color jokes. My hands are full, so I simply nod at the woman.

She thanks me and asks us to follow her down the long, wide corridor.

"Bethany is so excited. She really wanted to see you in concert last night, and we were trying to make that work. But her doctors couldn't give the okay for the outing."

"I'm sorry to hear that," Shelby says.

We stop at a nursing station and Elaine confers with a woman in scrubs. They ask Shelby a few questions before allowing us to continue.

We walk to the end of a long corridor before stopping outside the last room on the left. A big window at the end of the hallway looks out into the parking lot. Elaine knocks on the door. Shelby turns and leans up on her tiptoes. "Can you send me the video you took last night?" she asks in a low voice.

"Sure."

"Thanks." She takes her guitar case from me, tucking it close to her body, careful not to knock into anything while entering the small hospital room.

Not wanting to intrude on the moment, I hang back, setting the bags on the windowsill behind me.

"Bethany, someone's here to see you," Elaine says in a cheery voice.

"Hi!" Even from where I'm standing, Shelby's bright smile lights up the whole damn room. "Are you Bethany?"

"That's me!" a little girl squeals.

The mom, who doesn't look much older than Shelby, rests her hand over her heart. "Thank you so much, Shelby," she says. "This means a lot."

"I'm glad it worked out."

"She's having a good day, so..."

Shelby puts her arms around the woman's shoulders, leaning close to say words that don't reach me.

"Hi." Shelby approaches the bed and Elaine hurries over to push a chair next to it for Shelby.

There's not a lot of room to move around but somehow, Shelby sets her case down and pulls the guitar out. Their conversation's soft and easy; most of it I can't make out and I don't dare move any closer or intrude. If my big ass could blend into the wallpaper, that'd be ideal.

Instead, I pull out my phone and send Shelby the videos from last night. Why didn't I think to bring something with a bigger screen with us? We were right at the mall. I could've grabbed something.

"I wrote a song for you. Do you want to hear it and tell me what you think?" Shelby asks.

By the excited noises, I'm guessing Bethany's answer is an enthusiastic *yes*.

Shelby strums a few upbeat notes and launches into a cute tune that consists of a bunch of words that somehow rhyme with Bethany in Shelby's sassy twang. Her talent keeps on amazing me.

With tears in her eyes, the mom wanders into the hallway.

Even for a cynical bastard like me, this whole scene's overwhelming.

The mom sniffles and then startles when she notices me leaning against the wall. "Are you Shelby's husband?"

"Uh." Fuck, I feel shitty even being here. "Her boyfriend." What an inappropriate moment to test out *that* word for the first time. "And driver." I force a smile, trying to keep things light. I'm sure the woman has enough darkness in her life.

"Well, thank you." She sighs and glances into the room again. "When Bethany first got diagnosed, we were in the hospital a lot and somehow we got hooked on that show. We watched episodes of *Redneck Roadhouse* constantly. Bethany was obsessed, and she adored Shelby. This means a lot to her."

Words. Think of some. How do I respond to that? "I'm happy we could make it work out," I finally say.

Awkwardness crawls up and down my skin. I'm not good at small talk in regular situations, and certainly not in ones when I'm intruding on a stranger's suffering. "Can I get you anything? A soda, coffee?"

Not that I want to run away. It's more that I want to do something...useful.

"A Pepsi? There's a vending machine at the end of the hallway." She points in the opposite direction. "If you don't mind."

"Not at all. I'll be right back."

The heavy feeling from Bethany's room chases me down the hallway. It takes a second to locate the small lounge full of vending machines. And when I finally do, I stop and stare at the machines for a few seconds, not looking at anything in particular.

How the hell does Shelby do this?

How many visits has she made? One? Two? Ten?

I feed the machine and punch the button a few times, grabbing a couple of cans to take back with me.

When I return, Shelby's showing the little girl the video of the duet with Dawson, explaining how nervous she was and how nice he is. The kind of behind-the-scenes information that makes Bethany's eyes go wide.

"I'm so sorry you couldn't make it last night," Shelby says. "But I brought you a couple things." She turns and raises an eyebrow at the mom. "Is that okay?" she whispers.

Mom nods quickly.

That's my cue. I set the soda cans on the windowsill and grab the bags we brought. I hadn't noticed last night, but apparently Shelby packed T-shirts and other concert merchandise with her before leaving the venue.

After the presents, they take a bunch of pictures. Shelby hugs the mom and Elaine before stepping out.

"I've got this." I take her guitar case from her and wrap my hand around hers.

Shelby's quiet as we navigate our way out of the hospital. The heels of her sandals click over the shiny tiles, emphasizing how little there is to say.

Inside the truck, she bursts into tears.

"Shhh. Shelby, come here." I don't bother asking what's wrong. Seeing such a sweet little girl so sick and in pain would be rough on anyone, let alone someone who's lost her little sister. I flip the middle console out of the way and slide closer, pulling her into my arms. "Shhh. I got you."

I hold her while she trembles and sobs for several minutes. Finally, she takes a deep breath and draws away.

"Here." I reach into the back seat and snag a box of tissues, then hold them out to her.

"Thank you," she whispers and dabs at her eyes. "Shoot. I'm so sorry."

"Don't be sorry." I set the tissue box on the dash, so she can grab more if she needs them. "That was sweet. What you did. You made that little girl so happy."

She sniffles and dabs at her cheeks.

"Do you want to talk about it?" I ask.

After blowing out a long breath, her gaze darts everywhere, never landing on me. "About what?" Her bottom lip trembles.

"'Empty Room?'"

Finally, she meets my eyes. "You're an attentive one, aren't you?" Her words come out flat. Not teasing. Not hostile.

I brush my knuckles over her cheek. "If you're talking, I'm listening."

After a few more seconds of silence, she says, "My sister's name was Hayley..."

"Shelby and Hayley. That's pretty."

One corner of her mouth curves up. "She was almost four years younger than me but we were tight as ticks when we were little. No one messed with my baby sister without gettin' an ass whoopin' from me."

"I can picture that."

When she doesn't continue, I hug her a little tighter before asking, "She got sick?"

"Yeah," she whispers. After a few seconds, she seems to find her voice again. "At first she was just tired or didn't feel like eating. She was always a picky eater, so our parents didn't think much of it. Then she was in pain but doctors couldn't figure out what was wrong, so they said she must be making it up for attention." Her hands ball into fists. "I *knew* Hayley. She wasn't a liar. She was suffering and no one would listen. Made me so damn mad that they didn't take her seriously until it was too late."

"What about your parents?"

"They believed the doctors."

"Didn't they take her somewhere else? Or to see another doctor?"

"You've been to my house. You know I didn't grow up with no silver spoon or nothin'."

"I know you and your mom both work hard."

She shrugs. "My dad had a decent job at the time. Okay insurance. But it still didn't cover everything. Put my parents into a load of debt. When Hayley was in the hospital, they'd fight constantly. Momma couldn't work because she needed to be with Hayley."

"I can't imagine how hard it was on them."

She hums and shifts to the side. "Hayley always wanted to sing with me. We were going to be a duo. I'd bring my guitar and sing to her in the hospital." She lets out a sad laugh. "I guess that's why it hit me so hard today."

"Today would've been rough on anyone."

She pulls away from me and grabs another tissue, wiping her face. "Sorry."

"You don't have to apologize."

"I miss her. She would've been eighteen. Just graduatin' from high school. I can't even…"

My own uncomfortable memories of loss bubble to the surface. I open my mouth to say I'm sorry but it's such a useless sentiment, I reach over and squeeze her hand instead.

"Anyway," she continues, "Dream Makers did a lot for us when Hayley was sick. They sent our whole family to Disneyland. To this day, I think that trip helped Hayley hang on a little longer. I saw what a huge difference they made for a lot of other kids too. So the first time they contacted me, there was no way I'd turn them down."

Admiration for Shelby fills my chest.

But who looks after her when she makes these visits? It has to take a toll on her spirit. Who holds her in the car afterward? Does Greg even know about Shelby's sister? Does he realize these visits might be painful for Shelby? He must, right?

"I think it's great that you work with them," I say carefully. "But who takes care of *you?*"

She blinks at me. "I'm okay."

"You're more than okay, but that's not what I'm asking."

"I don't get asked *that* often, Rooster. Maybe a handful of times since *Redneck Roadhouse* ended. There's no wait list to meet Shelby Morgan or anything. I'm not that—"

"Woman, if you say *not that big a deal* again—"

"What?" she challenges.

"You're bigger than you realize, but that's not the point." I tap her chest, over her heart. "You need to take care of yourself too." *Or you need me to protect you.*

She reaches over and tugs on my beard. "I'm okay, really. Thank you for being here with me today. It really helped."

I cup her cheek, running my thumb over her bottom lip. "Let me know next time you're doing a visit. I don't want you to go alone."

"Rooster. That's crazy. Sometimes they're set up in advance but other times, it's like this one—I get the message on short notice."

"You *can* say no."

"I can't." She drops her gaze and shakes her head. "It's not an option for me, Logan."

I wrap my hand around hers, dragging it closer, running my lips over her knuckles. "Then let me know. Please. If I can't go with you, I'll at least talk you through it after or something."

"Okay," she whispers. A soft laugh passes her lips and she tugs her hand away. "That tickles."

"I thought you liked my beard?" I pull her close and rub my chin against her inner wrist and up her arm.

"Oh, I do." She laughs harder. "Still tickles."

I lean over and rub my face against her cheek until she's giggling uncontrollably and pushes me away. "Stop! Stop!"

"How do you feel about bonfires?" I pop a kiss on her cheek and move back to my seat.

"Love 'em. Why?"

"That's what they're planning at the clubhouse tonight."

"When do I get to see *your* clubhouse?" she asks.

"We can go now if you want. I have to warn you—downstate's place isn't quite as fancy."

"But I'd still like to see where you spend most of your time." She closes her eyes. "So when I'm on the road, I can picture you in your natural habitat."

"My *natural habitat* is on my bike, riding the wind."

She closes her eyes and tips her head back. "Hmm. Yeah, I can picture that."

After a few seconds, she opens her eyes, the full weight of her gaze bearing down on me.

"All right." I start up the truck. "If you're sure that's how you want to spend your day. You're on the road so much, thought you'd want to be still for a little bit."

The sadness in her expression doesn't lift. "I just want to soak up as much time with you as possible."

As if I needed the reminder that tomorrow she'll be gone.

CHAPTER TWENTY-TWO

Shelby

The sadness that always follows me after a Dream Makers visit still lingers but it doesn't threaten to crush me into a million pieces the way it did when we first left the hospital. Talking to Rooster helped. Sharing a little bit about Hayley lifted me up, even though a dull ache still throbs through my chest whenever I think about her.

I reach forward, studying the radio. "Am I allowed to play with the music or are you a 'driver rules the tunes' kinda fella?"

Rooster chuckles and glances over. "Fiddle away. I'm sure Murphy's got all the country stations in the area dialed in."

"I listen to more than just country, you know." I flick the knobs and punch a few buttons, finally landing on a hard rock station on satellite radio. "Never know where inspiration will strike, so I listen to a lil' bit of *everything*."

My phone buzzes and I pull it out of my pocket and thumb the screen on.

Greg: This isn't the publicity you need right now.

"Shoot," I mutter.

"What's wrong?"

"I'm not sure." I click on the link Greg added. It leads me to an article on the *Sippin' on Secrets* blog—the bane of entertainers everywhere, especially country musicians.

The ridiculous headline in bold, hot-pink letters reads, *Sweet and Sassy Country Singer Shelby Morgan Getting Cozy With Biker Backstage.*

Seriously?

There are a few fuzzy pictures of Rooster picking me up and us kissing. I squint and try to blow up the photos. While his black leather vest is visible—and how I assume they knew he was a biker—thankfully, only a portion of his vice president patch is legible. Nothing specifically identifies him as a Lost King, thank heavens. I can't imagine his club would appreciate the exposure.

A quick scan of the accompanying "article" shows it's just as silly as the dumb headline.

Shelby Morgan, country music's newest sensational sweetheart, was caught in a compromising position backstage at the Back Road Dreams tour in upstate New York. An eagle-eyed fan snapped several steamy pics of the couple engaged in a heavy make-out sesh after Shelby's thirty-five-minute set.

The buxom blonde songbird is best known for appearing on the reality television show Redneck Roadhouse, *where her red-hot show-mance with co-star Austin Mates famously blew up her friendship with co-star Ruby Nolan.*

Morgan's team had no comment but it's easy to see Shelby and her new mystery man have the look of love brewing in their eyes.

Morgan is currently the opening act on the Back Road Dreams tour headlined by the newly single country super stud Dawson Roads. Concertgoers report later in the night, Morgan and Roads performed a romantic duet hot enough to light a thousand fires.

Hopefully, sassy Miss Shelby learned her lesson from the Redneck Roadhouse *disaster and isn't entering another love triangle.*

Wow. Way to bring up one of the most humiliating moments of my life while insinuating I'm slutty. I'm never going to live down *Redneck Roadhouse*, am I? Worse, I'll forever be mentioned in relation to my connection to some man. Never be taken seriously as an artist. Always reduced to my tit size and hair color.

I grumble a few curses under my breath and fire off a text to Greg.

Can we do anything about it?

Better to ignore.

"Then why'd you send it to me?" I mutter.

"What's wrong?" Rooster asks.

I sigh. Should I even tell him about the article? While this particular blog's a big deal in my world, I doubt it's something Rooster is even aware exists. Then again, some of these so-called reporters are relentless and I should probably warn him that people might try to track down his identity.

His attention's focused on the road, so I don't bother showing him my screen. "Just a stupid entertainment and gossip site. Someone snapped a few pictures of us last night and sent them in."

"Who's *us*? You and me, us?"

"Yeah." I read him the dumb headline, and he roars with laughter.

"Getting cozy, huh? What's the picture?"

I reach over and shift my screen in front of him, and he flicks it a quick glance. "Nice."

"You're not mad?"

"Why would I be mad?"

"What if they had named your club?"

"That wouldn't be ideal." He shrugs. "I'm more worried about *you*, though."

"They might try to track you down, Rooster. You can almost make out the vice president patch." I squint at the screen again. "How many motorcycle clubs are in the area?"

"It's not exactly like we publish a yearbook." He grunts. "Let 'em track me down. Ain't gonna like what they find."

"I'm sorry."

"It's fine." He's quiet for a minute. "Jigsaw is coming out to the show with us tomorrow. Dex is coming too."

"He's the serious, quiet one, right?"

"That's Dex." He glances over. "Actually, Z asked them to go with me. Is that gonna cause problems for you?"

I blow out a long breath. "More people might try to grab pictures now. Why did Z want them to go with you?"

He drums his fingers against the steering wheel for a few seconds before answering. "It's in another club's territory. We're friendly with this club. Pretty close relationship that extends before my time, actually. There's also some business we need to take care of on the way home."

"Oh."

"Since he's coming anyway, I asked Jiggy to help me out at your meet and greet."

I blink. "You did? But I can't pay him—"

"He's not taking your money." He dismisses it like it's a non-issue.

"Rooster, I appreciate that, but I can't ask him to work for free. I felt bad enough having you do it." I reach over and run my hand up his thigh. "But I had a form of payment in mind."

He closes his hand over mine. "I don't like what you're implying on several levels." He raises my hand, kissing the back of it before letting go. "*You* didn't ask. *I* did. If the roles were reversed, I wouldn't hesitate to help him out. It's what we do for each other."

"Greg's going to shit himself." I smile with glee.

"Tough. He needs to do a better job protecting you. You're his artist. Your safety should be his top priority."

"Pfft. Every now and then I get some crummy, creepy letter or weird present. Besides that, and the occasional guy who wants to play grab ass, I'm fine."

"Wait, what? What letters? And no one should be grabbing your ass. Jesus Christ, we don't allow ass-grabbing at our strip club. It sure as fuck shouldn't—"

"What strip club?"

He glances over. "I told you upstate runs a strip joint. Crystal Ball."

"Do *you* hang out there a lot?"

"I *work* there when the club needs me to help out." He glances over and gives me a playful smirk. "You're not jealous, I hope."

"Nah. I was thinking if this singing thing doesn't work out, maybe I can audition at your place since I'll have an in with the owners."

"Fuck that," he growls. "That's not even funny."

"Why? It's honest work."

"Yeah. Hard work too. High turnover rate." He flicks his gaze my way again. "You got a need to dress up and twirl around a pole, you can do it for me. And only me."

"I was kidding. But it's cute that you're all riled up."

He makes more growly noises, which make me laugh harder.

"I'm way too shy to get naked in front of a room full of people, Rooster. So settle down."

"You have nothing to be shy about. Trust me."

"Are you *trying* to talk me into it?"

"Fuck no." He glances over. "How can you say you're shy? Don't you basically take the stage and get emotionally naked every night?"

Unsure of how to respond, I stare at him. From someone not in the entertainment business, it's an awfully accurate description. "That's exactly what it feels like sometimes."

He reaches over and rests his hand on my leg. "I think that's why people relate to you so well."

"You think they do?"

"I know you don't draw the same crowd Dawson does—*yet*—but yeah, you captured their attention last night and kept 'em hanging on 'til the last note."

My eyes water and I turn to stare out the window. Huh. Must be allergic to something in New York. "Thank you. That's really sweet."

"Hey, what's wrong?"

"Nothing. I appreciate what you said is all."

"I wouldn't say it if I didn't think it was true."

"Oh, I know you wouldn't. You've already been in my panties. Several times."

He busts out a laugh. "I've been in *more* than your panties, chickadee."

No joke. Rooster's slowly, but surely, taking up residence in my heart.

CHAPTER TWENTY-THREE

Rooster

Shelby and I don't run out of things to talk about on the way downstate. Usually this much conversation would have me crawling the walls, but I can't get enough of her voice and stories.

She reaches for her water bottle, taking a long sip. "I should probably pipe down or I won't be able to sing a note tomorrow."

Shit, why didn't I think of that? "I should do a better job holding up my end of the conversation, huh?"

She laughs softly. "You're a good listener. Even my mom can't listen to me for long without offering an opinion." Her gaze shifts to the window. "Whether I want it or not."

"You two have a fight this morning?"

"No."

Obviously, that's a topic of conversation she wants to avoid. Which probably means I should investigate it more.

The overgrown grass and shrubs lining the clubhouse's property comes into view. Much to Z's irritation, we keep things looking a little raggedy around the edges to deter visitors. I flick the blinker on. Outside the newly installed gate, I have to stop and punch in a code.

"So much security," Shelby comments.

"We just added this a little while ago."

"Was there a reason?"

"Nothing specific."

Shelby accepts that answer, which I appreciate. Few things she's encountered about MC life seem to bother her. Unusual attitude for a woman who's never been around a club before.

I park in the spot reserved for the VP, noting that Tawny's big, black Cadillac is parked right in front of the large wooden clubhouse doors. Of course, the one chance I get to bring Shelby by the clubhouse the old president's wife would be prowling around. Stirring up trouble, no doubt.

Upstate likes to joke about using Tawny as some sort of test for whether a woman will survive as a Lost Kings ol' lady. Used to think it was kind of funny until right this second.

We haven't been...whatever we are...long enough for Shelby to be subjected to Tawny yet.

I walk around and open Shelby's door.

"Thought you said everyone was upstate?" She glances around at the few bikes and cars in the lot.

"Couple brothers stayed behind, and a few girls live here and help us take care of the place."

A flash of...annoyance, maybe suspicion, crosses her face, but she doesn't question me.

I pull open the heavy front doors and motion for her to go inside.

At least the place is clean and doesn't smell like ass the way it used to.

"Give me a second." I squeeze Shelby's hand and duck into the office I share with Z.

Someone tossed a stack of envelopes on the desk. The red light on the phone blinks a steady, annoying red.

Junk mail.

Spam phone calls.

Nothing that needs my attention.

"You work here?" Shelby asks, leaning against the doorframe.

"*Work* is probably stretching it."

She raises her hands to her face, forming a little square. "Click."

I set the phone down and come around the desk. "What's that, chickadee?"

"Just taking a mental snapshot for my collection." She mimes shaking out a Polaroid and tucking it in her pocket.

I grab her hips and yank her closer. "You're fucking cute, you know that?"

She opens her mouth.

"Rooster!"

I cringe. Somehow Tawny's husky voice—that I'm sure she thinks is sexy—is more like nails down a fucking chalkboard. "What are you doing here? Thought you boys were gone all weekend?"

Without bothering to introduce herself, she hip checks Shelby aside to hug me and press a kiss to my cheek, no doubt leaving hot-pink lipstick marks.

Sway may not be our president anymore, but it's still customary to show his ol' lady respect. No matter how much I'd rather not. "Where's your ol' man, Tawny?" *Why are you running around unsupervised?*

She points at the ceiling. "Upstairs. Resting."

"Tawny." I slip my hand around Shelby's and tug her closer. "This is my girlfriend, Shelby. She's only in town for the weekend, so I thought I'd bring her by and show her around."

She rakes her gaze over Shelby. "Where you from, Shelby?"

"Texas." Shelby slathers on the southern twang. Is she nervous or annoyed?

She curls an arm around my waist and pats my chest. "Rooster rescued me from drowning."

Tawny nods. "Sounds like our Rooster."

"Rooster!" one of the girls shouts. "Can you help me out a second?"

I glance over my shoulder at Delilah. "Be right there."

Hopefully Tawny can behave for five minutes. And if she doesn't, hopefully Shelby will forgive me.

SHELBY

"Aren't you a cute little thing," Tawny says, slowly assessing me after Rooster dashes away.

I study her tight red jeans, high-heeled sandals, ample cleavage, and helmet of shellacked red hair, and want to answer, *"Well, aren't you a scary bitch?"* But my momma raised me better than that.

"So, what do you do in Texas?" she asks like Texas is located in the sewer instead of the south.

"I'm a singer."

She raises an eyebrow. I'm guessing she's not a fan of reality television or country music, which is oddly comforting. I'd rather she not have any pre-conceived ideas about me.

"You must be special." Her lips curve into a cruel smile, and a lump forms in the pit of my stomach. "Rooster's never brought a girl to the clubhouse he didn't intend to share with his brothers."

Eww. Gross. Really?

I flashback to the scene at upstate's clubhouse last night. She's probably not lying.

Doesn't matter. Rooster and I can discuss it later. I can't let this lady think she's rattled me. This woman's giving off serious spotted hyena vibes. If she smells fear, she'll probably claw me to ribbons.

I shrug, all casual, like I couldn't care less. "Well, he's pretty snarly around most guys I encounter. And I *don't* share, so, guess those days are over for him."

"Well, just make sure they know it too." She points one manicured finger in the direction of the two girls perched on bar stools watching Rooster carry a heavy stack of boxes. "They've probably both fucked your man at some point. You'll want to make it clear he's no longer free dick."

Tawny's still chuckling to herself—*miserable old bitch*—as I stomp over to the bar.

The spark of jealousy burns maddeningly hot inside me. This right here is what I don't need in my life. Why I shouldn't be in a relationship.

I catch the eye of the darker-haired girl and she beams at me, throwing a little wave. The urge to slap her scares me, it comes on so strong.

Rooster's mine. I don't care who he's banged in the past.

What a whopper of a lie. I care way too damn much.

Thinking about him with either of these broads has me madder than a three-legged dog trying to bury a bone on an icy pond.

"Hey." I boost myself up on one of the bar stools and none-too-subtly drape my arm over Rooster's shoulder.

To my great relief, he slips his arm around my waist. "Hey, chickadee." He leans down and kisses my cheek. "This is Delilah and..."

"Sheila," the blonde answers for him.

Phew. So either he's never slept with her or he's slept with so many girls he can't remember all their names.

Oh, this is so bad.

"Right. Sorry, hon." He squeezes me closer. "This is my girl, Shelby. We're actually headed upstate again tonight, but I wanted to show her around."

"How'd it go up there?" Delilah asks.

"Good. You could've come up."

"Nah, I had to work." She winks at him. "My real job."

Rooster chuckles. "Appreciate you lookin' after things here for us."

"No problem." She nods to the staircase in the corner. "Sway and Tawny have been here to 'monitor' things as well."

She says it in a neutral tone but I sense she's not too thrilled. Maybe Tawny's full of "helpful" tips for all the women who stop by.

Rooster finishes and walks me down the long corridor off the main room. At the end, we take a left and he pulls out a key to open one of the doors. "This is my room," he explains.

"Oh." I step inside, admiring the dark gray, weathered hardwood floor that matches the rest of the clubhouse. The walls are painted a lighter shade of gray than the hallways, except for a deep blue accent wall behind the bed. While the colors are calm and soothing, the masculine vibe is reinforced with leather and metal details in the bedframe and a reading chair in the corner. "This is nice."

He shuts the door behind us. "What'd Tawny say to you?"

Biting my lip, I back into the room, not wanting to answer the question. Now I feel a little silly for letting that woman bother me.

"She's the last president's ol' lady," he explains. "So I still gotta show her respect, but she's not always kind to the girls."

The last flames of jealousy flare and die out. "Some stuff about you liking to share girls? And that you'd probably fucked both bartenders at some point."

"Jesus." He pinches the bridge of his nose and drops his head. "Fuckin' pain in the ass."

After a beat or two, he glances up, meeting my eyes. "For the record, Sheila just started hanging around here, helping out, more recently. Delilah's more like a kid sister than...anything else."

"Oh." Funny how he sidestepped the first part of what Tawny told me.

"To me," he clarifies. "What she does with anyone else isn't my business."

"Well, I don't care what anyone else does."

"Good."

We stare at each other for a few beats.

"Tawny loves to stir up trouble."

Rooster's frustrated tone plucks my guilt strings. I shouldn't hassle him for horseshit someone else said to me.

"I'm sure she's still salty that she's not in charge of the girls around here anymore," he continues. "Lilly's too nice to say anything, so I'll talk to Z."

"I don't want to start trouble."

"It's not a big deal. I told her you were my girl—that should've been her warning not to start shit."

"No wonder she styles her hair so damn high. Gotta hide them horns somehow," I grumble.

He bursts out laughing and holds out his arms. "Come here."

I can't get to him fast enough. The ugliness still lingers in my belly, mocking me for thinking this long-distance thing is possible.

I peer up at him. "Rooster, I'm not interested in anyone besides you." In a stronger voice, I add, "And so we're clear, I *don't* share. With anyone."

He cups my cheek, rubbing his thumb over my bottom lip. "I thought we talked about this last night?"

"We did. This is just for clarification purposes."

His lips twitch.

"Those stories about southern girls being crazy bitches are all true, Rooster. I got no problem taking a bat to your truck, bike, or shins if you ever cheat on me."

His cheeks puff out with the effort of holding back his laughter.

"Don't laugh at me."

"I'm not. I like this side of you."

A whole bunch of drunk butterflies flutter in my stomach. "Do you bring girls back here?"

Why do I keep insisting on ice-skating over such dangerous territory?

He groans. "Not since the re-model."

I glance around at the shiny laminate floors, crisp painted walls, and stiff curtains. "Was that recent?"

This wild, twitterpated feeling seems determined to make me stick my boots in my mouth this afternoon.

"Right before our run to Texas." He settles his hands on my hips. "What I said last night was the truth. I don't see the point in lying, Shelby." His eyes narrow and he shifts his jaw from side to side, like he's not sure if what he wants to say will land well.

Probably means it'll be bad.

"When I left Texas, we didn't make any promises to each other, right?"

"Yeah." Oh, how I'd wanted to, but I'd kept my dang mouth shut, convinced I'd never see or hear from him again. Color me shocked when he texted me hours later from the road. And the next day. And the next... No making me wait seventy-two hours or whatever stupid rules some guys have. Rooster doesn't play games.

"So, if I'd been fucking around all this time, I would've said so. Wouldn't be any reason to lie, would there?"

I blink, considering how much I'd hate hearing it. But there's comfort in knowing that Rooster's not the kind of man to lie or sugarcoat things to spare anyone's feelings. Not even mine.

Still feeling petulant for some reason, I stick out my bottom lip. "I guess."

"Pouty Shelby's even cuter than scary Shelby." He pulls me closer. "And now you've got me thinking, the lack of action this room has seen is pretty pathetic."

My heart kicks, but I arch a brow and keep my tone disinterested. "That right?"

His hands fist in the material at my hips, slowly dragging my skirt up. "You have no idea how many times I wanted to pull over on our trip down here, yank this little skirt over your sexy hips, and have you ride my dick."

I'm already fantasizing what that would've been like. "What'd I tell you about ruining my panties?"

He cocks his head, pretending to think on it. "Guess you'll have to remind me."

His hands grip my hips harder, and he walks us backwards until my butt meets the edge of his bed.

I'm trapped.

Nowhere to go.

A thrill of excitement zips down my legs.

With a wicked grin, Rooster turns me so I'm facing the bed. I brace myself on the thick, soft gray comforter with a black and blue scroll design.

"Nice bedding. Who picked it out?"

He laughs softly, his warm breath tickling my shoulder. "Murphy helped us with the remodel while Z was out of town. So, I'm pretty sure Heidi picked 'em out, I okayed them, and Hustler placed a bulk order of bedding for the whole clubhouse." He leans down, kissing my neck. "You really want to question my decorating choices right now?"

"No," I whisper, reaching back to run my fingers through his hair.

His fingers dig into my hips as he pulls me against him. "Feel what you do to me?" I bite my lip as his hardness presses against my butt. "Put your hands on the bed."

I hesitate, consider sassing back with a *"no"* or *"make me,"* but wanton, eager Shelby doesn't want any delays. Bending at the waist, I take my time laying my palms flat against the bed and arching my back.

He sucks in a deep breath. "Fuck." Rough fingers trace a line under

160

my tank top, all the way up my spine. He flicks the shirt over my head and unhooks my bra. I shimmy out of both and toss them by the pillows.

I move to unzip my skirt and Rooster closes one hand over mine. "No. Put your hands back where they were."

Moving in closer, he pushes my skirt all the way until it's bunched around my waist, and slowly drags my underwear down my legs. "Leave it," he orders when I try to kick them off.

Behind me, a drawer slides open, then shut. There's a familiar crinkling. The ticking of Rooster's zipper. He clutches my hips again and oh-so slowly drives into me.

"Every night I've slept in this room I've been imagining fucking you just like this."

Some sort of stuck-sheep bleat passes my lips.

He falls down over me, pinning my body to the mattress.

"Poor Shelby," he whispers in a sexy, rough mocking tone. His beard rasps over my shoulder. "Had no idea what a dirty bastard she was gettin' tangled up with."

"Uh." I twist my fingers in the comforter.

He covers my hands with one of his and slowly stretches my arms above my head, holding me down.

"Oh." I gasp. Each thrust creates a delicious friction. Under the weight of him, I struggle to spread my legs wider and arch my back.

"You like that?" he teases. He slows ever so slightly, snaking his arm under our bodies, and gently rubs my clit. His touch is like fire and I'm ready to explode.

He picks up the tempo, pounding into me with quick, precise strokes. My stomach tightens. The electric jolt spreads from my hips to my thighs. My toes curl, and my legs shake uncontrollably. "Roost— oh my God."

"That's it." He releases my hands and grabs my hip. "Oh fuck. You're shaking."

"Can't stop." My vision blurs. The angle or the way he's pressing me into the mattress—something triggers the non-stop shock of sensation. It's like he's flipped some sort of electrical current to my clit.

"Keep coming," he encourages. "Fuck, you're strangling my cock." Breathing hard, he stops moving, his fingers digging into my hips, pressing his pelvis into me like he's trying to permanently fuse our lower halves together. After a few seconds, he collapses on the bed next to me with a contented groan.

My poor legs are still nothing but jelly, so I can't do much more than roll onto my side next to him. He loosely drapes his arm over me and turns to kiss my temple. "You okay?"

"I think so," I whisper, staring up at the soft gray ceiling. "Are you?"

He lifts up, peering down his glistening body. "My dick's still attached. Afraid you snapped it off for a second."

"Oh my God." Laughter spills out of me, and I turn so I'm facing him.

He grins at me. "Come here." He slides his hand into my hair, cupping the back of my head to drag me closer for a soft kiss. "Thanks for making my dreams come true."

Still laughing, I snuggle even closer, running my fingers over his beard and down his chest.

He kisses my cheek and gently shifts me, so he can sit. "Let me clean up. I'll be right back."

While he's gone, I strip out of my wrinkled skirt and underwear, stretching out on top of the bed, facing the bathroom.

"Oh, fuck me." He stops in the doorway to stare.

"What?" I ask innocently, running my hand over my hip.

He waves his hand at me. "Careful, chickadee. I don't think you can handle another round."

Shirtless and jeans unbuttoned, he's one very sexy man. "You're the one who can't handle it."

ROOSTER

At some point we fell asleep. I wake and find Shelby's golden hair spilling all over my pillows. What I wouldn't give to wake up to this every damn day.

I glance at the clock. Probably time to get going if we want to make it upstate before dark. I pick up my phone and send Z a text asking if he needs anything from here.

Even though I set the phone back on the nightstand quietly, I sense Shelby's breathing change. She slowly stretches and opens her eyes. "Hey."

"Hey."

"Can't remember the last time I napped during the day."

"Needed the rest. Your man rode you pretty hard." I hold out my arm. "Come here."

She scoots closer and rests her head on my chest.

"I'm not one for naps either."

"Didn't think you were." She traces an aimless pattern over my chest. "So this is where you live?"

"Most of the time."

"Where are your parents?"

Ouch, that's a painful topic. I swallow hard. "Dead."

She shoots upright, distress creasing her forehead. "Oh my gosh. I'm sorry. Why didn't you say so?"

I shrug and pull her still-naked body next to me. "Hadn't really come up. Seems like an odd thing to blurt out."

"I'm sorry."

"Club's the only family I need."

She's quiet, as if she's waiting me for add some details. Fuck if I feel like ruining the moment with such an ugly story.

"You ever hear from your dad?" Damn, what a dick way to deflect the attention from myself.

She blinks and shakes her head. "Nope. I fully expect him to come crawlin' out of the woodwork with his hand out if I ever become real famous. After the way he left us broke and almost homeless, I look forward to telling him to go fuck himself and not giving him one red cent."

"That's my girl," I whisper.

Her fire and fighting spirit pull me right into the present. The only place I want to be.

Shelby's light and warmth is all I need to chase away the ghosts that still haunt me.

CHAPTER TWENTY-FOUR

Rooster

The sun's almost all the way down when we arrive upstate.
Everyone's either heading out of the clubhouse or in the garage,
pulling out chairs, blankets, and other stuff for the bonfire.

The scent of burning wood drifts through the trees, drawing my
attention toward the woods.

"How'd the truck run?" Murphy asks, coming out of the garage and
setting down two camp chairs.

"Perfect. Thanks a lot."

"No problem." He ambles over and gives me a fist bump, then nods
at Shelby. "Heard you met Tawny."

Shelby purses her lips and shrugs.

"Sounds about right." Murphy laughs. "Heidi and the girls are
already at the fire." He gestures behind him. "Trinity got out the tent
for the little guys."

Murphy hands each of us a chair and a blanket. We wait to follow Z
and Lilly to the clearing where the bonfire's set up.

Hope, Rock, Wrath, Trinity, Teller, and Charlotte are already
situated around the fire. Z sets up a spot next to Hope's chair, while
Murphy plants two chairs next to Teller.

"Blanket or chair?" I ask Shelby.

"Blanket." She wraps her arms around me. "So you can keep me warm."

"Are you cold?"

"Not yet."

"Hi, Hope." Jigsaw braces his hands on the back of her chair and leans over. "You're looking lovely this evening."

"Hello, Jigsaw." She smiles up sweetly at him. "You're looking suicidal tonight."

Like he has radar for anyone trying to cop a peek down his wife's shirt, Rock body checks Jiggy away from his wife. "Control your RC, Prez," he growls at Z.

Z snaps his fingers at me. "VP, come get your boy."

Jiggy swipes one of the chairs out of my hands and flips it open next to us.

Eventually we're all scattered around the fire. Dex and Z strike up a conversation about Crystal Ball.

"We can talk stripper business inside at the table." Ravage claps his hands together to get everyone's attention.

Once the conversation dies down, Ravage rubs his hands together like an evil party mastermind. "This is always a fun one. Who's got the best losing their virginity story?"

"Who, exactly, is that fun for?" Teller asks.

Jigsaw and Ravage both raise their hands.

"Fuck this shit," Murphy growls. He pulls Heidi out of her seat and the two of them move away from the ring of chairs, spreading out a blanket and dropping out of sight.

Jigsaw's devious gaze bounces around the fire, landing on Shelby. "As the newcomer to the group, the respectful thing is to allow you to go first."

"Fuck off," I growl.

"No, no. I'm game." Shelby leans forward and snags a can of soda from the cooler at Jiggy's feet. "Too bad for you, it's not that exciting a story."

"Hey." I nudge her shoulder. "You don't have to do this."

"They're tryin' to test me," she whispers. "It's fine." She kisses my cheek.

Ravage raises his hand. "Jigsaw and I will be the ones to decide the merits of each story."

"Well," Shelby drawls, "I hate to be a southern cliché, but back of a pickup truck after a football game. Lasted about the length of a Dawson Roads song."

"So *that's* why there are so many country songs about tailgates?" Jigsaw snaps his fingers.

"Yup." Shelby nods. "No doubt."

"After a *football* game?" Ravage asks. "Not even prom or homecoming, or whatever you guys do down there? That's just sad, Shelby."

"I know." She lets out a long, dramatic sigh. "In my defense, we won the state championship."

The guys and most of the girls crack up.

"You're so quiet over there, Rooster. No comment?" Jigsaw grins at me.

"Fuck off." I know exactly what story he's dying to share. Dickhead.

Sure enough, he sits forward, elbows resting on his knees, grinning like a serial killer. "I volunteer to go next. Lost it to Rooster's girlfriend at her parents' lake house."

I roll my eyes.

Rav and Stash fall over laughing.

"*Ex*-girlfriend, shithead." I throw my empty, crumpled can at him and it bounces off the side of his head, landing on the ground.

"She talked about Rooster the entire fucking time." Jiggy adopts a high-pitched whiny tone that's remarkably similar to the voice of the girl in question. "'Rooster tongues my clit this way. Rooster makes me come in five seconds. Rooster's dick is three-feet long.' You wanna talk about a boner-killer for a young, desperate lad?"

Shelby snorts, sitting forward and spitting soda everywhere. "Serves you right," she coughs out.

That pulls a chuckle from me. I pat her back and hand her a paper towel.

"I didn't do it on purpose," Jigsaw whines.

"Bullshit," I mutter.

"What happened?" Teller lobs a marshmallow at Jigsaw. "You tripped and your dick fell into her by accident?"

"Not quite."

A few of the ol' ladies squirm and shift their gazes away from the group. Don't blame 'em. I'm not exactly loving this 'game' myself. "Can we move on to another topic?"

"No, no, no." Stash wags his finger at me. "We're missing some vital pieces of information. This is a serious violation of bro code. How'd Jigsaw ever earn his patch? You voted him in to the club after that?"

Laughing, I reach over to smack the back of Stash's head. "What fucking bro code? This pre-dates the club. She and I had already broken up weeks before this went down." I glance over at Jigsaw, who's still grinning like an idiot. "I was thrilled he finally lost it so he'd shut the fuck up about it."

"See?" Jigsaw nods. "My bro always has my back."

Ravage turns his trouble-making face Hope and Rock's way. Can't wait to see how this ends. Maybe with a knife in his gut.

"Prez?" Ravage presses his fists together in a demented prayer pose and focuses on Rock. "We've never heard your story."

Rock's death glare should melt Rav into a puddle of goo any second now.

After a second or two, he answers, "Seduced my babysitter."

"*Daaamn*. Respect." Ravage holds out his fist, which Rock ignores. "How old were you?"

Rock's gaze settles across the fire on Teller. "Old enough, apparently." His stone-cold tone leaves no doubt he's done contributing to the game.

Ravage doesn't seem to be able to read his prez's mood too well. His gaze lands on Hope next. "First Lady, care to share?"

Rock throws him a threatening scowl, but his wife is also game tonight. She laughs and rests her arm on his chest, not that she could hold him back if he decides to permanently shut Ravage up. "Afraid I'm another teenage cliché. Prom night. High school boyfriend."

"How very all-American of you." Ravage nods his approval.

Hope lifts one shoulder in a careless shrug. "Nothing to write home about."

Lilly leans out of Z's lap and turns toward Hope. "Let me guess—fast, awkward, and orgasm-less?"

"Pretty much."

Jigsaw raises his hands toward the sky, sermon-style. "Except for Rooster's girlfriend—"

"Ex-girlfriend, jackass," I snarl.

"Yeah, yeah. His ex." Jigsaw jerks his thumb in my direction, "Except for her, I've *never* left a woman hanging."

"That you *know* of," Charlotte adds.

"Yeah, I highly doubt you could tell the difference, bro," Z says.

Ignoring the digs to his manhood, Jigsaw searches the group for his next victim. Ravage leans in and slaps his shoulder. "Skip Sparky. He's still a virgin."

"That's not what your mom said," Sparky retorts with a raised middle finger.

I choke on my own laughter.

Steer volunteers next. "Fifteen with the preacher's daughter."

"Nice." Ravage tips his beer in Steer's direction.

"Murphy, you're awfully quiet over there," Jigsaw sings out, ignoring the murder faces from half the group.

"Fuck off," Murphy growls without lifting his head.

"His math tutor," Teller answers in a bored tone.

"English!" Murphy corrects.

"Little Hammer?" Jigsaw calls out to Heidi. Brother just doesn't know when to quit. Asking Heidi a question like that's bound to get him knocked out by either Murphy or Teller.

Heidi doesn't bother to sit up either. "Prom night cliché."

Teller's eyes widen, and he slowly turns his head. "I fuckin' knew it, you little liar."

"Get over it, big brother." She flicks her wrist in his direction in a dismissive gesture.

When the rest of us stop laughing, Charlotte waves her hand in the air, catching Jigsaw's eye. "Not to rain on your pervert parade, but you realize not everyone's first time might have been as pleasant and humorous as yours, right?"

That wipes the smile off Jiggy's face. Yeah, he's an asshole but he's not completely insensitive.

Trinity raises her hand. "Mom's bed with her thirty-five-year-old boyfriend when I was thirteen."

Wrath squeezes her to his side and whispers something in her ear.

"Fuck," Jigsaw mutters. "Where's that dirtbag now?"

Rock's the one who answers. "In the ground where he belongs."

And that closes the coffin lid on *that* conversation.

"Football's big in Texas, right, Shelby?" Sparky asks, smoothing over the awkward moment.

"Practically a religion."

"Do you even know which one football is, Sparky?" Ravage asks.

"Yeah. There's a ball." Sparky's indignant tone cracks us all up.

"Were you a cheerleader?" Jigsaw asks Shelby. "I bet you were. You have that cheerleader look."

"Nope." She shakes her head, blond curls flying around. "Couldn't afford to buy a hummingbird on a string for a nickel, let alone those cute little cheerleader outfits. Besides, I was too busy workin' and singin' where I could." She points her soda can at Jiggy. "I *did* sing the national anthem at several games, though."

"How long are you on this current tour, Shelby?" Z asks.

She hesitates and darts a nervous look my way before answering. "Couple more months. Then I'm supposed to go into the studio. After that, my manager's trying to get me on another tour."

All those plans are news to me.

Doesn't really matter, though. Shelby's given me the green light to visit her while she's on tour and I plan to take advantage of it as often as possible.

"With the same old dude?" Jigsaw asks.

"Dawson's only thirty-eight," Shelby says. "That's not old."

"Thank you, Shelby," Z says.

Rock and Wrath both chuckle. Steer lobs a pine cone at Jigsaw's head. I'm not even sure if Jigsaw realizes he just insulted half the club's officers. On the other hand, I don't care for Shelby sticking up for Dawson in any capacity.

"Anyway, no. Greg's lookin' into other options." She shrugs. "I've got my bucket list of artists I'd like to tour with. Hoping he starts there."

As much as I want her to achieve all her goals, I can't deny how much I love having her right here with me.

I glance over at Shelby wishing like hell I had more to offer her.

While tonight's been fun, even I have to admit, bonfires in the boonies with my club pales in comparison to touring the country and being on stage every night.

Shelby's on her way to becoming a star. But the best nights I have to offer her are around a campfire *under* the stars.

CHAPTER TWENTY-FIVE

Rooster

The next morning, much sooner than I'd like, I'm watching Shelby pack up her stuff and helping her carry it all downstairs.

"I feel bad you can't ride," she says, staring at the truck.

"I'll live." I glance down at her bare legs and tiny denim shorts. "Looking over at your sexy legs for the next couple hours helps a lot."

She wiggles her eyebrows and prances over to the truck, putting on a good show of climbing on the running board and bending over to "fix" stuff in the backseat.

I walk up behind her and run my hands from her thighs to her hips. "Why you trying to tease me? Hmm?"

"You two planning to go at it right here in the parking lot?" Jigsaw calls out.

I squeeze my eyes shut and count to ten before flipping him off.

"Those are some mighty fine shorts, Shelby," Jigsaw says, "Always had a thing for daisy dukes."

I stare him down. "Do you want to die? Painfully?"

"Thank you, Jigsaw." Shelby turns and jumps off the truck, her boots crunching against the gravel.

My best friend will be begging for death if he keeps staring at her tits like he's some damn homeless street dog.

"The fuck's wrong with you?" I reach out and smack him upside the head.

"Paying the lady a compliment. Is that so wrong?"

"The compliment was lovely. I think it's you droolin' over my tits that's gettin' Rooster all peeved," Shelby drawls. She cups her chest and stares down. "I know they're fabulous, but have a little respect."

Jigsaw's mouth twists with amusement. "I like her."

"Get out of here." I shove him toward his bike and he laughs the whole way.

"You two really are like brothers," Shelby says.

"He certainly works my last nerve like a little brother."

Dex pops out of the garage for a last-minute review of the directions. At least he's nothing but respectful to Shelby.

Once we're on the Thruway headed west, Jigsaw and Dex pull in front of me.

Shelby's been quiet for a few miles.

"You all right?" I ask her.

"Just thinking about tonight. Will it be weird for you if I warm up my voice a little?"

"Not at all."

I wasn't expecting a free concert but I also wasn't expecting her to launch into humming. She works her way up to singing vowels from a low to high range. Every few minutes, she stops and sips her water.

"You all right?"

"The AC and the smoke from the weekend has me a little raspy."

"Why didn't you say something?"

"What was I gonna say? Put out the bonfire? Tell your brothers they can't smoke in their own clubhouse?"

Well, now I feel like shit. "Is there anything I can stop and get for you?"

"Heidi packed some grapes and watermelon for me. I need the hydration." She taps the side of her thermos. "Trinity sent me with some tea. We got lots of water back there. I'll be okay." She glances over at me. "Well, I might ask you to stop so I can pee a few dozen times."

"Whatever you need. You should've told me, though. I don't want you to be uncomfortable or do anything to risk your voice."

"And yet you're always trying to make me scream your name."

My mouth twitches. "That's different."

"Psh." She waves her hand in front of her face and throws me one of her teasing smiles that does weird shit to my insides. After a few more sips of water, she goes back to humming and vocalizing.

"I never knew singers had a process like this," I say when she finishes.

"Some probably don't. I didn't until I worked with a vocal coach on the show. I used to open my mouth and let whatever noises wanted to come out, out. Which is fine, if you're singing for fun or tips. But if I want to be able to do this night after night, I need to take care of my voice."

"And I want to help you do that. So next time, tell me."

She glances over and rests her hand on my thigh. "Thank you."

After a few miles, she fiddles with her phone. "We're gettin' close."

Tonight, we're all going in blind. None of us have ever been to this place.

"Hope the directions are good."

I signal to the guys a couple miles before our exit. At least it's not a state park.

"It says we should be able to drive right up to Gate 9A and let them know we're on the list."

These fairgrounds have much clearer signs letting us know where to go than the last one. Unfortunately, that also means the security will probably be on the ball.

Shelby and I are able to get past the gate because we're on the list. Jigsaw and Dex have to wait outside.

"This is so ridiculous. Greg has to be able to get more passes for me," Shelby fumes.

Especially if he can't even provide decent security for her.

After a flurry of texts, Jigsaw and Dex are added to the list and allowed to roll past the security gate.

Greg meets us at the entrance to the theater.

"More bikers?" He rakes his gaze over the four of us, finally landing on Shelby. "Are you kidding me?" Greg's face is so red, I'm waiting for steam to shoot out of his ears.

"Easy, Greg." I step up, placing myself between Greg and Shelby. "I asked some of my brothers to join us so we don't have a repeat of the other night."

"Well, I..." He backs off, blows out a breath, and drops the disrespectful attitude.

"And watch how you talk to Shelby," I add, giving Greg a dose of lethal biker stare.

"There's no money in the budget to pay for security."

What a load of shit. Dawson's got money coming out his ass, and he can't afford to protect his opening act? What-the-fuck-ever.

"I don't need her money." I sneer at him.

"I'll get you some extra passes so you can move through the venue without being hassled." He turns and jogs down the hallway.

Good choice. Although I think it has more to do with not wanting to draw attention to Shelby's biker entourage than our comfort.

Jigsaw's shaking with laughter when I turn around. "You sure scared the piss outta him." He lifts his chin at Shelby. "He get surly with you like that all the time?"

She glances at me before shrugging. "I pick my battles."

Considering the unwanted attention and gossip article from the other night, I'm not expecting her to reach up and loop her arms around my neck. "Thank you," she whispers, kissing my jaw. "I'm real happy you're here tonight."

Jigsaw clears his throat in a particularly loud, obnoxious way.

Shelby releases me. "I'm happy you and Dex are here too, Jiggy."

"Thank you, darlin'."

She giggles at his attempted southern accent, then turns serious. "I mean it. I'm sure you have better things to do. And I know you hate the music. I don't want to take advantage of—"

"Don't sweat it, Shelby." Jigsaw grips my shoulder and gives me a shake. "I always got his back." He shrugs. "Besides, *hate's* a strong word. I never *appreciated* country music before."

"Don't let him fool you, Shelby," Dex says. "He's here to lure desperate girls into the shadows."

"That's hella creepy," Shelby says.

"For a mutually pleasurable good time." Jigsaw glares at Dex. "Stop making me sound like a serial killer."

"Eh." Dex wobbles his hand in the air and Jiggy smacks it away.

Greg returns in a calmer mood. He hands passes out to the four of us, then hands me two extras without comment.

"You guys can go check out the fair," Shelby says.

I'm shaking my head before she even finishes the offer.

She curls her finger, inviting me to dip down closer. "I need to change and get my hair and makeup done. I assume your brothers won't find that as entertaining as you do."

She has a point.

"Seriously, go ahead," she encourages. "I'd say bring me back some cotton candy but I can't have the sugar before I go onstage."

"Is there anything you *do* want?"

She casts a longing gaze toward the fairgrounds. "Nothing that's good for me."

I confirm the time of the meet and greet with Greg, then lean down and press a kiss to Shelby's forehead. "Text me if you need anything."

"Thank you."

"What are we supposed to do?" Jigsaw asks as we're leaving the music center. "Take a few spins on the merry-go-round?"

"I'm gonna spin you around with my fist if you keep running your mouth," I threaten.

"So testy." He shoves me to the side.

"Feel free to be the creepy adult on the rides by himself, Jiggy." Dex points toward a row of brown shacks straight ahead. "I'm going to grab some Dinosaur Bar-B-Que."

Jigsaw searches the line of food trucks. "Sparky said there should be a chicken and waffle pizza at one of these places."

"Sounds like Sparky," Dex says.

I clutch my stomach. "That's disgusting."

"Don't go yucking someone's yum." Dex smacks me on the back.

"Whatever."

As we shoulder our way through the crowd of fairgoers, one small white tent catches my attention. "Give me a minute. I'll catch up." I slap Dex's shoulder to get his attention.

Unfortunately, they both follow me into the tent.

"Since when are you into all this hippie shit?" Jigsaw casts a look at the incense, candles, bells, soaps, scarves, tapestries, and embroidered wall-hangings. "This place looks like the inside of Sparky's head."

"Shut up." My gaze lands on the jewelry case and I step up, not quite sure what I'm searching for.

"Can I help you?" a soft voice asks from behind a wall of scarves. A few seconds later, an older woman pushes her way through. She doesn't even blink at the three giant bikers taking up all the available space in her little tent shop.

Shit, I don't know what Shelby likes. She doesn't even wear a lot of jewelry. "Do you have tarot cards?" No, that's stupid. Shelby already has a deck of them. Does she need another one? I'd probably get the wrong kind.

"Not here," she says. "Are you looking for your girlfriend?"

It doesn't exactly take a clairvoyant to tell I don't belong here, so her question doesn't shock me. "Yes."

"She reads tarot?"

"I think so," I answer, painfully aware my brothers are so damn close to this conversation.

"What about crystals?" she asks.

"Uh, I think she has a purple one."

"What does she do?"

"She's a singer."

Her lips curve into a smile. "A free, creative spirit?"

"Sort of. She works hard though. Dedicated."

She runs her hand over the glass counter slowly. Back and forth. "Much judgment and stress in her world."

I think about the article Shelby showed me. "Yeah."

She reaches into the case and pulls out a long, clear stone suspended from a purple silk cord. It's simple but pretty. "Clear quartz.

To absorb negativity and bring harmony. It also has many healing properties."

"That's one hell of a multi-tasking rock." Jigsaw scoffs.

I glare at him and he grins.

"Bro, come on. It's probably a hunk of melted glass," Jigsaw says.

"Would you shut up?" Dex slaps Jiggy's shoulder and pushes him toward the front of the tent.

The owner casts a look that drills home the meaning of *evil eye* Jigsaw's way, wiping the goofy look off his face.

Ignoring him, she returns her attention to me. "Hold it."

"What?" I scoop it off the counter. The stone's cool and smooth in my hand.

"Real quartz is still cool to the touch, even if it's a hot day. See the markings and imperfections?"

I study the small swirls and patterns of the stone and nod.

"Fake ones would be symmetrical and perfect."

Since I honestly don't believe in any of this shit, it doesn't matter if it is a hunk of glass. I just want to give Shelby something pretty.

The woman quotes what seems like a reasonable price—not that I'd know the difference. I hand her some cash. She wraps it up in a box and tucks it into a bag.

"Thank you." I stuff the little bag into my inner jacket pocket and meet my brothers outside.

"If you open your mouth, you'll be eatin' your chicken and waffles with a straw tonight," I warn Jigsaw.

He fights to wipe the grin off his face. "I didn't say a word."

"You didn't have to be a dick to the woman."

"I was just messing around. She could tell that I'm a jovial spirit."

"She probably put a hex on you." Dex says. "I'd be careful for the next twenty-four to forty-eight hours. Your dick might turn green and fall off."

"What? That's not true. Why would she do that? My dick didn't do anything."

"I don't know." Dex shrugs. "You were pretty rude. Maybe your tongue will fall out instead."

The panicked expression on Jigsaw's face is too irresistible. I *must* fuck with him. "Yeah, I heard about this guy down in Virginia once who gave some fortune-teller lip and his dick rotted clean off a few weeks later. No one could explain why it happened."

"Now I know you're lying. You wouldn't go to a fortune-teller."

"Never said it was me, jackass. Met the guy after it happened and he told me the whole story. Why do you think I won't go to one?"

His expression falters and I barely keep a straight face. God, I love when he falls for shit I make up on the spot.

"Fuckers," Jigsaw grumbles before stomping ahead of us.

Dex elbows me and the two of us bust up laughing.

"That was almost too easy." Dex wipes a few tears from his eyes when we're done laughing.

While all this fucking around has been fun, it's time for me to get back to Shelby. I can screw off with my brothers whenever I want, but who knows how long it'll be until I see my girl again?

CHAPTER TWENTY-SIX

Rooster

Not wanting to leave Shelby alone for too long, I part ways with the guys after the food court and head back to the theater. Ahead of me, a biker in a black cut catches my attention. I stop, recognizing the three-piece patch on the back.

He turns and I wave, pushing my way past people.

"Rooster." Chaser holds out his hand as he approaches me. "Good to see you."

We shake hands and he pulls me in, slapping my back a few times. "Good to see you too."

Out of the corner of my eye, I catch movement. Security guards pile up next to each other, talking while keeping an eye on us. I'm sure they see two different MC cuts and assume we're rivals about to kick off a turf war. At the fair. Fuckin' idiots.

Chaser follows my line of sight and huffs out a laugh. "Rent-a-bouncers don't look like they have more than three brain cells between them to rub together." He returns his attention to me. "How you been? Who else is with you?"

"Dex and Jigsaw. I was hoping I'd run into you while I was out this way, but never thought it'd be *here*."

He smirks and gestures toward the stage. "My daughter likes the opening act a lot."

"You don't say." I run my hand over my chin. Looks like tonight's going to work out well for me in several ways. Z wanted me to make sure relations between our clubs are one hundred percent solid, and here I am with two backstage passes burning a hole in my pocket.

"Think she'd want to meet her?"

He cocks his head, as if he's assessing me before answering. I don't have a reputation as a joker, so he must realize I'm not fucking around. "You have a connection?"

"Kinda." I grin and pull out the passes. "Shelby's my girlfriend."

His eyes widen and his expression slides into a slow, knowing grin. "No shit. Let me text her."

While he slips out his phone and sends his daughter a text, I pull out mine and text Shelby.

You mind if I bring a friend backstage? His daughter is a big fan of yours. She answers right away: *Sure!*

Chaser's daughter joins us a few minutes later. It's hard to say if she favors her mom or dad more, but she's a pretty woman maybe a few years older than Shelby if I remember right.

"What's up, Dad?"

He lifts his chin. "You remember Rooster?" He smirks at me. "It's been a while since he paid the clubhouse a visit."

"Uh..." She gives me a blank expression. "I'm sorry, I don't. Hi, Rooster."

"That's all right. Good to see you, Angelina. Shelby's right backstage if you want to meet her?"

"Sure!" She bounces up on her toes, her excited gaze dancing between her father and me. "Thank you so much." In an instant, she went from a woman being polite to her dad's friend to an over-excited fan.

As we walk backstage, I nudge Chaser's arm. "You were all heavy metal back in the day, weren't you? How'd your daughter rope you into this show?"

"No matter how old your kids get, they always have you wrapped around their finger. Remember that." He laughs. "No, seriously, her friend flaked out, and I didn't want her coming to a show this big by herself. And I listen to a little bit of everything."

Angelina's an adult, but the overprotective dad thing from Chaser doesn't shock me one bit. "Good call. Lot more assholes than I expected."

"No kidding. I honestly think it's worse now than when I used to play."

We reach Shelby's door, and I knock before pushing it open. Shelby sets her guitar down and shines one of her smiles our way.

"Hi!" She blinks and stares at Chaser, then me.

"Shelby this is a friend of mine, Chaser A—"

"Chaser Adams! Oh my gosh." She hurries over and holds out her hand. "*In Your Hands* was one of my daddy's favorite albums. I listened to it over and over growing up. Gosh, you were a phenomenal guitar player. I mean you are a...shoot. Sorry. So nice to meet you."

Jesus. When Shelby said she knew all years and genres of music, she wasn't kidding.

Chaser takes her gushing in stride. "Thank you. Must be mutual appreciation night. You're very talented. And my daughter's a huge fan of yours as well."

Poor Angelina's cheeks turn red and her eyes bug out. She seems... shocked...or maybe embarrassed. After a second or two, she raises her hand and wiggles her fingers at Shelby.

Shelby pulls her in for a hug. "Thank you so much for coming tonight."

Angelina blinks and finally smiles. "The day those tickets went on sale—"

"She begged me to get them for her," Chaser finishes.

Angelina rolls her eyes. "I'd defend myself but Dad's absolutely right."

The girls move over to the couch to talk and I lean against the wall. "You still get recognized a lot?" Damn, that must be awkward as fuck when he's on club business.

"Fuck no." He glances over at Shelby. "Shit, she couldn't even have been born yet, the last time I put an album out. I'm just as shocked as you."

I chuckle and slap his shoulder. "She surprises me every day."

"How long you known each other?"

"Not long. We met down in Texas." I shrug. "Visiting with her while she's in town." The smile slides off my face as that last part comes out of my mouth. After tomorrow, who the fuck knows when I'll see Shelby again?

"They rolling out tonight right after the show?"

"I'm not sure yet."

"Well if you're gonna be in the area, you're more than welcome to stop by the clubhouse. Welcome to stay if you need a place to crash too."

"Appreciate that." If Shelby was sticking around, I planned to get a hotel room. If they left tonight, I planned to unroll a sleeping bag and spend the night in the back of the truck. A room at the Devil Demon MC's clubhouse might be slightly more comfortable.

Someone knocks, prompting Chaser and me to move away from the door. I open it to find Greg. Poor bastard's really gonna flip his shit when he finds yet another biker in Shelby's circle.

"Hey, they'll be ready for her in fifteen minutes or so," he informs me before ducking out again.

"Okay." I pull out my phone and send Jigsaw a text.

Chaser raises an eyebrow but he's too respectful to ask any questions.

"Meet-and-greet thing. Fucking security is a joke," I mumble, waiting for a response.

He glances over at Shelby. "Entire industry is different now. I don't envy her at all."

"How so?"

"First, she's probably getting paid peanuts. Don't get me wrong—suits took advantage of musicians back in my day too, but it's even worse now. Doubt they'll cough up much money for shit like security. Or if they do, they'll take it out of her royalties. She'll still be paying off her first album when she's recording her third."

"Fuck." My gaze lands on Shelby. I've never asked or stuck my nose in the business end of her career...because it's really not my business. But I fuckin' hate the idea of anyone taking advantage of her.

"I kept my fingers in the publishing end for a long time. Writing for other artists. Suited *me* much better. I don't know what her deal is." Chaser shrugs. "Some go hybrid and keep more control of their catalog. A tour for a big name like Dawson Roads, she probably has label support of some kind. The exposure they can get her is a blessing but the rest can be a curse."

"She came off one of those music reality shows."

He nods. "Yeah, that definitely wasn't a thing back then. Mallory and I got approached by a bunch of those lowlife reality shows maybe ten, fifteen years ago. Thank fuck we always turned 'em down."

"Shit." I shake with laughter. "I could see your dad blowing a gasket, bringing exposure like that to the MC."

"Right?" He laughs with me. In the biker world, Stump's not exactly known for his easygoing personality. "The club's not the only reason we turned 'em down, though." He tips his head toward Shelby. "If she got her deal that way, I'm sure it's exploitative as hell. Hope her manager's got her looking into other streams of income."

"I'm not sure *what* he does to earn his keep."

"Well, you're not exactly objective either."

"True."

Shelby approaches both of us, with Angelina trailing behind her. "I'm sorry, I have to—"

"No problem, sweetheart." Chaser holds out his hand. "Appreciate you taking the time."

"You're more than welcome to hang out here if you want." She glances around the dressing room. "It's nothing fancy."

"We're fine." He lifts his chin. "Told Rooster you two have an open invite to stop by the clubhouse while you're in the area. If you need a place to crash or just want to visit."

"Thank you."

He shakes my hand. "Offer extends to Dex and Jigsaw too, obviously. Mallory would love to say hi."

"Careful. Jiggy will take you up on it for sure."

Chaser's jaw twitches. Yeah, maybe that wasn't the smartest comment. It's no secret Chaser's one hell of a vigilant caveman when it comes to his wife.

There's another knock at the door. "Bet that's them now," I say as I twist the knob.

But it's Dawson.

This dude. *Again.*

"Hey, Shelby." He glances at me. "Logan, good to see ya tonight." His gaze shifts to Chaser and Angelina, lingering on Angelina too long for Chaser's taste if his narrow-eyed expression is any indication.

Fuck, this could get awkward.

"Hey, Dawson." Shelby threads her arm through Angelina's. "These are our friends, Angelina and Chaser—"

Dawson shakes himself out of his Angelina-induced trance. "Chaser? Chaser Adams." He squints at Chaser. "I bought a few songs from you in my early days." He grins wide and sticks out his hand.

"Sure did." Chaser quickly shakes his hand and motions to Angelina. "My daughter and I were just heading out. Thank you, Shelby."

Dawson actually tips his baseball cap to Angelina as she brushes past him. Thank fuck Chaser's already out of the room.

Shelby tosses me a wide-eyed what-just-happened expression, and I shrug.

"Did you need something, Dawson?" I ask to get his attention off Angelina's ass.

"Huh. Oh, yeah." He throws a quick scowl my way. "Shelby, you up for another song with me tonight?"

"Oh my gosh. Yes! Yes, of course. Thank you."

"Apparently, it got some good play in the press, and, well, you know." He shrugs. Big name or not, sounds like Dawson has to answer to higher-ups too.

Honestly, it eases my annoyance with the guy. Seems like he's giving her the opportunity to appease his record label, not to get in her pants. It'd be nice if he was doing it purely to help out a fellow artist but I'm not dumb enough to think that's the way this business works. Plus, I'm impressed he came to ask her himself instead of sending one of his minions.

"All right. I'll see you later." He ducks out, closing the door behind him.

"Sorry," Shelby says. "I thought we'd get to spend more time after my set—"

"Don't apologize. I'm thrilled for you." Yeah, I wanted to soak up every last second with her too but this is a great opportunity and I'm not going to ruin it by being a sulky dick.

I hold out my hand. "Ready?"

She peers into the mirror and fluffs her hair. "I think so. Does this dress look okay? It's vintage." She reaches down to swish the skirt around. "My mom wore it in high school. Everything old is new again, right?"

"Sure, I guess." I glance down at my plain T, leather cut, jeans, and boots. "Not sure you want to take fashion advice from me, though."

She tips her head back and pats my chest. "I like your look. Casual and sexy."

"Glad you think so."

"If I ever get nominated for a CMA or an ACM, or something, I promise I won't ask you to wear a tuxedo."

Well, shit. Escorting Shelby to some high-profile event never occurred to me. The idea of mixing with that sort of crowd turns my stomach. My disgust must be written on my face, considering the way Shelby recoils.

"Never mind, that's silly. I'm sure it'll never happen anyway." She scoffs. "No one's nominating the bimbo from the reality show for any awards."

"Hey, don't talk about yourself like that."

"Rooster, seriously, that's how everyone sees me." She balls her hands into fists. "A joke."

"Shelby, I don't think Dawson would be asking you to perform with him if he thought you were a joke."

She snorts. "It's probably to fuel rumors that we're a couple or something stupid like that. He just broke up with another country artist so the gossips are all fanning the flames over who'll be warming his bed next. I'll send you the link for *that* blog post. You'll see."

I couldn't give a fuck about Dawson's love life. "I'm serious." I grab her hand and force her to look at me. "Don't let a stupid post written by some slob living in his mom's basement do this to you.

You're damn talented. Even I can see it, and I know dick about any of this."

"You're biased."

"I know what I see when I look out in your audience." I press my hand to my chest. "I know what I feel in here when you get onstage and open your mouth."

"Thank you."

"Now, knock this shit off and let's get you ready for your show."

Her lips twitch. "So bossy."

"I'm told it's one of my more desirable qualities."

She chuckles as I open the door. Normally, I'd have her go ahead of me, but I'm not sure what she'll step into, so I block her with my arm while I check out the hallway. Crew members move around equipment. Most I recognize from the other night. Others have shirts indicating they work for the fairgrounds. To my right, Jigsaw and Dex are muscling their way through the crowd.

"Took you long enough," I say when they reach us.

Shelby pokes my side. "Rude."

I grin down at her. "That's me being polite."

Jigsaw slaps my arm. "Yo, Chaser's daughter—"

"Don't go there. For the love of fuck. Don't."

"What? She's really nice."

"Yeah, I'm sure that's what was on the tip of your tongue."

Dex elbows Jigsaw in the ribs. "He behaved. Thought he was going to explode with the effort of keeping his mouth shut."

Jiggy rubs the side of his head. "I think I blew a fuse or something."

"Jesus." I jerk my head to the side and step into the hallway, motioning for Shelby to get in the middle between us. "She's going to be late."

The three of us form a semi-circle around Shelby—a good thing since the line to get into the meet-and-greet room is long. No one really notices her until we're already past them.

Once we're in the room, Greg rushes over to us. "You're all set up in here. No photos with guests tonight." He gestures toward the table. "Just stay behind the table. Answer questions, smile, sign stuff."

"You know I can't say no to pictures," Shelby protests. "That'll break the kids' hearts. They want to post that stuff online. Half the reason they come to these things is to take a picture with me."

He turns and searches the area. "There's no setup for it."

I gesture to Jigsaw. "We'll move the tables. She can come around to the side if someone wants a picture. Three of us will make sure no one gets out of line."

Greg takes a long, deep breath, clearly not in favor of my plan. Not that I really give a fuck. "Please keep to the background."

"Last thing I want is to make a scene, Greg. Trust me." Z will kick my ass up and down the Thruway if I bring unwanted attention to the club. Especially with Priest breathing down his neck.

I'm still not letting anyone mess with Shelby, though.

CHAPTER TWENTY-SEVEN

Shelby

Tonight, there were no incidents while meeting the fans, and my set went off without a hitch. I'm almost starting to believe I'm an actual professional.

I rest my hand over my stomach, willing the butterflies to settle. Waiting through Thundersmoke's set and most of Dawson's is torture. Usually by now, I'm in my jammy pants, winding down in my hotel room or on the road to the next destination.

And tonight I've got one hot hunk of man I desperately need some alone time with before we have to say goodbye.

"Shit, I forgot to give you this earlier," Rooster says.

"Give me what?" I turn and he's pulling a small white paper bag from the inner pocket of his cut.

He shrugs. "I hope she didn't feed me a line of bullshit," he mutters, shaking a small white box into his palm.

"What is it?"

"Open it."

I slip the top of the box off and stare at the clear quartz stone suspended on a fine purple silk cord. "Logan," I breathe out, "It's so pretty."

"The woman told me it was supposed to absorb negativity and bring peace of mind." His brows draw down, suggesting he thinks it's all hogwash. "Thought it would help you tonight and then I forgot to give it to you before your show."

Aware that he thinks esoteric, spiritual stuff is silly, I'm touched he even considered buying a crystal, let alone talked to anyone about its healing properties. When did he even have the time? I thought he went off with his brothers for dinner but he found me a present instead?

"Thank you," I whisper. I hold the box up. "Will you put it on for me?"

"Sure." He carefully lifts the necklace out, works the small clasp loose and drapes it over my head.

The cool weight of the crystal settles against my skin and I glance down. "Thank you," I whisper. Why am I getting so choked up over a gift?

I turn to show him.

"You like it?" he asks. "Is that what it's supposed to do, or did I get taken?"

I chuckle at the note of uncertainty coloring his question. "Yes, clear quartz is supposed to remove negativity and promote harmony. Thank you."

We don't have much longer. One of Dawson's roadies grabs my attention. I steal a last kiss from Rooster.

Clutching my microphone, I follow the roadie down the long metal walkway leading to the platform under the stage. I slip in my earpiece and wiggle my jaw, humming a few notes to calm my nerves.

"Ready?" one of the techs shouts.

I flash a thumbs-up.

Dawson's booming voice is slightly muffled, but it sounds like he's announcing my appearance.

The platform shakes before rising into the air. Mist dances around my feet as the contraption lurches to a stop. Stage lights blind me, then disappear. Fake-smoke smell tickles my nose. *Please don't let me sneeze.*

"Miss Shelby Morgan!"

Blinking, I raise my hands over my head and smile wide.

Nerves have no place here. I'm Shelby fucking Morgan, and I've got this.

Slowly, so I don't bust my ass, I sway down the metal staircase.

"Ain't she pretty?" Dawson piles on the good ol' southern charm. "Y'all enjoy her show earlier?"

The crowd responds with a thunderous 'yes.' I'm sure it has more to do with pleasing their country music idol than admiring my talent, but I smile and gush an extra twangy, "Thank y'all *so* much!"

Dawson leaps up the last few steps and offers me his hand.

"Such a gentleman," I coo into the microphone, batting my fake lashes.

"Anything for a pretty lady, darlin'."

Oh, he's really ramping up the cheese factor tonight.

He stares at a spot above my head, but I'm sure that to the audience it looks like he's staring deep into my eyes. Slowly, he croons the first line of the song into his microphone.

My heart thumps with nerves, listening carefully for my cue. I'm determined to nail every word this time.

Tonight, Dawson wants to play it up for the crowd more. He holds onto my hand longer than seems necessary while singing all the sweet words to convince me to stay wrapped up in his arms all night long. I get into the role, making cow eyes at him and belting out every note of the excuses for I have to leave perfectly. Every time Dawson swaggers closer, I sashay away—a perfectly choreographed game of cat and mouse.

Before I know it, the song's over. The stage goes dark, then the lights blink on. "Shelby Morgan, everyone!"

Sweat rolls down my forehead and into my hair and I'm still panting from bopping around the stage but I smile bright and wave big to the crowd.

Dawson kisses my cheek. "Thanks, darlin'. You were fantastic," he whispers in my ear before sending me on my way.

"All right, Shelby!" Rooster picks me up as soon as I clear the stage. "You nailed it."

"Yeah?" My laughter rings out as he gives me a quick spin.

"Yeah. You were incredible."

I glance down, and there's nothing but pride shining in his eyes. No jealousy. He understands that was all for show.

I wrap my arms around his neck and fuse my mouth to his. He lets out a surprised rumble and my back hits something hard and cool. The wall.

Rooster draws back. "Careful." He sets me down. "You don't need more pictures leaking on the Internet." He takes a quick glance around the corridor. While it's busy, full of workers, roadies, and other people lingering, no one seems to be paying attention to us.

"Good job, Shelby!" Greg shouts.

"Were you watching?" I ask when he gets closer.

He jerks his head toward the stage. "Out front. I set up an interview for you after the Columbus show. Wanted to send them a video clip."

"Oh, sweet. Thank you."

Greg glances at Rooster. "Thank you for your help tonight."

"No problem." He squeezes my hand.

"We're not rolling out until tomorrow morning, Shelby," Greg says. "We're all staying down at the Hilton." He glances at Rooster. "I didn't know if—"

"I got her." Rooster doesn't bother to hide his eagerness. "What time does she need to meet you?"

Greg's either tired or given up trying to corral me. He texts the information to Rooster, including the hotel's address.

"Thanks, man." Rooster shakes Greg's hand.

I'm wired and buzzy while we walk down to the dressing room to grab my stuff, excited I have more time with Rooster.

Except I'm afraid it will make it all that much harder to say goodbye tomorrow morning.

CHAPTER TWENTY-EIGHT

Rooster

I'm here for Shelby, but I can't forget that my president also asked me to handle business while I was in Chaser's territory. Since Shelby's dressing room wasn't the appropriate place for that conversation earlier, it'll have to be now.

"Hey, you heard Chaser invite us to their clubhouse before. You mind if we stop by?" Shit, I hate asking, since all I want to do is be alone with her.

"Really?" Her eyes go big and her lips curl up. "Sure. Maybe I can pick his brain." She wiggles her fingers. "About technique."

I huff out a laugh. "Maybe."

"Shoot." She slaps her hand over her mouth. "He's president of his club? So...would that be rude, if I ask him about...music stuff?"

I love that she seems to understand how important respect is in my world, but also hate her being so nervous. "We'll see how busy it is, but I don't think he'll mind." I hesitate for a second. "I do have a few things I need to discuss with him, though."

Her lips curl into a teasing smile. "Biker business?"

"More or less."

"That's okay. I know how to entertain myself."

"I need you to stick with Dex or Jigsaw. Or Chaser's wife if she's around. It's not the kind of place I want—"

"Me roaming around by myself." She leans in and nudges me with her shoulder. "I understand."

"Thanks." I press a quick kiss to her forehead.

SHELBY

When Rooster said the clubhouse wasn't far, that wasn't quite accurate. After leaving the bustling area around the fairgrounds, we drive through a lot of dark, twisty back roads with Dex and Jigsaw ahead of us.

Finally, light spills through the trees. The guys slow.

A large metal gate stands wide open. Two men in black leather cuts step out of the shadows with flashlights and approach Jigsaw and Dex's bikes.

Rooster tenses, his hand straying toward the middle console.

"Everything all right?" I ask.

He doesn't take his eyes off his brothers. "Yeah, they'll know who we are." His flat tone doesn't exactly comfort me.

Rooster's a dangerous man. Why is that shocking? I never gave the risk of dating a biker a lot of thought before.

Yes, he's big, heavy, muscled, thick, and hard. But he's always been sweet and gentle—almost reverent—in the way he treats me. Yes, I've seen him take action to protect me from men when they've been inappropriate. But that didn't strike me as odd or dangerous—more like the gentlemanly thing to do.

Tonight, the danger seems to be all around us. And dangerous men tend to hang out with other dangerous men.

Jigsaw and Dex are allowed to pass the two guards and continue into the compound.

Rooster eases the truck up a few inches.

"Name?" one of guards barks. He casts a dismissive look at the truck.

"It's Rooster." His deep, rumbly voice forces the guard's head to snap up, eyes narrowing while he studies Rooster for a quick second.

"Fuck, man. Sorry." He ducks his head and waves us forward. "Go on. Chaser said to look out for you."

Rooster dips his chin. "Thanks."

The truck bumps over the uneven ground, the headlights bouncing up and down and illuminating the area in bits and pieces.

A glimpse of the sign on the front of the building announces the clubhouse belongs to the Devil Demons MC.

I sure am getting an education on the outlaw clubs of New York tonight. Red Storm MC ran Texas for years, and those were about the only bikers I ever saw until Savage Dragons MC and Iron Bulls MC showed up and pushed 'em out. Now here I am, discovering more about this world.

Rooster parks near Dex and Jigsaw and turns to me. "You okay?"

"A little nervous."

"Don't be. We've been friends with this club for years."

Jigsaw and Dex are laughing as we approach.

"You make the prospect piss his pants?" Rooster lightly punches Jigsaw's shoulder.

Jigsaw touches his chest briefly. "Who, me? Naw, I was nothing but sweetness."

Dex rolls his eyes. "Poor kids. Surprised a full-patch isn't supervising them." He lifts his chin at me. "Didn't think you'd be seeing this much of backwoods, New York, did ya?"

I let out a soft laugh. "Not really. It's pretty out here, though."

"Hey." Rooster leans closer to the guys. "Keep an eye on her, okay?" His gaze shifts to Jigsaw. "I know you're dying to fill your wet dick bingo card but control yourself."

Jigsaw blinks. One corner of his mouth curls up. "Always, brother."

Together, we approach the front of the club. Two more bikers in cuts study us under the bright security lights before pulling the doors open wide for us to enter.

It takes a second for my eyes to adjust to the dim interior. The entryway opens up to a wide main room full of bikers and scantily clad women. I glance down at my denim skirt, flamingo tank top and cowgirl boots. Maybe not the best biker girlfriend's outfit.

Men acknowledge us as we pass.

The threat Rooster poses is reflected in the eyes of the bikers of this club—in the respect they offer when they nod and shake his hand. The tension that ripples through the air as we move through the clubhouse.

In Rooster's world, these men know who they can and can't fuck with. In my world, some men are too stupid to figure out when danger's walking among them.

If my father could see me now, hanging out at Chaser Adams' motorcycle club. The thought of my father dampens my enthusiasm for the evening ahead. Pisses me off too.

Chaser's imposing figure is easy to spot by the bar. Even his own MC brothers keep a respectful distance around him and the blonde at his side.

Rooster taps Jigsaw and Dex. When he has their attention, he jerks his head in Chaser's direction.

"We need to say hello." Rooster leans closer to me. "Pay our respects to our host."

"Sure."

"Rooster!" Chaser shouts over the crowd when he spots our little group. He raises his hand high in the air, motioning us over.

"Glad you made it." Chaser takes Rooster's outstretched hand and pulls him in for a friendly pat on the shoulder.

"Thanks for the invite."

Chaser wraps his arm around the beautiful blonde woman next to him. "Mallory, this is Shelby. Shelby, my wife, Mallory."

Mallory reaches for me before her husband even finishes the introductions. "Welcome. It's so nice to meet you. Angelina came home all excited from the show." She squeezes me tight.

At least this president's wife is nothing like Tawny. Mallory's bubbly and kind, turning us toward the bar and signaling for the girl behind it to bring us drinks. "This is your first tour, right?" she asks.

"Yup. So far it's been an adventure."

CHAPTER TWENTY-NINE

Rooster

Whether or not it was calculated to give Chaser and me space to talk, I appreciate Mallory being so friendly to Shelby.

"Everything go all right at the show?" Chaser asks.

"I think so." I slap Jigsaw's shoulder. "He helped scare the gropers away."

Jigsaw laughs.

"You ever need some help when she's traveling in one of our areas, say the word. I can ask a few brothers from one of our other charters to help you out."

No doubt there will be strings attached but I appreciate the offer. "Thank you." Fuck, I don't have all night to initiate the delicate conversation we need to have. Any second, he'll probably grab Mallory and take off. "How are things around here?"

His friendly smile freezes in place.

He's gonna make me get specific first. It'll annoy Chaser more if I beat around the bush, so I guess I'm diving in. "How's your father-in-law? We kind of cut off our assistance abruptly."

Chaser snorts. "He's not holding a grudge against your club. Don't worry."

And yet, I don't have a warm, fuzzy reassuring feeling in my chest.

"How are things with Z at the head of your table?" he asks.

It's unusual for bikers to stick their noses in other club's business. Since I poked into his business first, he must've decided to break the code. "Good. We're lucky to have him." Even if that were a lie, it's not like I'd talk shit about my president to another club. Chaser knows that.

Chaser sips his drink slowly. "Can't imagine that's sitting well with Sway."

Bold statement. I shift my jaw from side to side as a few answers roll through my mind. "He's still focused on his recovery."

"That's good. Fuckin' miracle he survived." He gives me another pointed look. "You ever catch the shooter?"

Jesus Christ.

I keep my expression blank and shrug. Explaining such a troubling internal battle to an outsider isn't happening.

Still, Chaser's not dumb. I'm sure he can put the pieces together without me drawing him a damn map. Sway got shot...old VP went "missing"...I'm suddenly wearing the VP patch. A two-year-old could connect the dots. It only helps our reputation. If the Lost Kings are willing to brutally punish a brother for misconduct, what the hell would they do to an outsider?

Chaser moves in closer. Jigsaw shifts his body, brushing his arm against mine.

"Settle down." Chaser smirks at him before focusing on me again. "Truth is, my father-in-law is retiring."

"Well, shit. Never thought that would happen."

"You and me both." He laughs.

"He planning to head down to Florida and get a place next to your father?"

He busts up laughing. "Fuck no. They'd both be dead within a week."

"DeLova gonna move into your house?"

Mallory reaches over and flicks my arm. "Bite your tongue."

Obviously, she's keeping tabs on our conversation. I grin at her.

"He's staying close," Chaser says.

That must be a delight.

"Who's taking over their action?" Jigsaw asks.

Chaser doesn't blink at the nosy question. "We'll see." He nods at Mallory. "Her cousin's been running some aspects for a while. My club obviously has a large part of it." He studies us for a few beats. "There will be room for Lost Kings at the table."

That's not something I can consider without talking to the rest of the club.

"Not the collection bullshit Sway was doing for my father-in-law before," Chaser adds when I don't respond right away.

Devil Demons have always been into riskier ways of earning money than Lost Kings, at least as far back as I remember. With Priest pushing us away from stuff that might bring law enforcement knocking on our doors, I can already guess what Z's answer will be. But I don't want to insult Chaser after his generous offer.

"I can take it to the table. We have a lot going on right now, though," I add.

His mouth curls up. "How much are you really earning with the *film* company?"

You'd be surprised. "It's lucrative. Low risk." I hook my thumbs in my pockets. "Lot of pain-in-the-ass maintenance, though."

"I can imagine." He slaps my shoulder, then Jiggy's and Dex's. "Enjoy the party." He reaches for Mallory's hand, tugging her closer. "We need to check on a few things. You want a room later, talk to Stoner. He'll hook you up."

I have no idea who the hell that is but I nod anyway and shake his hand one more time.

Jiggy waits until Chaser and Mallory are out of earshot before moving close. Dex closes off the circle.

"The fuck?" Jiggy says in a low voice. "You know that's getting a thumbs-down from Z."

"No shit. Thought it would be rude to say that right to his face." I lift my chin. "You catch all that, Dex?"

"Every word."

I glance over. Shelby's a few feet away, facing the bar, fidgeting with her can of soda. "We'll talk about it later." I reach over and curl my finger in the waistband of her skirt, dragging her closer. "Sorry about that."

"Pfft." She waves off the apology. "You've spent the last couple days waitin' on me. I know you have business to take care of. I'm fine."

I lean down and press a quick kiss against her lips. "Thank you."

Something hard slams into my arm and I growl. I turn and Jigsaw grins at me. "Am I off the clock now, brother?"

Dex meets my eyes. "Bingo time."

I chuckle at the joke. "Yeah. Go on. But for fuck's sake, stay away from anyone's ol' lady or—"

"Bro." Jiggy waves his hand at the room. "Pretty sure Mallory was the only ol' lady in attendance at *this* party."

"Go on."

Dex watches Jigsaw for a second before clapping me on the shoulder. "I'll be back."

I don't bother issuing any warnings to Dex. He doesn't need 'em.

"You all right?" I ask Shelby.

"I'm fine. Mallory was so sweet. Like, polar opposite of Tawny."

I snort at the comparison. "You're not kidding. She's definitely got more in common with Lilly and Hope." I run my gaze over Shelby again. I'm dying to be alone with her, acutely aware we're running out of time. Since I took care of what Z asked me to do, I feel entitled to take off.

Shelby

I haven't felt this relaxed in months. It's an odd feeling to have at an MC clubhouse. But no one's gawking at me, I'm not expected to serve the drinks, and Mallory assured me no one would try and sneak pictures here. I'm free to blend into the scenery.

Guilt presses down on me. Am I really bellyaching about being recognized? Everything I've wanted since I was ten years old is slowly coming true. I have no right to complain.

But it sure does feel good to have time off.

"You want to go outside?" Rooster asks. "It's a little smoky in here."

Touched he remembered what I'd said about my voice, I nod and take his hand. Two younger bikers hold the front doors open for us. The cool wash of night air slips over my skin and I inhale deeply.

"They have some tables and stuff set up around back," Rooster says. Our boots crunch over the gravel. Voices carry through the night. The bright orange glow of a fire lights what looks like a picnic area. We climb up on a wooden table near the trees and I lean on my hands to stare at the sky. "I don't want this night to end." I turn and stare at Rooster. "Is that selfish?"

"If it is, then I'm selfish too." He kisses my cheek. "We can stay here or grab a room at the hotel your crew's staying at. Up to you."

While I'm enjoying our time here, I won't be able to sleep if I'm worried I'll be late tomorrow. "Hotel. Are you sure you don't mind?"

"Let's go." He jumps off the table, boots rustling the grass, and holds out his hand. "I need to say good night to Chaser. And I'll give Jiggy and Dex the option to come with us—and get their own rooms."

"Shoot. I feel bad making them spend extra money—"

He presses a finger to my lips. "Dex is always up for a road trip. Jigsaw's up for anything—if you hadn't noticed. Don't sweat it."

Inside the clubhouse, Rooster wastes no time locating Chaser and Mallory.

One corner of Chaser's mouth hitches up as we approach. "Headin' out?"

Rooster squeezes my hand. "Yeah, she's rolling out early."

"I remember those days." Chaser nods at me. "Thanks for coming."

"Sure." My tongue's all tangled. "Thanks for havin' me."

"Anytime, Shelby," Mallory says.

Chaser holds out his hand and pulls Rooster in, slapping his back. "Good to see you, brother. Don't be a stranger."

"I won't," Rooster promises.

"And tell Z to get his ass out here." He snaps his fingers. "We're doing a big thing for our thirtieth in a couple months. You'll have to come."

Mallory's face brightens. She clasps her hands together. "I already talked to Hope and Lilly about it a little while ago. We'll send official invites soon." She squeezes my hand. "Of course, you're also welcome to come, Shelby."

She sounds awfully confident Rooster and I will still be together in a few months. "Thank you."

Rooster curls his arm around my waist without hesitation. "Thanks, Mallory."

"If you can...with your schedule," she adds. "I know how hard it is when you're on the road so much."

After a few more pleasantries, we say good night. Rooster searches the club but can't find Jigsaw or Dex.

"I'll text them. Let's go."

In the truck, he pulls out his phone.

"You guys really look out for each other, don't ya?" I ask.

"Leave no man behind. I just want to hear back from one of them before we leave."

"Sure thing." I slip my phone free of my pocket and scroll through my emails. One subject stands out.

WILL YOU MARRY ME?

I click on it.

Dear Shelby,

Roses are red, violets are blue,

I really want to marry you.

Tomorrow night would be better,

For us to get together.

You'll always be mine.

I promise you, the sex will be fine.

Please say yes.

Don't respond with rejection.

You don't want to miss out on my massive erection.

Love, Floyd. 937-555-9375

"Eww!" I click delete but scrubbing my brain of that creep-tastic poem won't be as easy.

"What's wrong?" Rooster asks.

"Nothing. Just some creepy fan mail. I'll never understand why they think being gross will work."

His face pulls into a frown. "Gross how?"

I retrieve the email from my trash folder and show it to him.

"What the fuck? You've gotten more messages like this?"

"All the time." I squint at him. "Me and every other female who has a social media account. At least there's no dick pic attached this time."

"What?"

"How can you be so unaware?"

"I assure you, never in my twenty-eight years has it occurred to me to send a picture of my dick to a stranger."

Something about his serious tone sends me into a fit of giggles. "So, you send them to your friends?"

"No." He glances at my phone again and taps the screen.

"What are you doing?"

"Forwarding that to my account."

"What? Why?"

"Don't worry about it."

"Rooster!" I lunge to his side of the truck, grabbing for my phone. "Give me that."

"Here." He hands it over. "All done."

"You can't go harassing my fans."

"That's not a *fan*. That's a creep who needs to learn some manners."

"He's not the only one," I grumble. I open my Instagram account. Takes less than a second to find some perv's comment on my most recent post.

"Shelby," I read out loud. "I bet you'd ride my face like a mechanical bull. What do ya say? Cowgirl up?" I click my phone screen off, in case Rooster gets any ideas. "You can't go after all of them, Rooster."

"That's fucking bullshit."

I squint at him. "I can't believe you're so shocked."

He shakes his head. "Actually, I'm not. Some of the girls we work with get some pretty twisted messages, but—"

"Oh, you think because I'm a sweet, sassy little country singer those kinda guys will treat me nicer than they treat a stripper? Nah. All women are whores dying to see a dick in their inbox to them."

He busts up laughing. "I still don't like it."

I reach over and tug on his beard. "And I wouldn't like *you* so much if you did."

"Seriously, though." He takes a deep breath. "I want you to be careful."

"I am. I never post pics until after I leave the location. I don't answer those creepy messages. I don't go off exploring by myself when we're in a new city—"

He leans in and presses his mouth to mine—a soft kiss that whips into something wild and demanding.

And then it's over.

Woozy from the kiss, I'm slow to open my eyes.

"I know this is…new and we're still figuring out how this long-distance thing works, but I can't help wanting to protect you. Can't help wanting to beat the shit out of anyone who disrespects you. It's just who I am."

"I understand that." I force a quick smile. "I kinda like that about you."

"Good."

"It's a little weird for me, though." The intensity between us feels too heavy, so I stare out the window. "My momma's fierce."

He chuckles softly. "I remember."

"Well, I watched her fall apart after my sister…after Hayley…"

He reaches over and squeezes my hand.

"Then my dad just walked out. Not that he was some super-dad even before Hayley got sick. He was one of those 'fetch me a beer while I sit and watch television all night' kind of dads when he got home from work. Never paid all that much attention to us in the first place. It broke her a little. I had to fend for myself and look out for her."

I risk glancing up and find him staring at me, beard twitching from grinding his jaw.

"Sorry, I didn't mean to take a detour there."

"I'm listening."

I wipe my hands against my skirt, trying to force the thoughts in my head into words on my tongue. "What I'm trying to say is, I'm not familiar with someone else looking out for *me*. My mom worries about me but it's different."

"Shelby. Look at me." He waits until I comply, then trails his knuckles down the side of my cheek. "You're not alone anymore."

CHAPTER THIRTY

Shelby

The next morning, I'm fighting tears as Rooster and I leave our hotel room and quietly walk through the silent hallway to the elevator. It's early. If I hadn't been woken by Greg's text, I'd assume no one in the building was awake yet.

The sun's barely peeking over the mountains and the sky matches my gloomy mood. At least the air is still cool. As my protest against the early morning wake-up, I'm still in my fluffy mint-green fleece jammy pants and a T-shirt with two lambs kissing on the front. In the name of decency, I slipped a bra on underneath my shirt and stuffed my feet into my Converse.

Jigsaw and Dex are parked next to Rooster's truck, leaning on their bikes, sipping cups of coffee. Rooster rips a shrill whistle and they wave to acknowledge the greeting.

The three tour buses for Dawson's crew and Thundersmoke line the edge of the parking lot.

Hmph. Doesn't look like any of *them* are awake yet.

Our sad little van is parked along the curb. Rooster taps on the door and our driver, James, opens it. "Mornin', Shelby."

"Morning," I grumble.

"I got her stuff," Trent says, walking up behind us. He scowls at Rooster and I scowl right back.

Rooster doesn't bother engaging.

"You leaving right away?" Rooster asks James.

"You got time."

"Thanks." Rooster rests his palm at the small of my back and guides me over to the truck.

"Morning, Shelby." Jigsaw grins at me.

"Morning." I nod at Dex. "Morning."

"You stay at Chaser's?" Rooster asks.

"We grabbed a room here earlier this morning." Jigsaw yawns and stretches.

"Someone should've warned me he sleeps naked," Dex says.

Jigsaw grins. "Nah, that was just for you, buddy."

Rooster groans and steers me toward the tailgate where we have some privacy. I lean against the cool metal, trying not to look up at him or all the heartache gathering in my chest will pour from my eyes.

"What's wrong?" He rubs my bare arm. "Are you warm enough?"

"I'm fine." Such a lie. "The air feels good."

"Talk to me," he pleads.

"Rooster," I whisper, finally daring to look up at him.

He stares into my eyes and I search his face, trying to commit every bit of him to memory.

"What, chickadee?" he says lightly.

I can't fake the same light cheeriness. Not when I'm coming apart inside. "I'll miss you."

His smile fades. "I'm gonna miss you too."

It seems so unfair to ask *when* he'll visit. I don't want to go months without seeing him again. I'd ask him to follow us onto the highway right now, today, and for the rest of the tour if I could.

He traces his finger over the curve of my cheek. "When can I see you again?"

His question unravels the tightly knotted ball of sorrow in my heart. "I don't know."

"You got your tour schedule?"

I release him and pull my phone out, searching for the document with all the dates listed.

"I have a copy I printed out at home somewhere," Rooster mutters. "You're headed to Virginia at some point, right?"

Thrilled he remembered, I scan the dates as soon as the document pops up on my screen. "Yup. End of next week."

"Can you forward that to me?" He nods at my phone.

I send it and his phone pings a few seconds later. "Done."

He brushes my hair off my cheek and leans down to capture my attention. "I have some business down in Virginia. Why don't we meet up there?" He glances over at our van. "When you're moving from show to show, you don't *have* to ride in the van, right? I mean, are you doing special musical bonding stuff with the band?"

Sweet relief that we have a plan to see each other frees my spirit with laughter. "Not really. Sometimes we work on a song. Mostly everyone stares at their phones or sleeps."

"So, maybe you ride with me for a bit." He runs his hands through his hair. "I'm really not trying to fuck things up for you or invite myself along, but—"

"No. I'd like that, Rooster." I try to control the excitement in my voice. "But I can't ask you to drop everything. It's not fair."

The corner of his mouth curls up. "It sounds to me like we both want the same thing."

"Is that awful of me?"

He leans down and brushes his lips over mine. "No."

"What business are you up to in Virginia?" I ask.

"We have a charter there. Z wants me to help them with a few things."

"Anything fun?" I still don't know what he actually does for the club.

His face slides into that expressionless mask I noticed last night when Chaser probed about the club. "Never mind," I say quickly. "You don't have to tell me."

"It's nothing major," he says without elaborating.

A sharp whistle splits the air. The chug-roar of the van rumbles to life.

"Shelby! Let's go!" Greg shouts.

"Dammit." Tears prick my eyes. I'm not ready to say goodbye.

"Come on. I'll walk over with you."

"No. Don't." My protest is a blunt hammer, stopping him in his tracks. "I want to remember you like this. Next to the truck we spent the weekend in. Together." I sniff. "If you come over there, I might drag you onto the van with me."

His firm hands grip my waist, yanking me closer. Without a word, he leans down and presses his mouth to mine. Hard.

It's not a sweet kiss. It's one of need and desperation, longing and goodbye. He groans and lifts me, pushing me against truck, and deepens our kiss. My legs wrap around him, squeezing his hips. I loop my arms around his neck, hanging on tight. His beard tickles and scratches my chin and above my lip.

Another piercing whistle pulls us apart.

Rooster growls and shifts his focus toward the van.

"I'm sorry. I have to go."

His expression softens as he faces me. "Be awesome tonight." A smile teases the corners of his mouth. "I hate that I'm missing your show."

My heart flips at the sincerity in his voice. No one in my life besides my mother has ever taken my music so seriously. "I'll miss you being there."

He sets me down gently.

We step around the side of the truck where Jiggy and Dex are still waiting at their bikes. How much did they overhear? Will Jiggy razz Rooster terribly?

Dex notices us first and flashes a friendly smile. "Bye, Shelby. Good luck." He holds out his fist to me and I tap his knuckles with my own.

"Thank you for coming out all this way with Rooster."

"Not a problem." He lifts his chin. "I'm sure I'll see you again soon."

Jigsaw's more subdued than I expected. He also holds out his fist for a bump. "Be safe, Shelby."

"I'll try."

He flicks his gaze toward Greg, who's on the verge of having an apoplectic fit, and curls his lip in a snarl. "He better do his job and look out for you."

"I'll be okay," I promise. "Thank you."

I jump up and hug Rooster one last time, kiss his bristly cheek, and dart away. Good thing the parking lot isn't busy at this hour. I don't bother looking for cars as I sprint to the van.

"Let's roll." I stop in front of Greg.

We're not close enough for him to ask many questions. "Cincinnati, here we come!" he says in a cheerful voice.

I pump my fist in the air with appreciation at his attempt to cheer me up.

The guys are in their designated spots, and I murmur hellos. Trent tosses my favorite blanket at me, hitting me in the face with it. I hug it to my chest and stick my nose in the cozy fleece. "Did you wash it?"

He shrugs. "They had a washer and dryer on our floor."

"Thank you."

His shoulders jerk in another *whatever* shrug. I curl up in my seat, pulling my blanket around me. As much as I try to resist, I can't help pressing my face against the window to spy on Rooster. The glass is tinted, so he can't see me watching him as he talks to his brothers, flicking a glance at the van every couple minutes.

Come on. Hurry up. Why'd Greg call me over here if we were just going to idle for minutes?

James finally drops into his seat. Greg smacks the van door before jogging off to his own vehicle.

Even though he can't see me, Rooster lifts his hand as the van pulls out of the parking lot. I press my fingers to the glass and choke down a sob.

Maybe *this* is what my momma meant. This moment. Right here. Lost in the time Rooster and I were able to spend together, my brain buried how much it hurt when we'd said goodbye in Texas months ago.

Maybe she remembered how sad I'd been after Rooster left.

Back then, I had the upcoming tour and hours of rehearsals to pull me out of my funk. Now, I've got nothing but miles of road ahead of me to miss him and only warm memories to keep me company.

CHAPTER THIRTY-ONE

Rooster

Watching Shelby's van pull away is harder than I'd expected.

Can't remember ever feeling this way about someone.

"You all right?" Dex asks quietly.

"Yeah. We made plans. I'll see her soon."

He claps me on the back. "That's good."

I side-eye him. "You're not gonna tell me how whipped I am?"

"Nah, that's Jigsaw's job."

"Who's giving me a job?" Jigsaw wraps an arm around each of our necks. "What kind of job? Hand job? Blow job?"

"I'll give you fuckin' job." I shake him off and stretch, already dreading the long drive ahead of me. Without Shelby by my side, being cooped up in a cage is intolerable. "Y'all ready to head back?"

"Aw, listen to that. Rooster said, *y'all*. Startin' to sound like your girl," Jigsaw says. "Is *yeehaw* next?"

"Fuck off." I push my middle finger in his face and he slaps my arm away.

"You gonna be okay?" Jigsaw's mouth turns down as if he's feeling sorry for me. "You need to go to the bathroom and have a cry about missin' Shelby? We'll wait."

"You're extra-strength asshole today." Dex pulls his keys from his pocket.

"Rooster knows I'm fucking with him." He adopts a more serious tone. "Be straight with me. You all right?"

"Yes. Fuck. I'm fine."

Jiggy crosses his arms and rests his chin in one hand, tapping his fingers against his jaw. "You worried she's meetin' up with her Ohio boyfriend next? I mean, she could be like most bikers we know and have a stud stashed in every state."

"Fuck this." I give him a quick shove and head toward the hotel. "I'm gettin' a coffee for the road."

Behind me, Jigsaw's laughter rings out, then there's an, "Ow! What're you hittin' me for?"

Dex's heavy steps thud over the pavement until he catches up to me. "How have you not killed him yet?"

"I ask myself that every day, brother."

"I'm sorry!" Jigsaw shouts as he hurries to my side. "Didn't know you'd get so bent. I like Shelby. Any asshole can tell she's into you."

"And yet..."

"I'm not just any asshole."

"Amen to that," Dex mutters. "More like a special kind of jackass."

The hotel clerk doesn't look thrilled to have us in his establishment again. Ignoring him, I head for the snack bar and fill an extra-large coffee cup to the top. "You wanna stop for breakfast on the road?" I ask Dex. "Or wait 'til we get to Johnsonville?"

"Who's riding my johnson?" Jigsaw quips.

"Did you strike out with the Demons' club girls last night?" I ask. "You seem awfully frustrated this morning."

Dex smacks Jigsaw's shoulder. "The scary thing is, he didn't. He terrorized...I mean, *romanced* at least two from what I saw."

Jiggy scowls at him. "I don't *romance*, bro."

I let out a long, irritated sigh. "I honestly don't care."

"Sure, now that you have a steady supply of p—"

"Don't," I warn him.

"*Pleasurable* communication," he continues, "you can afford to be smug. Don't judge me. I'm a healthy young man. I need frequent release with various females as often as possible."

"Christ, you're disgusting," Dex mutters, handing the scandalized cashier a couple of bills and telling her to keep the change.

Outside, I stop to sip my coffee and notice the other tour buses. Guess Dawson didn't get an early wake-up. What the fuck was the rush for Shelby? I glance back at the hotel...

"You thinking of finding Dawson and pounding on his door?" Jigsaw asks.

This fucker knows me too well. "No. What are you, eight?"

"More like nine, nine and a half inches."

I roll my eyes. That ride in the car is looking better by the second. "Shut up."

We stop at our vehicles and I check my phone. "Texting Murphy to let him know we're on our way back. See where he wants to meet up before we head to Zips."

Dex takes out his phone, flips through a few screens. "We should hit Exit 28 in about three hours. Four if we stop for breakfast somewhere. Have him meet us at the gas station right off the exit."

"Sounds good."

"How'd you leave it?" Jigsaw asks.

I finish sending the text before glancing up. "Leave what?"

"Things with Shelby."

"None of your fucking business."

"Seriously?"

I blow out a breath and squeeze my eyes shut. Why am I even bothering? "We're gonna meet up in Virginia next week. Z's got a few charters he wants me to visit and that one was on top of the list." I lift my shoulders. "So, it works out."

"Aw, fuck." Dex groans. "Priest's still poking around?"

"Apparently."

Jigsaw frowns at me. "You can't go alone."

"Why not? It's one of *our* charters."

"Yeah, but unless you're planning to take some long way around, you'll go right through Viper territory."

"And having you with me will help? Pass. I'll go through Harrisburg. Done it before. Only adds an hour or so."

"You still need someone to help you out backstage. Fuck, I'm surprised you let her go as it is, knowing the shit she puts up with."

"He's got a point," Dex adds.

"You think I'm an asshole too?"

"No, brother. Just sayin'. It would drive me nuts thinking she'd be unprotected at those shows."

"Her schedule says she only has one meet and greet coming up." I take out my phone and scan the schedule Shelby sent me.

"She really does need a security team," Dex says.

"Can't afford it yet. Fucking pisses me off no one will do shit for her." I hold one hand about chest level. "She gets to this point of fame but she ain't making this level of money yet to afford the shit she needs to stay at that level or go any higher."

Jigsaw bounces up and down in a circle. "That's where knowing some bikers will come in handy."

I aim a cool look his way. "*Some* bikers?"

"Sounds like Jiggy's itching to hit the highway," Dex says.

"Fuck yeah." Jigsaw punches his fist in the air. "We used to have the most epic time on the road back in the day."

"This is my girlfriend's tour, not a road trip."

"Close enough." Jigsaw stops his manic dancing around and shrugs. "Just has a stricter schedule than we used to keep."

"Bro, it's fucked up for me to ask you to do that."

"Why? You like Shelby?"

I tilt my head. As if I need to answer that.

"You thinking you might patch her one day?" Dex asks.

Patch Shelby? I can't fathom what that would look like.

Fuck, who am I kidding? I've been picturing *Property of Rooster* on her back since the first time she hung out with my club.

"Maybe."

"Coming from you, that's as good as a yes." Jigsaw grins.

CHAPTER THIRTY-TWO

Rooster

The ride east drags. Maybe it's because my body knows I'm moving away from Shelby. No amount of internal rationalization that I'll see her soon seems to lessen the nagging pull.

As promised, Murphy's waiting for us by the gas station off Exit 28. I signal to Dex and Jigsaw as I change lanes. Murphy nods at me as I roll up next to him.

"'Sup, brother?" he asks, clutching my hand and pulling me in. "How'd it go?"

"Good." Although, I doubt Murphy would make a joke about it, I'm not in the mood to whine to him—or anyone else—about how much I'm already missing Shelby.

After a quick run inside, we pull out of the parking lot and head to Zips. I've only been to the racetrack Eraser owns a handful of times. Racing doesn't interest me all that much. Seems more like an excuse to piss away money on car parts and betting to make a guy feel better about his dick size. Since I'm pretty confident in the dick department, the whole posturing, trash-talking, and gambling scene bores the shit out of me.

Beyond my lack of interest in racing, I'm not as convinced as

Murphy and Z that we even *need* a support club. Support clubs have always been more trouble than they're worth in my experience. The thought of having to ride out here on a regular basis to "mentor" these little punks couldn't be more unappealing when there's a certain little sassy singer on the road I'd rather visit.

But I'm here to observe and assist my brothers, so I'll keep my opinions to myself. For now.

When the time comes, though, what's right for the club will have to be my priority whether it fucks up my plans or not.

We take the turn down the long-forgotten road leading to Zips. I'm guessing back in the sixties or seventies, this place was rockin'. Eraser's maintained its charming overgrown, neglected appearance on the outside. Cracked asphalt, wild grass, trees in desperate need of pruning almost obscuring the entrance. No one finds their way here by accident or without an invite.

Inside's been maintained better—hard to convince people to drop hundreds of dollars a night if they're worried they're gonna break an axle on the track.

Eraser's the first one to greet us as we make our way over to the snack shack. "How you been?"

I shake his hand. "Can't complain."

Remy and Griff follow to greet us and bump fists.

Eraser reaches for Murphy next, pulling him in with a quick slap on the back. "How's the head?"

Murphy knocks on his skull. "Harder than ever."

"Good."

Ah, nice little reminder. These three had our backs when it counted. Without them, we might still be wasting our time tracking down the asshole who whacked Murphy upside the head with a baseball bat and put him in the hospital.

Maybe I shouldn't be so quick to dismiss the support club idea after all.

While Murphy and Remy pull away to gossip about underground fighting, Griff hooks his thumbs in his pockets and lifts his chin at me. "Was I mistaken or was that Shelby Morgan at the clubhouse the other night?"

I knew he recognized her. "Surprised you know who she is."

He shrugs and tilts his head Remy's way. "Molly's a big fan."

Remy glances over and scowls at the mention of his little sister, which Griff ignores.

"Tried getting tickets but they sold out quick."

"Shit, I wish I'd known. I would've tried to get you in. We just came back from her show in Kodack. Should've had you ride out with us."

He raises an eyebrow. "You're *with* her, with her?"

"Why are you probing into my love life, son?" I reach out and pat his cheek.

He swats my hand away, flirting with the thin line between not taking any shit and maintaining respect. "I ain't young enough to be your son. Just curious."

Out of the corner of my eye, I catch Jigsaw's mouth twisting with the effort of holding back his laughter. He won't rib me in front of these guys but he's definitely storing up ammunition for later.

"How's that work between you two, with her on the road all the time?"

"You looking for dating advice or something, Griff?"

He shrugs off the taunting question. "No, I'm all set."

I decide to ease up since he doesn't seem to be asking for dickish reasons. "Don't know yet. Haven't been with her long. Headed down to see her in Virginia next week."

Jigsaw swaggers closer and slaps my shoulder. "We're also headed to Virginia to expand our porn empire."

I shoot a glare at Jiggy.

"Now *that's* a venture I would be happy to help support," Remy volunteers.

Murphy gives Remy a quick shove. "You'll need to earn your way up that particular ladder."

Eraser's gaze darts between them and he backs up a step, like he's questioning his choice in friends. "That's what your club's into, Murphy?"

Murphy's face settles into a more severe expression. Yeah, we're looking to form a support club out here, but it's still not their place to question club business. Although, I don't blame the kid for wanting to be clear about what he's getting into.

"It's mostly downstate's action." Murphy puts one hand on my shoulder and the other on Jigsaw's. "But we always help each other out."

Remy grins at me. "You ever need someone to chauffeur your stars around or maybe fluff 'em up before a shoot, I'm your man."

Griff side-eyes his best friend. "Don't you get enough fluffing around here?"

"I'll keep you in mind." My flat tone should make it clear he'll be at the bottom of the list.

Murphy's got his chin to his chest, silently laughing.

Jigsaw slaps Murphy's arm. "What's so funny?"

"Nothing. We got Rock and Z trying to pass off overseeing the porn biz like a hot sack of shit and Remy here's all, 'Pick me! Pick me!'"

"Uh, to be fair, I'm also in the 'pick me' camp." Jigsaw elbows Murphy's side.

Eraser's gaze moves to Dex. "You compensate for that *help* or do you treat it like asking a buddy to come move some furniture?"

"If you're asking if we pay in pizza and beer, the answer's no." Dex crosses his arms over his chest. "Vapor can tell you that. He's always been paid for any work he's done for the club. Everyone gets taken care of so it's worth their time."

Remy raises his hand. "I'm cool with being paid in pussy."

"And *that's* why we'll never ask you to help out in that area," Dex shoots back.

"Well, fuck."

"Upstate has the strip club?" Eraser asks, ignoring Remy.

"Along with some other businesses," Murphy answers. "We like to maintain diverse revenue streams."

"Smart." Eraser nods at Remy and Griff. "We've been talking about that. Besides the bar Remy owns, none of us have any other legit income to show."

"You wash your cash through the bar?" Murphy asks.

"Yeah, but you've seen the place." Remy stands up straighter, dropping the horndog act. "Where it's located, it's hard to claim it does *that* much business with a straight face."

"Another legit business wouldn't be a bad idea," Murphy encourages him. "What else interests you?"

"I'm saving to open a garage for classic cars," Griff says.

"You've seen the work he does." Remy slaps Griff's back. "Even Eraser's wife plans to help out at the shop."

"Ella's getting her welding certificate," Eraser explains. "So, we'll have that base covered."

Murphy nods. "Good idea. Keep it in the family."

Aw, look at Murphy. He's like a legit mentor now.

"That's the plan," Griff agrees.

"Well, if you want, I can have Teller talk to you. Maybe help figure out some of the financials," Murphy offers. Sounds like upstate will be investing in a classic car garage in the near future.

Maybe now isn't the best time to consider going on the road with Shelby.

Because it looks like a Lost Kings MC support club is inevitable.

CHAPTER THIRTY-THREE

Shelby

I yawn and stare at my face in the mirror on the wall of tonight's dressing room. "Sure wish I'd had more sleep this morning," I grumble at Greg. "Hope you've got extra concealer in there, Cindy." I tap the top of her rolling makeup case.

"Don't worry about a thing, sweetheart."

Behind me, Greg flicks a look at the ceiling.

"I saw that. Why'd we have to get here so dang early, anyway? Dawson didn't roll in until an hour ago." Six hours on the road hasn't made me any less crabby about missing Rooster.

"They needed you early for sound check. I wasn't going to argue with the venue." He shrugs and pats my shoulder before walking out.

Cindy squeezes my upper arms. "You're going to be fine tonight."

"Thanks."

"Where's your man?"

"He had to go home. We're going to meet up next week."

"Oh. Sounds serious."

My cheeks warm. "It could be."

"I like the way he treats you," she says softly. "Attentive and protective."

"That's Logan."

We chat about the tour. Actually, I listen while Cindy gives me the scoop on Thundersmoke and Dawson's ex. "Rumor is, she's been pitching one hell of a hissyfit after she saw the video of you two singing *their* song together."

"Aw, shit. Really?" Why didn't it occur to me that the woman Dawson wrote and originally recorded the song with might get a bee up her butt seeing him perform it with someone else? "Damn, I never thought of that. I feel bad."

"Don't you dare feel bad. She knows this business better than anyone."

A worse thought occurs to me. "He's using me to piss her off, ain't he?"

She sighs and gives me a sympathetic shoulder squeeze. "Yeah, probably. She cheated on him with his best friend, so give him a pass." In the mirror, I watch her bite her lip. "You did *not* hear that from me."

Holy smokes. "Surprised *Sippin' on Secrets* hasn't spilled it yet. Guess they're too worried about posting fuzzy photos of every guy who stands within five feet of me," I grumble. Another unflattering piece had posted to their site earlier today.

"Well, she doesn't need the bad press and he doesn't want his manly-man image tarnished, so it's in both their interests to keep their yaps shut."

"But he's using me to needle her." I'm startin' to think everyone in this business sucks.

"Yeah, it's not great," she agrees. "But it's still good for you. Honestly, that's why I don't think *Sippin' on Secrets* posting those stories about you and Logan is so awful. Shows everyone you got a fine man of your own. You don't need to chase after her sloppy seconds."

Laughter bursts out of me followed by a wave of guilt. Whatever the reasons, Dawson's treated me well and I'm lucky to even be on this tour. Singing with him has brought me a lot of attention and boosted album sales.

My phone chirps and I happily reach for it, hoping it's Rooster. *Rooster: Just got home.*

Me: Are you in your sexy gray and blue bedroom? Because that's where I'm picturing you.

Rooster: In the parking lot.

I close my eyes briefly. He took me a lot of different places during my visit but I can imagine his clubhouse perfectly. I just need to mentally clip Tawny the hyena out of the picture.

Me: Will you send me a pic?

Rooster: Dick or regular?

Me: Well, Cindy's working on me at the moment so...

A picture of his serious face framed by the evening sky pops up next.

Rooster: Your turn.

Cindy chuckles and steps clear of the frame while I stick out my tongue and snap a picture. It's goofy as all get-out. My hair's all half-up, half-down and my face a clean canvas of primer that gives me a ghostly appearance.

Rooster: Beautiful. I miss you.

Me: Miss you too.

Rooster: Gotta go.

I set the phone in my lap.

Behind me, Cindy sighs. "Missin' him?"

"Yeah," I admit.

She's quiet after that, working quickly to transform me into my onstage persona while I hum a few scales.

After she's finished, I have a few minutes to myself. Jittery and anxious about the show, I pace back and forth, focusing on some favorite deep breathing techniques.

A scratch-whoosh noise draws my attention to the door in time to see a black envelope with a glint of silver pushed underneath. It sails across the floor. I frown at it before scurrying to pick it up.

My name's scrawled on the front in some kind of silver pen. Reminds me of the black notebooks and gel pens I'd loved in high school. The writing's neat, precise, like a child trying to impress his parents.

I rip open the flap and pull out the piece of paper tucked inside. Expecting it to be from a kid, I smile.

Dearest Shelby,

For your sake, I hope the rumors of you cavorting around with two men isn't true.

M

What the heck?

I'm not smiling any more. That's not a note from a sweet little kid.

Cavorting? Who says crap like that?

I glance at the door again. Did security drop it off?

Whatever. I don't have time for this nonsense.

More annoyed than scared, I stuff the stupid note at the bottom of my purse and finish getting ready for my show.

CHAPTER THIRTY-FOUR

Rooster

I keep flicking my phone on to check out the silly pic Shelby sent me. I love that she trusts me enough to send goofy candids instead of filtered glamour shots.

As much as I love to be on the road, damn, it feels good to be home. Only thing better would be having Shelby here with me.

Jigsaw and I said goodbye to Dex and Murphy at Exit 24, promising we'd both fill our presidents in on the visit to Zips. Jigsaw and I continued downstate on our own.

The front door slams open and Z swaggers outside. I stuff my phone back in my pocket. Z greets us with hugs and hearty thumps on the back. "It's not the same around here without you two." He flashes a sincere dimpled grin.

It's nice to be missed and appreciated for a change. Sway always acted like all the brothers hanging around the clubhouse annoyed him and ruined his jolly good time.

I shouldn't compare Z to our old president. They're worlds apart. Sometimes it's hard not to, though.

I set my helmet on the seat of my bike. "I get why you miss *me*, but what's Jiggy add to the atmosphere?"

Jigsaw flips me off and I blow him a kiss.

"How'd it go?" Z asks, ignoring our antics.

"You want me to debrief you now?" I ask, following him inside. "Or at the table?"

He cocks his head and studies me under the clubhouse's new and improved lighting. "Something happen I need to call everyone to the table for?"

"No, nothing like that." I consider the conversation I had with Chaser. "Well, maybe."

"All right, let's chat."

He waves us into the chapel and stretches out in his chair, lacing his hands behind his head. "So?"

Jigsaw adopts a similar pose, adding an eyebrow quirk in my direction. *Dick.*

"I ran into Chaser at Shelby's show."

"Really? Don't picture him being into country music."

The corners of my mouth twitch. "His daughter's a fan of Shelby." Now I've got Z's attention. "No shit?"

"She's also smoking hot," Jigsaw adds. "Just like Mallory."

Z slides his gaze Jigsaw's way. "Please tell me you didn't—"

"No." Jigsaw points at me. "He forbid me from even talking to her."

"Good." Z nods at me. "Continue."

"Brought them backstage to meet Shelby. She and Angelina seemed to get along. I talked to Chaser a bit. All low-key friendly stuff. He invited us to the clubhouse, so we popped in after the show and hung for a while."

Z's eyes widen. "Good."

"He says DeLova's retiring."

"Fuck me. Never thought that day would come."

"No one did. Sounds like he's annoying the shit out of Chaser and Mallory while he's at it."

Z lets out a brief chuckle. "So, he's not upset with us then? For turning down DeLova's work? That didn't have anything to do with him retiring, right?"

"Fuck, never considered that angle. But I don't think so." I shrug. "Chaser's pretty straightforward. If he thought we'd fucked them over, he'd have no problem saying so, and I doubt he would've invited us to their clubhouse."

"True." Z squints and stares up at the ceiling for a few minutes. "Who's taking over for him?"

"Excellent question, Prez." I use my best game-show host voice.

"Chaser? I don't know all the intricacies of DeLova's operation but there has to be some mob stuff his club can't touch."

"Obviously, he didn't share details. He said Mallory's cousin has a piece. Demons have part of it. And..." I pause for effect. "He's offering some of the action to us."

"Fuck. Extortion—no thanks. Guns—Priest will bury all of us. Heroin—same problem."

"They run counterfeit crap from Russia," Jigsaw says. "Especially down in Bright Point. Move that shit right into NYC."

"Well, we don't speak Russian." Z grins. "I bet that piece is going to the cousin anyway."

"Maybe." I sit forward, capturing Z's attention. "Our concern should be whoever takes over for DeLova respects our boundaries and territory."

"That's why I want to make sure we stay friendly with Chaser's crew." Z's gaze shifts to Jigsaw, then me. Technically, we probably should've called Hustler and Steer in for this meeting. "Let's wait and bring this to the table when upstate's here. It's going to fall on both charters."

"Okay."

"Otherwise..." Z runs his hand over his chin and nods thoughtfully. "That's more than I hoped for. Thanks for going the extra mile, with the backstage invite and all. I like that your visit wasn't *all* about business."

"Not a problem."

"Shelby didn't mind?"

Interesting that Z gives a shit what Shelby thinks. Can't imagine many MC presidents showing concern about a female's opinion. But I respect his approach. Too many clubs have been brought down by forgetting or dismissing how important an ol' lady can be to their members' well-being. "Not at all. Like I said, she got along well with

Angelina. Chaser knows the headliner, so they talked a bit. It was all good."

"Shelby do all right at their clubhouse?"

Meaning did she see some deviant shit and pitch a fit. "She was fine."

"It didn't get really wild until after they left," Jigsaw adds.

"You stayed?"

"Dex and I stayed pretty late. Rooster wanted to get his princess a hotel room." He sings out the last part in a high-pitched wail.

I roll my eyes but don't bother responding to the taunt.

Z smirks but doesn't comment. "Moving on. How's our wee little support club?"

"Wee *little* nothing." I snort and sit forward, resting my elbows on the table and lacing my fingers together. "Still feeling them out. This isn't something we should jump into lightly. Oh and Remy offered to help with any of our porn needs."

"Dex shot that down quick," Jigsaw says.

Z rolls his eyes. "He want to star in them or something?"

"No, just meet the talent."

"Yeah, we got plenty of that here. He can fuck off," Z dismisses that easily. "What else?"

"Eraser didn't seem as enthusiastic about the porn but we *did* discuss their money-laundering needs. Griff wants to open an auto body shop or something. Sounds like Murphy's gonna have Teller handle that."

Z chuckles. "Like Teller doesn't have enough to do. That sounds good. You get a read on how they're feeling about the support club?"

I catch Jigsaw's eye and shrug, giving him a chance to jump in if he wants. He answers with a quick headshake.

"Honestly, none of us brought it up directly. It was more like a, 'Hey, how's everything?' kind of visit. Letting Murphy reel 'em in slow with some assistance in their business ventures is a solid play."

"Build that trust and loyalty," Jigsaw agrees.

Z sits up and claps his hands together. "Thank you. That's good."

His gaze lands on the small silver burner phone in the middle of the table and he grits his teeth. "I got another fuckin' call with Priest this afternoon." He flashes a devilish smile. "I'm looking forward to siccing him on Murphy next."

"I'm sure he'll appreciate that, Prez." Guess I better text Murphy later and let him know what's coming his way. VPs gotta look out for each other and all.

Hustler pushes the door open. "Z, you got a minute?"

Z slaps the table and stands. "We good?"

"Yup."

Jigsaw follows them out.

My phone buzzes and I pull it from my pocket. The corners of my mouth automatically curl up when *Chickadee* flashes across the screen.

Almost finished.

Another picture comes through of Shelby. This time she's fully made up in her supermodel persona.

I like the first picture better, but there's no fuckin' way I'd say that to her. Especially—I glance at the clock—an hour before she's going onstage.

Me: You are smoking hot.

Shelby: Where are you?

Me: Clubhouse. Was having a sit-down with Z.

Shelby: Sorry.

Me: Don't be. We're done.

"What're you up to?" Z's voice breaks through my thoughts and I quickly turn off my phone, shoving it in my pocket.

"Nothing. Thought we were finished?"

"Missing Shelby already?"

Busted.

I sit back and tap a finger against my cheek. "Why are you asking?"

He jerks his chin. "The phone you just shoved so far down your pocket I wouldn't be surprised if it landed on the floor." He closes the door behind him while he waits for my answer.

Z's not a soft guy. You can't be soft and run a motorcycle club. I've literally committed murder with this man. More than once. But he's also one of the most involved family men I've known. Has crazy love for his wife and son. Treats the other club kids as if they're his own. Would kill to protect his brothers' old ladies.

Still, it feels weird to get all touchy-feely with my president. "Yeah, I miss her."

"Then why are you here instead of on the road with her?"

I snap my head up. "What are you talking about? I don't have time for that when you're trying to force me into mentoring a bunch of teenyboppers out in the woods and set up porn networks all over the country."

Z snorts. "As if anyone can *force* you to do anything."

"You know what I mean, Prez. Club first." I tap my VP patch. "Still feel like I need to earn this."

"You've more than earned that patch, brother. No doubt. You've been putting the club first more than anyone. Murphy can handle the support club." Z glances around. "Things are calm here. Might as well take advantage of it while it lasts. You should benefit from all your hard work too."

"I'm not the only one working hard. Everyone's finally pulling their weight."

"And again, you're partially responsible for that. So, go spend some time with your girl."

"I made plans to meet up with her in Virginia next week."

A genuine smile curves his mouth up. "Good."

"Plannin' to check in down there. See what I can do to help them out."

"Appreciate that, brother. I'll call Ice after my chat with Priest and let him know you're droppin' in."

"Thanks." I lift an eyebrow. "You mind if I take Jiggy with me?"

"Christ." He laughs. "You gonna subject poor Shelby to more of him?"

"He was actually helpful at her meet and greet. Keeping the pervs away."

His expression darkens. "That a regular problem for her?"

"More often than I think she wants to tell me. She downplays it, like it's part of the job—"

"Fuck that." Z's bloodthirsty nature already extends to Shelby and she's not even officially my ol' lady yet.

"Yeah, my reaction too."

"How many dates is she playing in Virginia?"

I'd only briefly looked at the schedule this morning. "Two, I think."

"Then what?"

"Depends on how much help Ice needs to get his crew set up."

"Go early." He hesitates for a second. "But do me a favor and keep it on the down low." He gestures toward the closed war room door. "I don't need Stella catching wind of this and throwing a tantrum."

"She's smart enough to know if porn's making the club money, we're going to set up more sites."

"Yeah, I wouldn't be so sure about that. To her, it's 'art' and she's going to be offended if you're replicating the same setup with another girl."

"For fuck's sake. She didn't *invent* porn or even the sex-with-strangers reality version she does. People have been doing that shit for eons."

"I'm not disagreeing, I'm just warning you."

"Tell Sway to keep her ass in line, then."

His lips twist with amusement. "I think he's got his hands full."

Sway's recovery from the bullet to the head he took earlier in the year has been going well. Now that I've straightened out the mess he made with the film companies and they're profitable, maybe he should start handling it again.

"I'd like to turn over the maintenance for the sites back to Sway at some point, you know." Preferably before I have to tell Shelby how often my work for the club involves the business end of amateur porn. I had the perfect opportunity when we briefly talked about Crystal Ball, and let it slip away. Shelby won't care. She was pretty chill about the strip club. Porn is almost the same thing, right?

He snorts. "Good luck convincing the rest of the club Sway won't fuck it up again. You're better off grooming Jigsaw to take over or maybe Steer."

"Jiggy *does* have an annoying knack for detail."

"Good, so get him up to speed while you're in Virginia. Show him how to build it from the ground up. Like I said, keep it off Stella's radar."

"I'm not exactly in the habit of updating Stella on my whereabouts, so I don't think it'll be a problem." I'm trying really hard not to judge Z too harshly for ever gettin' involved with her.

"Good." He slaps his hand on the table. "Head down early. It shouldn't take long to scout some locations, set things up, then you're free to continue on to the next date with Shelby until I have another assignment for you."

Z hasn't dealt with the technical side as much as I have or he'd know it's not always that simple.

"Are you encouraging me to *stay* on the road?" As soon as the words are out of my mouth, I'm into the idea. "Don't you need me here at some point?"

"You'll still be helping out. Besides," he shrugs, "some things are more important."

CHAPTER THIRTY-FIVE

Rooster

A few days later, Jigsaw and I roll into the parking lot of our Virginia charter.

"*Fuuuck*." Jigsaw groans and stretches as he slips off his helmet. The last leg of our trip had been rough.

"Still happy you joined me?"

"Fuck, yeah. Just felt every fuckin' bump and pothole ripple up my spine the last few miles."

"You might wanna check the air pressure on those shocks."

"No shit, genius."

"Told you before we left switching them out for the progressive shocks would've been better."

He rubs the back of his neck and sneaks a glance at the clubhouse. "You know what will help even more?"

"Let me guess. Asking the first random girl you see inside those doors to rub you all over."

He points to his forehead and then mine. "It's like you can read my mind, brother."

"Yeah, because you're pathetically transparent."

"What'd I tell you about gettin' smug with me?"

I scratch my beard and pretend to think it over. "Is it smugness if I'm just pointing out that you're a degenerate?"

"Rooster! Jigsaw!" T-Bone's booming voice bounces over the parking lot, interrupting our post-ride conversation.

"What's up, brother?" Jigsaw calls out.

"Long time, dickheads."

"I can go right back home if you're planning to bust my balls all night." I take his outstretched hand, yank him close and slap his back a few times. "How you been, brother?"

"Can't complain." He lifts his chin at Jigsaw. "How you been, ya scary fuck?"

"Life's good." Jigsaw knocks knuckles with T-Bone. "Nice ride down. Hot as fuck here, though."

"This is nothing, you whiner." T-Bone waves at us to follow him into the clubhouse. Place looks like a big, rustic cabin. It's nestled deep in the woods sort of the way upstate's clubhouse is but not as hard to find.

For a Thursday afternoon, it's tame inside—but not *so* quiet that a pretty dark-skinned girl doesn't immediately attract Jigsaw's roving eye.

"Focus," I growl at him.

"But—"

T-Bone, of course, waves her over. "This is Shonda. Anything you need around the clubhouse, she's your girl. Shonda, these are our brothers visiting from New York."

Jigsaw might as well be Roger Rabbit with his lust-crazed eyes popping out of his head.

He rubs his hand over the back of his neck. "Hurtin' bad after a bit of rough road. You think—"

"I'll take care of you," she coos. She lifts one perfectly sculpted eyebrow at me. "How about you?"

Jigsaw slaps my shoulder, drawing her attention back to him. "Don't worry about my brother here. Rooster's girlfriend took his balls with her on tour, so he won't be needing any comfort during our visit."

T-Bone busts up laughing. Jigsaw grins like a puppy looking for a reward for peeing outside.

Poor Shonda glances at the door leading upstairs, like she's rethinking her offer to give Jiggy a rubdown. Can't blame the girl, really.

"I'm fine, sweetheart," I assure her. I reach over and slap Jigsaw hard enough to push him forward. "This one's laid his bike down one too many times. On his head. So, be gentle with him."

"Rooster! Jigsaw!" Ice shouts, jogging down the stairs. "Hey, honey." He kisses Shonda's cheek before sending her away.

"Welcome, home, brothers." We go through another round of hugs and handshakes with the president of our Port Everhart, VA charter.

"Thanks for letting us drop in."

"You're always welcome here." Ice scratches his chin and rocks back on his heels. "Z said you'd be able to help us set up a site for one of my girls. Maybe create a membership-based service to distribute films we're producing. Think you're up for it?"

"Yup. We have several sites and I'm running all of them at the moment. One's more successful than the others, but she had a huge following to begin with. Sway bankrolled her project and it kind of snowballed from there," I say with complete confidence.

"Good. Let me show you one of the areas we might use," Ice offers. "Then we'll visit the house we're setting up."

Damn, sounds like Ice has this thought out a hell of a lot better than we did.

"Joke's on you, by the way," Jigsaw whispers as we follow Ice and T-Bone over gray tile floors into a narrow, stark-white hallway. "Now she'll want to tend to my boo-boos even more after you basically told her I'm brain-damaged."

"You're here to listen and learn," I growl.

The sooner I turn over the porn production to Jiggy, the better. His obsession with female anatomy makes him perfect for the job.

"So you're all wifed up now, Rooster?" T-Bone asks.

"I've got a girl," I answer carefully.

"She's actually pretty cool," Jigsaw says. "Don't know what she sees in Rooster, though."

Ice glances over his shoulder. "You patch her yet?"

Why does everyone keep asking me about patching Shelby? "Not yet."

"Keep an eye on her if you bring her by," he warns.

Great.

I hadn't decided if I was going to even bring Shelby here. Yeah, it's another Lost Kings MC charter, but I haven't visited enough lately to know if it's somewhere I'm comfortable taking Shelby. Especially when our time together is so fleeting.

We step through a wide open door and Ice flips on a light. We're standing in a cool, mostly empty cement basement that resembles something out of a *Saw* movie more than a biker clubhouse.

"Z said you're good at setting stuff up?"

"Depends what we're talking about."

Ice hooks his thumbs in his pockets and turns to face us. "Already got the talent."

I bet you do. "That's the hardest part."

"Anya's my star. She's accumulated a huge fanbase in a short amount of time."

"Even better."

"She hot?" Jigsaw asks.

T-Bone side-eyes him. "Here I thought Rooster was joking about you taking some knocks to the head."

I cover up my laugh with a cough.

"Anyway," Ice says, giving Jiggy a final warning scowl, "she's been camming for a while but wants to focus on film."

"Smart move," I answer. "Camming's a lot of work. If she starts creating content instead, she can spend a day or two filming, then have a finished product to sell forever."

"Right." Ice waves his hand in the air. "I don't care about the details. I just want her safe, happy, and making bank."

T-Bone glances down at his boots and chuckles.

"So you have female talent covered." I'd really rather not know the details about Ice's relationship with his "*talent.*" "What about male performers?"

Both of them sort of gag as if I'd asked *them* to fuck random dudes. Working hard to control my eye roll, I elaborate, "Our star was in the industry before so she already had access to talent. Then she does this other thing where she takes applications from her audience."

"Yeah, I don't want Anya doing *that*," Ice says quickly.

"She can work it out later." For fuck's sake, I'm sorry I even mentioned it. Unless he's planning for her to only film solo stuff, logic dictates dudes are an obvious ingredient. *Whatever.*

I move on to some other ideas. "Custom stuff will sell big. Customers get off on thinking they're the director. She can also do some content trade with other performers."

As much as Z wants me to leave Stella out of this, her numbers were down last month. Nothing alarming, but some exclusive scenes from a newcomer might help boost interest. If they partner up, it could benefit both girls and both charters in the long run.

"We can build her own website where she controls everything, or upload to a platform that will store and deliver for you. Those places usually take a hefty commission, but it can be worth it for the traffic they generate."

"Let's keep it in-house."

"All right. I'll still get her set up on a few platforms. She can post short clips there and direct them to her site where they can pay for the full ones."

"Yeah, I like that idea."

"Having your own location simplifies things. No reason to get permits to film, but she's going to have to keep some records of anyone she shoots with." Outlaws aren't so fond of paper trails. While this whole operation's quasi-legit at best, that's a basic requirement that needs to be addressed whether Ice likes it or not. Again, it was simpler setting up this stuff with Stella because she'd already been in the business for years.

"Yeah, that'll be my job too." T-Bone raises his hand slightly.

Ice glances over his shoulder. "This is one space we're considering using. Like, some fetish, dungeon shit." He shrugs. "But I've got a rental house not too far from here. Anya's working on decorating 'theme' rooms."

Meaning she's out shopping with the prez's credit card.

Cool.

Any second, my eyes are gonna roll right the fuck out of my head.

"Great. If she can make it look like she's mixing up locations without having to spend a lot on travel and renting space, even better. We can also generate income with advertising and sponsorships."

"Whatever brings in some cash to replace what we've lost recently."

That's almost a golden opportunity for me to probe into what sort of direction he's getting pushed in by our national president.

Ice crosses his arms over his chest. "Gettin' real sick of Priest breathing down my neck."

Gee, I didn't even have to ask.

He and T-Bone share a look. "We had an issue with Vipers trying to expand into our territory."

"Surprised they'd mess with us down here when we *helped* them move out of New York," I say.

T-Bone shrugs. "They've never been the brightest."

"We had an understanding with them for years." Ice's cold, hollow voice would probably send a shiver down the spine of anyone else. "Then they burned one of our tattoo parlors down."

"Arson seems to be a theme with them," Jigsaw says.

Ice nods. "Right. Forgot about Furious. Wrath's rebuilt the place, though, right?"

"Fuck yeah," I answer. "Bigger than before but it took a while."

"Yeah, I'm still sorting through fucking ashes. We *handled* the Vipers, but the attention brought ATF sniffing around."

"Fuck."

"We *fixed* that issue," Ice adds with a maniacal smile.

Lord, that's not a confession I want to hear.

"Priest's aware," Ice assures me, reading my don't-make-me-an-accessory-to-murder-after-the-fact expression correctly. "The problem's been solved."

Jiggy better not decide now would be an optimal time to crack a joke.

"That's good." I take a second look at the basement. It's probably stored a body or two. Bet they've used it to store guns at some point too.

"Let's just say that soon, ATF will be busy focusing elsewhere and we'll be free to handle whatever action we want, and Priest can't say shit about it."

Bad sign.

"You *want* back into guns?" I ask against my better judgment.

"I don't *like* Priest telling us what we can and can't do. Doesn't that bug you?"

Yeah, but I'm also not eager to sign up for an extended prison stay, which running guns will bring us eventually.

"Doesn't matter." He shrugs. "We've taken care of it."

Uh, can we dig into that?

"Come on." Ice slaps my shoulder and turns me toward the door. "I'll take you to the house and show you around."

Can't wait. "I'll start making up a list of the equipment we need."

"Corporate names have all been filed. Bank accounts opened. Domain names registered. I'll get you that info so you can order whatever you need."

"Perfect."

We follow Ice down the hallway. I yank Jigsaw closer. "Pay attention, brother."

"Wouldn't miss a minute."

"Asshole," I growl under my breath.

The main area's filling up with more people. Mostly girls. T-Bone gestures to a cluster of women sitting on top of the bar. "We have our choice of talent right there. Every night of the week, brother."

"Yeah?" I sweep my gaze over the group. "Every one of them cool with filming themselves and throwing it out there for the world to see?"

"You'd be surprised." Ice flicks his presidential glare T-Bone's way. "We're trying to run this thing as professionally as possible. Signed contracts, profit splits. I want everything spelled out. No wiggle room."

Smart man. "That's probably for the best."

Priest sure as fuck won't be happy if they go from ATF watchlist to getting sued by random club girls who catch a case of porn star's remorse after their parents find their biker bangfest online. A story that salacious might actually bring *more* than the prying eyes of ATF.

CHAPTER THIRTY-SIX

Rooster

The rental house Ice takes us to is nothing remarkable. There's no neon sign outside announcing it's about to be turned into a den of sin. Four bikers tearing through the quiet, suburban neighborhood probably isn't appreciated, though.

Ice pulls into a long, wide, freshly blacktopped driveway and shuts down his bike. The rest of us pull up next to him in a neat line. I survey the area—large yard, lots of space between the house and the nearest neighbor. Good signs.

How long's Ice been planning this porn paradise? Or did he buy the place for some other reason?

The answers don't matter and have nothing to do with why I'm here. *Help the club set up their new business.* That's all I need to do. The rest isn't my concern.

"Nice area," I say to Ice when he approaches. "Neighbors aren't too close. Should cut down on noise pollution and any complaints."

He glances around at the manicured lawns and perfectly planted shrubbery. "That's the idea."

He pulls out a key and leads us in through a side door. "Anya's not here right now, but she's been working on each room."

Kitchen—complete with counters at a fuckable height. Table and chairs—sturdy. Laundry. A room in the back set up like an office, with an ornate desk, high-backed leather chair, and built-in bookcases. Plenty of office "romance" potential. I flick a few switches. Decent overhead lighting.

"Bar stools for anal scenes," T-Bone points out as we return to the kitchen. "Adjustable height."

I flick my gaze to the ceiling. "Classy."

He smirks and hurries to catch up with Ice.

Jigsaw shakes with laughter and gives one of the stools a spin.

I elbow him and we find our way into the living area.

T-Bone spreads his arms wide. "Orgy room."

Jiggy studies the low, flat L-shaped sectional. "Looks like a giant bed."

"That's the idea."

Upstairs is more of the same. Three bedrooms and even the bathroom staged with filming in mind. A pink, frilly room with a double bed covered in stuffed animals—which is honestly more creepy than anything. One room with two twin beds and a desk, which I suppose resembles a college dorm.

The last bedroom on the right has a more lived-in feel. It's decorated in white, peach, and soft tan colors. A leather jacket tossed over the back of a chair. An ornate vanity overflowing with cosmetics. Closet doors open wide, with clothes, purses, and shoes spilling into the room.

"Does she live here too?" I ask.

"Most of the time," Ice answers evasively.

The room across from that one is the largest and still empty. "Not sure what she has planned in here," Ice says.

I check out the wide, bay windows. Probably has good sunlight early in the morning.

"Well, what do you think?" Ice asks.

"You're further along than I expected. Place looks great, honestly. She has a good eye for detail." I glance at the windows again. "You're going to need more lighting throughout the house. Really blow out each location you're going to film in with light."

"You mean install them or buy lamps?" he asks.

"Lot of low-budget sets are using LED panels. They're pretty reliable. This is a big place. She'll need a lot of them, unless you're going to be hauling them from location to location."

Ice shrugs. "Whatever she needs."

"Who's actually doing the filming? Directing?"

His expression remains blank. "She is."

Man, he has a lot of faith in this chick. Spending an awful lot of cash for what amounts to an amateur production.

Downstairs, a door slams. "Ice, is that you?" a woman calls out.

"Upstairs." He motions for us to follow him the way we came.

We find the star of this escapade waiting in the kitchen.

Anya's about what I expected—young, tall, skinny, long blonde hair, big tits, giant name-brand purse on her shoulder, and a tiny dog tucked under her arm.

She flashes a quick warm smile at all four of us that makes me feel a little shitty for my snap judgment.

"How'd you do?" Ice asks, leaning down to kiss her cheek.

She bends over to set the dog down, giving the four of us a clear view down her shirt. "Good. The stuff for the big bedroom should be here Friday."

The little dog runs over and scratches at my boot.

"Aw, he likes you," Jigsaw says.

"He likes everyone." She drops her purse on the counter and flicks her questioning gaze between Jigsaw and me. Sure enough, the dog scampers over and scratches at Jigsaw's leg next.

"Babe, this is Rooster. He's gonna help you set up some of the technical side this week." Ice leers at her and tucks her hair behind her ear. "Whatever he needs, you give it to him, got it?"

Uh, make it sound like I expect to be paid in blow jobs, much, Ice?

"Jigsaw's here to help out too." Ice lightly punches Jiggy's shoulder. "I promise he's not as scary as he looks."

She flashes another genuine smile. "You don't look scary at all."

Jigsaw's lips quirk. Great, he's already smitten for the second time in two hours.

God help me.

She focuses on me again. "You're the one who's worked with Stella, right?"

"My club has."

"I like her style. I'm trying to create a similar feel without traveling to different hotels and stuff."

"What you have here looks great." I nod to Ice. "Location's one of the hardest parts. Not a lot of places to film outside of Florida, Las Vegas, or LA. And even then, people aren't always open to having a film crew defile their house. Having your own space is smart."

Ice snorts. "Figured it'll be less trouble than renting out the house to deadbeat tenants."

Sure, hire someone to clean the jizz off the walls once a week and you're all set, Prez.

"I've been working on promotion." She taps her phone. "I'm up to over five hundred thousand Instagram followers."

Not bad for a chick I've never even heard of. Too bad only a small percentage of those followers will be willing to pay actual money for content. Even so, it's a damn good start.

"I have a few things in the works." She taps Ice's chest and purses her lips into a pouty little smile.

I'm sure you do.

HOURS LATER, I'M TUCKED AWAY IN ICE'S OFFICE AT THE BACK OF the clubhouse. I finish placing orders for some of the supplies I need. Tomorrow, I'll set up accounts on the different platforms we'll use to upload the videos.

For now, I'm done.

I log off of Ice's computer and shut it down, tucking the business credit card he'd handed me back into the desk drawer and locking it.

In the main room, music's pumping. Brothers and club girls fill the place, engaged in various activities.

That whole ATF thing Ice mentioned before our trip to the porn palace is still nagging at me. At some point, I need to discuss it with Jigsaw, see if it gave him the same bad feeling.

I jog upstairs to the room I'm using at the clubhouse and pull Shelby's schedule out from my pocket. I'd been so focused on Virginia because of our charter here that I missed a closer location.

Baltimore.

A few days apart and I'm missing Shelby more than ever. While there's plenty to keep me occupied around here, I should be able to slip away for a day.

CHAPTER THIRTY-SEVEN

Shelby

Sweat rolls down my forehead and into my eyes as I finish soundcheck. Another outdoor, open-air pavilion. The sound's better than the last two places but the air-conditioning is non-existent. Can't seem to go anywhere to get relief.

The solid *click-thump* of my boots accompanies me off the stage.

"You all right, Shelby?" Greg's hand settles on my shoulder, stopping me in the hallway. "You look pale."

"I'm hot."

"I'll see if I can find a fan or something for your room." He jerks his head toward the stage. "There's a bit of a breeze out front. Why don't you stand up there for a minute or two and cool off?"

"All right." I push past a few people. The scent of fried dough hangs in the air. My stomach growls. When was the last time I ate? Maybe that's why I'm feeling all sweaty and shaky.

"Miss Shelby? Can I have your autograph please?"

I glance up, seeking the source of the question. A man, probably older than Dawson, on the other side of the waist-high fence thrusts a black marker at me. Something about him seems familiar and I squint, studying him for a second. Tall, round in the middle, graying hair, black polo shirt tucked into neat khaki pants. Brown plush bunny backpack hanging off his shoulder.

Okay, that's weird. Unless it belongs to his kid. My gaze searches the area behind him. Families, kids, adults, and teenagers. This tour draws fans of all ages.

"Shelby?" he prompts, waving the marker at me again.

"Oh, sorry." I work some extra Southern charm into my voice. I fan my hand close to my face. "The heat's gettin' to me today."

"We can't have that. You're going onstage in a couple hours." He pulls the plush bunny backpack off his shoulder and unzips it. "Here, take this." He hands me a miniature, battery-operated neon-green fan.

"Oh! I can't take that from you. You're gonna need it."

"I have another one." He thrusts it into my hands. "Go on. Take it."

Easy, Mr. Pushy. I accept it, flicking on the switch and holding it close to my face and then lift my hair and run it over my sweaty neck.

"Better?"

It's a drop in the bucket but I don't want to be rude to this stranger who's been nothin' but nice. Even if he is a bit odd. "Much. Thank you." I flick the switch off and hold the fan to him. "Are you sure you don't need it?"

"Nope." He pulls a pink T-shirt out of the bunny backpack and pushes it at me. "Would you mind signing this?"

Must be for his daughter. "Sure. Back or front?"

"Anywhere that makes you happy, Shelby."

My mouth twitches into a half-hearted smile as I search for a way to smooth the material out enough to sign it without making a mess.

"Here." He turns around and points to his back. "Use me."

"Uh." His dark shirt's stained with sweat. Not exactly the most appealing surface. *Suck it up and get it over with. He's a fan. Don't be rude.* "Thanks." I press the shirt against his back, trying to ignore the moist sensation soaking into the edge of my hand and arm as I quickly scrawl my signature.

"Thank you." He faces me and takes the shirt from my hands. "I can't believe I got you alone and all to myself."

Yeah, me either. Sure, people are everywhere but no one's *with* me or even paying attention to what I'm doing.

"Do you mind taking a selfie with me?" He waves his phone at me. "Oh. Sure.."

I turn and try not to cringe when he drops his arm across my shoulders. Thank the lord for the fence keeping us somewhat apart.

"Smile." He sticks his arm out and struggles to get both of us in the frame and take the picture.

My smile's so big and fake, it probably looks like someone propped my mouth open with a toothpick.

He digs his fingers into my shoulder. "Let's try that again. Nice smile, Shelby."

This is ridiculous.

Finally, he seems satisfied and tucks his phone into his bunny backpack. "That was nice. Can I cook you dinner?"

"Shelby!" Trent shouts before I have a chance to process the question. I turn and find him jogging up to me. "What are you doing?" He glances at the guy. "Greg found a fan for you. Come on."

I hand the marker back to the man. "So nice meeting you. Enjoy the show!" I hold up the little fan. "Thank you so much for this."

"Wait! Trent, would you sign this for me too?" the man asks.

Trent hesitates for a second. He doesn't get asked to sign stuff often. "Sure, man. Then I really need to get her backstage."

My phone buzzes in my pocket and I yank it free.

Rooster: How'd rehearsal go?

"Shelby?" the man's voice interrupts and I shove my phone back into my pocket.

Trent takes my hand, cutting the man off. "We need to go. Nice to meet ya. Enjoy the show." He tugs me away without another word.

I wave over my shoulder and breathe out a sigh of relief. Once we're backstage, Trent pushes me in front of him as we navigate our way to my dressing room. "What the heck's wrong with you?" he seethes. "Don't go runnin' off talking to weirdos like that."

"He's a fan." I elbow him. "I didn't want to be rude."

"Sometimes it's okay to be rude, Shelby." He grabs the fan out of my hand. "He give this to you? Shoot, dude probably wiped his balls all over it. Or dosed it with something." He swipes his shirt over every inch of the little plastic fan.

"Eww, don't be gross." I snatch it back.

He pushes the door to the green room open. Greg found a jet engine of an industrial fan that's louder than it is cooling. All it's doing is blowing dust around the room. I reach up and flick it off.

My body shakes with a violent sneeze.

"You all right?" Trent asks, resting a hand on my back. "You're not gettin' sick are you?"

"Hush your mouth," I scold. That's my worst damn nightmare. No time for colds on this tour. "It's the fan. You know I'm allergic to dust and a million other things." I twirl my finger in the air. "The fan stirred up a lot of crap."

"Shit. Sorry." He steers me toward the makeup chair. "Go sit. I'll look for some tissues. Cindy should be here soon."

"Thanks." I reach out and grab his hand. "I mean it. Thanks for coming to look for me too."

"You're the star."

It sounds hollow. Or maybe I'm feelin' guilty. I stare at the closed door for a few seconds after Trent leaves.

My phone buzzes and my heart gallops off to the races.

Rooster.

"Hey," I answer.

"How's it going?"

"All right."

"What's wrong? You sound sad."

The immediate concern in his voice melts me. "It's hot as blazes here."

"What happened to the sassy Texan girl who said us Northerners didn't know the meaning of hot?" he teases.

I groan-laugh into the phone. "I stand corrected."

"What else is going on?"

I don't want to tell him I went off by myself and encountered an oddball fan, or that Trent found and scolded me. Nope. Because from the second I heard Logan's smooth voice, only one thing has been on my mind. "Just missing you."

"Yeah? Been thinking about you all day, chickadee."

"You were?"

"Yup. Not sure how I missed it before, but I saw you have a show in Baltimore. I'm only four hours from there."

My heart stutters. Baltimore's three days away. Not the ten I thought I'd have to wait to see him again.

"Shelby? You still there?"

"I'm here."

"You all right with me coming to see you sooner than we said?" A bit of worry creeps into his tone.

Pull it together and let him know how much you want to see him. "Yes," I yelp.

His warm, rich laughter floats through the phone and wraps tight around my heart. "Good."

Be brave. "I miss you."

"Miss you too."

"I mean it." *Say it. Stop being so damn scared of gettin' hurt.* "The only thing that stopped me from bawling my eyes out when I left you in New York was knowing I'd see you in Virginia. So if I can see you even sooner . . ."

"Shelby," he breathes out.

"Is that okay?"

"That's more than okay."

"Good." I move away from the makeup chair and plop down on the couch, tucking my feet under me. "What've you been up to?"

"Helping the president get a project off the ground."

"Anything exciting?"

Silence. I pull the phone away from my ear to check if I lost the call. "Rooster?"

"Nothing exciting to me."

What's that mean? Maybe club stuff I'm not supposed to ask about? "How's Jigsaw? He rode down with you, right?"

"More helpful than I expected." He chuckles. "I'll let him know you asked."

"Sounds like you're busy. Sure you can come up to Baltimore?"

"To see my girl? Fuck yeah, I can."

253

"I can't wait." My breath hitches and another violent sneeze shakes me out of my seat. "Dammit."

"You okay?"

"Yeah, it's dusty, and it stirred up my allergies."

"You gonna be all right to sing?"

"I think so." Someone knocks and the door swings open. Cindy waves and rolls her case inside. "Cindy's here."

"Send me a picture later."

"I will."

There's a beat of silence.

"Talk to you soon."

I open my mouth. An *I love you* almost rolls off my tongue.

Lucky for me, the call already ended.

CHAPTER THIRTY-EIGHT

Rooster

One little sneeze and I'm ready to dump everything and ride to Michigan to see my girl.

Shelby's been on tour for months. She's more than capable of taking care of herself. But I can't help the instinct. Really glad she sounded excited about me coming to visit in a couple days.

My phone pings. Expecting a picture from Shelby, I flick the screen on.

Z: How's it going?

Me: Good. Few things we should discuss.

Z: ???

Me: Not sure yet.

Z: Keep me updated.

I send him a thumbs-up emoji and flick my screen off.

It's time to kick back and hang out with brothers I haven't seen since our national conference. See who's feeling chatty once half the club's drunk and scattered around away from the watchful eye of their president.

I pound downstairs, passing club girls and brothers in the narrow hallway. Give out a few nods hello and quick handshakes. Living room's full but I find a free spot and tuck myself into a corner of one of the couches where I have a decent view of most of the room.

One of the girls hurries over and drops a bottle of beer on the table in front of me without asking or offering anything else. Doesn't really matter. I'm not feeling picky tonight. "Thanks, hon."

Jigsaw throws himself down next to me. For the moment, we're alone. He leans in, digging his elbow into my side. "You get that bit about ATF?" he says against my ear. "Earlier?"

Aw, my boy's growing up. Figured after the porn overload, he would've forgotten all about the earlier, more important conversation.

"I caught it." I gesture to the room in front of us. "Let's see if someone's tongue loosens up as the night goes on."

We shouldn't outright *ask* but one of our brothers is bound to get sloppy eventually.

"How about that porn house?" he asks. "Think Sway shouldn've gone that route with Stella, instead of all the hotels?"

I take a sip of beer. "The only thinking Sway put into it was with his dick."

"True story."

"But the house is a good idea. A lot less risk. We should let Stella do her thing however she wants. But for the new girls, we should consider a house."

"Teller will probably say, 'Real estate is always a wise investment,'" he says, imitating our upstate treasurer's cocky advice-giving voice perfectly.

"House of the same size will cost a fortune in Union county."

"Could always look out near Johnsonville."

I side eye-him. "And what? Let the support club kids run it? You saw the attitude Eraser had. Besides, good luck getting any of the girls to spend time there. It's so far out in the middle of nowhere."

He shrugs. "Fuck that. They go where we tell 'em to go or they're free to find someone else to finance them."

"Good point." Except, it pays to keep the talent happy. He'll learn. "By all means, say that to Stella and let me know how it works out for you."

"She's got attitude because she's so wrapped around Sway's dick."

"I think you have that backwards."

He scratches the side of his head. "Never mind. You know what I mean."

A mountain of a man everyone calls Pants lumbers over and drops into a chair across from us. "Been a minute, Rooster." The SAA for this charter reaches out his hand and we shake.

"Good to see you, brother."

"How ya been, Pants?" Jigsaw salutes.

"Can't complain." Pants lifts his chin at me. "You helping with the porn palace?" Judging by his mocking tone, I'm guessing he's not a fan of his club's new business venture.

"Doing what I can."

He half stands and pulls his chair closer. "Ice tell you he's got hidden cameras all over that place?"

"I thought that was the point?"

"No, so *we* can keep tabs on *her*. Make sure she's not fucking over the club."

"I think she's fucking *for* the club," Jigsaw quips.

Pants chuckles. "True."

Shonda wiggles by in a short red dress on the arm of a local brother. Jigsaw's sad puppy eyes follow them to the bar.

"Easy come, easy go, brother." I slap his leg.

"Yeah, except I didn't get to come *or* go yet."

"You got a thing for Shonda?" Pants grins and throws his arm wide. "We got a club full of bunnies, brother. Take your pick."

"Yeah, but she's..." He turns, searching the room for a second. "Got those nice wide hips and ass." He curls his fingers in the air like he's gripping, well, a pair of wide hips. "What's with all the bony bitches, bro?"

I hang my head. "Jesus Christ."

"What?" Jiggy leans over and punches my arm. "You like 'em thick too, so shut your mouth."

Pants roars with laughter. "Bony girls need lovin' too. Give it time, though. It's still early."

Jigsaw elbows me and I'm seriously reconsidering my earlier

thoughts about his helpfulness. "Why couldn't your girl be out on tour with some chick bands instead of that sausage fest?"

"What does that have to do with anything?"

"Then I wouldn't be so desperate."

"You're *always* desperate."

Pants cracks up and slams one of his meaty paws on the low table in front of us. "Fuck, I've missed you two."

"Well, why don't you get your big ass up to New York and visit more?"

The smile slides off his face. "How are you handling things since Z staged his coup?"

"Z didn't stage a fucking coup," I reply. Shit, Z was right. Good thing he didn't come with us.

"No?" He raises an eyebrow. "You were all cool with him coming in and taking over?"

"He didn't 'come in and take over.' He busted his ass to prove himself and win our trust," I answer with a tad more hostility than appropriate.

"Sway trust him too?"

Fuck Sway.

"Look, I got mad respect for Sway." *Lie.* "But he was getting sloppy and it was causing issues." *Truth.* "And that's not me talking shit behind his back. I've said that straight to his face." *Also true.*

"A-fucking-men." Jigsaw raises his palms toward the ceiling. "Preach it, brother."

Pants stares at Jiggy. "Whole club feels that way?"

"Fuck yeah." Jigsaw glances at me. "The two brothers who didn't, left."

Left is a bit of a stretch. Shadow's in the ground and Smoke hightailed it down to Florida to cause trouble with the other retired Lost Kings.

"Yeah." Pants rubs his hand over his jaw. "Heard something about Shadow going nomad. He always was a dick, though."

If you only knew how much of an asshole he really was.

"Tawny's the one who took it the hardest." I smirk, sidestepping getting into details about Shadow's whereabouts.

Pants bursts into laughter, slapping his hand on his thigh. "Yeah, I'm sure the queen bee was all sorts of pissed. Fuck her."

"Far as I know, Sway supports Z one hundred percent," I add. This rumor that Z took over our charter needs to fucking die here and now.

Pants shrugs. "Guess if he didn't, he would've taken off to Florida with Smoke."

"Right." I sit back, resting one ankle across my knee.

Now that Pants seems to trust us a little more, he loosens up. I sip my beer slowly while he pounds down shot after shot.

Jigsaw's shot glass remains untouched.

"What else is lucrative these days?" I flick a dismissive glance to the ceiling. "Besides the porn."

He pushes his mop of blond hair back and flashes a maniacal grin. "Hog farming."

"Come again?"

Clearly excited about this topic, he sits forward. "Organic, pasture-raised piggies fetch a fortune. Hippies love that shit and will pay top dollar for it."

Hog farming? Is that a euphemism for something else?

"Plus, hogs will eat *anything*. Makes disposal of *certain* items much easier."

Ahhh, figures their SAA would come up with a creative way to dispose of bodies.

"I should have Teller come down and talk to you about it. He's started raising chickens in his backyard."

"Fuck, yeah. Anytime. Chickens are a gateway drug. Tell him pork is where the real money is made." He rubs his fingers together in the universal cash-is-king sign.

"Porn and pigs. Sounds like appropriate MC money earners," Jigsaw deadpans.

"Right?" Pants slaps his leg. "People gotta eat and jerk-off. We're meeting basic human needs."

Jigsaw slides a look my way. "Can't deny that."

"Opened a second tattoo parlor too." Pants shoves his sleeve up over his shoulder, showing off an impressive swath of blackwork-style graphic art with pops of blues and greens.

"Damn. How long'd that take?"

"Couple sessions." He smooths his shirt into place. "So fucking busy, they're booking eight months out."

"That's good." I scratch my beard. "This new shop replace the one Vipers—"

His stone-cold killer expression returns. "Ice told you about that?"

"He mentioned it."

He leans in closer and grins. Somehow his smile is scarier than any other expression that's flickered over his face. I've never doubted the story that he got his road name by making a guy piss his pants with just a look. "We have someone on the inside at the ATF now. So it worked out in the end."

I struggle to keep my face impassive. "He mentioned something about having them under control."

"Fuckin' A." He sits back. "Moving a few people into strategic places."

A *few*.

"You sure you can trust 'em? Anyone working in that environment day after day eventually might be compromised."

"Ice has insurance."

Blackmail—yippie.

"And the other's a blood relation."

"No one can fuck you over more than blood," Jigsaw points out.

"Truth." Pants raises his shot glass. "But in this case, we're confident."

"That's good, brother. Sounds like it will benefit the whole organization."

"Absolutely." He reaches over and slaps my boot. "Virginia's always looking out for you."

While Lost Kings has a decent presence across the US, we're certainly not the largest outlaw club. Known for ruthlessly defending our territory *and* respecting the territory of other clubs, only the stupid or baby outlaw clubs ever attempt to fuck with us. Those challenges have always been dealt with swiftly and harshly.

"That's good, brother," Jigsaw says. "LOKI East Coast needs to stick together."

"Amen!" Pants raises his shot glass, sloshing brown liquid all over his hand.

Until more recently, our two New York charters have kept to themselves and weren't real plugged in to what everyone else in the LOKI network was up to. Kicking up our percentage to National, sure. No one escapes that obligation. Keeping tabs on who's getting raided and arrested is just common sense. Hell, until Sway's shooting, the two New York clubs operated extremely independently of each other, so we sure as fuck weren't sticking our noses in the business of charters outside our state.

Maybe we should have.

One thing Rock's done that's benefitted both NY clubs is cultivate alliances within New York State. No one ever talks about it, but we all know he's well-connected to important people. Something he never abuses, which is probably why, with the exception of a few incidents, we've operated undisturbed.

We've never had clout at the federal level. Everyone's heard the rumors that larger clubs have infiltrated all sorts of important places and now it sounds as if our Virginia charter has found a way in too.

I can't decide if that's reason to celebrate or piss *my* pants.

CHAPTER THIRTY-NINE

Rooster

"What. The. Fuck?" Jigsaw whispers as he closes my bedroom door behind us.

I press a finger against my lips. The way Pants oh-so casually mentioned the hidden cameras at the porno palace has me wondering if the clubhouse is rigged up too.

Sure enough, after a quick search, I find a camera pointed at the bed.

Classy.

To be fair, I'd have to be an idiot *not* to see it, but still.

Shutting it off will only raise Ice's suspicions. He'll either think Jiggy and I want some *alone* time or that we're in here conspiring against him. Neither are real helpful.

"You want to ride down to the store with me?" I ask, tilting my head toward the camera.

"No, I want to get my dick sucked. You offering?"

"Not if you were on your deathbed, brother."

He lets out a big, dramatic sigh. "Yeah, I'll go with you, ya big, needy bastard."

We move through the clubhouse slowly, invite a few brothers to come along with us. Everyone's shitfaced so no one bites but at least we've made the offer.

Outside, we're quiet. We nod hello to a few people hanging around the parking lot. Thank the prospects for looking after our bikes. Then get the fuck out of there.

Jigsaw follows me down the mountain road into town. We pass a few other bikes. Probably headed toward the clubhouse. Flash a two-fingered hello at each one. A cloud of paranoia clings to me as we escape the clubhouse.

Finally we reach the closest town. I pull into the only place open at this hour, a small gas station. No doubt Ice has his hooks in everything around here, so I search for a spot away from prying eyes and big ears.

My gaze lands on an ancient playground across the street. Large, swaying willow trees provide privacy.

"Want me to push ya on the swings, big buddy?" Jigsaw asks as he follows me.

"Sure, then I'll spin you on the merry-go-round, dick."

Except for a few empty brown bags fluttering over the grass, the park is clear. I stop and peer up at the large metal frame of the industrial-size swing set. The contraption lets out a long metallic groan as I throw myself into one of the soft, black seats.

"Aw, it's like the day we met all over again." Jigsaw squeezes himself into the swing next to me, digging his boots into the dirt and launching himself sideways. "You feeling nostalgic?"

"You want me to break your arm so we can find out?"

He stares at his right hand. "No, I'm good."

"What the fuck did we step into here?" I ask.

"I don't fuckin' know. But I'm thoroughly creeped the fuck out that he has cameras in the bedrooms. That seems like very un-bro-code behavior."

I snort. "We're way past worrying about bro code. You hear what Pants said?"

"Uh, that Ice is probably blackmailing some government officials? Yeah, got that."

"That ain't gonna end well."

"No shit." He twists the swing around and lets it spin him a few times. "Who do you think the blood is?"

"Could be anyone. I don't know a lot about Ice's family."

"Think Z does?"

"Texted him earlier. But fuck, I can't call him with this. I gotta tell him face-to-face."

Jigsaw shivers. "Christ, better not piss off Ice. He'll have fuckin' Pants feed us to his hogs."

"Guessing that's where those Vipers ended up. Maybe an ATF agent or two?"

He's quiet for a few blessed seconds. "Not a whole lot we can do if Ice has already set it into motion. At least, until the warrants for all our arrests start coming when the mole gets caught and the government wants to set an example."

The hairs on my arms prickle and stand up. Jigsaw nailed every one of my concerns in a few sentences.

He grunts and stays silent for a few seconds. "I get why you didn't want to turn the camera off with *me* in your room, but I think Ice will understand why if Shelby's with you."

"Fuck," I groan. "I didn't even think of that."

"He's not stupid. Creepy as fuck, yes. But not dumb. You know how to find hidden cameras and shit. And by the way, you're coming up to my room with me to do a search when we get back. Just FYI."

"Any sane man's gonna shut it off."

"Yeah, well it's a dick move for him to have 'em and not warn a brother, anyway."

I've certainly never worried about shit like that in either of our New York clubhouses.

CHAPTER FORTY

Rooster

Ice never said a word about the cameras I disconnected in our rooms. Maybe I'm overthinking the whole thing and they're only there as some extra insurance when people outside the club visit.

The irony of it is Jigsaw and I have been spending all week setting up cameras and lights at the house during the day. At night, I've been working on the website. Anya wants everything operational before some radio interview she has scheduled. And I'm eager to finish so I can get the fuck out of here.

"You sure you don't want me to ride up with you?" Jigsaw asks after breakfast the morning I'm leaving for Baltimore.

"I've ridden by myself before, you know."

He slaps my hand away.

"Seriously," I add. "I have more boxes arriving today. I'll feel better if you're around to accept the delivery."

"She's filming, you know." He wiggles his eyebrows.

"For fuck's sake, please behave. Don't be a leering creep. Keep your mouth shut and stay out of the shots."

"I'd be offended but—"

"Yeah. Exactly." I slap his shoulder and walk down to Ice's door, then rap my knuckles against the wood.

"Come in," he hollers.

"Hey." I poke my head inside. "I'm runnin' up to Baltimore for a bit. Probably be back tomorrow afternoon."

He stands and walks around his desk. "You don't have to check in with me. Appreciate everything you've been doing around here."

"Not a problem."

He leans his ass on the desk and crosses his arms over his chest.

A muscle in my leg twitches. Really wasn't planning to settle in for a chat. "Things going okay with Anya at the house?" he asks.

"I think so. I'm waitin' for a few more packages, so Jigsaw's headed over there to handle it while I'm gone."

"Appreciate that too."

"You need something or have any questions, call me or ask Jigsaw."

"All right, brother." He steps forward and shakes my hand. "Shiny side up."

"Thanks."

I haul ass out of the clubhouse before anyone else delays me.

Finally, I'm on the road on my way to Shelby. Can't wait to get my hands on her.

It's early enough that traffic isn't awful until I get near DC. It thins out enough that I'm turning off I-295 sooner than I expected. The arena's in the city, and my inner country boy shudders.

Shelby had sent directions this morning, telling me where to park. I miss the turn for the one-way street leading to the loading area. Muttering a bunch of curses, I circle the block and finally pull into the lot.

The knots in my chest unravel when my gaze lands on her van. My girl's here somewhere.

I tuck my bike into a spot near her van and trailer. No signs indicate you need permission to park here.

I better not get fucking towed. I briefly study the trailer. Doesn't look big enough to haul my bike. Probably at capacity with all of her equipment and stuff anyway.

My gaze searches the area. Plenty of roadies moving instruments and boxes inside. Dawson's fleet of buses and trucks. I recognize a few people, but not enough to ask them where to find Shelby.

"Logan?"

My eyes narrow as I search for whoever called my name.

Trent.

I lift my arm in a half-assed wave. What is it about this kid that bugs me so damn much?

As if I don't know. He's a guy who spends a lot of time in close proximity with Shelby. That's more than enough for my inner grizzly bear to wanna shred him to pieces.

"Hey." He holds out his hand as I approach. "Shelby asked me to come meet you." I shake his hand and he gives me a pass. He leans in. "They've been dicks here, so keep that on you."

"Thanks." I slip the lanyard around my neck.

"This, too, for your bike." He hands me an orange tag with the name of the tour and "guest" in black ink. Someone punched a hole through one end and tied a hair elastic through it. My lips twitch. Had to be Shelby. I wrap the tag around the handlebars, not feeling reassured that the flimsy piece of orange cardstock's gonna keep my bike from getting towed, and return to Trent.

"Where is she?"

"Follow me." He jerks his head toward the glass doors and pushes his way inside. "How was traffic?"

"Not bad."

It's early enough that none of the concession stands are open—something my growling stomach doesn't appreciate. The only people milling around seem to work at the arena.

"We're in the basement," he says, leading me to a set of wide metal doors. "Caught her talking to some sweaty creeper fan the other day. Didn't want her wandering around here while she was waiting for ya." He jabs at the elevator button.

"What are you talking about?"

"She does it all the time." He lifts his shoulders. "Afraid she'll offend someone and they'll rip her apart online. But shoot, people are gonna do that anyway."

"When's Greg gonna hire some security?"

He shrugs again. "We keep an eye on her."

The air's cooler when we step out of the elevator. It's not really a basement. Just a lower level that isn't accessible to the general public. Trent moves fast but it's still not enough. I'm ready to come out of my skin with the need to get my hands on Shelby.

A cluster of people blocking the hallway come close to getting a body-check from me.

"Logan." Dawson steps away from the circle to greet me. Which is nice and all, but...*motherfucker, don't slow me down.*

"Hey, good to see you," I say, and we share a quick handshake.

"I'm taking him to Shelby," Trent says.

Dawson backs up a step. "Don't let me stop ya."

Smart man.

Finally, Trent stops at a white door with a gold star smack in the middle. About time someone acknowledges her properly.

He knocks twice and pushes the door open. "Catch you later." He doesn't bother sticking around. Not that I'm complaining.

My gaze lands on Shelby. Hair in a half-up style, long curls spilling over her bare shoulders. Thin straps hold up a black dress with big blue flowers. Tight on top with a skirt that flares out. A wide, shiny blue belt accentuates her waist. Might as well be a sign announcing, "Rooster's hands go here."

Her face explodes into a radiant smile the second our eyes meet. Her eyes shining brighter than the damn sun. Something shifts inside my chest. Thaws.

I put that look on her face.

"Logan." She rushes forward, hitting me square in the chest and wrapping her arms around me. "I'm so happy to see you."

I squeeze her just as tight and move us out of the doorway, kicking the door shut. "Did I miss your pre-show yoga routine?"

She laughs and hugs me tighter. "Sorry. Next time."

Shelby

Rooster's actually here. His warm, solid, comforting body. My heart's all frantic, performing a happy two-step.

After a few seconds, I step back and peer up at him.

"Cindy's coming back to do my lipstick later." I blush and glance down. "I wanted to be able to kiss the hell out of you when you got here."

"Well, get kissing, chickadee."

I throw my arms around his neck, leaning up to press my lips to his. He meets me halfway, responding with the same intensity.

He groans and draws back, resting his hands on my shoulders to hold me at arm's length. "Let me look at you."

I glance down at my dress and wrap my hands up in the puffy skirt, swinging it from side to side. "I hope it looks more rock-country than square dance."

The corners of his mouth lift. "You look cute and sexy."

"That works." I'm nervous and can't stop moving.

"What's wrong?" he asks.

"I'm anxious tonight. Don't know why."

Actually, except for the shows in New York, I've been like this *every* night since the tour started. None of my yoga, meditation, or pre-show routines helps quell the storm the way Rooster's presence does. But I can't admit that. I don't want to sound like a scared little girl who can't handle her business.

"It's a big arena," he says.

"Yeah, that's probably part of it."

"When is Cindy coming back?"

"An hour or so, I think."

"Plenty of time." He pulls me into the bathroom and locks the door. This one's a lot cleaner and neater than the last few have been.

"Time for what?" I really don't have to ask. His smile is pure seduction, his eyes full of smoldering heat.

A long mirror lines the wall. Rooster turns me to face it, slipping his arms around my waist and leaning down to kiss my neck and shoulder. "Missed you."

I sigh and rest my head against his chest. "Missed you more than I thought was possible," I whisper.

He slides his hands down my belly and over my dress, slowly lifting the skirt. Rough hands glide up my thighs.

A smile teases over my lips. I open my eyes and peer up at him. "What are you doing?"

"Helping you relax."

His fingers skim the waistband of the little shorts I'm wearing under my dress and I jump. "That's going to get me more worked up."

"Shh." Warm breath skates over my shoulder. Beard whiskers tickle my skin. Lips kiss and suck at my neck. His fingers travel lower, and he rumbles with laughter. "Shorts *and* panties."

"You can never be too careful covering the goods."

He hums. "I approve."

"I wasn't asking."

He rumbles with more laughter and slides his hand lower.

"Oh!" I gasp, and my body jolts as he rubs the material directly over my clit.

"These are already wet." His voice drops to a seductive rasp.

"Second I saw you." My breathing picks up. "That feels nice."

"Nice, huh? I can do better than *nice*."

My hips jerk as if my body understood his words and wholeheartedly agrees.

"Spread your legs," he demands.

"You make those words so sexy."

He kisses my neck up to my earlobe and nips. A shiver of pleasure shoots down my back and I hurry to move my feet apart.

A soft whine spills out of me as he sneaks his fingers under my panties.

"I can't wait to fuck you later," he whispers against my ear.

I suck in a sharp breath. "Me too."

He slides one finger between my lips, teasing. "Gonna eat your pussy first."

I can't form any words but I nod eagerly.

"You like that, don't you?"

"Yes. God, yes. You're the best I've—" I snap my mouth shut. *Don't compare him to anyone else!*

He doesn't seem offended. Laughter rumbles out of him for a brief second. "Good to know." He keeps sliding his fingers in my wetness, teasing around my clit but not quite touching where I'm throbbing the most. I whine again and he squeezes the arm around me tighter. "What do you need?"

"Make me come. Please? Oh God. I really, really need…" He slips one finger inside me and my panting breath steals the rest of my words.

"Fuck," he groans.

I open my eyes and watch him in the mirror. Sexy, tortured man. Eyes shut tight.

"Let me take care of you too," I whisper.

"You will." He kisses my cheek. "Later."

He slowly pumps one finger inside me, pressing the heel of his hand into my clit.

Off-balance, half-crazed with need, I stumble forward, pressing my palms to the mirror.

"That's nice." He grips my hip. "Stick your ass out and spread your legs more."

A delicious tremble shimmies up my legs as he continues stroking. My whole universe centers on the point of pleasure. He slips his finger out and finally circles my clit, lightly pinching, the right amount of gentle but firm pressure I need to be set free.

"Oh!" I gasp and slap my hand against the mirror.

"That's it. Come for me, Shelby. Let go."

I whimper and shake as he continues working me into a wobbling mess. My knees buckle and Rooster's there with an arm around my waist to keep me upright. My head drops forward, my cheek resting against the cool glass. Breath. I can't catch it. Rooster takes a moment to smooth my dress into place.

Warm satisfaction replaces the anxiety that was flowing through my veins.

"Thank you," I whisper.

After a heartbeat, I turn and rest my palms against his chest. "Don't laugh at me."

He chuckles and places a finger under my chin, tipping my head back. "What's on your mind?"

"I never knew there were different kinds of orgasms."

He chokes down a laugh. "How so?"

I should've kept my mouth shut. *That* orgasm will have to be added to the list under the heading *ones that make me say stupid stuff*.

"Shelby?" he prompts.

"Nothing." I shake my head and try to pull away, but he holds me in place.

I sigh. "I don't know. Sometimes it feels like you've stuck my clit in a light socket and others are an out-of-body meditative experience."

His eyebrows draw down. No longer laughing, he studies my face. "That first one sounds painful."

"It is almost." I squeeze my eyes shut, throbbing from the thought. "But bliss too." Shoot, maybe I've insulted him. "Every one is amazing, though. No matter what."

Instead of answering, he leans down and brushes his lips against mine.

Rooster

I'm not sure how to respond to Shelby's description. For lots of reasons.

One, I've never been with a woman quite like her. Responsive and so damn honest. But comparing her to past fucks is a dick move, so I can't say that.

Two, I'm tempted to strip her naked and perform a scientific experiment. One where we discover *exactly* how many different kinds of orgasms I can give her. Maybe even have her write me a song about each one. But we don't have enough time.

So I kiss her instead. Unfortunately, that seems to leave her more unsure. When I pull away, she fiddles with her dress and hair, her gaze darting around the small room.

I squeeze her hips to get her attention. "Shelby, that's both the sweetest and hottest thing a woman's ever said to me."

Fuck, that wasn't helpful. At all.

She doesn't seem offended, thank fuck. Nope, she meets my eyes. "Really? I feel silly. Maybe I should add that as a third kind—the orgasm that makes me say dumb stuff."

"It's not dumb at all. I love the way you express yourself. I can't come up with pretty words the way you do." I tuck her hair behind her ear. Good thing Cindy's returning to fix Shelby's makeup, since I kinda messed up her hair too. "All my brain can conjure up are words like, touch. Lick. Kiss. Mine. The basics."

A full-body shiver sweeps over her. "Well, that's something, I guess."

"Beautiful. That's another word. But it doesn't seem adequate to describe you. Sexy doesn't quite cut it either." No, I need a whole new word. Her skin's all flushed, her golden curls a little mussed from where she'd been leaning against me. The crystal I gave her glitters against her creamy skin. Her plump breasts almost spilling out of the tight, low-cut dress are begging for my hands. My gaze drops to her lush, curvy hips exaggerated by the wide, shiny blue belt wrapped around the dip of her waist.

I shift, adjusting myself. My damn cock's ready to bust through my jeans and wave at her.

"Rooster." She sighs and wraps her arms around me, hugging me tight, not helping my imprisoned cock one bit. "I'm so happy you're here." She tips her head back. "For *you*. Not the orgasms. Those are a fantastic bonus, though."

Forget my tortured cock—there's that strange sensation pulsing through me again. That *L* word that's getting harder and harder not to say every time I'm with her. "I'm happy I'm here too. Made a hotel reservation at a place down by the water for us tonight."

"You did? You didn't have to do that."

"Yeah, I did. And I want to take you to an early lunch or something before you leave tomorrow." Fuck, why am I bringing up that she's leaving when I just got my hands on her?

"Why? You don't have to do any of that."

I squeeze her hips, seeking her softness under the layers of dress in my way. "I *want* to." Seems like whenever we're together we're racing off somewhere or fucking. "I want to take you out on a normal date."

"What's normal for *us*?" She presses her hand over my heart. "You do so many sweet, helpful things that mean so much more than a dinner date."

I wrap my fingers around hers, lifting her hand and brushing my lips over her inner wrist. "Just want you to know you're special."

"You always make me feel special." She titters with laughter. "That tickles."

Someone knocks on the dressing room door, cutting off our conversation. Judging by the persistent pounding, they're not leaving.

"Dang." Shelby spins away, curling her hand around the doorknob. She hesitates then turns and reaches up to give me a quick kiss on the cheek.

Like a complete sap, I press my fingers to the spot briefly before following her out of the bathroom. Good thing she's tiny. My long legs make it to the door faster. I hold out my arm to keep her behind me while I open it.

She huffs. "I answer my own door all the time."

"Humor me."

Cindy holds up her makeup case. "Just me." Her gaze shoots to Shelby and she wiggles her eyebrows. "Good to see you again, Logan."

I run my hand over my beard, opening the door wider for Cindy to come in, amused as hell. Sounds like they've been chatting about me in my absence. Good stuff, if Cindy's beaming smile is any indication.

"You need anything?" I ask Shelby. "Want your tea?"

"If you don't mind."

"Nope. Be right back."

SHELBY

"What have you been up to since I left?" Cindy touches my shoulder. "You're all flushed."

My cheeks burn even hotter under the pounds of makeup. I peer in the mirror. Splotches of pink stain my chest. Might as well hang a "got some" sign around my neck. "Nothin'."

"Hmm." She smooths the messy curls at the back of my head. "Someone got lucky."

"Maybe a little."

"Can't blame you." Her gaze darts to the door. "I'd ride that man like a mechanical bull."

It's a teasing comment, meant to be a compliment to Logan, I'm sure. Still, a white-hot prick of jealousy stabs my heart.

"Shoot. I'm kidding, Shelby." She squeezes the tops of my arms.

I force a smile.

Rooster returns with my tea while she's fixing my hair. I have a few quick swallows before she starts lining my lips.

"I hate this stuff," I mumble. "My lips are always so dry after I take it off."

"I know," she murmurs. "Hard to find something that'll stay put during your set. Open. Now blot." She stands back, running her gaze over me, and I flash a bright smile. "Perfect."

She wags her finger in Rooster's direction. "Don't mess up my work."

He rumbles with laughter and holds his hands in the air. "I'll do my best."

"Good luck tonight, hon."

"Thanks."

The jitters pop up as soon as she leaves.

"Come here," Rooster says softly.

"You heard Cindy," I say as I approach.

"I'll behave." He holds out his hands to me, and I curl my fingers around his. "You look amazing. How's your throat feel?"

I hum a few notes. "Okay."

"Good." He pulls me down into his lap, draping my legs sideways over his. Carefully, I rest my head on his shoulder, the steady thump of his heart grounds and reassures me.

"I could go to sleep like this."

He kisses my forehead. "Relax for a few minutes."

"Okay."

My set list, the things I want to say to the crowd tonight all float through my head. I picture myself strong, and hitting every note perfectly. Eventually, I drift away, hovering somewhere between sleep and awake.

Vaguely, I'm aware of someone knocking and the door opening.

"She feelin' all right?"

Dawson's voice.

"Yeah," Rooster rumbles.

I drag myself back to consciousness, blinking and sitting up. Only mildly embarrassed to be caught taking a catnap in my boyfriend's embrace.

"You all right, little lady?" Dawson flashes me a warm smile.

Great. The last thing I need is him thinking I can't handle the stress of the tour. "Just resting before my set. What's up?"

He closes the door behind him and drops into the chair across from us. Guess he's sticking around to chat.

Feeling a bit unprofessional sitting in Rooster's lap, I slide down until my butt hits the couch cushions and face Dawson. "What's on your mind?"

He shoots a look Rooster's way before speaking. "Would ya be offended if I took the stage with you instead tonight? Last song. Mix things up a little?"

I blink and sit back, trying to digest that.

Dawson Roads wants to perform with me? During *my* set?

The star of the tour is lowering himself and going on stage early? With the opening act?

He seems to take my hesitation for disagreement, sitting back and holding up his hands. "Won't cut you short, promise."

"No, no. It's not that. Just...why? I'm the opener. Seats aren't even full during my slot."

"Let's teach those fuckers a lesson." He grins. "They oughtta be here earlier."

Next to me, Rooster chuckles.

"Sure. Of course," I answer. Why the heck am I questioning Dawson Roads, anyway? I work a little more graciousness into my tone. "I'm honored to share the stage with you anytime."

He rubs his hand over his chin and leans forward, resting one elbow on his knee. "I didn't get a chance to discuss this with Greg yet, but you're going into the studio right after we get off the road, right?"

"Uh, yeah." I glance at Rooster. "Planning to spend a few days at home. Visit my momma first."

"How would you feel about recording something together?"

"I'd love to!" I wince from the enthusiasm in my voice and try to settle down. "That would be great."

"Not 'Let the Night Go.'" He lets out a humorless laugh. "Glenna

would sue me to hell and back if I re-recorded it with someone else."
His expression turns sour for a second before his gaze lands on Logan.
"It was good seeing your friend the other night. Got in touch with his
people. Going to see if we can work on something together."

Rooster's eyes widen a touch, then his expression flattens. "Wasn't
aware Chaser had 'people,' but that sounds good."

Dawson shrugs. This is all kinds of weird.

"Dawson, I appreciate the opportunity. A lot." I drop my gaze. "I
don't mean to sound ungrateful, but you're not just offering to work
with me to, you know, piss off Glenna, are you?"

When he doesn't answer, I lift my gaze and find him stroking his
chin, staring at me in a thoughtful way. Not mean or angry at least.
"Shelby, I think you're one of the most talented singers to come offa
one of those foolish reality shows in years. You got chewed up and spit
out in the name of drama and ratings. Hated to see it."

I wasn't aware he'd actually watched *Redneck Roadhouse,* and I
cringe, remembering some of the worst moments.

"You attract a slightly younger audience," he continues, "and you're
getting some mainstream airplay, which I've never really managed to
crack."

I blink and stare. He's dominated the country charts for close to
fifteen years. Who knew Dawson Roads gave a crap about mainstream
anything?

"And I think you working with me helps expose *you* to an older
audience, so they can discover you're more than a cutesy teenager
singing about ponies and boy troubles."

"Of course. You're right. I'm—"

"But if it happens to piss Glenna off at the same time, I ain't mad
about it. God's honest truth." He raises his left hand, then shrugs. "I'm
only human."

Dang. That's a bummer.

But I respect his honesty. At least he didn't try gaslighting me for
asking the question.

He slaps his hands against his knees. "Good. You know 'Friends in
Low Places?' Everyone knows it. We'll do that tonight. That all right
with you?"

"Uh, sure. I'll let the guys know."

"Don't cut your set. Just add it in after your last song."

"Okay."

"Thanks, darlin'. Good seein' ya, Logan." He waves at us over his shoulder and leaves.

I blink and stare at the door. After a few seconds, I glance down and pinch my arm. "Did that just happen?"

When Rooster doesn't answer, I peer up at him. He's watching the door.

"I can't believe I asked him that."

"What?" He turns his attention to me.

"About his ex. Oh my gosh. Here he is doing me a huge favor. That wasn't polite."

A scowl slashes across Rooster's forehead. "Fuck polite. I woulda asked the same thing. Is that even normal?"

"Yeah, I've seen a few shows where the bands mix it up like that. Usually if they're friendly or whatever. Cindy and I were talking the other day." I lower my voice. "And it hit me that the only reason he was asking me to come out and sing with him was to get back at his ex."

"I don't think that's the *only* reason. But it seems to be a bonus. Least he admits it." He squeezes my leg. "It's good you spoke up. He'll respect you more for not kissing his ass. And respect goes all around. You gotta respect yourself. Don't let anyone bullshit you."

I turn that over in my head for a bit. "I'm so new at the business. I've never even met Glenna Wilson, and now I'm making an enemy out of her. Feels kinda anti-girl-power to be singing with her ex."

Being VP of a motorcycle club—not exactly all about female empowerment—I almost expect Rooster to laugh. But he tilts his head, studying me for a few seconds. "You said it yourself. Never even met her. You don't owe her shit. Besides, this is *business*. Nothing personal." He leans in and kisses my cheek. "You already have a man," he says against my ear. "You don't need hers."

Warmth sweeps over my skin, chasing away the unsettling sensation lingering in my belly from the talk with Dawson. "I sure do."

And I can't stop falling head over boots for him either.

CHAPTER FORTY-ONE

Rooster

Watching Shelby and Dawson belt out 'Friends in Low Places' is a thousand times better than the 'let's fuck all night' song they've been performing.

So fucking proud of the way she handled it too. I bit the inside of my cheek so hard I drew blood trying not to laugh when she asked him about his ex.

The arena's so damn big, it's hard to find a good spot to take my video of their duet. Lynn's gonna be getting a side-stage view. It's the best I can manage.

The song winds down and Dawson wraps an arm around Shelby's shoulders. "Shelby Morgan, everyone. I'll see y'all later."

The building shakes from the screams of the fans as he walks offstage. Fucking brilliant move, honestly. I bet all the seats will be filled for Shelby's show tomorrow.

Kinda pissed I'll miss it.

Shelby says a few more words, then the lights blink out and a curtain drops.

"What'd you think?" Dawson asks me.

Not sure why he gives a shit about my opinion. I hit stop on my phone, shut off the screen and jam it in my pocket. "Sounded good. Recorded it to send to her mom."

"Ah." He slaps my shoulder. "You two have fun. Take her someplace nice."

"Thanks."

Shelby runs straight for me, bright-eyed and breathless. "What'd you think?"

"You were amazing." I pick her up for a quick kiss but she loops her arms over my head and her legs around my waist, hanging on tight. "Easy," I groan into her mouth. "People around."

"I don't care," she whispers against my lips.

Next to us, someone clears their throat.

I growl at the intrusion. Shelby unwinds her body from me and I set her down.

Greg's exasperated scowl pulls a laugh from me.

"I suppose you're taking off?" he says to Shelby.

"If that's all right, yeah." She slips her hand into mine. "I'm done, right?"

"Yeah, go on."

"I need to change first and load up my stuff." She tugs me forward.

Greg stops me with a hand against my chest.

Slowly, I drop my gaze. "Careful, Greg. Last man who did that is walking around with a bloody stump."

He snatches his hand away. "We're at the inn behind the arena. She needs to be there by ten a.m."

Fuck, that's earlier than I'd planned. "Yeah, okay. We'll be at the Crown on Water Street."

He raises an eyebrow. Where'd he expect me to take her? Some fleabag motel that rents rooms by the hour?

His attitude evaporates and he squeezes Shelby's shoulder. "Good show tonight. I think it was your best one yet."

"You liked 'Friends in Low Places?'" She grins.

"Yes, that was a great ender. But I'm talking about *your* performance. Good job."

"Thanks."

"See you tomorrow."

Trent's waiting in her dressing room. "I wasn't sure what you wanted me to put in the van?" He gestures to her trunk and the different bags scattered around.

"Shoot." Shelby bites her lip. "The trunk definitely. I have my backpack ready for tonight, so I'll keep that and my purse." She glances down. "But I need to pack up my dress."

"I'll bring the trunk with us, Trent," I offer. "You're not leaving right now, are you?"

"Nah, we'll be here for a bit." He gathers up some of her other things. "Guitar's already up there. You don't need it, right?"

"Nope. All set." She walks him to the door and locks it after he leaves.

"What do you need me to do, Shelby?" I ask, sorting through the stuff spilling out of her trunk. "You got a hanger or something you want the dress on?"

"Take out your cock."

"What now?" I turn my attention from the trunk to her.

She kicks her shoes in the direction of the trunk, hitting the side with two solid *thumps*. "You heard me." Her hips sway as she closes the short distance between us. She presses her hands against my chest and pushes.

I smile down at her. "You're gonna have to be stronger than that to take me down."

"That right?" She slides her hands lower, cupping me through my jeans.

"Fuck." My eyes close. She gives me another shove and this time I topple onto the couch.

"That's better." She gathers her skirt and slips her hands underneath it. A few seconds later, her little shorts and her underwear sail toward the trunk.

My heart hammers. "What are you doing?"

She bends her leg, gently setting it on the couch cushion next to my thigh, and lowers herself onto my lap. "I said, take out your cock."

"Told you I wanted to eat your pussy first." I grin at her and lace my fingers behind my head, easing into the couch.

"I'm all sweaty and need a shower."

283

"I'll take you any way I can get you."

"Hmm. You're being awfully difficult." She shifts back and attacks my belt, pulling it loose and diving for the button of my jeans.

"You're not worried about someone—" I flap my hand toward the door, all words falling out of my brain as she starts stroking my cock. "Fuck."

"Door's locked." She sneaks her hand in my pocket and pulls a condom free. "Good man."

"I like to be prepared." I wink at her and pluck the packet from her fingers.

I barely have it rolled on all the way when she rests one hand on my shoulder and uses the other to hike up her dress, hovering over my lap and lining herself up.

"Oh fuck," I groan and squeeze my eyes shut. "I'm glad you're primed and ready, because this is going to be short."

She laughs softly and rakes her nails over my shirt, slowly easing her way down.

"Oh." She lets out a soft grunt when she bottoms out.

I slide my hands up under her dress, appreciating the muscles in her legs straining. "Come on," I encourage, grabbing her ass cheeks and pushing her forward. There's too much dress in my way. My hands go to the zipper at her back and tug. "This needs to come off, right?"

"Y-yes."

Tight, tiny little fucking zipper.

Finally, I tug it down enough that the straps fall off her shoulders. I drag the top down and flick the clasps of her bra loose. "Much better." I cup her tits, holding them up for my eager mouth, and suck one nipple, then the other.

"Shit!" She stabs her fingers through my hair, yanking a fistful. "Oh my God, Logan."

Her movements turn frantic as she loses her rhythm, her body crashing into mine in a chaotic frenzy.

"Already?" I kiss and lick at her neck, savoring the salt on her skin.

"Close," she whispers.

"Yeah?" I suck my thumb in my mouth for a second and bring it to her clit, rubbing in quick, firm circles.

"Yes, yes, yes." She rides me faster and faster, digging her nails into my shoulders.

That sexy trembling quiver takes hold of her legs. Fuck, if that doesn't trigger my own orgasm.

I clamp my hands over her hips, holding her down while I hammer up into her. The shaking in her legs increases. "Fuck," I roar through my release.

Breathless and pulsing with pleasure, I fall back against the couch. She slumps over me, our sweaty bodies clinging together.

I pinch the material of her dress. "We're going to ruin this."

"Don't care," she mumbles against me.

I run my hands up and down her back. She jumps and wiggles her hips. My softening cock, still inside her, perks up. "Careful," I warn. "You're so fucking hot. If you give me a minute, I'll bend you over the end of the couch."

She laughs softly and sits up, carefully extracting herself from my lap.

I crack open one eye and stare at her. Carefully curled and pinned hair—disheveled. Makeup—obliterated. Dress wrinkled and twisted around her waist. Pink blotches stain her chest and neck. All from our frantic fuck. "You are *wrecked*, woman."

She glances down and giggles, pushing her dress off the rest of the way. "Never felt better, though."

"Never looked better, either." I groan as I sit up. "Was that one of those light-socket orgasms you mentioned?"

She ducks her head, her tangled hair obscuring her face. "Definitely."

I reach for her hand, tugging gently. "I could tell. Your legs shake. Your eyes roll back in your head."

"You make me sound demonic."

"It's hot as hell."

She giggles again and I tickle her side. "Give me a second to clean up and I'll help you pack."

"Okay."

I'm finishing up in the bathroom when she joins me. Sadly, she's covered—jeans that hug her curvy legs, a long-sleeve T-shirt, and boots. Ready to ride. She holds up a few bottles of liquid or lotion. "I'm going to wash this crap off my face before we go."

"Probably a good idea."

She gasps when she glances in the mirror. "Why didn't you tell me I look like a freakshow?"

"You look fucking hot to me." I pat her ass as I squeeze past her.

The second band must have taken the stage. Loud beats rumble overhead and the dull roar of the crowd pulses through the walls.

"You want your dress in the trunk?" I call out.

"Sure."

Inside the trunk, I find her laundry bag and I stuff her clothes in there. I toss the shoes in too, hoping that's where they go. "Anything else?"

She steps out of the bathroom and scans the couch, dressing table, and chair. "Nope. That's all of it."

I snap the trunk closed and hoist it into my arms.

"I can ask Trent to bring the hand cart down," she offers.

I'm insulted she thinks I can't carry her coffin-sized trunk of dresses and shoes. "The one with the flamingo stickers all over it? Pass."

"My stickers are adorable." She pouts as she slips the straps of her backpack on.

"You're adorable." Can't take my damn eyes off her.

"Hey," I wait until she lifts her gaze, "come here."

She stops in front of me and peers up. "What's wrong?"

"Nothing. Kiss me." Holding the trunk out of her way, I lean over and steal a quick kiss. "That's better."

"Was that okay?" Her nervous gaze darts to the shaggy olive green couch and back.

I laugh so hard the trunk slides from my grip and I catch it with my knee. "Anytime you feel like jumping on my cock, say the word." I tilt my head toward the door. "Let's go."

Thank fuck I paid attention when Trent brought me down here. Shelby turns left instead of right. Clearly, she has no clue where she's going.

"All these places look the same after a while," she says when I question her.

"I know. But you should pay better attention. I can't have you getting lost when you're someplace unfamiliar."

She squints at me.

Yeah, that sounded harsher than I meant. "Not trying to be bossy."

"And yet, you're so good at it."

SHELBY

Tonight, the wrongness of leaving the tour doesn't chase me from the arena. My show kicked ass. I'm entitled to have a night with my boyfriend.

The hotel Rooster chose is the fanciest place I've ever been. The valet allows Rooster to leave his bike right in front and opens the door to the hotel for us. Several uniformed employees offer respectful low-toned greetings.

"Where'd you find this place?" I whisper once we're alone in the mirrored elevator.

"The magic of the Internet?" He shrugs. "We don't have much time together. I wanted to take you someplace nice."

My pulse pounds harder. I open my mouth but the words in my heart stick in my throat. "You've never really told me what you do," I say instead.

The elevator chimes and the doors open. Our floor has thick carpet that mutes our steps. We're not far from the elevator when Rooster stops and slides the key card into the panel on the door.

"To afford a place like this," I continue.

"I'm a simple man, Shelby. If I was by myself, I'd probably camp outside or check into the first place I saw."

I shudder at the word *camping*. "Humans evolved for a reason, ya know. Sleeping outside is like flippin' off all our ancestors who busted their butts to learn how to build houses and stuff."

He roars with laughter. "You like nature. I've taken you to a few bonfires."

"Yeah, bonfires near a dwelling with indoor plumbing."

He chuckles and hooks his arm over my shoulders. The room's even nicer than I expected. A wall of windows looks out over the harbor, and I'm instantly drawn to it. Rooster flicks on the lamps, and in the glass I follow his reflection as he pulls out his phone, and taps out a message or two.

"Rooster?"

He glances up and flicks his phone off. "Sorry, I wanted to send that video to your mom before I forgot."

Dang.

My heart pounds for different reasons. First, that he's so sweet he remembered to film me singing with Dawson, knowing that my mom would want to see the clip. Second, now she'll know Rooster's visiting me on the road and I can—

My phone buzzes in my pocket.

Expect a call from her any second.

"Guess she got the video," I mumble.

He chuckles and drops into one of the chairs to unlace his boots.

"Hey, Momma," I answer. What are the odds she'll be happy I'm with a man who's worried about sending her videos? Every other boyfriend I've had acted like I hatched from an egg.

"Why is Rooster still on tour with you?"

"Hello to you too." While the room's all kinds of fancy—from the plush carpet to the television that raises out of a platform at the end of the bed—it doesn't offer enough privacy for this phone call.

I wander down the line of windows until I'm in the opposite corner from Rooster.

"Don't sass me," she says.

I turn so I'm facing the wall and lower my voice. "He wasn't far from this show and came to visit me, that's all."

"Shelby." She sighs. "We talked about this."

"No, *you* talked. I listened." I lower my voice. "Then I followed my heart."

"Hearts are foolish. Listen to your head like I taught you."

"Well, my head's thinking, my momma oughtta be a little more grateful someone even thought to take a video *and* remembered to send it without me even asking." Each word shoots out of my mouth like a bullet.

She's silent. Holy hell, did I finally win an argument with my mother?

"That was nice of him," she concedes. "I sent a thank you."

"Good. Now let me tell you my news."

"What?"

"Dawson asked if I'd like to record a song with him when we're done with the tour."

"Oh, Shelby! That's wonderful." In a lower voice, she adds, "I see the gossip sites are trying to link you two romantically."

"Shoot. Really?"

"Shelby, you're not...are you?"

"No. Jeez."

"Well, it wouldn't be the worst thing. Look what he did for Glenna Wilson's career."

I pull the phone away and stare at it for a second. Did she really just say that? "Are you *drunk*? I wouldn't sleep with that producer to win *Roadhouse*. Why the fuck would I do it now?"

"Shelby! Language!"

"Fuck that. I can't believe you'd even suggest—"

"I was kidding. Calm down."

Kidding my ass.

"I need to go. Rooster and I have plans."

She sighs. "Please. Guard your heart."

"*You're* the only one hurting my heart right now."

"Don't say that. You know I love you."

"Yeah, I know. Night, Momma."

I click the end call button and contemplate tossing my phone out the window.

Expecting to find Rooster still across the room, I force a smile on my face and spin around.

He's right in front of me.

I jolt back a step.

In his plain black T-shirt, jeans and bare feet, he's absolutely mouthwatering.

My gaze travels up to his face again.

He's not smiling.

And those aren't his smoldering "I want to eat your pussy" eyes either.

"You scared me. I thought you were over there." I jut my chin toward the small chair.

"You sounded...unhappy. What's wrong?"

"Nothing."

"Is she upset I'm visiting you?"

I stare down at my phone and the notification that I already have a text from my mother. Dammit. Instead of reading it, I turn it off and set it on one of the nightstands.

"Honestly?"

He reaches for my hands. "I always want you to be honest with me."

Shame—that shouldn't be mine in the first place—trickles down my spine. How the hell do I explain her specific brand of crazy? "She'd prefer I don't let myself get distracted...with a relationship...and blow the tour or any other opportunities."

"Huh." He tips his head to the side. "And here I thought Lynn liked me."

"Oh, she likes you. As a person. Just not as a boyfriend for her daughter right now." I blow out a breath. Shoot, this is embarrassing to talk about. And yet, Rooster's the only person I feel comfortable talking to about everything. "She has it in her head that I'm...that I'll get so twitterpated over you, I'll drop everything and become your baby-making slave and blow off the career she's worked so hard for me to have."

He stares at me for a few blinks. "Twitterpated?"

"So crazy in love you can't think straight." I squint at him. "Didn't you ever watch *Bambi*?"

"The kid's movie?"

"Yeah." I stomp my foot on the carpet. "Thumper the bunny? Flower? None of that's ringin' a bell?"

A smile tugs at the corners of his mouth. "*Bambi* is bullshit. A wise old buck is more likely to spar with another male deer than save him from a forest fire. Even if it is his son."

"Aha, so you have seen it!"

He flicks his gaze toward the ceiling. "I *may* have been in the room when Chance and Alexa watched it at Z's house. By the way, it's not a toddler-appropriate movie. The two of them bawled their little eyes out. And Uncle Teller explaining to them that "venison is delicious" didn't help the situation. A fun time was *not* had by all."

I double over laughing until tears roll down my cheeks.

When I finally have control of myself, I straighten.

Rooster's grinning. "Glad I could cheer you up." He works his jaw from side to side. "And I needed a second to digest the rest of what you said."

The lightness in my heart turns to lead.

"First, I don't want a slave. Baby-making or otherwise. Second, *you're* the one who works hard. Your success belongs to *you*. No one else."

The instant need to defend my mother burns hot. "You don't understand. She's sacrificed—"

"Maybe I don't know every detail, Shelby. But I've watched you bust your ass. If your mom gave up her singing career, that's not on you."

My temper spikes. "You're talking over me and not listening."

He slips on a patient expression. "I'm listening."

"It's been the two of us for a long time now. She's just protective." The words feel wrong as they roll off my tongue.

"She shouldn't try to live vicariously through you."

"She's not," I protest, even though my heart's whispering in agreement.

CHAPTER FORTY-TWO

Rooster

Waking up next to Shelby needs to happen more often.

Like every damn morning.

I can't remember ever having the urge to watch a woman sleep. Usually, I'm praying they disappear in the middle of the night and I'm relieved to wake up alone.

If Shelby ever vanishes in the middle of the night, there's a good chance I'll burn the city to the ground trying to find her.

Listening to her defend me to her mother last night was the final straw.

I'm in love with this woman.

Her mom? Not so much.

Not because she doesn't want me hanging around Shelby. Other than it stressing Shelby out, I don't give a fuck what Lynn thinks about me.

Hinting that Shelby should fuck Dawson to get ahead? That's the part that pissed me the fuck off.

I overheard a *lot* more of their conversation than Shelby realizes.

What am I going to do about it?

Not a damn thing.

Shelby and her mom are tight. I get it. However misguided, she thinks she's looking out for her daughter.

Only one way to handle this. Keep supporting Shelby however I can and showing her how I feel. Eventually, Lynn will come around. And honestly, I'm relieved her opposition to me has more to do with Shelby's career than, say, me being VP of a motorcycle club.

I snort to myself. At least Lynn won't be asking us when she can expect some grandbabies.

"What are you laughing at?" Shelby mumbles.

"Nothing. Didn't mean to wake you."

"Hmm." She snuggles closer, her warm breath drifting over my arm.

I twist and glance at the clock. She can have another fifteen minutes tops.

Flashing and blinking from my phone catches my attention. I swipe it off the nightstand and check the messages.

One from Lynn, thanking me for the video.

I flip my middle finger at the screen.

Jigsaw asking how my trip's going.

I send him a quick reply.

Z wants to know what I'm up to.

I respond to that right away.

Me: I'm about two hours from Allentown. Wanna meet up?

Z: Why do you want to meet in Allentown?

Me: To kiss your ass. What do you think?

My phone vibrates. *God dammit, Z. If I wanted to talk, I would've called.* I toss the covers back and step into the bathroom, closing the door behind me. Learned last night there's no privacy in our room.

"What, old man?" I answer. "Texting giving you arthritis or something?"

"You're awfully grouchy for someone shacking up with his little songbird." Z's voice flows with amusement.

Deep laughter rumbles out of me. "Jiggy's such a snitch."

"Nope. Lilly spotted your big ass on Instagram."

"Well, shit."

He chuckles.

"I'm headed back to Virginia after she leaves."

"Don't need to explain it to me." He waits a beat or two. "Why you want to meet up?"

"Well, *obviously* it's not something I want to discuss over the phone, Prez." Z's not that dumb; he just enjoys fucking with me.

He blows out a long breath. "You're working my last nerve, motherclucker. Hang on."

There's a muffled scratching noise. Some sniffing. A slurping sound. Guessing Z's home and the dogs are looking for his attention.

"Rock and I will meet you. Text me an address."

Shit, I don't know the area all that well. "Why you dragging Rock with you?"

"He and Hope were staying at our place this weekend anyway."

"Oh, shit. Sorry."

"It's fine. Rock's been dying for a bro trip with me." He laughs again. "Should I invite anyone else along?"

"Nah." We talk for a few more minutes, setting up a time, and I promise to text him a location.

As soon as I hang up with Z, my phone buzzes again.

Greg.

Why's this fucker calling *me*?

"Yeah?" I flip the taps in the sink on and run my toothbrush under the water.

"Shelby's phone is off."

"Good morning, Greg," I mumble around a mouth full of toothpaste. "How are you?"

"Why is her phone off?"

I lean over and spit, rinsing my mouth before answering. "I don't fucking know."

I slam the bathroom door open harder than I meant to and search the room until I find her phone. "Got it."

Shelby grumbles and shoves her head under her pillow.

"Make sure she keeps it on. See you two in a little bit."

"We'll be there."

Greg hangs up.

Asshole.

"That had to be Greg. What'd he want?" Shelby mumbles.

"Guess your phone was off and he freaked out."

She huffs an annoyed noise and reaches for her phone, quickly checking her texts.

"Oh, jeez." She turns her phone toward me. "That's what he's fussin' about."

Another picture of us from last night. Making out backstage.

"Good thing they didn't see what we did in your dressing room." I wiggle my eyebrows at her.

She laughs softly.

"Z's wife must have seen it too. He knew I was with you."

"Gotta love social media."

That's why I've avoided it for so many years. But I'm not trying to guilt trip Shelby so I don't say that out loud.

"Come on. Let's grab breakfast. Greg will have a stroke if you're late."

ONE MINUTE BEFORE TEN, I PULL INTO THE PARKING LOT. I'M NOT giving Shelby up a second sooner than I have to.

The bike rolls to a stop next to the van and I toe the kickstand down. Shelby hops off and hands me her helmet. "Thank you."

I take her backpack and follow her to the van.

"Sup?" Trent says, grabbing her pack and tossing it inside. "Greg's grabbing coffee. You eat?" he asks Shelby.

"We had breakfast."

Since it seems we have a few minutes after all, I tug her over to my bike, resting my butt on the seat and pulling her between my knees. "You want coffee or something for the road?"

"No." She loops her arms around my neck. "I'm sorry about last night."

"What about it?"

"My mom. I...I know you're right. It's just..."

"Hey." I tip her chin up with my finger. "I get why she worries about you. She's been through a lot."

"I don't want you to be mad at her."

"I'm not." I curl my arms around her waist and kiss the tip of her nose. "Fucking loved the way you stood up for us."

Her eyes widen. She tries to pull back but I tighten my hold on her. "I love you, Shelby."

Of all the places to tell this woman I love her. A cheap motel parking lot isn't my first choice. But now that I've figured out what that warm sensation spreading through my chest is every time I think about her, I can't stand another second of her not knowing exactly how I feel.

"Logan." She leans in and kisses me. "I love you too. Been fighting it for a while."

I draw back. "Why?"

"I don't have a lot of myself to give right now." She waves toward the van. "You deserve...more."

That sounds a lot more ominous than I'm prepared for. "All I need is you. I knew this going in. I'm here for all of it, Shelby."

"You mean that?"

"I do." I push her hair back. "Hate leaving you right now. Wouldn't do it if I hadn't promised to finish up some things down in Virginia."

Every word's the truth. My body's already protesting the idea of heading in the opposite direction.

"We'll meet up in a few days." She bites her lip. "You'll still be down there, right?"

How can she even ask? I just told her I love her and she's worried I won't make the effort to see her? That visit's the only reason I'm willing to let her go today.

"Fuck yeah. Planning to roll out with you."

"Really?"

"Think you'll be okay with that?"

"I'm more than okay with it." She shifts her gaze and picks at a loose thread on my shoulder. "Tour ends in Texas. I'm supposed to go home for a few days, then up to Tennessee to record...then another tour."

"I don't mind dropping in to say hi to your mom." I grin down at her but she doesn't laugh.

"I'm sure she'll be thrilled." She shakes her head quickly.

"I'll win her over." Yeah, I'd been pissed about what I overheard. But the woman's been through some of the worst tragedies life can throw at you and still managed to raise this strong, incredible woman. I can't blame her for wanting the best for Shelby.

"While you're recording, I'll head home to take care of stuff so I'm not in your way." I have no idea what her recording process entails. I'm damn curious though. Want to worm my way into every single crevice of her life.

"You could never be in the way."

"Think somewhere in there we can schedule a few days to spend in New York?"

"I'd like that. A lot."

Relief flows through me. I kiss her forehead. "Good."

Shelby

Once again, Rooster waits until the van pulls away.

He loves me.

Now he knows exactly how I feel about him too.

"You two looked intense. Everything all right?" Trent pushes my blanket to the side and drops down next to me.

"Better than all right."

"Good." He glances out the window. "He seems to make you happy."

"So far, so good."

"Can you give us a minute, Trent?" Greg jerks his head to the side, dismissing Trent.

Trent pats my leg. "We'll talk later." He brushes past Greg, knocking into his shoulder.

I scowl at Greg's tense face. "What's going on?"

"I got a call from your mother this morning."

Sadly, this isn't the first time she's called Greg. It's embarrassing as all hell. "I just talked to her last night."

"She had some...strong opinions about Logan visiting you on tour."

Anger and frustration bubble up, threatening to leak from my eyes. "That's not her decision to make." I stab him with a look. "Or yours."

He holds his hands up. "I told her that. I'm not sure why she's so adamant. Logan seems to treat you well. You're happier when he's around. He gets you back to us on time. Helps out when he's here. She doesn't seem to care about the biker thing—which would be my concern."

"They're his family," I say, annoyed he brought up something he knows nothing about. "And they've always been kind to me."

"Good. That's all that matters."

"I'm sorry she called you."

"Don't be." He huffs a short laugh. "That's my job."

"Dealing with your twenty-two-year-old client's mother?" I roll my eyes his way. "Come on, Greg. That's not in your job description."

"Will we see Logan again?"

"Uh, yeah. The Virginia dates." I don't want to let Greg know Rooster's planning to join me on the tour after that. If it doesn't work out for some reason, I'll feel silly.

Forget my mother's meddling. Sure, I'm annoyed about it. I'll have some choice words for her when I calm down. But I can't worry about her antics right now.

My heart thumps.

I admitted to Logan that I love him.

Few things scare me more than a broken heart. This morning, with three little words, I set my foolish heart free.

And I'm more terrified than ever.

CHAPTER FORTY-THREE

Rooster

Two Harleys I recognize are neatly backed into spots in front of the diner.

Fuck. Can't wait for Z to bust my balls for making him wait.

Two hours was overly optimistic. Took more like three to get here.

Still, I stop to check my phone before going inside.

A picture of Shelby staring out the van window flashes on my screen.

Missin' you already.

Damn. Why the fuck am I up in Allentown instead of following her to Louisville?

The club comes first.

I stroll into the diner. Place doesn't look quite as bright and shiny as it did on Yelp. My boots make a scraping noise over the chipped, dirty tile. The hostess is pleasant enough, though. She beams up at me. "I bet you're looking for the two gentlemen in the back. Let me show you to their booth, sir."

"Thank you."

Figures the two presidents found a spot far away from anyone else.

I spot Z's broad shoulders and the top of his Lost Kings top rocker first. Rock's sitting across from him in the large, red vinyl booth and lifts his chin when he notices me.

"Here ya go." The waitress hands me a menu. "Holler when you're ready to order."

"Thank you."

Rock slides out and stands, motioning for me to take a seat. Super. Wedged between the two of them with no escape. I awkwardly shift over the seat, grunting when my hand brushes over something sticky.

"Classy joint you located." Z grins at me.

"You couldn't get a normal table?" I bitch.

The woman who showed me to the booth returns with a pot of coffee for the three of us.

After she leaves, Z sits back, spreading his arms out. "What are we doing here, bro?"

Rock's more serious. "Things all right down at Ice's place?"

"Yeah. It's quite a setup." I turn toward Z. "He's deeper into the porn game than we thought. Has himself a sweet little house set up for his girl to film in. Something we might want to explore."

"Real estate's always a wise investment," Rock says. "It would sure be better than Stella's hotel schtick."

Z winces at the mention of his ex's name.

"I wouldn't mess with her theme," I assure Z. "It works for her. But for the other girls, we should consider it."

"Yeah, whatever you think is best." Z waves his hand over the table. "That really why you brought us down here, though?"

"No." I clasp my hands on the table in front of me. "You know they had issues with Vipers?" I turn toward Rock. "Same problem you had. They burned down one of their businesses."

Rock sits back and nods slowly. "Yeah, that was a while ago. Jersey, right?" He flashes a grim smile at Z. "No Vipers left in NY."

"Fuckin' A," Z mutters.

I lean in again. "Ice says that event triggered a visit from the ATF."

"No shit." Z shrugs. "Not shocking, though. Wrath had to put up with an arson investigation."

"That was contained locally," Rock says, his tone turning sharper. "Maybe it's time for you to move on if Virginia's on ATF's radar."

Rock's not my president, so it's not an order. More like a strong suggestion. While we haven't openly discussed it, I'm sure he's aware I helped Z plant the car bomb that blew the late Senator Kelly sky-high. It's in all of our interests that my name doesn't come across the desk of anyone at ATF.

"If their clubhouse is under surveillance, they've probably already identified you," Z says in a flat tone.

"I'm planning to take off and travel with Shelby as soon as I finish up the website for Ice."

"Good." Rock sits back.

My gaze skirts to Z. "That's not what concerned me and why I asked to meet up."

"Christ," Rock mutters. "What else?"

I scan the room quickly. Neat rows of Formica tables and empty red vinyl chairs. No lingering waitresses or busboys. We're still the only ones in this section. "Ice claims he has the ATF problem solved."

"Fuuuck," Z groans. "Do we want to hear this?"

"I don't know. Let's find out," I quip before turning serious again.

Rock flicks a quick glance at the ceiling, his mouth twisting like he's trying to hold back his laughter.

Under the table there's a soft thump. "Keep thanking Buddha, fucker," Z grumbles at Rock. He jerks his thumb at me. "I was never this disrespectful."

"Please," Rock draws out the word to dismiss Z's comment. "Go on, Rooster."

I grin at both of them. "So happy I could be the catalyst for your presidential bonding trip."

They both glare at me in return.

"Anyway, Jiggy and I pulled the story out of Pants."

"How is that scary mountain man?" Z asks.

"He's apparently a *hog farmer* now. Doesn't seem as excited about the porn as Ice and T-Bone."

"Not surprised. About either of those." Rock says. "Go on."

"He says they have people inside ATF now. Sounds like blackmail for one, and another might be family to Ice or someone at their charter."

"Fuck me." Rock focuses his stare on Z. "That's new territory."

Z runs his hand over his jaw. "They think that's gonna give 'em enough cover to do what?"

"I think they want back into guns."

"Priest won't go for that. Even if ATF is covered. Too much potential to go wrong."

"Right. That's what Jigsaw and I thought."

"Although..." Z says.

"Here we go," Rock mutters.

"Demons never got out of guns that we know of. Maybe we can work this situation to their advantage. If we don't want to split what's coming to them after DeLova retires, maybe we can hook them up with Virginia."

"I thought you were worried we'd all get swept up in that?" I ask.

Z shrugs. "Sounds like we will one way or another."

"Might as well roll with it," Rock adds. "That what you're suggesting?"

"If Ice already has this set up, he's not going to back off just because we ask him nicely. And if we rat him out to Priest, that's not good for anyone either. Sounds like it's a done deal."

"Might as well do what we can to make it beneficial for everyone." Rock focuses on me again. "If they come at us for RICO at some point, they're going to want the ones directly involved. They'll dick all of us around, no doubt, but I think we can manage to minimize our risk."

"All right." I'm not as convinced as they seem to be. "Still thought you should know."

"Fuck yeah." Z slaps my arm. "Thanks for keeping those big ears open."

"Anything else?" Rock asks.

"Oh, Ice has cameras stashed all over the clubhouse."

Z shrugs. "So do we."

"No, bedrooms too."

He cracks up, slapping his hand on the table. "Didn't warn a brother?"

"No," I growl. "Pants said something about the porn house being wired so Ice can keep tabs on his girl. Prompted me to take a closer look at my room."

"That's probably the answer to how he managed to hook someone at ATF," Rock says.

"My thoughts too."

"Better be careful if you bring Shelby there," Z warns. "She doesn't need a 'country superstar railed in biker clubhouse' video all over the Internet."

"Fuck off," I growl.

"Just sayin'." He holds up his hands in a "no harm" gesture.

Rock side-eyes him. "Extorting law enforcement is one thing. Betraying a brother that way is something else entirely. You think Ice is capable of that?"

"These days, I think anyone's capable of anything." Z's dimples vanish, his face turning dead serious. "Only brothers I trust with my life have *New York* stitched on their bottom rockers."

Rock lifts his coffee cup in Z's direction. "Amen to that, brother."

CHAPTER FORTY-FOUR

Shelby

Another dressing room in another city.

I stare at myself in the mirror, waiting for Cindy to begin her magic.

Greg knocks and pushes the door open. "How are you feeling tonight?"

"Good." I bit my lip. "You haven't gotten any more calls from my mom, have you?"

His mouth twists down.

Bad sign.

"She really wants you to call her," he finally says. "She's worried about you."

"Well, then I hope you told her I'm peachy."

"Yes," he answers slowly.

My gaze drops to his hands, narrowing on what looks like a black envelope in one.

My stomach drops.

"Oh, yeah. Someone dropped this off at the ticket office for you." He tosses the envelope in my lap.

Not again.

"Where'd it come from?" I stare at the envelope the same way I'd stare at a rat swinging by its tail.

"Don't know. Probably fan mail." He shrugs and walks out.

Cindy frowns at the envelope. "Looks kinda like a kid's handwriting."

No doubt whatever's inside won't be kid-friendly.

"Aren't you going to open it?" she asks.

"I guess." I pick it up and rip open the flap. Just like before, there's a piece of black paper inside. Slowly, I tug it out and unfold it.

Same silver writing.

This time, the note's longer and scrawled on the page from top to bottom. Fear twists my insides.

My Shelby,

I hope you enjoyed your time with your new boyfriend. Soon you won't have any need for men in your life besides me. I was so disappointed to see you cavorting around with some strange man again like a whore. But that's what your industry does to young, beautiful girls, isn't it? Turns them into whores.

It's a conundrum because your music is how I met and fell in love with you and yet your behavior disappoints me.

I don't want to hurt you, I promise.

I just want to make you happy. And I will.

Soon.

All my love.

M

By the time I'm finished, fear has melted my brain into a puddle that can't form any rational thoughts.

With my heart racing, and what-the-fuck alarm bells clanging like crazy in my head, I toss the letter and envelope on the counter. "Holy shit."

"What is it?" Cindy reaches over and picks it up. A few seconds later, she gasps. "Shelby. Oh my God."

She flings the door open and hollers, "Greg!"

"Cindy, don't." It's a weak protest.

"Shelby, this isn't a joke." She rests her hand on my shoulder. "I'm scared for you."

Greg stops in front of my open door. "What?"

"Who left this for her?" Cindy insists.

He shrugs.

Cindy grabs his arm and drags him into the room.

"It's just some creep." I shrug, but I'm shaking so hard it probably looks more like a zombie twitch. "I've gotten them before."

"What do you mean you've gotten these before?" Cindy scolds.

Greg snaps the paper out of her hands and scans it. "Jesus. I knew those pictures were a bad idea," he mutters. "You've got to be more careful."

"So what?" I snap, anger burning a hole in my fear. "I'm never supposed to have a life because some creep thinks he's in love with me? That's ridiculous."

"One of Dawson's guys needs to watch her, Greg," Cindy insists.

"Where's Logan now?" Greg asks me.

"I told you we're plannin' to meet up in Virginia. He can't just upend his life to play bodyguard for free. He has a life. A job." I'm trying to keep my voice calm. I can't afford to stress out my vocal cords before I go onstage, but it's hard not to scream in frustration—and terror.

I have gotten letters like this before. Not these black and silver ones. But ones with similar creepy undertones. Some guy who probably needs medication, thinking he's in love with me or that I "spoke" to him through the television. Or that my songs contain coded messages only he can decipher. I've always cringed, then tossed 'em in the trash. What else can I do? I don't have the money to hire investigators every time I receive a twisted love note.

"I need to talk to the record company. They'll have to hire someone," Greg says.

"I'm never gonna see a penny in royalties if they keep sticking stuff on my tab," I grumble, staring at the ceiling. Why'd I have to open that dang letter with Cindy here?

"Shelby, honey, we've talked about this. You're never gonna see a dime from this album. Your downloads are through the roof after all the exposure you've been getting. I'll be able to weasel more stuff from them."

That's exactly what I don't want—to owe the record company

another red penny, or I'll never get my mother out of that damn tiny house. As much as she's burning my biscuits these days, it's the one thing I've wanted to do more than anything. I always promised myself that if I made any real money with my music, I'd set her up someplace nice before indulging in anything for myself.

"We need to find you some endorsements," Greg says. This has been a frequent topic of conversation lately. "Maybe have you audition for films. I've had a few inquiries. Something to bring in money outside of music."

"But music's all I wanna do."

"We need to capitalize off your fame some other way." He glances at my boots. "Maybe a line of Shelby Morgan cowgirl boots."

"Cheap shit made in China that'll fall apart in two weeks? No way."

"Jessica Simpson had a clothing empire."

I grunt at him.

"Listen, you need to center yourself for the show tonight. I'll talk to Dawson. Tomorrow, I'll be speaking with the record company."

"Great." I reach out and grab his arm on his way to the door. "Thank you."

His gruff manager face softens. "Of course."

Cindy's hands are shaking when she returns to work on my hair. "We need to take that letter seriously, Shelby. I've seen this get out of hand with celebrities before. It starts small with a letter or phone calls. Next, they're showing up at your front door with a knife."

Chills race down my spine and I scowl at Cindy. "I'm not a celebrity. Stop trying to scare the piss outta me."

"Honey, you need to wrap your pretty little head around the fact that you *are* a celebrity." She squeezes my shoulders. "I'll feel better when your sexy beast of a man is here to look out for you. I don't doubt he'll keep the creeps away."

My lips curve into a smile. Dang, I'm missing Rooster something fierce.

Someone knocks on the door so hard it rattles on its hinges. Cindy reaches over to open it.

Dawson and one of his bodyguards step inside.

"What's goin' on, Shelby?" Dawson's concerned face helps chase some of my embarrassment away. "Greg said you got some sort of threat?"

"Not a threat, exactly." I hand him the letter and he scans it before passing it to the guy at his side.

"Shoot, that's creepy," Dawson mutters. "All right." He claps his hands together. "Here's what's gonna happen. Bane's stickin' with ya tonight and until Greg figures something else out. You're not to go *anywhere* without him. Understood?"

His tone leaves me feeling like a naughty puppy who peed on the carpet. "Thank you, Dawson." I peek up at Bane. His severe expression softens. "Thank you, Bane."

Dawson glances around my dressing room. "Where's Logan?"

"Home."

"You tell him 'bout this?"

"I just opened it. But I don't want him to worry." I shrug. "I've gotten stuff like that before."

"If it was me, I'd wanna know." Dawson holds up his hands. "Not sticking my nose in your personal business. Just sayin'."

"Thanks, Dawson."

He slaps Bane's shoulder. "Stay on her."

"You got it."

Bane parks himself on the couch facing the door after Dawson leaves.

Great.

Cindy goes back to work on my hair.

My phone chirps and for the first time ever, I hesitate to pick it up. That letter rattled me more than I want to admit. Or maybe I'm uncomfortable having Bane watch my every move.

I flick the screen on to find a text from Rooster.

Rooster: I miss you.

Me: Miss you too.

Rooster: Love you. Be awesome tonight, chickadee.

A few seconds later, a selfie of Rooster pulling a sad face appears on my screen.

I finally smile.

"Did you tell him?" Cindy asks.

I set my phone in my lap facedown.

Fear swoops into my belly again. A few seconds of texting with Rooster and I forgot all about the creepy letter. What can I do, though? If I tell him, he'll want to race right out here and beat someone up. While that might make me feel better, I can't make him drop everything and come hold my hand every time some psycho sends me a note.

"Nah I told you, it's probably harmless. No need to make him worry."

Wow, that almost sounded believable.

CHAPTER FORTY-FIVE

Rooster

It's late when I return to the Virginia clubhouse. Parking lot's full of brothers and the usual assortment of visitors—hanger-ons, club girls, and prospects.

Jigsaw's heavy boots crunch over the gravel. He slaps my shoulder. "How'd it go?"

"Good."

"Take a detour? What took so long?"

I give him a hard look meant to shut him up and hook my arm around his neck, pulling him in close. "Met up with Z and Rock. Heads-up about what's going on here," I say against his ear.

"I missed ya, bro, but no need to slobber on me." He shoves me away but gives me a quick nod to acknowledge what I said.

Music and loud voices from the clubhouse pour into the night.

"All the stuff came," Jigsaw says. "I didn't want to mess with it, but it's locked up at the house."

"Thanks."

As I step into the clubhouse, someone lets out a 'cock-a-doodle-doo', alerting the whole place that I've returned.

"Welcome back, brother!" Ice shouts.

The brothers and even a few of the girls surrounding him lift their arms in the air and cheer.

I walk up to Ice and slap his outstretched hand. "Missed me that much, huh?"

"Don't worry. Anya said Jigsaw held things together."

I wasn't worried but okay.

Anya pops up at Ice's side. "Do you think we can be ready to open the online store by Friday?"

Sure fucking hope so. Shelby's supposed to roll into town late Thursday night or early Friday morning. After her shows and couple days off, I'm planning to follow her out of here. "Shouldn't be a problem."

"What's the hurry?" Ice asks.

"I set up that interview." Anya pouts. "I need you to take me there Thursday morning."

"No can do." Ice shakes his head and doesn't offer any more of an explanation for his refusal.

Her bottom lip quivers and the corners of her mouth turn down. Is she going to cry? I don't wanna see this.

"Please?" she whines. "I'm worried they're gonna be dicks."

"I really can't." Ice turns to me. "You mind taking her? She's got this thing with the radio station."

"The DJs are really crude and gross," Anya explains. "But their audience is basically who I'm trying to target."

"Yeah." I glance at Jigsaw. *Speak up anytime, bro.* "One of us can do it."

Never mind that it's not what I signed up for on this trip and Ice has an entire clubhouse of other brothers he could ask.

She claps her hands together. "Thank you. I'll feel better having you there."

"No problem."

"Thanks, Rooster." Ice pats my back and moves on to talk to someone else. Jigsaw catches Shonda's eye and swaggers her way. Lord help the woman.

I'm really not in the mood to party, especially since I need to have all this stuff set up before the weekend.

I take Anya aside.

"Are you sticking around tonight?" I ask her.

She bats her eyelashes a few times and answers in a breathy voice. "I can if you want me to."

Yeah, no.

"I could use your help with some of the website sign-ups," I clarify so there are no misunderstandings about my expectations.

Her shoulders drop and a softer, more natural smile curves her lips. "Oh. Sure."

Party noises fade away as she follows me down the long, narrow hallway to Ice's office.

She frowns when I pull out a key to open the door. "Ice doesn't allow me in here."

"You're with me. He knows I need your help with this."

She bites her lip and glances back the way we came. Shit. Is she worried Ice will be pissed at her or worried about being alone with me?

"Okay."

My gaze strays to the corner and the tiny red, blinking light. Ice even has cameras set up in here. Really couldn't give a shit less if he's somewhere else in the house watching us. Actually, knowing we're being filmed is a relief. This way, there's no chance of him accusing me of hitting on his girlfriend—or whatever she is to him—later.

I drop into the chair behind the desk and motion for her to take the one across from me. "You got your license on you?"

"Give me a second." She pulls her big purse into her lap and searches through it.

While I'm waiting, I jot down a bunch of addresses and passwords she'll need. Ice has a copy of everything I'm giving her, and I'll keep a third copy. Just in case.

Finally, she hands me her license. It's real—or one hell of a fake. I snap a quick picture of her holding the license up to her face, then she sets it down on the desk next to me.

One after the other, I fill in the same tedious information at each film distribution platform.

"So, five to seven minute clips on the free sites seem to do the best to reel people in," I explain so she knows why the fuck I dragged her down here. "At least for Stella. Yours might be different, so you can play around with the length until you find something that consistently works for you."

"Okay." She nods eagerly. "I never give the pop shot away."

"Probably a good strategy. Give 'em blue balls."

She chuckles.

My gaze won't stop straying to her license sitting next to the keyboard.

I'm not judging. She seems to be into this business venture. It's not like Ice is forcing her into anything. But God damn. She's a year younger than Shelby. Old enough to make her own choices, sure. Luckier than most girls, I guess. Found someone to bankroll her business. Still, some of the stupid decisions I made at her age flood my memories.

Not your concern.

"How long you been doing this, Anya?" I can't help myself.

Her eyes widen. Shit, maybe she mentioned it at some point and I forgot. Or maybe no one's ever given a damn before. "Uh, since I was eighteen, why?"

"Just curious."

She sits forward and drums her nails over against the desk, her gaze darting around the room. "Actually..."

Please tell me Ice hasn't been banging this chick since she was a teenager.

"My stepdad posted videos of me before then..."

Fuck.

"I didn't find out until some kids in school were passing around the links. It took me forever to get the sites to take them down." She jerks her chin toward her license and the paperwork I've been filling out. "That's all bullshit. They don't really give a damn."

"Shit, I'm sorry. Is your stepfather at least in prison?"

She frowns, as if prison had never been an option. *Holy fuck, tell me her pedo stepdad isn't still running around?*

"Well, no...uh..." She lowers her voice. "Ice *took care* of him." She raises her eyebrows in a catch-my-drift sort of way.

So, stepdaddy's six-feet under somewhere. I'm certainly not losing sleep over the information.

Her gaze drops to my VP patch. "You're a brother. I can tell you that, right?"

"Of course." On second thought, Ice might not appreciate her sharing that with anyone, brother or not. "But let's pretend you didn't."

She snaps her mouth shut.

"Go on," I encourage her. "You got those videos down?"

"Yeah. They still pop up from time to time. I get sick of chasing them, though."

I stare at her, trying hard not to ask the obvious question.

"A boyfriend posted some clips without telling me maybe a year later." She lifts her shoulders. "I figured the whole world's seen me anyway. Might as well profit off it myself."

Christ, that's fucking sad.

I'm overcome with the urge to bang my head against the desk. For fuck's sake, I'm a fucking biker who really shouldn't give a shit about any of this.

I struggle to keep my face neutral. Seems as if life's given her one shitty choice after another. I don't want to make her feel bad about the decisions she's made.

"Is there anything else you ever wanted to do?" I tap my pen against the desk, debating my words. "You know it might be hard to find a different line of work later on."

"I think that ship has sailed." She flashes a pained smile. "Ice is letting me keep fifty percent ownership of all my content. That's better than the five hundred a scene I used to get paid and own nothing after."

"True." I'd gone over the contracts and paperwork setting up the corporation. Honestly, I'm shocked Ice was so generous. Is he using club funds or personal for this business?

Doesn't matter. Not your business.

"Maybe counseling or something," she says. "Ice made me finish my associates in psychology."

I guess that's something.

CHAPTER FORTY-SIX

Shelby

Dawson has been true to his word. Bane's like superglue. Can't pry him off my ass. I swore up and down I wouldn't leave my room but I bet if I opened that door, I'd find him sittin' out in the hallway.

The hum of the hotel's air conditioner blunts the city noises drifting into my room.

I center myself in the middle of the bed and clutch the crystal around my neck. The nominations for the Country Music Awards are coming soon. Afraid to let anyone know how much I secretly long for at least a nomination, I haven't breathed a word.

I don't need to win. But just a nod would be nice. So maybe people would stop writing headlines like the one posted on *Sippin' on Secrets* this afternoon.

Buxom blonde songbird parts ways with biker

I mean, what the heck? Now I don't even get a name? Deeper down, in a place I don't feel like acknowledging, it prickles at my insecurity about being so far away from Rooster.

You're going to see him in a couple days. You've talked to him every day. Quit being a baby.

The corners of my mouth tug up. At least that article will keep my mother off my back about Rooster. Maybe I should send *Sippin' on Secrets* a thank you note.

Ha! Talk about puttin' a positive spin on something negative.

Feeling a bit better, I shuffle my tarot cards through my hands and close my eyes.

What do I need to do right now to be taken seriously in this business?

The cards flow through my hands, one after the other. I open my eyes and stare down at them as I shuffle.

One card pops out, landing facedown in front of me.

Huh. I'm not the best shuffler in the world, but even so, I don't usually have jumper cards.

Card on the floor means check your door. Momma says that all the time. Jumper cards are serious business—something happening soon the universe really wants you to know about. She usually says to treat it as a special card outside of the message of the spread and sets it aside.

Resisting the urge to turn it over, I pick it up and set it next to my knee.

A chill runs down my spine.

I flick my gaze to the air conditioner.

The negative energy surrounding me from missing Rooster is gonna throw off my reading. And if that doesn't do it, the stress of receiving another creepy letter last night sure will. Same black paper. Same silver ink. It was shorter than the last one but creepier than midnight at summer camp in October.

DEAREST SHELBY,

It pleases me when you're a good girl and behave yourself.
Soon.
All my love.
M

CLEARLY M IS A FEW BRICKS SHORT OF A LOAD.

Focus.

Forget the stupid letters and concentrate.

What do I need to do right now to be taken seriously in this business? I repeat the question softly to myself while I continue shuffling the deck.

When I'm satisfied, I lay out my three cards and turn them over one by one.

Three of Swords.

Ten of Swords.

Justice.

I stare at the cards.

Breathe. Don't freak out.

There are no "good" or "bad" cards. They represent a spectrum of meaning. At least, that's what some people say. It's trendy to try and put a positive spin on the cards that lean negative. But my momma always insists I read the hand I'm dealt the way it's dealt.

I pick up the booklet that came with the deck and flip through the pages. These all seem related to interpersonal relationships or...I don't know what.

I was asking a career question.

Maybe the universe doesn't give a crap about your questions.

Three of Swords—the card depicts three swords piercing a full heart. Representative of unexpected painful events. Heartache, separation, sadness.

Well, I miss Rooster. That's not a surprise.

I set aside other interpretations that say the card can indicate infidelity and breakups.

Ten of Swords—a man facedown with ten swords in his back.

A sign of an unwelcome surprise in the future. So, I *won't* get nominated for a CMA? That's not exactly a surprise either.

Again, I ignore that it can also indicate a breakup.

Or the obvious interpretation that someone's going to stab you in the back.

Justice. Okay, this isn't a bad card. Unless you're a serial killer or something. Justice can also restore balance and order in some way if you've been wronged.

I sweep my gaze over the cards again. Maybe whoever's going to stab me in the back will get what they deserve? And the painful events can be a learning opportunity?

Dammit, why can't the universe be a little more direct?

I bite my lip and continue studying the cards. Who would stab me in the back? Except for Trent, I'm not really close to any of the guys in my band. They were hired specifically for this tour. We get along okay but Trent's closer to them than I am.

Greg hasn't been my manager for long. I don't always trust him. Then again, it's hard for me to trust *anyone*. Always has been.

Except Rooster. I trust him more than I probably should.

Don't go there. I asked a career question. This ain't a love reading.

I jot down the cards and their positions in my notebook to study later.

The jumper card catches my eye and I flip it over.

The Devil.

My heart thuds louder, drowning out all the other noises. Never gotten that one before. It's not as evil as it seems. But it can indicate addiction, obsession, or negativity of some sort in my life. Sometimes it can hint at self-destruction.

I jot a few notes and close my journal.

Another chill races down my spine and this time it's got nothing to do with the air-conditioning.

CHAPTER FORTY-SEVEN

Rooster

The morning of Anya's interview, the clubhouse seems to be empty. Guess Ice wasn't lying when he said he had somewhere else to be.

I meet her at the bar. She keeps rocking from side to side on her feet and startles when I approach.

"Easy, it's just me. You ready to go?"

"Are you sure you don't mind taking me?" She drops her head, her long wheat-blond hair covering her face. "I just never know what I'm going to encounter. . ."

It's not on the top of things I'm in the mood to do today but the whole point of me coming down here was to help out. Eventually, Ice needs to pick a brother he trusts to escort his stars but today, I'll handle it.

"No problem."

She glances toward the parking lot. "You got an extra helmet?"

"You're not riding on the back of my bike." That came out harsher than I intended. I tack on a, "sweetheart," to soften the rejection. But no fucking way is anyone except Shelby claiming that spot.

Her wide eyes meet mine. Her slick red lips part but no words come out. Guess guys don't say *no* to her often.

"Back of my bike's for my ol' lady." Not that I owe her an explanation.

"Oh. Of course. I didn't realize. I thought." She blows out a breath and snaps her mouth shut.

"You ready?" I nod to her oversized, long-sleeve shirt and jeans. "We don't have a lot of time if you want to change."

"Oh." She tugs at the hem of the shirt and laughs. "Yeah. It's a radio interview. Those fuckers can pay if they want to see me naked."

Can't argue with that logic.

I grab the keys to one the club's extra trucks and head outside. Anya hurries to catch up to me, her sneakers grinding over the gravel and sending little rocks skittering out in front of us. I point the remote at the line of trucks and hit the unlock button. A black Ford F-150 beeps and flashes its lights.

After a quick check that the lights and everything seem to be working—fuck knows so many arrests could be avoided if people bothered to check their damn tail lights—I motion for Anya to get in on the passenger side.

"Thanks for doing this." She hands me her phone with the address for the radio station so I can plug it into the GPS.

"Are you nervous?" I ask.

"A little." She laughs. "I've only done one or two other interviews and the guys were gross."

I grin at her. "Maybe don't say that in the interview."

"I won't."

"You know not to get into specifics about who bankrolls you, hosts your site, or anything like that, right?"

"Oh yeah. Ice was clear I shouldn't ever mention the club."

"Good." This isn't technically illegal. Still, the whole Lost Kings organization prefers to stay out of as many mouths and off as many radars as possible.

I pull into the parking garage and back the truck into a spot near the stairs. Anya blinks at me when I follow her into the stairwell.

"You're coming in with me?"

"That was the whole point, wasn't it? Otherwise, I could've just called you an Uber."

"Oh, well." She tips her head toward my cut. "Your patches. You said you didn't want the club connected..."

Aw, ain't that sweet? "Nah, *financially* the club doesn't want to be linked. Don't really care who knows you have the club's protection."

"Thank you." Her tense smile fades. "I mean it."

"No problem." I gesture toward the stairs. "Let's go."

AN HOUR LATER, I'M THOROUGHLY BORED AND RECONSIDERING MY love for our Virginia brothers. One of those motherfuckers could've played chauffeur today. I glance at my phone. I can't wait to be done with Mission Porno, VA edition.

I've only been half-listening to the interview. Every time I glance up, Anya has an attentive look on her face, or she's laughing and twirling her hair around her finger.

My phone buzzes.

Shelby: Miss you. Driver says we'll be there around one a.m.

Shit, that's later than I expected.

Me: I'll be there.

Shelby: You don't have to. It's so late.

Me: I'm not exactly an early-to-bed guy. Send me the address.

She doesn't answer right away, so I assume she's finding the info for me. Greg's probably planning to have them sleep in the van. I'll either take Shelby back to the clubhouse or go to a hotel.

"So, you're into the bad boys?" one of the interviewers asks.

I snap my head up.

Anya lets out a flirty giggle. "Of course."

The other interviewer leers at her. "You ever give nice guys a chance?"

I snort. *Nice guy.* That's usually code for a passive-aggressive dude who feels entitled to a woman's attention—or more—because he's so "nice." This guy has *jerk* written all over him.

"I mean, it depends." Anya giggles again. A fake, bubbly sound that's more grating than cute. "A *truly* nice guy, sure. But someone who's *pretending* to be nice just to get in my panties? Hell no."

Good answer, Anya. I chuckle and go back to my phone.

"—biker boyfriend?"

What now?

I narrow my eyes. The jerk interviewer's watching me with a smirk that's about to get punched off his face.

"No, that's my bodyguard," Anya says.

Jerk opens his mouth and the other interviewer cuts him off. Guess he carries the common sense for the pair.

"That's all we have time for today. Anya, you want to give out your website or any other info?" the sensible one asks.

"Sure." She rattles off the website and a code for people to use that will rope them into a recurring subscription.

"Tune in tomorrow morning. We'll be interviewing country music's newest sweetheart, Shelby Morgan."

Wait, what?

"Oh, she's hot," Jerk interviewer groans into the microphone. "Now *there's* a girl who should be in porn."

Motherfucker. I stand up, ready to crack open his skull.

My phone buzzes again and I check to find an address from Shelby.

Me: Are you doing some radio interview tomorrow?

No response.

She's mentioned Greg setting her up on surprise interviews before. Maybe she doesn't even know about it yet.

Anya's interview seems to be over. Some pop tune floats over the speakers. Sounds like someone dropped a bunch of soup cans over a piano with a sack full of cats screaming in the background. But what do I know?

My gaze zeroes in on Anya's uncomfortable smile as she inches her way toward freedom.

That's what I'm here for.

Not giving one absolute fuck, I open the door to the studio.

"You sure I can't take you out tonight, sweetheart?" Jerk says to her.

"Sorry, I have plans." Anya's nervous gaze darts to me.

"We need to get some promotional photos," the sensible guy says.

Fuck.

I drop back into my chair and wait for someone at the station to pop in with a camera and snap some shots of the three of them standing in front of a wall with a full-color painting of the station's tacky logo.

Jerk keeps asking her questions, trying to convince her to go out with him.

"We done?" I interrupt the conversation. She's too nice to cut them off and I have no problem playing the bad guy here.

I curl my hand at Anya. "Come on. Time to go."

Anya wiggles her fingers. "Bye. Thanks so much for having me." She skirts away from the two men while I stare the jerk down.

"Thanks, Mr. Bodyguard." He smirks at me.

I don't bother responding, just shut the door behind us.

In the elevator downstairs, Anya shivers and rolls her eyes. "Yuck, that guy was *so* gross."

"Yeah, he sounded like a dick."

"Did I do okay? I didn't sound like an airhead, did I?"

Shit, I barely even listened. "The parts I caught sounded good to me."

Once we're in the truck, I pull out my phone.

Shelby: Yup. Two shock jock D-bags.

My mouth curls up. Fuck, I miss Shelby's sassy mouth.

"What's wrong?" Anya asks.

"Nothing." I toss my phone in the middle console.

Guess I'll be paying the radio station another visit tomorrow.

And you bet your ass I'll be listening to every word of *that* interview.

CHAPTER FORTY-EIGHT

Rooster

Sure, *now* the clubhouse is full with awake and functioning brothers.

Ice greets Anya and me in the common area. "How'd it go, princess?"

"Good," she coos and curls her hair around her finger, rocking her hips from side to side. All she needs is a schoolgirl outfit and some bubble gum and the two of them could go film a video right now. Jesus, this is Sway and Stella all over again. Starting to wonder if that president's patch makes your brain leak out through your dick or something.

Jigsaw wanders in, bleary-eyed and hanging onto a small, dark-haired girl. Even in her five-inch fuck-me pumps, she barely clears his shoulder.

He lifts his chin at me. "Why didn't you wake me up? I would've come with you."

"It's fine."

Anya squeezes my arm. "Rooster was so badass. That fucker Scotty kept hassling me to go out with him tonight, and Rooster scared the piss out of him."

"Thanks, brother." Ice jerks his chin toward the hallway. "Got a minute?"

"Sure." I point to Jigsaw. "Don't go far. I need to talk to you."

"Yeah, okay."

I follow Ice into his office and he closes the door behind us. "How'd it go?" he rumbles in a flat, disinterested tone that probably inspired his road name.

"Fine." Fuck, I agreed to go as protection, not to return with a fucking full report of events. "She handled it well. Gave out the info for the site. Station said they'll keep it up on their website too."

"Good. They treat her with respect?"

"Eh." I shrug. "One was a bit of an asshole, like she said. But I think that's their schtick."

Maybe if you want people to be respectful, don't send her to the prick and dick show.

He reaches into his desk drawer and pulls out a wad of cash.

"Ice, come on. You don't have to pay me."

He levels a frosty glare my way. "Don't start that shit with me, Rooster."

I did the respectful-decline-the-money-first routine, so now I feel comfortable reaching for the cash. "Appreciate it."

"How long you in town?"

"My girl gets in late tonight. Probably leaving with her early next week."

"You bringing her by tonight? Probably gonna be rowdy. Celebrating the launch of the site and all."

"I might get a room downtown, but I'll definitely bring her by the next night."

"It'll be a party all weekend but anyone you want to bring is fine with me."

"Thanks."

After I leave Ice's office, I pull out my phone and text Shelby.

Me: Make it to Philadelphia?

Shelby: Just finished rehearsal.

Me: How'd it go?

She responds with a few thumbs down emojis.

330

Instead of answering, I jog upstairs and slip into my room to call her.

"Hey," she answers right away.

"What's wrong?"

She laughs softly. "Nothing's wrong. I just didn't like the sound setup. It'll be okay."

"I miss you," I blurt out.

"Miss you too," she says softly. "Whatcha been up to? I don't have any mental pictures of you in that clubhouse."

Yeah, my day isn't one any woman wants mental snapshots of. *Here's my boyfriend escorting a porn star around town. Oh, look, a shot of my boyfriend spending his afternoon setting up accounts on adult film sites. Here he is deciding which bare-assed photo will bring in the most subscribers.*

Nope.

"Nothing you want in your mental photo album." Points for honesty, right? But I really need to come clean about what I'm up to when I see her. Not the intricate club-business details but at least the broad strokes.

"Hmm. That sounds ominous."

"Club business. Nothing exciting." Not to me, anyway. To Shelby? Yeah, I think she'll have an opinion or two.

"You really want to pick me up tonight? You don't have to. I can—"

"What are you talking about? Of course I'll be there." Somehow, I need to make it clearer to Shelby that I mean what I say and she can trust me.

"Shoot. I have to go. Sorry, Rooster."

"Hey, before you go, any more creepy messages?"

"Wh-what do you mean?"

It shouldn't be that hard of a question to answer. "Like that 'marry me' one you got the other night?"

She lets out a high, thin laugh. Not like Shelby at all. I pull the phone away from my ear and stare at it for a second.

"Probably dozens of 'em. I haven't checked my email yet," she finally answers.

Hasn't checked her Instagram either, or she might have noticed the King of Cocky Roosters profile that started following her recently. Still not sure how I'll explain all the porn stars I'm also following. But those are for business reasons. The way I'm stalking Shelby's pervy admirers is purely personal. I've already zeroed in on at least three grown-ass men who seem to be obsessed with her.

From what I've seen, her social media's full of bullshit that Greg should be keeping better tabs on. Someone needs to go through and delete the shitty comments, report and investigate the creepy ones, and answer her genuine fans.

Not my business.

Not yet anyway.

SHELBY

After my set, Greg walks me to my dressing room, Bane close on our tail.

I'm buzzing to get the heck out of here. We have a long drive ahead of us.

Greg drops down on the couch while I pack my stuff.

Paper crinkles and I glance over. "What's that?"

"Your schedule for tomorrow."

"My *schedule*?" Except for this dumb interview that got tacked on, my only plans were to spend time with Rooster. He better not have added anything else. "Email it to me."

"You need to be at the interview early. Are you sure you'll be ready? I'm not comfortable having Logan take you."

I pace the length of the couch, throwing glares at Greg each time I pass. "Well, I really wish you'd consulted me before you set it up."

"This is a big deal for you, Shelby," Greg says in his "be reasonable" tone that usually has the opposite reaction from me. "This isn't a country station. 'Big Lies' has more of a mainstream feel and they've been getting tons of requests for it."

"Then why didn't you tell me about it ahead of time?" I stop pacing and squint at him. "And why don't *you* look more excited?"

"They had a last-minute spot to fill," he hedges.

"And?"

"They're shock jocks." He sighs. "Have a bit of a reputation for being obnoxious."

"Wait, shock jocks are still a thing? I thought all those tools moved to podcasts and satellite radio."

He frowns at the question. "This duo's still popular. They got fined into oblivion a few years back but returned with a bigger audience than ever. They do a variety of interviews, from porn stars to pop stars."

"And you think that's good for my image?"

"I do. You're getting airplay on mainstream radio. I know your roots are country but we'll go anywhere the money's green, right?"

"If you say so, I'll do it."

Another frown. In Greg's head, this wasn't up for debate.

"Bane should be the one to escort you. Keep it professional. Your boyfriend's got a hair trigger for anything he deems offensive against you."

I snort and then full-on belly laugh. "I'm not sure what it says about you that you think that's a negative quality in a man, Greg. But I'll tell you one thing: I'm sure as shit not going without him."

He sighs and stands. "Just keep him on a leash."

As if anyone could leash Rooster. Or I'd insult him by asking him to sit there and say nothing, denying his true nature. "I'm sure it'll be fine."

"It would be a better use of his time if you'd tell him about the letters."

"Why? How's he supposed to track the guy down? With the power of his mind?" I scoff. Greg just wants to use Rooster as free labor, and I'm not havin' it. Nor am I gonna worry him by telling him what's going on. I snap a quick picture of the schedule and send it to Rooster, so he at least knows what to expect.

After Greg leaves, I poke my head outside the door. Bane's standing guard like he has been every night since Dawson assigned him to me.

"Need something?" he asks.

"Just help moving my stuff out." I'm not bothering to change out of my dress. Rooster said he's picking me up in a truck so I can bring my guitar to the radio station tomorrow, and I want to look pretty for him.

"I'll find someone. Stay put."

As if I'd bother with an escape attempt.

I haven't personally received any more letters but between Bane's constant vigilance, Dawson stopping by to check on me every night, and Greg's arguments with the record label, I have a feeling more have been delivered and no one wants to tell me.

I shut the door with a quiet click and face the empty, lonely dressing room. Eagerness to see Rooster shoots through my belly. If I could sprout a set of wings, I'd take flight right now.

A few minutes later, Trent's usual rapid-fire three knocks hit the door. "It's me," he calls out.

"Come on in."

He and Bane grab my stuff and sandwich me between them for the long walk to the van.

The fire of a dozen bees are stinging my eyes tonight. *Sleep.* I just want to sleep in a reasonably comfortable bed.

We reach the van and I help the guys load everything, remembering to take my backpack and another bag up front.

"Go ahead, Shelby. We've got the rest of this."

Stretching out on the thin mattress of my tiny bunk, I groan and close my eyes.

Rooster. Can't wait to see him.

An instant replay of tonight's show flashes behind my eyelids. It was good, but not my best. Besides my stinging eyes from whatever pollen is floatin' in the air, my throat's raw and scratchy. Dawson hadn't asked me to perform with him, and instead of being insulted, I was relieved.

I pop a lozenge in my mouth and roll to my side. As I'm drifting off, the guys step into the van. Poor Bane's been riding with us in our less luxurious surroundings but hasn't complained.

How the heck am I supposed to explain his presence to Rooster?

CHAPTER FORTY-NINE

Rooster

The spot Shelby asked me to pick her up from tonight is a few rows over from where her van's parked. The lot's empty at this hour. I'm about to start up the truck and move closer when she pops out of the van, hoisting her backpack on her shoulder.

A big mountain of a man follows her. Dude could give Pants a run for his money in the scary fucker department. Why the fuck's he following Shelby?

I step out of the truck, keeping my eye on both of them. She turns and stops him, speaking a few words I can't catch. She points my way and motions with her hands.

Mountain man nods, and she races across the blacktop.

She turns and waves at the guy before flinging herself at me. "Hey. I'm so sorry about that—"

I slam my mouth over hers, swallowing the explanations she doesn't owe me. When we part, she's fidgety and keeps glancing around the parking lot.

Shelby's smiles are usually sunlight melting my frosty corpse heart. But tonight, her face is tight. Strained. Is she tired? Not thrilled to see me?

Headlights sweep over the parking lot and the van honks twice as it drives away.

I hold her door open, my hungry eyes roaming every inch of her. A hint of her lemon-sugar scent teases my nose. I fit my hands on her waist and boost her into the truck.

"Rooster."

One more kiss, then we'll get going. She twists in her seat so her boots are resting on the running board. Her dress grazes her knees, hiding enough to annoy me. I step closer, slide my hands up her legs, under her dress, until my hands are on her hips.

She tilts her head to the side. "What're you doing?"

"I need another kiss." The pull is too strong to ignore. I push my big body between her knees and she squeezes my sides. I brush my nose along her temple to inhale her sweet scent again.

She loops her arms around my neck. "So kiss me."

I brush my lips over hers. She lets out a sharp sound that ratchets up my need for her. Her tongue flicks against mine.

"Shelby," I groan, barely leaving her lips.

She lets out a softer moan, clinging to me tighter.

How does this woman always taste so good?

A wild need-to-have-her-*now* fever consumes me. We're a tangle of limbs and clothes, and too many car parts in the way, but I finally squeeze my big body into the front seat with her and slam the door shut, locking it.

Shelby wastes no time straddling my lap. I run my hands up under her dress again, savoring every inch of skin. My fingers tease the edge of her underwear, trace the small of her back.

"Fuck, I really didn't plan to do this in the parking lot," I mumble as I kiss a path from Shelby's ear to her neck. "You smell so good. I missed you."

"I missed you too." She gathers her dress in her hands, tugging it up even higher so I catch a glimpse of peach thong. "Why do you think I'm wearin' a dress at midnight instead of my jammy pants?"

"Clever girl." I fumble with the top button of her dress, torn between getting my mouth on her tits but not wanting to leave her exposed in case someone knocks on the truck window.

I slip my hands under her dress, shoving it up around her waist. "I love how perfectly you fit in my hands."

She presses her palms to my cheeks and swoops in for another kiss. Her hips roll, crushing her soft center against my hard cock. I thrust up, giving her something to really grind against and groan. I haven't ached for a woman this painfully in years. Maybe ever.

"We can do foreplay later." She reaches for my belt. "I want you inside me."

"Not arguing." I suck in a stuttering breath as she frees my cock and wraps her fingers around me. "Fuck."

I'm so wild for her, my hands get tangled in the long fabric of her dress and the tiny strap of her underwear.

"Logan, wait." She groans as I rub between her legs.

"You're so wet." I continue exploring, slipping my fingers underneath the tiny strip of satin between her thighs.

She rocks her hips back and forth. Short, quick movements, chasing the friction of my hand. "I...I know."

Her plush little body radiates heat. That thong's so damn tiny, I can slip it to the side. No reason for her to leave my body for a second. I dig my fingers into her hip, pulling her closer.

Oh fuck, I need to be inside her.

She braces her hand against my chest, pushing me away. "Condom, condom," she chants.

Well, fuck.

This is the first time I've ever completely forgotten about wrapping my dick. "I, uh. Are you on the pill or something?"

She stops cold.

That's not good. "What's wrong?"

Her body trembles as she tries to shift off my lap.

I clamp down on her hips harder. "No. Talk to me."

Having this conversation with my naked dick so close to her soaked pussy isn't the wisest choice.

"That's a deal-breaker for me."

Huh?

"I'm terrified of getting pregnant," she adds.

Why are we talking about—oh, *right.*

"Okay." I'm having trouble clearing the fog of lust from my head and catching up.

"I'm serious," she says. "It would ruin my career right now. And—I can't take the chance."

"Hey, shh. I hear you." I run my hand over her shoulder, cupping the back of her head and sliding my fingers in her hair. Dragging her closer until we're almost nose-to-nose, I stare into her wild eyes. "I don't want to clip your wings, chickadee. Promise."

"Logan," she whispers.

"I have bad news, though." My heart fists at the uncertain way her eyes widen. Guess it wasn't clear I'm teasing. "I don't have any on me. I really wasn't planning this."

"Oh." She covers her mouth with her hand and laughs softly. Arching and twisting, she leans back and reaches for her purse. "I have some."

"Fuck, woman. Why didn't you say so? Hurry up."

She laughs harder, not doing a damn thing to soothe my aching dick. "Here."

I tear into that sucker so fast it's not even funny. My whole body's shaking with need. I roll it on and squeeze her hip again. "Come here."

Her body pulses like a live wire as she sinks down. She bites her lip. Stares straight into my eyes.

"More," she whispers.

A flash of pleasure fires over my skin. She sinks her nails into my shoulders, easing herself inch by agonizing inch. I flick my gaze down. Wish I had more light to watch her take me.

"Fuck, that's good." I squeeze my eyes shut. "Stay like that for a sec."

My sassy girl slowly rolls her hips, ignoring my desperate plea for mercy. The sensation's a gentle wave in my turbulent ocean of need.

A frustrated noise passes her lips and she scrabbles to lift my shirt. I have to lean forward and yank the damn thing off. Not even sure where it ends up. "Better?"

She runs her hands over my shoulders and down my chest. "Much."

"Good." I squeeze her hip. "Get to work." I glance out the window. I hadn't parked under any of the functioning lights. Truck's windows are tinted. It's unlikely anyone can see us. Still, I don't like taking the chance with Shelby.

But there's no stopping her now.

"Uh." She rocks her hips faster. Leaning back, she braces her hands on my knees.

I've never needed anything the way I need to see more of her. Fuck it. I flick open the few top buttons of her dress. The flowy material flutters and falls to the side. Still greedy, I push the cups of her bra down.

There's enough light filtering through the windows for my eyes to follow the outline of her body. I splay my hand across her chest, right between her breasts, feeling the thump of her heart against my palm. Sliding to the right, I cup her breast, brushing my thumb over her tight nipple.

"Oh!" she gasps.

"What do you need?"

"More."

I shift lower in the seat and she leans back, resting her elbows on the dashboard.

"Nice," I mumble, licking the pad of my thumb before dipping under her dress to rub her clit. "How's that?"

Her hips buck and jerk. "Good." There's a frustrated catch in her voice.

"Slow down. We've got all night." That's not technically true. Any minute, someone could ruin our reunion party and I think that's what's messing with her.

"You feel so good," she pants. "This feels..."

"Keep going." I roll my thumb around her clit in slow circles, listening carefully for the hitch in her breath saying she's close. "Stop trying so hard. Relax."

"I...I can't."

"Where's that little bullet you were telling me about?"

"Huh?" She tips her head up, staring at me with dazed, desperate eyes. Her movements slow.

I pinch her hip. "Keep riding. Where is it?"

Please don't say "in the van."

"In...in my purse." She drops her arm and twists her body, reaching for it.

I say a quick, silent prayer for her magical bag that seems to have everything.

Her body jerks and trembles with the effort of searching in the dark at a weird angle. Honestly, every movement goes straight to my cock, making the situation even more critical.

"Got it." She thrusts her hand between her legs.

"No. No." I pry the slim, smooth wand from her fingers. "My job."

She laughs softly as I study the toy for a second. It's small. Maybe the length of my pinky. "This really gets you off?"

She stops moving and squints at me. "My clit's sensitive, thank you very much."

"I'm aware." I finally locate the on button and click it. Strong vibrations ripple through my arm.

With my free hand, I tap her ass. "Did I say you could stop?"

She falls forward, wrapping her arms around my neck and laughing against my shoulder.

Pressed tight to my front, she starts that slow, maddening roll of her hips again.

"That's it," I whisper, kissing and sucking at the sensitive skin below her ear. "Lean back for me."

She cups my cheeks, brushing the softest kiss against my lips.

Gone. I'm so fucking gone over this woman.

"Like this?" she teases, resting her hands on my knees and thrusting her hips forward.

"Fuck yeah." I lick my thumb again and rub her clit a few times before adding the little vibrating bullet.

"Oh!" Her hips jerk. "Too much."

I slide it an inch higher, to the side, then the other side, avoiding direct contact until I locate a spot that makes her thighs quiver.

Her pussy fists around my cock so damn tight. "Fuck," I groan.

"Right there. Don't move," she pleads. Desperately, she reaches for me, hooking one hand over my shoulder, frantically bouncing up and down. "Oh my God."

"Good girl. Come for me." I roll the vibrator right over her clit and she spasms around me, digging her nails into my back.

"Yes."

For several heartbeats I'm suspended in time, solely focused on the pleasure of her coming apart.

Finally, she slumps against me, panting, shaking, and sweaty. "Thank you," she mumbles, kissing my neck and cheek.

Time for holding back's over. I curl my hands over her shoulders, pinning her down, and let loose. My hips snap up into the sweet, tight clutch of her perfect little body over and over. All rational thought has been ripped out of my brain. My body bows up off the seat as I explode.

Mind-blowing.

Thump.

I peel my eyes open. Shelby has her hands braced against the roof of the truck and her neck at an awkward angle.

"Sorry," I groan, still coming so hard, white spots dot my vision. I ease my ass back down to the seat so I'm not ramming her head in the roof. She laughs softly and rubs the top of her head.

"Oh, fuck. Come here." I wrap my arms around her, burying my face against her shoulder.

Frantic hearts beating, panting, and sweaty, we stay pressed together.

I'm not ready to let go.

CHAPTER FIFTY

Shelby

I don't want to leave Rooster's embrace.

Although we are a little sticky.

He presses kisses to my cheek and forehead. "Let's get out of here."

Slowly, I extract myself from him, throwing myself onto the passenger seat. With love-drunk puppy eyes, I watch him search the truck for napkins to clean himself with, finally tossing everything into a paper bag and throwing it behind his seat.

"So, uh, whose truck did we defile?" I ask, reaching over to touch his shoulder.

He leans into the seat, arching his back and lifting his hips to buckle his belt. It's a damn sexy move.

"Ice's. He's the president of this charter."

"Oops." I cover my mouth with my hand and giggle.

"Mmm." He swoops in and kisses me. "That's better. You didn't look happy when I got here."

"I've never been happier to see anyone in my life."

Buzzing hums through the air, drawing our attention to a crack in the seat. Rooster digs my little bullet vibrator out, clicks it off, and hands it to me.

Heat stings my cheeks. "Thanks."

"What's wrong?"

"Sorry, I...uh."

He stops and stares. "Sorry about what?"

"Nothing." I hurry to return the vibrator to its hiding spot in my purse.

"Shelby? What's the matter?" His hand lands on my arm, gently tugging until I turn toward him.

"Nothing's wrong. I just don't want you mad at me."

He shifts closer, brushing his knuckles over my cheek. "How could I ever be mad at you?"

"I don't want you to be insulted."

"About what?"

I swear every time I open my mouth, I'm just jamming my boot farther down my throat. His beard twitches with confusion as he studies my face.

"You know." I gesture toward my purse.

He swivels his head, staring out the window for a second. "Aren't you the same girl who told me to whip out my cock in your dressing last time I saw you? And then, I'm pretty sure a few minutes ago you said we could skip foreplay because you needed me inside you so bad." He brushes his fingers over my knee. "Why so shy all of a sudden?"

Thank God it's dark. My face is about to burst into flames. "That I needed—you know..."

"I asked you for the toy, Shelby. You worried you insulted my manhood or something?"

"Well, none of my other—"

"Don't." He squeezes his eyes shut. "I fuckin' love getting you off. Any and every single way I can. Like, I want to spend weeks holed up with you somewhere private so we can experiment. Learn every single way to make your legs shake, toes curl, and your eyes roll back in your head."

What do you say to something like that? "Wow."

"You have no idea." He snorts out a laugh. "Anyway, didn't Heidi tell you about her side hustle? I can't wait to get home and order a whole bunch of gadgets from her catalog."

"No, she didn't. What side hustle?"

"She's been supplying the whole clubhouse with sex toys for months."

"Really? But...she's a *mom*."

He side-eyes me. "I'm pretty sure moms have sex too. Actually—"

"All right. I get it. Stop makin' fun of me."

He twists the key in the ignition and sneaks a glance my way. "Anything else?"

I bite my lip so hard I wince. "Thanks for understanding, about..."

"You wantin' me to wrap my dick?" Blunt as usual. "I'm not exactly eager to have little baby roosters clucking around either."

How can he make me laugh when I'm so tangled up inside?

He reaches over and strokes my cheek. "As long as I get to love you up, I'm happy."

My heart melts, and I lean into his touch. "You'd be the first who doesn't bitch about a condom," I mutter. "Shoot, my last boyfriend kept trying to slip 'em off during. As if I wouldn't notice."

Silence.

Why did I say that out loud?

Rooster's brimming with anger—fists tight, voice down to a low rumble. "I *knew* I didn't kick that motherfucker's ass enough."

"Forgot you'd met him," I mutter.

"Shelby, look at me, please."

He waits until I meet his eyes. "I know I can be a crude motherfucker, but I'm not the guy who ever wants to make you uncomfortable. Or do something you're not a hundred percent into, okay?"

"I know that."

"Good." One corner of his mouth quirks. "And don't ever compare me to any of your piece-of-shit exes again."

I open my mouth to protest, then stop myself. Even if I didn't mean to, that's kinda what I did. Twice now. Lordy, how does he put up with me?

He tucks my hair behind my ear. "Let's get going. You must be exhausted. And we need to be up early for your interview."

Again, here he is, runnin' all over for me. Picking me up late and gettin' up at the butt crack of dawn to take me to the radio station. "Ugh. I'm so sorry about that." I twist in my seat, grabbing the seatbelt and clicking it into place. "I'm so mad at Greg for scheduling that without telling me."

He slips the truck into gear. "These guys are dicks, from what I know of 'em. Jigsaw's going with us. Just in case."

He doesn't leave it open for debate. And I'm okay with that.

"Do you listen to them? Greg said their show is syndicated across the country."

"Ah, yeah. I've caught them once or twice. Not really my thing, though." He grips the steering wheel harder. "Uh, don't freak out but I need to warn you about something."

"Uh, okay."

"I can't get into a lot of details, but this club's a little different from mine."

"You say that every time you take me to a new clubhouse."

"Shit, I guess I do." He laughs, a loud *ha* that punches the air between us. "Nothing bad. But they're a little overzealous with their security. Found a camera in my room. I disconnected it, but I'm guessing they're all over the house."

I'm not sure what to say to that.

"Are you thinking of asking me to take you back to the van?"

"Heck no." I quiet down for a second "That's kind of a club business-y thing to share with me, isn't it?"

"I guess so."

"Are there toilet cams?"

"Fuck, I hope Ice isn't that twisted. I'll check when we get there."

"Found one of those in a dressing room one time." I shudder. "So gross."

"Are you fuckin' serious?" Fury seeps into his tone.

I shrug, even though he's watchin' the road, not me. "Sometimes I feel like someone's spying on me twenty-four hours a day. At least this time, I won't be wondering if I'm crazy."

Rooster

How the fuck do I digest the fact that someone's stuck a toilet camera in my girlfriend's dressing room? Never mind the other shit she confessed tonight. More than ever, I want to tuck her in my pocket and keep her safe from everyone. The world doesn't deserve her sweetness.

"Wow. Bikers sure are fond of middle-of-nowhere places, huh?" she asks as the truck climbs the mountainside.

"Not all of 'em. But yeah, we like our privacy."

"Can't imagine why," she says, using her light, teasing tone.

Fuck, there goes that warmth sliding through my chest again.

After a few seconds of silence, I glance over. Her head's against the seat and awkwardly rolled to the side. Breathing's soft and even. Shit, she must be exhausted. Instead of fucking her in the parking lot like an animal, and then dragging her out into the woods, I should've taken her to a damn hotel so she could get some sleep.

Finally, the clubhouse comes into view and I flip on the blinker. From the glow of the bonfires and number of shadows filling the parking lot, it looks like they took the party outside tonight.

Brothers wave and slap the hood as I pass. The noise doesn't stir Shelby. I park around the side of the building to keep Ice's truck out of the way of these rowdy motherfuckers.

Shelby's still sound asleep. Hate like hell to wake her.

I text Jigsaw, letting him know I'm here, then haul my ass out of the truck. Slowly, I ease Shelby's door open, not wanting to startle her. "Hey, chickadee." I keep my voice low and in a soothing range. "We're here."

"Hmm?" she mumbles, drools on herself a little. Just makes her even cuter.

Reaching over her, I unclick her seatbelt and kiss her cheek. "We're here."

She blinks, her gaze bouncing around the truck. "Did I fall asleep?"

"You did." An amused smile curves my lips. "Want me to carry you inside?"

Still bleary-eyed and a little dazed, she shakes her head. "I have all my crap to carry in."

"I got it." I offer her my hand. "Come on."

She jumps out of the truck, a soft huff passing her lips. I grab her bags and guitar case, not comfortable leaving it in someone else's truck overnight with all these people.

"I'll show you around tomorrow. Let's get you to bed."

"All right." She follows me in the front door.

"Cock-a-doodle-fucking-do!" Jigsaw shouts from the bar. "Where ya been?"

I tilt my head at Shelby. "You knew I was going to pick her up."

"Oh, yeah." He slides off his stool. "Hey."

"Hey, Jiggy." She reaches up and hugs the asshole.

He hangs on to her long enough to annoy me, then adds an eyebrow wiggle to really piss me off. "Welcome to Port Everheart, chickadee."

"Why are *you* calling my girlfriend that?" I infuse enough menace into my tone to make my irritation clear.

Jigsaw pulls away. If he had feelings, I'd worry I'd hurt them. "I didn't know if you wanted me to use her name." He lowers his voice and casts a look around. The music's not the usual drown-out-conversation level. Plenty of couples are inside. A few brothers are scattered around the bar sharing drinks and stories. "Thought you might be worried someone would recognize her."

Shit. Yeah, I probably should be concerned about that. "Thanks, brother." I really need to calm my territorial urges when it comes to Shelby. "We're headed to bed. You're still coming with us tomorrow, right?"

"Fuck yeah." He gives me a hug and slaps my cheeks a few times. My hands are full so I tolerate the abuse. Barely.

SHELBY

My confused brain tries to make sense of my surroundings. I vaguely remember arriving at a clubhouse.

What the heck am I wearing?

Rooster must have undressed me. I run my fingers over the soft blue T-shirt. Smells like detergent and Rooster.

"I didn't want to rummage through your bags last night."

I turn and find him awake, staring at me with a soft a smile. "Have you been watching me sleep again?"

"Feels good waking up next to you. I like to enjoy it."

"Same," I whisper.

An alarm chirps and Rooster rolls over, scooping up his phone. "Time to get ready."

"Ugh, I don't wanna." I grab one of the pillows and shove it against my face.

"I'd rather have you get more sleep. But you can't miss stuff because you're with me, either."

"I'm not dressing up," I protest, even though I doubt Rooster really cares about my wardrobe issues. "And the only makeup I have with me is a couple tubes of lipgloss."

"It's radio." He throws the covers back and I yelp.

"Yeah, but they'll want to take photos and post 'em online and probably make fun of me. Say I look nothing like my pictures and I'm a hag in real life."

He stares down at me. "If anyone says that about you, they'll be eating through a straw for the next six to eight weeks."

"Careful, Logan. You'll be taking me to all of my appearances if you keep up the sexy talk."

He hesitates, the menace sliding off his face. "You know I'll take you anywhere you need to go."

"Yeah, I do."

I end up squeezing myself into a pair of skinny jeans, a teal tank top with a *flamazing* flamingo on the front, and my electric teal cowgirl boots.

Downstairs, people are scattered everywhere. I vaguely remember a party last night, running into Jigsaw...and not much after that.

"Do you want breakfast?" Rooster asks, checking his phone.

"After the interview."

He searches the bar area. "Where the fuck is Jiggy?"

We continue outside, Rooster furiously tapping on his phone.

I head for his bike.

"Hey, Rooster!" a high, feminine voice calls out.

I spin around so fast, my hair sticks to my gloss-slicked lips. I sputter, spitting out hair and trailing sticky gloss down my chin.

A tall, slim blonde jogs over to us. I should ask her what kind of bra she's wearing. Her giant boobs barely even bounce as she navigates over the uneven ground.

"I'm so glad I caught you," she says in a breathless rush. "I really appreciate all your help this week." She hands him a tiny green envelope. "I wanted to give you this to say thanks." She's so completely focused on *my* boyfriend, she doesn't even seem to notice me standing there. Holding his hand.

"Thanks, hon." He slides the envelope in his cut pocket without opening it and squeezes my hand. "Anya, this is my girlfriend, Shelby."

Finally, her dizzy eyes swing my way. She smiles even wider. Damn, she's pretty. Has at least three inches on me too, with those freakin' flamingo legs of hers.

"Oh, hey!" She yanks me into her arms, crushing me against her chest and huggin' the stuffing outta me.

"Uh, hey," I mumble around a mouthful of her blouse.

"Sorry." She releases me so fast, I almost fall on my ass. Rooster steadies me with an arm around my shoulders. She glances at his bike and giggles. "You should've seen Rooster. I thought he was taking me to my interview on his bike. And he almost bit my head off. 'Back of my bike is for my girlfriend,'" she says in a deep, angry voice meant to imitate Rooster.

My lips twitch. Did he really say that to her?

An image of her pressing her giant tits up against his back and hanging onto him dances in my brain and my blood boils. *Nope. Nope. Nope.* I shake my head, willing the mental snapshot away.

Damn right that's my spot.

I force a smile. "Sounds like something my man would say."

"Morning, Anya," Jigsaw calls out. "Hey, guys. Ready to go?"

"Thanks again, Rooster." Anya waves at us. "Good meeting you, Shelby. Hopefully, we can chat more later."

Unlikely.

She disappears inside the clubhouse.

Jigsaw's gaze bounces between Rooster and me. "Yeah, you two look tense. I'm gonna go..." He executes a sharp left and hightails it into the clubhouse.

"That's what you've been doing here all week?" I ask in a low, tight voice once we're alone. "Hanging out with Chesapeake Bay Barbie?"

Damn, why does that bug me so bad?

Logan's chest rises and falls. Deep breaths. In and out. The silence goes on for so long my stomach goes into free fall.

Finally, he answers, "She works for the club and the president needed me to help her with a project."

"What kind of project?"

"Club stuff."

"She sure seems awful friendly with ya," I grumble.

He yanks the envelope she'd handed him and opens it, pulling out a plastic gift card.

"You think she'd give me a twenty-five dollar Starbucks gift card if I'd been busy fucking her all week long?" He shoves the card in my face. "I'm at least worth fifty."

Yeah, that *would* be weird.

But the gift card isn't my proof. Anya's friendliness toward me isn't either. Rooster is. He's already shown me in so many ways that he's an honorable man.

"You're worth a million." Shame stabs me in the chest for the momentary frenzy of jealousy. I move closer and slide my arms around his waist. "Sorry," I mumble, resting my cheek against his shirt.

He doesn't hesitate to hug me to him. "I didn't know what to say about it over the phone. It was all club business. Nothing more."

Is this what normal people do? Talk stuff out? I've never had a boyfriend who didn't love stroking up against my jealous streak.

Not Logan. He recognized my jealousy for what it was and immediately snuffed it out with calm, straightforward reassurance.

"You've had to watch me sing a love song with another guy several times and never, ever complained," I whisper.

"I get it. Believe me, I do." He grips my shoulders gently and bends down to look me in the eye. "I'm not the guy who wants you worried and wondering all the time, okay?"

"Okay." I glance toward the clubhouse and wrinkle my nose. "She's really pretty, though. Can you blame me?"

He chuckles. "She is."

My eyes narrow.

"Will *lying* about something obvious help you trust me?" he asks.

I honestly consider the question before answering. It wouldn't. Over time, I'd start wondering what else he was lying about. "No. It wouldn't."

"Shelby," he rasps. "Look at me."

He doesn't say another word until I slowly lift my gaze to meet his.

"You're *more* than pretty. You're everything. You're mine. Okay?"

"Okay," I whisper.

My phone buzzes and I groan. Rooster watches as I check the text. "It's Greg. He wants me at the arena earlier."

For a second, disappointment clouds his eyes, but it passes quickly. "Okay. I'll go grab your stuff so we can head there after breakfast." He twists his fingers through my hair, tugging gently. "Shouldn't take the bike and get you all windblown anyway."

"I like riding with you, though."

"We'll have plenty of time to play, Shelby. Today's a work day."

Something about his words reassures me so much, I'm not sure how to respond.

Rooster

Crisis avoided.

Still, I had a really good opening to mention that the "project" I've been working on is setting up Anya's budding porn empire. And didn't. Again.

Fuck me.

If Shelby reacted like that to a girl handing me a fucking gift card, she's definitely not going to take the news of my job description well. And what are the odds those dickhead radio DJs don't mention that I was just there yesterday with a porn star?

Pretty damn slim.

Embarrassment still stains Shelby's cheeks. It shouldn't, though. As much as I never want to hurt her, I can't deny seeing that little spark of jealousy light up her eyes only made me want to pin her against the truck and fuck her until she understood she's the only woman I want.

It'll have to wait.

"Stay here. I'm gonna grab Jigsaw." I jog back to the clubhouse.

Jigsaw's right inside the door, talking to Anya. "Let's go, brother."

He says a few more words to her and then follows me outside. "Damn, she and Shelby were hot together when they were hugging." Jigsaw rubs his hands together. "Think they would—"

"Do *not* finish that sentence," I warn.

"I'm not talking about filming it."

"Shut the fuck up."

"Come on. It's not cheating if it's another girl and you're right there watching."

I turn my head slowly and stare at him. "For the love of fuck, mind your own business. And if you *ever* suggest something like that to Shelby—even as a joke—I will motherfucking gut you."

He takes a step back and raises one hand. "My bad. I didn't realize threesomes were now off the table."

"Stop being an asshole."

His gaze drops to the truck keys in my hand. "We're not riding together?"

"I need to talk to her."

"Don't you two yap enough?"

"Why are you testing my patience today?"

"Don't I do it every day?"

I pinch the bridge of my nose and take a deep breath. "I need to explain *what* exactly I'm doing for the club before she hears it somewhere else."

The joker smile slips off his face. "Club business isn't *her* business."

"Yeah, I get that. Except the two assholes interviewing her this morning are the same ones who interviewed Anya yesterday. You think they're not going to remember me and have some commentary?"

He roars with laughter and slaps my shoulder. "Good luck with that."

"Thanks, dickface."

Shelby's waiting by the truck and smiles when she sees us. "I feel so bad dragging you out this early in the morning, Jigsaw."

"It's fine. No amount of beauty sleep's gonna help him," I say.

"Logan Randall, that's not nice."

"He's vicious to me, Shelby. All the time." Jigsaw pulls a sad droopy-dog face that's pure bullshit.

"Aw." She pats his shoulder. "I'm sure you're totally innocent in all of it too."

He flashes a wicked half-grin at her.

"Enough." I wave him off. "Let's go."

"I'll follow you since you know where you're going," he says over his shoulder.

Shelby cocks her head and stares at me.

Motherfucking Jigsaw had to say it, didn't he? Sad thing is, I don't even think he did it on purpose.

Shelby waits until we're on the road to speak up.

"What'd he mean you know where the place is? Did you check it out when I told you about the interview?"

That would be an excellent excuse, wouldn't it?

But I can't lie to her.

"No, the girl you met—Anya. She had an interview with them yesterday and Ice asked me to go with her."

Please let that be sufficient.

"Really? Is she a singer too?"

"Uh, she's in entertainment."

Shelby seizes on my bullshit answer immediately. "Entertainment? Is she a dancer or something? Does this charter own a strip club too?"

If only.

"No, but they do have a successful tattoo parlor. They have a wait list but I could probably get you squeezed in if you want some ink while you're here."

Real subtle change of subject.

"Rooster, you've seen every inch of me and know I'm ink-free. I intend to stay that way."

I glance over at her. "Really?"

Her eyes glitter with amusement. "It's totally sexy on *you,* but it's not something I'd do."

Huh. "Is it frowned on in country music or something?"

"Maybe a little. I don't know. I haven't come up with anything I wanna stick on my body permanently." She reaches over and pokes my side. "Besides you."

"Same, chickadee."

"Doesn't it hurt?"

"No." I glance down at the intricate tribal pattern inked into my arm. Annoying, maybe, but not painful. "But I have a high tolerance for pain."

"Of course you do." I can practically hear the eye roll in her voice. "Is that a deal-breaker or something for you?"

"What? No." I reach over and squeeze her leg. "Love all your perfect, smooth skin just the way it is."

She twines her fingers with mine.

"Are you nervous?"

"A little."

"Don't be. Jigsaw and I will be right in the next room listening to the whole thing."

"Oh, great. What if I make a fool out of myself in front of Jigsaw?"

"You've met him, right?"

"You're terrible."

But she's smiling now, instead of fretting.

I steer the truck into the parking garage, taking a ticket and tossing it on the dashboard. Jigsaw's bike rumbles behind us, echoing throughout the parking garage.

I'm so focused on Shelby, I forget about the two DJs about to ruin our morning.

CHAPTER FIFTY-ONE

Shelby

I'm wound tighter than a cuckoo clock.

The radio station's small but clean and full of new equipment. Not as fancy as others I've been to but not shabby either.

"Shelby Morgan, it's so nice to meet you. This is Scotty and I'm Junior." He pauses as if he's expecting me to gush and say I'm a fan or something.

"Thanks for havin' me."

Scotty—*or Slimy*, as I've renamed him in my head so I can tell the two of them apart—leers down at me and offers his hand. Reluctantly, I take it. He brings it to his mouth, brushing his oily lips over my knuckles.

Gross.

Germs.

I should've brought hand sanitizer.

Next to me, Rooster growls.

I snatch my hand back, giving it a quick swipe against my jeans.

Junior—*Jolly in my head*—stares at Rooster. I guess I should be flattered. Apparently, I'm so dazzling they didn't notice the four hundred and fifty pounds of bikers who've followed me into the studio.

Jigsaw's been studying the wall of photos behind us. But Rooster hasn't left my side.

"Weren't you here yesterday?" Junior asks.

"With the porn star!" Scotty cackles and thrusts his hips in the air. "Considering a career switch, Shelby?"

Huh?

"No," Rooster growls. "Shouldn't you start the show?"

"So, what do you do, Mr. Biker Man?" Scotty asks. "Run a bodyguard service for porn stars and pop tarts? How can I get in on that?"

That draws Jigsaw's attention. He steps up to Scotty, conveniently blocking Rooster from killing the stupid DJ. "What'd you say 'bout my baby sister?" he says in a low, hollow voice that's downright terrifying.

Uncomfortable laughter rolls out of me. "Easy, big bro." I pat Jigsaw's rock-hard shoulder. "I'm sure Scotty just thinks he's funny."

Junior slaps his partner's chest. "Knock it off. Let's get ready for her segment."

An assistant comes in and guides me into a seat across from the two DJs.

Greg's lucky he didn't accompany me to this interview, or I mighta kicked his ass. I'm already hating it.

"Good morning!" Scotty's morning announcer voice is just as cheesy as I expected. "We're proud to say the lovely Shelby Morgan has graced us with her presence this morning."

I lean in closer to the microphone. "Thanks for havin' me."

"So tell us, Shelby, what was being on a show like *Redneck Roadhouse* like? That's how you got your start, right?" Junior asks.

"Well, technically I got my start at the local honky-tonk." I let out a soft laugh that I hope sounds more warm and friendly than brain-dead.

They take me through *Redneck Roadhouse*, thankfully avoiding some of the less-flattering moments. I doubt it's to spare my feelings. More like they didn't research much about me besides my cup size.

"Rumor has it you're very involved with the children's charity Dream Makers," Junior says. "Why'd you decide to do that?"

The question tumbles over me like a bucket of bricks. I guess they did their research after all. But these jerks don't deserve to hear stories about my beautiful baby sister. "They, ah, approached me when I was on *Redneck Roadhouse*, and whenever my schedule allows, I like to do what I can." Good Lord, if I sprinkle any more Southern sweetness into my voice, I'll have to change my name to Sugar.

"Isn't that depressing, visiting cancer kids?" Scotty says in a dismissive tone. If he keeps it up, I'm fixin' to jump this table and snatch him bald. "Is there a charity for teenage boys who want to lose their virginity to a hot chick? Now, *that's* a worthy cause."

Junior lets out an uncomfortable laugh. "Sounds like something *you* probably still need to sign up for."

They banter back and forth while I sit there with a polite smile etched on my face, trying not to roll my eyes.

"So, you're on tour with Dawson Roads right now?" Scotty asks when they finally settle down.

"That's right. We've got a show in town tonight."

"What's that like?" Scotty turns toward Junior. "That guy's a stud. You ever see some of the hot babes he...*dates?*"

Junior grunts in agreement.

"Are you and Dawson...*tight?*" The inflection Scotty uses sounds more like he's asking about the elasticity of my pussy than my relationship with Dawson.

"Dawson's been kind to me. The tour has been a wonderful learning experience," I answer carefully. "I'm thankful for the opportunity."

"I'm sure you are," Scotty says.

Jerk.

"Tell us about tour life," Junior says, before Scotty can open his mouth again. "This is your first national tour, right?"

"Yes. It's been an adventure."

"Do you have any pre-show rituals you have to do before you go onstage?"

"Well, I like to do a little yoga, meditate and center myself. I'll do some vocal exercises. Mostly, I just like to stay calm and focus on the show."

"Are you a diva?" Scotty's deep tone drips with sarcasm that grates on my nerves. "One of those singers who demands fancy artisan spring water from five-thousand-year-old caves and stuff?"

I huff out a soft laugh. "Hardly."

"Nah, you're a down-home Texas girl, right?" Junior teases. "Probably trying to get some sweet tea and lemonade."

"Well, days I'm singing I usually stick to plain water and a little hot tea with lemon."

"You don't let loose after a show and down some shots?" Scotty asks, eyebrows crawling all the way up his forehead.

"I've been known to knock back a paloma or two back home." I force out another friendly, girlish laugh. "Maybe after the tour, that's what I'll celebrate with."

"What the heck's a paloma?" Scotty gags. "Sounds super-girly."

"It's tequila, grapefruit juice, lime juice, simple syrup and club soda. The unofficial drink of Texas."

"Oh, now I want one," Junior says.

Scotty leans in close to the microphone. "Does tequila make your clothes come off, Shelby Morgan?"

What a waste of such a smooth baritone voice. I roll my eyes as he sits back in his chair and preens like the dumbest peacock in the flock, proud of himself for the cheesy song reference.

"Not even if you were Joe Nichols himself," I answer with a tart snap to my tone.

"Is there someone special in your life, Shelby?" Junior says.

I duck my head, trying to stop the heat spreading over my cheeks.

"Aw, she's blushing." Scotty giggles like an idiot. "Is it Dawson? Oh, even better, is it a woman? There are no lesbian country singers, are there? What a shame."

How the heck did Greg think this show would be a good move for me?

"Is it hard being in a relationship when you're on the road so much?" Junior asks.

Nice try at injecting some normalcy into this stupid interview.

"It is. But I'm incredibly blessed that he's able to visit me with some frequency."

"That must bum your male fans out, no?" Scotty asks.

"I guess."

"Rumor has it, you have an obsessed fan. Is that true?" Junior asks.

And I thought you were the nice one.

So far, I've done a good job of staring straight ahead and not checking to see if Rooster's watching or not.

As if he's physically compelling me to turn around, my body shifts. He's standing at the window staring at me with a whole lot of *what the fuck* burning in his eyes.

That'll be a fun conversation to have later.

"My fans are lovely. I'm grateful to have them," I say softly into the microphone.

I'd have to be nuttier than a squirrel turd to risk pissing off the creepy letter writer just so these two can get their jollies off.

ROOSTER

"Rumor has it, you have an obsessed fan. Is that true?"

What the fuck?

The whole time Shelby's been in there with those two jerks, I've been tense. Edgy. Ready to break down the door and crack their skulls together for the stupid shit they're saying.

Obsessed fan? Did they make that up to fuck with her? I've been stalking her social media like a fat kid waiting for the ice cream truck during summer break and haven't seen any mention of it. I've even been checking that stupid gossip blog that seems to be obsessed with her love life.

"What's he talking about?" Jigsaw asks. "Shelby has a stalker?"

"First I've heard it." I take out my phone and check out one of her accounts. "She's got a bunch of creepy fucks who follow her and send her weird DMs."

Jigsaw's eyes widen. "Did you hack into her Instagram account?"

"*Hack* is such an ugly word." I shrug off the question.

"Glad I won't be in the truck with you two later," he mutters.

"Fuck."

"What?"

"I recognize *this* guy." Middle-aged, sweaty, black polo shirt, khaki pants—he defines out-of-place at a country concert in the heat of the summer. "He was at the Wellspring show. I'm almost positive."

"So?"

I flick through the photos he's posted. "Shit, he's seen her in concert more than I have."

"Everyone needs a hobby. Don't be so judgmental."

I grab a few screenshots of the guy's page and shove my phone in my pocket. "What's with you saying she's your sister, by the way?"

He shrugs. "I figured that would shut them up and take the attention off you."

I slap his chest with the back of my hand. "Thanks."

"You need me to go to the show with you tonight?"

"If you don't mind."

"She's playing there tomorrow, right?"

"Yeah."

"Should be fun."

Finally, the inane interview ends. Scotty boy tries the whole "let me take you to dinner" thing with Shelby but she shuts him down fast. I'm so eager to get her alone, I'm practically vibrating out of my skin.

"Thanks so much, Shelby." Junior shakes her hand as they step out of the studio.

The assistant who'd set Shelby up with her microphone and headset earlier returns with a camera. The three of them stand in front of the station logo, posing for a few shots.

My eyes are glued to Shelby, so the second Scotty drapes his arm over her shoulder, my whole body tenses.

"Easy," Jigsaw warns. "Jesus."

Easy nothing. Five seconds later, Scotty "accidentally" brushes his fingers over Shelby's breast. Back and forth. The twitch at the corners of his mouth announces it's a deliberate move.

"Get off me!" Shelby's outraged shriek propels me across the room.

But I don't have time to wrap my hands around Scotty's neck. Shelby reels back and brings her knee straight up into his groin.

"*Oof.*" He doubles over.

Jigsaw bursts out laughing. "Good job, Shelby."

Junior backs away from Shelby with his hands in the air, like she randomly decided to go on a ball-breaking spree for no reason.

"You need a leash on your boy, Junior," she snaps.

Scotty's still wailing over his aching balls. I lift my foot and press my boot to his chest, kicking him onto his back. I lean over and grab a handful of his shirt, yanking him up into my face. "You're lucky she got to you before I did. That kick to your nuts is gonna feel like a tickle compared to what I'll do if you ever come near her again."

"She's a crazy bitch!" he gasps.

I release his shirt and wrap my hand around his throat. "You wanna repeat that?"

He gasps and scratches at my hand.

"I saw you try to cop a feel, motherfucker," I snarl right in his face. "Pretty sure your assistant got it on film."

"It was an accident! I didn't mean any harm. Everyone knows we joke around here!"

I squeeze his neck a little harder. The edgy, off-color jokes were bad enough. But that's the show's gimmick. I don't like it or respect it, but it's business. "She agreed to sit through forty-five minutes of your shitty attempts at humor—not a grope from your fat little sausage fingers."

"I...I..." he gasps.

"What?" I release him and he falls to the floor, choking and coughing. "You got more excuses?"

"Call security!" he says to Junior.

"No need. We're leaving." I squat next to Scotty and lean in close. "If you even think of using whatever power you think you have to trash talk her or fuck with her career in any way, I'll be back." I stand and stare down at him, adjusting my cut and running my hands through my hair. "My next warning won't be as friendly, Scotty."

CHAPTER FIFTY-TWO

Shelby

The three of us are silent on the way to the parking garage. I'm too stunned to speak. Jigsaw's jittery, like he's eager to get the hell away from us. And Rooster's jaw is so tight I'm afraid he's gonna crack a tooth or ten.

Jigsaw slaps Rooster's hand. "Meet you at the arena." He nods to me. "Later."

"Thanks for coming." I'm still embarrassed that he watched that jerk grope me. But it was awfully nice of Jigsaw to get up so early to help Rooster protect me *and* watch that hot mess.

"Anytime, Shelby."

When we're alone in the truck, I rest my cheek against the window. The cool glass soothes my overheated face. "What a disaster."

"The whole interview was a joke from the jump." Rooster's snorting mad and picking up steam. "What was Greg thinking? You shouldn't have to lower yourself to answering bullshit questions and sleazy innuendos from disrespectful dicks."

"It comes with the territory."

"That's fucking bullshit."

"Rooster, it's my job. You can't—"

"You need to understand something." He pauses until I meet his eyes. "No matter how much I hated it, I wouldn't butt into the business end of your career and complicate things for you." He stares down at his fists. "But once that fucker touched you, he made it personal. And I will *not* tolerate anyone putting their hands on you. End of story."

I've tolerated with that kind of behavior my whole life, waiting tables, tending bar, and singing. Hell, just existing. It hadn't occurred to me until more recently that men *aren't* entitled to grab a handful of my ass whenever they feel the urge. "Thank you."

"You nailed him in the groin pretty good, Shelby. Turns out, you didn't need me." He shakes his head. "Real fuckin' proud of you."

"Must be years of built-up rage from putting up with that crap. I wasn't even thinking. My body reacted without my brain's permission." I glance at the building. "Guess that'll be the last airplay I get on mainstream radio."

Finally, he cracks a hint of a smile. "Nah, I warned him I'd be back if he tried fucking with you in any way."

"You did?"

"Fucking right I did." He starts the truck without looking at me.

My phone buzzes and I groan. Greg's probably calling to scold me. It's just a text though.

Greg: Interview sounded great. Are you on your way here now?

"Guess your threat stuck. Greg doesn't seem to know anything went wrong."

"Good." His tone suggests he really doesn't give a hoot about Greg's opinion. "Look up a place to grab breakfast."

"What are you in the mood for?"

He slides his gaze my way. "Whatever you're comfortable eating on a concert day."

That's a short list. I scroll through a bunch of places and finally choose a diner only a few miles from the arena.

He's quiet, so I continue fiddling with my phone, looking up the Scotty and Junior show to see if they've posted anything about my appearance yet.

Ugh. Someone had the nerve to upload a picture taken about two seconds before Scotty tweaked my nipple. His fat fingers straining toward my boob and a slimy smirk on his face. There's no way anyone can claim that was an accident.

I take a screenshot of the photo just in case it "disappears" later and anyone tries to sue me or Rooster.

"What are you looking at?" he asks.

"Oh, they posted a photo. Right before he tried to honk my boob."

"Son of a bitch."

"No, it's fine. I saved it. Just in case."

He glances over with a half-smile. "Smart girl. Forward it to me, please."

I send it to his phone, smiling when I hear the distinctive chirp. "Do I have my own personal ringtone on your phone?"

"Sure do."

I continue absently scrolling through the radio station's website, stopping on a familiar face. The caption above it reads: *Scotty and Junior go deep with porn princess Anya Regal.*

After the awful way the interview ended, I'd forgotten how it all started. That and I'd chalked up Scotty's comment about "porn stars and pop tarts" as an exaggeration of how he viewed *all* women.

But there she is—the girl Rooster's been spending all week helping do some project that he claimed he couldn't explain because it was "club business." Her bright, pretty face smack between Junior and Scotty.

"Anya—the girl I met this morning—she's a...porn star? *That's* why she was on their show?"

"I don't know about *star*, but she creates adult films, yes," he answers carefully.

Sweet Jesus. Blood thunders through my veins drowning out all the other sounds around us. "You've been 'working' with her all week? On a project? Doing *what* exactly?"

A hot flood of uncontrollable fear churns my stomach. I knew I fell too hard and too fast for Rooster. Were the cards right? Is this the breakup and infidelity coming? Am I a few clicks away from finding videos of the man who's stolen my heart fucking Chesapeake Bay Barbie online?

I'm going to be sick.

Rooster flips on the turn signal and veers the truck to the right. The tires bounce onto the wide shoulder, stopping so fast I'm jerked forward.

"What are you doing?" I gasp, bracing myself with a hand on the dashboard. "Drop me off at the arena. I don't want breakfast anymore." No, I'm about to puke up my guts all over the side of the road.

"Shelby, look at me."

How could I be so dumb? All those vague answers he gave me about what he does for work make a lot more sense now.

"Shelby," he says in a sharper tone. "I'm not fucking around. Look at me."

I snap my head up. The intensity in his eyes doesn't falter. He reaches for my hand, his touch warm and heartbreakingly gentle.

"This isn't how I wanted to tell you."

Lordy, here it comes.

"Tell me what?" Hot tears burn my eyes. "I don't blame you. You're *so* good at it. I bet you look even better on camera."

"Wait, *what?*"

"I get it. It's just a *job* to you. But I can't..."

"Holy fuck." He bangs his head against the steering wheel, his whole burly body shaking with laughter.

My sadness and fear twist into anger. I smack my palm against the seat. "It's not funny! How could you not tell me?"

"It's a little funny." He sits up straight. "That you think I'm starring in porn. I'm flattered."

"If that's not it, then, what?"

"Job or not, I would've been honest if I'd been fucking other people, Shelby."

"I don't understand."

He lets out a long sigh and stares out the windshield for a few seconds. "My club has a film company we bankroll. 'Quasi-amateur' is the best way to describe it. I run the technical end of things. *After* the films are made." He pauses. "Well, that's not completely true. I've had to be 'on set' a few times. As security for the talent, *not* as a performer."

"Oh." Some of the knots in my stomach loosen. "But you said *your* club. Is Anya from New York too? Did she come down here with you?"

"No. Our Virginia charter wants to build something similar to what we do. Z asked me to help them. Me taking her to the interview was a favor to Ice—not Anya. He couldn't do it and asked me if I would. That's it." He turns his hands palms up. "Sorry it's not more exciting."

"So, you spend your days watching videos of pretty, naked women having sex?"

"*That's* what you took from what I said? No, I spend a lot of my time staring at a computer screen, uploading files, filling out annoying forms, chasing down assholes who pirate our content, dealing with billing issues, looking at spreadsheets, and other mundane crap." He slants a look at me. "I'm not a horny thirteen-year-old boy. Whacking it to porn all-day long isn't that exciting anymore."

"Gross," I mutter. "Why didn't you just tell me?"

"Well, for one thing, I'm really not in the habit of sharing club business with anyone *outside* the club." He hesitates, drums his thumbs against the steering wheel. "I was worried you'd react...well, like this." He scrunches up his face. "Actually, no, I didn't expect you to think *I* was in the talent. I didn't see that coming."

"Shut up." I reach over and lightly smack his arm. "If you're going on the road with me, who'll manage this stuff for the club?"

"I can do a lot of it remotely. I'm also trying to train Jigsaw so he can handle some of it for me."

"Oh." I stare down at my hands, still not sure what to say.

"I should've mentioned it sooner. I meant to say something this morning after you met Anya. We got sidetracked...and the interview."

His voice never falters. Except for the brief laughter, his body remains calm and relaxed. The posture of a man with nothing to hide.

I've fallen so hard for this man. He treats me well. Shows me he cares in so many ways.

I want to trust him. But can't help that little piece of me still scared, still wondering if he's hiding something else.

CHAPTER FIFTY-THREE

Shelby

I'm two-stepping on shaky ground.

After a quick breakfast, we're back in the truck on our way to the arena and my anxiety shoots through the roof.

How can I judge Logan for not telling me about his job? Here I've been assigned a bodyguard twenty-four hours a day on the tour. That's the kind of detail he would've wanted the minute it happened.

"Are you okay?" he asks. "You're so quiet. Does your throat hurt?"

Actually, it does but that's not what's keeping my mouth glued shut.

I'm running out of time to warn Logan about the letters and my new bodyguard. Bane's kind of hard to miss, and I have no doubt he'll pop up as soon as I arrive at the arena. "Rooster—"

"Aw, fuck." He peers into the rearview mirror and curses again.

"What is it?"

"We missed the exit," he growls.

Darn. If I'd been paying attention instead of figuring out how to explain this hot mess, he wouldn't be driving around looking for a place to turn in an unfamiliar city.

I hurry to reset the GPS and help him find the new turn-off. Guilt knots my stomach. But he's trying to focus on the road while he's in the middle of doing yet another favor for me. Not the best time to blurt out that I have a stalker.

He follows the signs for the arena and I read him Greg's instructions for how to find the loading area.

As soon as we pull into the lot, I spot Bane's big frame hanging out by Dawson's bus.

You've stalled long enough. Time to fess up.

"Uh, Rooster. I, uh, have to—"

"Who is that guy?" Rooster asks. "He was with you last night when I picked you up."

"Well, that's what I wanted to tell you."

He blinks and waits. Doesn't accuse me of cheating or anything silly like that. "I got this letter the other night…it's stupid, honestly. But Cindy made a big deal out of it and got Greg involved. Then Greg told Dawson, who assigned one of his guards to stick with me."

"Whoa. Slow down." He closes his eyes for a second. "That obsessed fan thing the DJs mentioned was *true?*"

"I don't know about obsessed. It was, like, *two* letters."

"Now it's *two* letters?"

"Well, three. That I know of."

"Shelby, are you fucking kidding me? How long has this been going on?"

"Since right after Baltimore, I think."

"What?" His sharp question punches through the air. "Why didn't you tell me?"

"It was a letter! Paper, ink, and some stupid, creepy words. It's not like it was a bomb or something. Dawson assigned one of his guys to watch me. I didn't want to make you worry about something so silly."

"You let me decide what to worry about. Dammit." He stabs his fingers through his hair and won't even look at me.

"Rooster."

"Don't. I'm really fuckin' furious with you right now." While he claims to be furious, he's awfully gentle as he pulls me into his arms, crushing me against his chest. "I hate that you've been worrying about this and didn't think you should tell me."

"I didn't want you to worry or think you had to do anything about it."

He rests his hands on my shoulders and pushes me back so he can meet my eyes. "Of course I worry about you. And you're mistaken if you think I'm gonna sit around and do nothing."

"Rooster."

"You're a ballsy little brat, giving me grief about *my* job when your life's in danger. You know that?"

"My life isn't *in danger*. And I honestly think I took the news of your *job* rather well, considering."

He kisses the tip of my nose and flicks a glance at Bane again. "At least I know why ol' beefcake was following you around."

"Stop. Bane's been nice to me."

Rooster continues scowling.

"Don't you dare," I warn him. "You start pissing a circle 'round me 'cause you're mad I didn't tell you sooner, I'll kick your firm, sexy ass back to your porno ranch right this second."

"Love to see you try, chickadee." He smirks. "I'm not going anywhere."

Now it's my turn to growl some frustrated noises.

He hooks his arm around my waist and leans down to kiss me. I lace my arms around his neck, tugging him closer. "That's better," I whisper.

After one final kiss, he pulls away. "Let's go."

We unpack my stuff from the truck quickly. Bane meets us halfway, giving Rooster a serious once-over.

"Bane, this is my boyfriend, Logan."

Rooster sets my guitar down and shakes Bane's hand. "Thank you for watching out for her."

Gee, and here I expected Rooster to go all caveman and tell Bane he'd handle things from here and to get lost.

"Just doing what the boss told me to do," Bane says.

Rooster smirks at me. "My girl didn't feel it was important to tell me about this until just now, or I would've been here sooner."

"Still woulda been watching out for her." Bane's serious expression doesn't change. "Come on. I'll walk you guys back to her room. Greg was lookin' for ya, Shelby."

Rooster keeps his arm around me, tucked so tight to his body we keep bumping into each other.

"You wanna just pick me up and stick me in your pocket?" I ask.

"Yeah, it'd be easier." He squeezes my hip. "Quit being a smartass."

Bane stops at an unmarked white door and twists the handle, gesturing for us to go inside. "I'll be right out here if you need something, Miss Shelby. Good to meet you, Logan."

"Thanks, Bane." I pat his arm as I pass him.

He closes the door behind us.

Rooster immediately searches the room. It's not that big. Tiny window, way up high. Round table with two chairs. Long, steel rod for wardrobe. Small closet-sized bathroom with a large frosted-glass window big enough for a pony to fit through. Not much different from dozens of other dressing rooms.

Someone left my trunk on the table and I snap it open, pulling out dresses to hang on the steel rod. This is actually a nice change. I don't always have somewhere convenient to hang up my stuff.

"I'm surprised you didn't tell Bane to get lost."

He stops his search and narrows his eyes at me. "I may be an overprotective caveman, but I'm not fucking stupid, Shelby. I want as many people watching out for you as possible. I'd prefer to have brothers I know and trust, but I'll take what I can get right now."

"Well, I don't know how long I've got Bane, honestly. He's one of Dawson's guys. The label's been giving Greg the runaround about sending security."

"Motherfuckers," he grumbles. "That's fine. Jiggy's planning to come tonight."

"Rooster, I can't keep asking—"

"Shelby, we've already had this conversation. You're not asking. *I* am. Trust me, Jiggy ain't gonna complain about being on the road for a while, hooking up with chicks in every damn city."

"But I thought you were planning to train him to do your bow-chicka-bow-wow stuff." I punctuate the silly sentence with an obscene hip thrust.

He rumbles with laughter and yanks me closer. "Love you, chickadee."

I reach up and trace the lines around his mouth. "Even though you're still a little mad at me?"

He kisses my forehead. "You make it hard to stay mad."

Rooster

My anger with Shelby for holding back the letters gives way to fear for her safety.

That and the desire to find whoever scared my girl and rip their arms off. While she's downplaying the situation, I know it has to be bad if Dawson's loaning out one of his bodyguards.

And I wasn't lying. That warmth pulsing through my chest whenever I'm with her doesn't leave room for anger.

As soon as she's settled, I text Greg.

Me: We need to talk.

Greg: About time she told you.

"Even Greg said you should tell me, didn't he?" I ask Shelby after showing her the message.

She bites her lip and glances away. "Well, yeah. Dawson did too."

Huh. Guess I'll have to be nicer to those guys.

"You want me to find some tea?" I ask as she starts humming her scales.

"If you don't mind. Water too."

"You got it." I lean in and kiss her cheek. "Stay in here, okay?"

"Couldn't sneak away if I wanted to. Bane will be planted there all night."

"Good."

As Shelby predicted, Bane's standing in the hallway right across from her door. He'd have to be asleep for someone to slip in without him noticing.

"You're not going anywhere, are you?" I ask him.

"No."

"Where can I find Greg?"

"Logan!" Greg shouts from my right.

Bane's serious mouth shifts into a half-smirk and he jerks his head to the side. "Right there."

"Thanks." I sneer.

I turn. Greg's power-walking his way down the long white corridor, dodging several carts of equipment.

Without stopping, he grabs my arm, pulling me down the hallway and into the hospitality room. A few people wearing yellow and black polo shirts identifying them as employees of the arena are milling around, setting stuff up. No one even glances at us.

"What the hell?" I shake him off me. "You call and bug me when her phone's off for five seconds, but you can't give me a heads-up that someone's sending her threatening letters?"

He stares as if he never considered contacting me. "I don't know what the status of your relationship is exactly. She said she didn't want to worry you. I work for *her*." He scans me from head to toe. "Not you."

I stalk over to one long table and search for a bottle of room-temperature water. "If you work for *her*, then your job is to do what's best for her. And that's get her some fucking security and let her boyfriend know what's going on."

It seems to take him a second to swallow that down. "The record company wants to 'wait' and see if she gets more letters before they do anything."

"That's fucking bullshit."

"I'm working on it."

"Where are the letters? How bad are they?"

"Sheesh," he mumbles, pulling out his phone. "I had to dig the first one out of her bag. I have the originals somewhere safe." He swipes across the screen and pulls up photos of the letters.

It takes me a second to mess with the screen so I can actually read them. "What the...?" I mutter flipping between the three different photos. "He likes the word *cavorting*, huh?"

"Yeah, he's a weirdo with a big vocabulary." Greg snatches his phone back. "I didn't know about the first one until days later. The second one, the ticket office gave me. But they had no idea where it came from or who left it. Same with the third letter."

"What kind of bullshit is that? They must have cameras all over these fucking places."

"Not all of them."

"Can you forward those pictures to me? They were all dropped off, right? None were mailed?"

"Correct."

"So, he's coming to her shows." I pull out my phone and bring up the screenshots I took earlier. "This guy look familiar to you?"

He frowns at me before looking at the photos.

"He could be anyone." He squints at the screen. "Maybe. It's hard to tell. Where did you get that?"

"One of her followers who's a bit off." I shoot a glare at him. "She has a lot of weirdos following her. You really need to manage her social media better."

"I check some things but it's a losing battle. Trent maintains it sometimes. Shelby rarely looks at it."

Huh, interesting.

"It's better to ignore them anyway. Banning and blocking them only makes them nuttier."

"Maybe." I tap my phone. "This guy was at the Wellspring show and, it looks like, a lot of others. Don't you think that's weird for a single dude his age?"

"To be fair, *I'm* a single dude his age, and I've been to every show."

"You're her *manager*. Don't be fucking dense, Greg. I'm not in the mood."

"What do you want from me? You see how big these crowds are."

"Give me time to think on it." Staying at Ice's place has given me a few ideas. "I'm going to need at least one extra pass for tonight and tomorrow."

He reaches into his back pocket and hands me three passes on lanyards. "Those are for the whole tour. Keep 'em on you so you don't need a new one at each venue."

I slip one around my neck and stuff the others inside my cut. "This woulda been helpful a couple weeks ago."

His casual shrug is completely unapologetic. "I wasn't sure how often you'd be joining us."

I almost laugh at the edge of sarcasm creeping into his tone. Greg's brave, I'll give him that.

"Well, I'll be joining you a lot more often, so get used to my pretty face. I'll have one or two of my brothers here for these shows and then we'll go from there." I find the tea and pour some hot water into a cup. The lemon slices look like they've been sitting there for a few weeks, so I don't bother with them. Can't find any honey packets either.

Greg's still annoyingly close when I turn around.

"I looked into your motorcycle gang, you know."

I cock my head and stare him down until he glances away. He didn't research us too hard or he'd know better than to refer to us as a "gang." "Careful, Greg. It's a motorcycle *club*. Not a gang."

"Sorry, *club*. Lost Kings, New York. Except for a few random arrests here and there, not much information since the late nineties and early aughts."

"Told you," I shrug, "We're just a club."

"*But* I see some of your other charters have made headlines more recently."

Seems Greg isn't as dumb as he wants everyone to think he is. "Do you have a point?"

"My point is, I've been having nightmares about what kind of publicity your *relationship* will bring Shelby."

You and me both. "You can always say you hired me to protect her."

"Well, that won't hold water when you keep having photos taken where it looks like you're trying to eat each other's faces off."

I snort and glance away. "I already had a dad, Greg. I'm not lookin' to replace him."

He lets out a soft *pfft* sound. "I couldn't give a fig about handing out parental advice to you or anyone else. The CMA nominations are coming up. Shelby should by all rights be up for Best New Artist. Having a biker boyfriend hanging around might hurt her chances. She's afraid talking about the nominations will bring bad juju"—he waves his hands in the air dismissively—"or whatever, but I know how badly she wants it."

Well, fuck.

"There isn't another artist this year who deserves it more than Shelby. And I'm not saying that because I'm her manager." He laces his fingers behind his head. "This isn't the ideal time for her fling with a biker to be splashed all over the place."

Can't say I care for Greg referring to me as a *fling*. Like I'm a fleeting moment in Shelby's life instead of a permanent fucking fixture.

"Not to mention," he continues, "I now have her mother harassing me constantly."

Shock takes me back a step. "About what?"

"You. She expects me to somehow ban you from the tour."

Damn, Lynn. You're starting to piss me off. "You can try."

"I guess what I want to know is..." He drops his arms and spears me with a more probing look. "How serious is this between you two?"

For a second there, I thought he was going to try paying me to go away.

"Well, I've never dropped everything to follow anyone around the country before, so there's that." I cross my arms over my chest and cock my head. "Why don't you ask Shelby?"

"Because she gets prickly when I pry into her personal stuff," he answers in a tight, irritated tone.

I burst out laughing. "I think I'm offended that you're more scared of Shelby than me."

"She could fire me."

"Yeah, but I could *end* you." I keep my mouth in a straight line, with no hint of a smile to suggest I'm joking.

He screws his face into the scowl of someone who stepped in elephant shit. "I can't believe I'm going to say this after you just *threatened* me, but I *think* it's good for her to have you around."

Now he has my attention. "How's that?"

He shrugs. "Maybe it's a fluke. The nights you've been here, she seems less anxious. More confident onstage. Subtle differences. No one else probably notices. All her performances are excellent," he hurries to add, like he's worried I'll think he's insulting her. "Don't get me wrong."

Damn. Not that I particularly care what Greg thinks of me or our relationship, but pride still prickles through my chest. I like helping Shelby any and every way I can, and knowing I make things better for her is worth putting up with annoying shit—like this conversation with Greg.

"I'm not here to cause trouble. I see how stressful all of this can be," I say. "I want to help take the pressure off her where I can while spending time with her."

He stares at me, like he's weighing my words. "I'm also asking because I'm worried if you two break up it's going to be hard on her."

"And ruin your tour."

"*Her* tour."

He's basically asking me not to break her heart. Same as Shelby asked me in the beginning.

"Talent isn't enough in this business. She's a strong girl who has fought damn hard to get here," he says. "I don't want to see anything change her trajectory."

The guy isn't entitled to my feelings about Shelby. I don't owe him shit. But he's trying to look out for Shelby in his own weird way. When you get right down to it, we have the same goal.

"Neither do I."

He keeps staring at me.

"What do you want me to say? I care about her. I'm here for her. Unless she tells me to take a hike, I'm not going anywhere."

His eyes close and he blows out a long breath. "Then I'll do what I can to manage the press and spin your relationship in a positive way."

Well, fuck. I didn't expect that.

He grits his teeth. "And I'll keep dealing with Lynn. She means well. Even if she's a pain in my ass."

"You're not gonna get your boxers twisted if I have one of my brothers travel with us and help look out for Shelby, right?"

"The scary one, or the friendly one who's probably even scarier?"

I rumble with laughter at his descriptions of Jigsaw and Dex. "Jigsaw. He's down here in Virginia with me. He went to the radio show with us this morning, actually."

"How was the show?"

"Fucking awful. What did you expect?"

"I listened to the whole interview." He frowns. "It sounded good."

"Uh, it was crass as fuck. Not exactly great for her 'image' you're supposedly so worried about. The guy put down her work with Dream Makers, for fuck's sake."

"Yeah, that was a little tactless."

"The worst was him trying to cop a feel while they were taking pictures after the interview."

He drops his gaze and pinches the bridge of his nose. "Please tell me you didn't—"

"Nah, I didn't do a thing. Shelby kneed him in the nuts." I rub my hand over my chin, like I can't remember all the details. "I might have had a chat with him after the blow to his balls."

"Jesus Christ, Logan. What were—"

"He won't do anything."

"You're killing me. It's almost impossible to secure promotion for her as it is. If she gets a reputation for being difficult or as someone who can't take a joke—"

"He tried to squeeze her fuckin' tit, Greg. That's not a joke. If she hadn't kneed him in the junk, I would've broken his fucking hands."

He snaps his mouth shut but doesn't seem surprised.

"Are we done here?" I hold up the water bottle and rapidly cooling tea. "I need to get back to Shelby."

"Do we have a deal?"

"Sure, Greg."

As I watch Greg walk away, I can't help wondering what I've committed myself to, and I doubt this will be the last time I have to fight for us.

CHAPTER FIFTY-FOUR

Rooster

I almost make it to Shelby's door before I'm stopped again.

"Logan, good to see you back here." Dawson stops in front of me. My hands are full, so we skip the handshake.

"Thanks." I jerk my head toward Shelby's dressing room. "Appreciate you having your guy look out for her."

"Not a problem." He shrugs. "It's probably nothing. I get kooky shit like that too, but I'd rather not take any chances."

"Same."

His lips curl up. "I reckon you'll be on her like white on rice now, but I'm still gonna leave Bane with her for the time being."

If he thinks I'll object, he's dead wrong. I wasn't kidding about having as many people as possible looking out for her. "Thank you."

"You got it." He claps me on the shoulder. "I'll stop by and check on her a little later."

Finally, I'm free to be with Shelby. I'm more focused and determined than ever to keep her safe.

Bane nods at me, knocks on the door three times and pushes it open for me.

Shelby's on her mat, stretched out in what she's explained to me is extended child's pose. I still say it looks more like grab-me-by-the-hips-and-slam-your-cock-in-me pose, but what do I know?

"You all right?" I ask.

She hums a soft noise that sounds like a *yes.*

Not wanting to bother her, I take a seat at the table where I'm not staring at her ass.

"You can join me." She lifts her head and smiles.

"If I join you, we're going to create a whole new pose called 'Rooster mounts a chickadee.'"

She laughs softly and drops her head down to the mat again.

Cute that she thinks I'm kidding.

"Dawson said he's gonna stop by and check on you later." The conversation with Greg's still bouncing around in my head, so I don't share any of it yet. It'll probably just stress her out anyway.

She kneels, rests her hands on her thighs and twists to one side, then the other. "I hate that everyone's making a fuss over nothing."

Now that I've read the letters, I strongly disagree that they're "nothing." "Rather be safe than sorry."

Someone knocks and Shelby jumps up, leaning over to quickly roll her mat.

Greg opens the door a crack, popping his head in. "They need you to come do sound check a little early."

She glances down at her tight yoga shorts and tank top. "Let me change."

"Hurry." He slams the door shut.

Shelby sticks her tongue out. "Hurry," she mutters.

She searches through her trunk, tossing clothes around until she settles on a denim skirt and flowered blouse. I keep my ass planted where it is, watching her every move but staying out of her way.

"It's cute you're dressing up for a fifteen-minute soundcheck."

"This isn't dressing up."

I shrug, still amused. Shit, is there anything about her I don't find fucking adorable and charming?

She hurries into the bathroom and since I don't know who'll be walking in next, I restrain myself from following her. I use the time to text Jigsaw and remind him what time he needs to be here.

"Ready!" Shelby announces a few minutes later. She slips on her brown, fringed boots and holds out her hand to me.

Outside her dressing room, I let go of her hand.

"What are you doing?"

"Greg's worried about your reputation if you keep getting photographed with your big, bad biker." I try to keep my tone light and teasing, so she knows I'm not mad about it.

She blinks. "I don't care what anyone thinks." She snatches my hand back.

I draw her closer. "I appreciate that but I want to do what's best for you. As long as you're all mine when we're alone—"

"That's really sucky and not the way I want to live." She gives me a tug. "Come on."

I nod to Bane and he follows us down the hallway. Signs point us in the direction of the stage.

"Shelby!" Greg calls out. "Hang on."

His sneakers squeak over the shiny floors as he jogs up to us. "Guys are already up there. They're having a few issues."

He falls into step with us, explaining sound stuff I don't follow along with.

At the entrance to the stage, Shelby drops my hand and leans up to kiss my cheek. "Will you watch?"

"Absolutely."

Her band starts with "Big Lies" and she waits a few minutes before jumping in and singing the first line. She frowns and asks the band to start over more than once.

"Is everything all right?" I ask Greg.

"It'll be fine."

Once Shelby's satisfied, we head back to her dressing room. Outside her door, she stops to talk to Greg and Trent.

While the hallway's busy enough, no one watched Shelby's room while we were gone. Since she's occupied, I slip inside and do a quick sweep. Everything seems fine. Untouched.

Until my gaze lands on a black envelope with silver writing waiting on her makeup chair.

"Motherfucker."

I open the letter carefully.

DEAREST SHELBY,

I was so relieved to learn of your charity work with Dream Makers. I will admit that I had my doubts after all your indiscriminate behavior. Now I feel reassured that you will be an appropriate mother for our children.

See you soon.

M

"FUCK!" I DROP THE LETTER AND STORM OUT OF SHELBY'S DRESSING room, on the hunt for someone to fucking murder.

"What's wrong?" Greg raises his hand in a 'stop' motion.

Shelby's bottom lip trembles, fear dancing in her eyes. "There's another letter, isn't there?"

Shit. I need to control myself. She still has a show. I pull her into my arms and kiss the top of her head, then motion for Greg and Bane to follow us into the room.

"How the fuck did this get in here?" I point to the letter I'd left on the makeup table.

Greg leans over and scans the note. "Shit."

"Yeah. What the fuck? Can anyone just walk around backstage?"

"They shouldn't be able to," Greg says.

Bane studies the letter for a second. "Where was it?"

"On her chair."

He turns to Greg. "It could've been like before. Someone might have left it up front and one of the employees dropped it off."

"You're going to need to start calling ahead to each place and give them a heads-up," I say to Greg.

"Heads-up to what?"

"To be on the lookout for anyone dropping off fan mail for Shelby. Detain them or get a name. Something." Why is he so slow to see this as a problem?

"Detain them for what?" Greg places his hands on his hips. "They're creepy, sure. But there's no threat."

Shelby raises her hand. "Uh, the 'see you soon' feels like a threat to *me*. Not to mention this letter reeks of reproductive coercion." She hugs herself and shudders.

I squeeze her tighter. Forget my whole caveman brain shorting out over some psycho thinking he's going to have babies with my woman— I know how much the subject freaks her out in general and that's way more important than my inner barbarian's instincts. "I'm gonna kill this motherfucker."

"That's not helpful." Greg wags his finger at me.

"Sorry, Greg." Bane snorts. "I'm with Logan."

Behind us, there's a knock and Dawson pushes the door open. "What's everyone doing in here?"

"Just admiring the latest missive Mr. Creepy left for me," Shelby mutters.

"Shit." Dawson closes the door behind him. "Are you serious? How the fuck are they getting to her, Greg?"

Greg backs up at the accusatory tone in Dawson's voice. "I'm not responsible for what the venue does."

"Where were you?" Dawson slaps Bane's shoulder.

"With her at sound check."

"Oh. Sorry." He lifts his chin at me. "You sticking around tonight?"

"I'm not going anywhere."

"Where you taking her after the show? I'm thinking she shouldn't stay at the same hotel as the rest of the band and crew."

"My club has a charter not far from here. She'll be safe there."

Dawson nods. "Good." He focuses on Greg. "I need a word with you."

Bane follows Greg and Dawson out, promising to remain outside the door. Finally, it's just the two of us. Shelby buries her face against my shirt.

I curl my arm around her. "Come here."

"I'm so creeped out that this guy was in here."

I sit in the corner of the couch and pull her into my lap. "We don't know that. It could've been staff who dropped it off."

"I guess." She drapes her arms around my neck and rests her head on my chest. I hook my arm under her knees, pulling her legs up.

"Thank you," she murmurs. "For being here."

"Nowhere else I wanna be, chickadee."

"Don't feel...obligated to come on tour with me because of this."

"Hey." I pull back and wait for her to look at me. "We talked about this. I was already planning to come with you." I tickle her side. "Remember? You were hiding this from me and I didn't know until this morning."

"I wasn't hiding—stop, that tickles!"

"Why do you have such a hard time believing me when I tell you stuff?"

She shrugs and glances away. "There haven't been a lot of people in my life I could depend on."

"I get that, but—"

Someone knocks and Shelby jumps.

"It's me!" Cindy calls as she opens the door. "Ready?"

"Shoot. Yeah. Sorry."

Cindy's gaze pings between us. "Everything okay?"

"I got another letter," Shelby mumbles.

"Oh my God, are you serious?" Cindy sets her case next to the dresser. "Shoot, honey. I'm really worried about you."

"I'll be fine." Shelby forces a bright smile that doesn't quite reach her eyes.

While they're doing their thing, I check messages. I also take a look at Shelby's Instagram. Good response to her post about the radio interview. No creeps. I guess that's something. An announcement about the show tonight and what time she goes onstage. Lots of people responding with, "Can't wait" or "Wish I could be there," comments. I scan each one quickly.

My phone buzzes, and a message pops up.

Jigsaw: I'm here.

Thank fuck.

I slide my phone in my pocket and stand. "Jiggy's here. I'm gonna go meet him so he doesn't get into trouble." I rest my hand on Shelby's shoulder, watching her in the mirror for a few seconds. The tense set of her jaw pushes me into murderous rampage territory again. She needs to focus on her show not worry about stupid letters. "Will you be okay?"

"I'm fine," she assures me.

"I'll be here with her," Cindy adds.

"Thanks. I'll be right back."

On my way out, I check with Bane that he's not going anywhere. Poor dude's probably sick of me asking. Tough shit. I navigate the long corridors and finally find my way outside just as Jigsaw's coming up the concrete steps of the loading dock.

"Sup, brother?" He grabs my hand and yanks me closer, patting my back.

"It's been a fucking day."

"Same."

"Why? What's wrong?"

"Well, Ice put those cameras to use at the porn palace."

Shit. I haven't finished setting stuff up there yet. "Did he touch the stuff I bought?"

"No. The security cameras that Pants told us about are fully functional. Caught some guy breaking into the place. Anya was there. Thought Ice was gonna lose his fucking mind."

"Shit. Sorry I wasn't there. Is it taken care of?"

"Oh yeah." His eyes widen. "Big time."

"Is Anya all right?"

"She was shaken up but otherwise, fine. She's at the clubhouse now."

"What was he doing? Monitoring the feeds from his office?"

Jiggy pulls out his phone. "Phone and office, I guess."

"Huh. Interesting."

He slaps my chest. "We gonna stand out here yapping all night? Where's our little songbird?"

"Getting ready." As we make our way to Shelby's room, I fill him in on the stalker letters and everything else that's gone down.

"Holy fuck. Here I thought you were hanging out having a good ol' time."

"Yeah, it's been a blast." I roll my eyes.

I nod to Bane and introduce him to Jigsaw before stepping into Shelby's room.

Cindy's already sticking her makeup brushes back into their slots and tucking them into the train case she always carries.

Jigsaw stops in his tracks, eyes bugging wide, and clutches his heart. *Jesus Christ. Why didn't I see this coming?*

What passes for a flirty smile curves his mouth up. "Who's your lovely friend, Shelby?"

"Hi, Jiggy," Shelby drawls. "This is Cindy, our makeup artist."

Cindy flicks her gaze over Jigsaw and tucks her hair behind her ear. "Well, aren't you a lucky girl, Shelby."

"The luck's all mine," Jigsaw says.

"Please stop," I say under my breath.

"Ease up, fella." Cindy holds up one hand. "I'm pretty sure I'm old enough to be your mother."

Shelby cough-laughs.

"I don't discriminate, Cindy," Jigsaw assures her. "I'm a big fan of females in a more experienced age range."

"Oh, Jesus," I mutter.

Cindy chuckles and seems more amused than offended, thank fuck. I bet *this* would fall under behavior Greg considers inappropriate.

"What did I tell you?" I growl after Cindy leaves.

"I couldn't help myself." He shrugs. "She's hot."

Shelby stands and moves to her massive trunk, searching through her clothes. "Cindy's real sweet and she's had some shitty men in her life, so please don't."

"I'm not shitty." His outraged tone doesn't quite match the you-caught-me smile tugging at the corners of his mouth.

I give him a quick shove. "You're the definition of shitty."

"If a woman has expectations, then yeah, I suck. But a one or two-night thing? Totally five-star rated."

"Good grief," Shelby mumbles.

"I'm kidding. I won't bug her, Shelby. Promise. You doin' okay?"

A serious Jigsaw is terrifying. I whap the back of his head. "You feeling okay, bro?"

"Fuck off."

Shelby sets down the pile of clothes in her arms, comes over and gives Jigsaw a quick kiss on the cheek. "Thanks for being here tonight. I guess Rooster told you everything?"

"Just the highlights. He tell you he's stalking your social media and has a few names on his list already? My boy will find this creeper in no time."

I smack Jigsaw. Will he ever learn to shut his mouth?

"I thought you didn't like social media," Shelby says.

"I don't. I have to use some stuff for work. Decided to keep an eye on yours too."

"Trackin' me with the porno princesses. Great." Her mouth twists. *Huh*. Here I thought it didn't bug her that much.

It doesn't matter. She needs to get ready for her show. We can talk it out later.

"Finally told her about our porn empire? That's good. Fun day for both of ya, right?" Jigsaw grins at us. When neither of us return the gesture, the smile slides off his face. "No? Not fun? A little tense? Still working through it?" He edges toward the door. "You know what? I'm gonna go sit in the hallway with your mountain-man buddy. Give you two some alone time."

Shelby chuckles as she watches him walk out.

"Do you need help?" I nod to her pile of dresses, still determined not to touch the porno princesses comment.

She stares at the door like she's contemplating her escape. "I feel like a wet washcloth that's been wrung out one too many times."

Shit, I hate this. I'm smart enough to know that unless something major happens, she won't cancel the show, so I don't bother suggesting it.

"Don't let this get to you. It's going to be fine. I promise." I step closer. "What can I do to help?"

One way or another, I'll get her through tonight safely.

We'll worry about the rest of it tomorrow.

CHAPTER FIFTY-FIVE

Rooster

After Shelby's set, everyone follows us back to her dressing room. It's not a big space but I'm not willing to leave her side, and Greg apparently wants to go over a game plan for tomorrow.

Hate to break it to him but I already have a plan.

Bane leans against the wall by the door. Greg takes the chair at Shelby's makeup table. Trent sits in one of the chairs at the small round table. Jigsaw drops down on the couch, kicking out his feet.

Someone knocks and Bane cautiously opens the door. His tense posture relaxes when Dawson strolls in. Bane closes the door and puts his back to it.

Shelby's gaze bounces around the room. "Appreciate the after-party, guys, but I'm beat. Dawson, don't you have a show to get ready for?"

"I got time, darlin'."

Her pleading eyes meet mine and I slip an arm around her shoulders, walking her to the bathroom door. "You shower, change, get ready to go. Let me talk to them."

"Logan—"

"I promise I'll share all the details with you later."

She scowls up at me. "I don't know how I feel about you swooping in and trying to take over things, but I'm too exhausted to give a damn." She rubs her throat. "And my voice isn't feelin' right."

I lean down and kiss her forehead. "Even more reason you should let me handle this for you."

"Fine."

I wait until the shower screeches to life before taking a seat next to Jigsaw.

"All right," Greg starts the conversation. "The venue says they might have video. They won't be able to let us look at it until tomorrow morning, though."

"That's a start." My gaze shifts to Dawson, unsure of why he's even here, then back to Greg. "Is there any extra room in her merch booth?"

He eyes me suspiciously. "Why?"

Ignoring his tone, I go right for it. "I want to set up a small viewing booth. We'll post on her social media that Shelby has an exclusive message of some sort for her *special* fans. They can come check it out at her merch booth for free. A different video in each city. I'll set up some cameras and we'll record everyone who stops by. We'll keep a log and be able to check them against each location. See who shows up over and over. You know this guy won't be able to resist."

"Shoot, that's brilliant," Dawson says. "I should have you running my security team."

"Shelby's my priority," I say without looking at him. "We'll work out the details." I slap Jigsaw's back. "And one of us will review the footage each night." Jiggy's annoying attention to small details is about to come in handy.

Greg rubs his hand over his chin for a few seconds. "I don't know if the venue will allow—"

"It's not their fuckin' business," I growl. "This is a huge place. There's no reasonable expectation of privacy at a merchandise booth. And we're not cops." Nor are we going to turn the stalker over to the cops, but mentioning that won't help Greg accept my plan, so I don't bother saying it.

"Furthest thing from cops," Jigsaw adds.

"There's no issue." I ignore Jiggy's contribution. "If you ask their permission, they might stall us, and I'm not in the mood to deal with any bullshit. Not when these letters are escalating in the sicko factor."

Dawson slaps Greg's shoulder. "Ask forgiveness, not permission, buddy."

"Will you still be saying that next year when they won't let us book a show here?" Greg asks.

Dawson busts out laughing. "Please. We sold out two nights in a row. It's not an issue."

Greg knows he's lost this battle but he still needs me to give him an extra push. "It's not much different than having cameras to stop people from boosting her T-shirts."

"All right. I'll get you the space. What footage of Shelby are you going to use as your bait?"

"I'll think of an angle. It'll have to be video they can't find anywhere else. Something cute and personal her fans don't know about her maybe."

"Where are you going to get equipment like that on such short notice? We don't have that kind of money in the budget."

"Don't worry about it." I glance over at Jigsaw. "I know where I can get everything I need."

CHAPTER FIFTY-SIX

Shelby

Guilt washes over me with the lukewarm water in the dressing room shower.

Maybe this is what my momma wanted me to avoid. A man coming in and controlling my business. My father did something similar, taking over bits and pieces of her life until he finally knocked her up and bye-bye, singing career.

At least, that's her version of the story. Dad's not exactly around to give me his side.

I'm five years older than she was when she quit singing. Made it a hell of a lot further too. Rooster is nothing like my dad. Then again, my memories could be tainted with my mother's bitterness and my own heartbreak.

Rooster's not taking over. He's trying to help me—that's another important difference.

But what's it look like to Dawson? To have my boyfriend handle things? Is he going to think I'm weak and pathetic? This business is hard enough. I want to gain respect from my peers, not pity.

All the men are out there discussing me and I'm in here hiding in the shower.

There's some creep on the loose who thinks I'm going to have his babies.

My stomach twists. *So gross.* What kind of sicko thinks like that, let alone puts it in a letter and gives it to another human being? Oh, right. A man like that only sees me as a cute little blonde baby-making machine.

The tap squeaks as I twist it off. I snag my towel from the hook and wrap it around myself.

What are they talking about? *Poor Shelby. She really attracts the weirdos?* Is Rooster thinking this is too much and he shouldn't have gotten involved with me? Or maybe he really has some white knight complex and—

Shoot. I need to calm the hell down.

Leaning against the sink, I swipe my hand over the foggy mirror and study my face. I'm so dang pale. Spending way too much time inside.

Quit stalling. Get your ass out there, Shelby Morgan.

I shake my jeans and wiggle into them. They stick in weird spots where my skin's still damp. I braid my wet hair out of my face and slip on a T-shirt, then flip flop my way to the door. A cloud of steam follows me.

"Feel better?" Rooster asks.

My gaze darts around the room. "Where'd everyone go?"

Jigsaw spreads his hands in front of him. "The most important person is still here."

That actually makes me chuckle. "Thank you, Jiggy."

Rooster slides a half-smirk Jigsaw's way. "Dawson needed to get ready for his set. Trent wanted to go to the hotel. Greg had to take care of some stuff. Told Bane we had you covered for the night. I'm meeting with Greg, Bane, and Trent tomorrow."

"Wait, you're what? Why?"

He stands, a slight frown wrinkling his forehead. "I'll explain on the way to the clubhouse."

"We're not staying at the hotel?"

He stops and stares at me. "I didn't think you'd want to. We can stay anywhere you want. I *do* need to go to the clubhouse to get some things, though. Either tonight or tomorrow morning."

"We should stay there then."

"Are you sure?"

"Yes."

I hate having this conversation in front of Jigsaw. As it is, he probably hates that I'm causing his best friend so many problems.

"Come on." Rooster slings his arm around my shoulders. "You have to be exhausted."

We grab my stuff and the three of us walk into the hallway. The canned music they play between sets thumps through the air. Outside, I take deep gulps of the muggy night air. Rooster's right; I'm bone-weary.

Jigsaw pats my back and waits for us to get in the truck before firing up his bike.

"So what plans were you making with all the men while I was showering?" I ask as Rooster twists the key in the ignition.

"Can you help me out of here before we start talking about that?" He reverses out of our spot and points the truck toward the main road.

"Sorry," I mumble, pulling up the map and directions on my phone. When we're clear of the arena, Rooster fills me in on his plan.

"Wait, so between now and tomorrow morning, you want to take some cutesy video of me? Doing what?"

"I don't know. Something your fans haven't seen before. Something endearing that shows your personality."

"And you want to create new content like that *every night* for the rest of the tour or until we catch the creep?" Is he out of his dang mind? "Besides singing, I'm not all that interesting."

"That's not true." He drums his thumbs against the steering wheel. "What about your tarot cards? You could show off a morning reading or something."

"Rooster." I try to work my voice down to a reasonable tone. "Lotta country fans are kinda religious. I don't want to offend them with my new-agey stuff. It won't go over well."

"Oh." He glances over. "Are you mad at me?"

"No." I'm not mad at all. I'm impressed with his plan. It just seems like an awful lot of work.

"What about a short video of Cindy doing your hair and stuff for the show?"

"Who wants to see that?"

"I'm thinking an obsessive stalker would love to see it."

"Ick."

"Some of your female fans might get a kick out of it too. A behind-the-scenes glimpse."

"I guess. We'll have to check with Cindy and make sure she's okay with it, though."

"All right. If not, maybe you and Trent collaborating on a song. A little peek of your songwriting process."

"Don't you think filming me with another guy might tick him off?"

"Maybe. What about a simple yoga routine? That can't possibly offend anyone, right?"

"Oh, I like that idea."

Now that we seem to have a plan, Rooster reaches over and rests his hand on my leg. "You were amazing tonight. I forgot to tell you."

Maybe it's exhaustion or stress from the day but tears prick my eyes. "Thank you," I whisper.

"Your throat feeling okay?"

"Not great."

"You want to close your eyes and rest? I'll wake you when we get there."

ROOSTER

The clubhouse is quieter than I expected. No party in the parking lot tonight. Music still spills out the front door but it's nowhere near the usual volume.

I'm actually relieved. I need to talk to Ice, and I want Shelby to get some rest.

Jigsaw's boots crunch over the gravel and I open the truck door to meet him outside so he doesn't wake Shelby.

"She all right?" he asks.

"Just tired, I think."

"Tell her your plan?"

I glance back at the truck before answering. "Yeah. She shot down my first idea but I think we settled on something else."

He stares at me. "Planning to share?"

"No, because if you say something obnoxious, I'll punch you."

"How bad can it be?"

"We were thinking one of her short yoga sequences. Sharing how she prepares for a show, kind of thing."

Jigsaw bites his lip, and wiggles his jaw from side to side.

"Motherfucker, I swear to—"

"No, no, no. It's perfect pervert-catching material."

"Do you have to be an asshole?"

He scratches the side of his head. "It's why I was put on this earth."

"Lucky us." I jerk my head toward the truck. "Come on. I want to get her inside."

"Switch those last two words around, and I'll believe you."

"Christ, you're a fucking pain in the ass," I grumble, stalking to Shelby's side of the truck. "We're here, chickadee," I say in a hushed voice.

"Jesus." Jiggy leans on the truck and stares up at the sky. "I haven't seen you like this since high school."

"What's your point?"

He glances at Shelby. "I haven't decided yet."

"I'm *never* fucking you, so put that thought right outta yer head," Shelby rasps.

"You're awake." He slaps the side of the truck. "Listening in?"

"Kinda hard not to hear your big mouth." She slides out of the truck.

I'm busy laughing for a solid minute. Hell, even Jiggy's laughing.

"Now, why did your dirty little mind go there, Shelby?" Jigsaw asks with a big grin stretched across his face.

She waves her hands in the air. "That story you told about giving up your V-card to his girlfriend."

"Ex-girlfriend," I correct.

"Ex. Whatever."

"That was years ago." Jigsaw pulls a puppy-dog face. "I've matured since then."

"If you're not planning to help unload the truck, can you at least get out of my way?" I shove him to the side and yank open the back door, pulling out Shelby's bags.

She and Jiggy continue their verbal sparring all the way into the clubhouse. I can't help watching with a goofy-as-fuck grin. Nothing better than a sassy woman who can go toe to toe with my best friend.

We say hello to a few brothers we pass in the clubhouse. Ice and Pants are nowhere to be found. I'll have to try to catch Ice in the morning.

And catch myself a stalker tomorrow night.

CHAPTER FIFTY-SEVEN

Shelby

Tonight, I'm more alert, and I study the clubhouse as we walk to our room.

Jiggy gives Rooster a fist bump and says good night at our door.

Inside, I take my backpack and one of my totes from Rooster. "I'm sorry you're always schlepping my stuff around."

"It's fine."

I drop my bag on the bed and unzip it, searching for my jammy pants. "So, is this place where the *porno magic* happens?" I ask.

"Are you still pissy about my *job*?" He stalks closer, hands on his hips.

I snort. "Some job."

"Seriously?"

"Sorry, guess I haven't had a lot of time to process—"

"Don't," he warns me. "You got some motherfucker stalking you, and you lied to me about it for days."

"I didn't *lie* about anything."

"Are you fucking kidding?"

I hurry and dig through my backpack faster. Where are my damn pants? My fingers brush against something soft, and I pull out the velvet bag with my tarot cards. I've been too scared to do a reading since the last one where the devil card and his two buddies popped up *again*.

"Shelby?"

I blink back tears. Oh my God. Is this it? The impending breakup? I duck my head, not wanting him to see me cry.

"Hey." He brushes his knuckles over my cheek. "I didn't mean to yell."

I risk a peek at him. He's still tight with anger but love and concern also burn in his eyes. "I don't want to break up."

He frowns and takes a step back. "Where did you get *break up* from what I said?"

I shrug.

"Get over here." He pulls me against his chest, stroking his hand over my head. "Break up? You're not getting rid of me, woman."

"Don't stay because you think you have to protect me." I snuffle against his shirt. "It's not your job."

He sweeps his hands up and down my back, soothing a little of the storm inside me.

"Shelby," he says softly. "Why'd you go to breaking up?" He leads me over to the side of the bed and snaps on the table lamp.

I can't form any words and end up uselessly shaking my head.

"I don't like you thinking that every time we have a...disagreement or we're angry with each other that it means I'm leaving you. We can talk and work through anything."

I blink and turn over his words. *Work through?* Sure, Rooster's gruff on the outside. But he's always thoughtful and concerned about me. About us. But can I really trust that he won't walk out the door one day and never come back without telling me why?

"I hate that every time we spoke on the phone and I asked you if you were okay, you didn't tell me about the letters." He taps his chest. "But I'm right here."

"You're still mad at me?"

"Not *at* you. Just the situation."

"I didn't want to make you worry. And it didn't seem like a big deal." I sniff and pull away. "At least, it didn't until today. That was the worst letter by far."

He hums in agreement. "Okay, so why would you think we're breaking up after everything we did and talked about today?"

"It's stupid."

"Nothing about you is stupid. Tell me why you thought that."

I shake my head. He's going to think I'm even more ridiculous than he already does. "I keep getting certain cards in my readings."

He blinks several times. Poor logical, linear Logan. "Come again?"

I roll to the side and grab the velvet bag I'd laid on the bed and pull out my tarot journal and deck of cards.

A muscle in his jaw twitches. I can't tell if he's trying not to laugh or if he's about to blow a gasket. He slides one leg on the bed and turns to face me.

I flip through the notebook until I find what I'd written about the first reading that plunged this shaky sensation into my heart.

He leans over and studies the page. "What's this one?" He points to the Devil card I'd noted on the side of the page.

"It was a jumper card."

"What the fuck is that?"

"You know, when you're shuffling a deck and a card or two pop out?" I flip through an imaginary deck of cards in my hands to demonstrate. "I'm a slow shuffler, so that doesn't usually happen, but that time it did. And it's happened two more times since then. Same card." I stop my frantic rush of words and take a breath. "It's freaky as shit, Logan."

He scrubs his hands over his face and through his hair. "I don't believe this," he mutters.

"I know you think this stuff's stupid—"

"Here I'm worried I triggered some abandonment issue you've got over your dad walking out on you, but you're letting some pretty pictures on a deck of cards guide our relationship?"

"Abandonment issues?" I sputter. "I don't have *abandonment* issues. And you're not *that* much older than me, so don't you go sayin' I've got daddy issues either."

He snorts and then laughs.

"It's not funny." I shove him, and he falls to the side, still laughing. How dare he think I have abandonment issues. I got over my father leaving years ago. *Didn't I?*

A few more chuckles spill out before he finally stops and holds out his hand. "Can I see your booklet?"

"What? No. Why? You don't believe in this stuff anyway."

"But you do, so let me see if I can help you."

I don't know whether to hug him or smack him. "Why? So you can mansplain my cards to me?"

"Fucking hell. I can't win tonight." He leans over and scoops his phone from the nightstand.

"What are you doing?"

He snatches my journal off the bed and studies the open page for a second before typing on his phone. "Googling it."

"Googling what? You can't *google* tarot readings." I tap my chest. "They're guided by intuition and inner wisdom."

"Everything can be googled." He grabs a pen and paper off the nightstand and scribbles down his own notes. "Each one of these could mean one of a thousand fucking things," he grumbles.

"That's why you read the entire spread and use your *intuition. Not* Google."

"How's this?" His smile takes on a seductive gleam. "*My* intuition says I'm gonna be fucking you doggy-style right here in this bed forty-five minutes from now."

I blink and scoot back a few inches. "Like hell you are."

He shrugs. "My prediction is about as accurate as anything here."

I reach over and scoop up my stuff. "Get your negative energy away from my cards."

"Which ones do you keep getting?" He rests his hand over mine to still my movements.

"The Devil's jumped out three times."

"What else?"

"The Three of Swords. I guess those are the two consistent ones. And Justice."

He flicks through a few more screens on his phone and jots down more notes.

"Your handwriting looks like chicken scratch."

He ignores me.

"Fuck me," he breathes out, staring at the notes in front of him. "Your Three of Swords isn't just breakups. It's loneliness and rejection."

"I'm lonely on the road," I admit with a pathetic shrug. "It made sense."

He sighs and pulls me to his side, kissing the top of my head. "Chickadee, I'm going to be so far up your ass from now on, you won't have time to be lonely."

ROOSTER

"There's your faulty intuition again," she sasses. "You're not getting anywhere *near* my ass."

I snort. "Famous last words."

My gaze strays to the notes I made. Do I believe in this stuff?

Fuck no.

But I'll admit it's weird that she keeps dealing the same cards. But there's probably a perfectly logical reason for that. Maybe she ate a cinnamon bun one day right before touching the deck and a few of them are sticky. Or maybe one's bent a fraction in a way that makes it easier or more likely to be pulled from the deck.

But now that my initial surprise that she thought we were going to break up because some cards told her so has worn off, I genuinely want to understand.

Before we get distracted, I tap my pen on the notepad. "Your Devil card?"

"It's not as bad as people think."

"Few things are." I tap my pen harder on the word *Devil* to keep her attention. "Obsession. Negativity." I slide my pen to the Three of Swords. "Loneliness. Rejection."

"Oh my God." She slaps my arm a few times. "It's a warning about my stalker."

I glance at the cards again. I was going to say she needs to stop reading that stupid *Sippin' on Secrets* blog. But *her* interpretation actually makes more sense. "That works. He's a fucking reject who's fixated on you."

"Oh, wow." She covers her hand with her mouth. "I asked a career question the first time. Not a love reading. I should've known...He wouldn't know who the heck I was if I didn't have a career!"

This feels like the most fucked-up mashup of a YouTube conspiracy video and Mad Libs game ever. But fuck do I love her and I never want her to doubt us.

"Shelby." I squeeze her tighter, aware what I'm about to say will make me sound like a bit of a dick. "No more love readings. You don't need 'em. If I'm ever unclear, just ask me whatever the fuck you need to know. I'm much more straightforward than the universe will ever be."

"Where is this relationship going?" A smile teases the corners of her mouth up.

"Is that what you'd ask during a love reading?"

"Yup."

I cup her cheek, staring into her eyes. "Everywhere, Shelby. We're going everywhere. Together."

CHAPTER FIFTY-EIGHT

Shelby

The heaviness has left my heart. Sure, Mr. Creepy Letters is probably out there somewhere setting his silver pen of terror to black paper.

But tonight, I'm safe with Rooster.

I grab my bag and duck into the bathroom to wash up and brush my teeth. I still can't find my jammy pants so I slip on a T-shirt.

Rooster's shirtless with only a sheet covering him from the waist down when I return. It's impossible to stay mad at him. Not when he tucks his hands behind his head, displaying his body like some sort of Viking warrior determined to claim my heart forever.

I drop my bag on my side of the bed and flop down next him, trying not to stare.

"What's wrong, chickadee?" He doesn't even bother to hide his smug smile at catching me checking him out.

"You think you can lie there being all sexy and your manly muscles will make me drop my panties, don't you?"

"You're not wearing panties." In a quick move, he powers forward and wraps one big hand around my ankle, yanking me under him. He's so dang strong, I might as well be a rag doll.

I reach up, touching his cheek, memorizing every detail of his face. The chasm of love in my heart for this man scares me to pieces.

"You know how much I love everything about you?" He brushes his lips over my forehead, my nose, my eyelids, and finally, my lips.

"I love you too," I whisper against his mouth. "So much…"

"I need you in my life." He runs his tongue down the column of my neck, stopping to suck at the sensitive dip between my neck and shoulder.

"Gah."

He rumbles with laughter. "What's that?"

I can't form an answer.

Ribbons of desire uncurl and float through me as he licks the pad of his thumb. "I could come just from watching you do *that*."

One corner of his mouth hitches up. "That right?"

I'm hyperaware of his hand sneaking under my T-shirt, grazing my thigh, and finally, of him rolling his thumb around my sweet spot.

"It means you're going to do *that*," I whisper.

"Do what?" He slips a finger inside me.

"Touch me *there*."

He adds a second finger. "Where?"

My toes curl into the comforter, balling it up under my feet.

"Oh, God." He goes deeper, hooking his fingers to rub the sensitive spot inside he alone has discovered and claimed.

He pushes my shirt up with his free hand and rains kisses from my stomach to the tops of my thighs. I struggle to sit up and wrestle the shirt off, then brace both hands on the mattress so I can watch his fingers disappear in and out.

I sigh and fall back as he picks up the pace. Tendrils of pleasure ripple down my legs. Warm, gentle waves reverberate throughout my body.

"Do you have any idea how addicted I am to making you come?" He presses another kiss to my inner thigh.

I glance down at him. "Maybe a little bit of a clue." I let my head fall back.

The bed shifts. There's the crinkle of a condom wrapper and then he returns, covering my body with his, entering me in one long, slow stroke.

"Come here," he says softly, gathering me into a full-body embrace. I wrap my arms and legs around him, tipping my hips so he can thrust deeper.

I can't stop running my hands through his hair and down his back. Over his strong, sturdy shoulders. He dips down, taking my mouth in a blazing sweet kiss. When he draws back, he's wearing that feral smile again.

He pulls out. I gasp in surprise. "What are you doing?"

In a quick, determined move, he lifts my hips and flips me over. "Show me that pose that drives me fucking nuts," he demands.

I peer over my shoulder and arch a brow. "Which one?"

"Lady's choice."

I shift my knees hip-width apart and stretch my arms in front of me, pressing my chest to the mattress. This one always seems to make him the growliest.

"Fuck yeah." His rough palm skates over my back. Under me, the mattress dips. Strong hands grip my hips, pulling me toward him as he slowly slides home.

I gasp and squirm, shimmying my hips. "You're too big for my britches."

His deep, warm laughter bubbles over me. "Fuck, I love the stuff that comes out of your mouth."

He pushes forward and I gasp again.

"Easy," he warns. "Up, up." He tugs my hips, urgency bleeding into his voice. I press my palms into the bed, lifting myself.

He uses the new position to adjust his angle and slide in deeper, slowly at first, giving me time.

"Oh, fuck, that's better." I moan and arch my back, digging the heels of my hands into the mattress for leverage.

I'm panting, squirming, and pushing against him when he drapes his body over me, one hand resting next to mine to keep the bulk of his weight off me. He pushes my hair to the side and kisses my shoulder.

"Shelby." His raw, gritty voice spirals my desire even higher. "I'm fucking you doggy-style and it's not even forty-five minutes later." He rumbles with laughter. "Admit my intuition is on point."

I attempt to crawl forward but he won't let me, digging his fingers into my hips and pulling me back against him. The gesture says everything. Rooster may be sweet but he's in control. Exactly the kind of man I want.

Still, I can't help teasing him. "Actually, right now, you're being smug." I wiggle my hips and barely bite back a moan. "Not fuckin'."

"Yeah?" He lets out a deep growl and jerks his hips forward. Hard. "How about now?"

This time, I let go and surrender, stretching my arms in front of me again. I suck in a ragged breath. "Your intuition is king."

A growl of satisfaction rumbles out of him. He picks up a slow, steady pace, gliding along the perfect spot over and over.

"Oh. Right there."

He kisses the curve between my neck and shoulder, scraping his teeth against my skin. Tingles burst over me, joining the riot of sensations. He slips his hand between my legs, swirling his fingers around my clit. "You like that?"

"Y-yes." I tightly close my eyes, concentrating on the building pleasure.

He squeezes my ass, giving me a soft pop on each cheek before hammering into me with short, quick strokes. "Love your body. You drive me wild all day. Do you realize that?" He trails his fingers down my spine. "Love how soft you are all over. Fit me so well." He grazes my inner thighs. "Love how strong you are too."

Our bodies might be grinding and roughly chasing release, but he's making love to me with decadent words that leave me speechless.

"Logan," I gasp. He seems bigger, thicker than ever. Sparks light me up and I'm falling over the cliff into nothing but bliss.

His body shudders and he stops moving, pulsing inside me, his fingers digging into my hips, holding me still. "Fuck."

Closing my eyes, I fall against the mattress. He drops down next to me, curling his body around mine. His big, rough hands rub my hip, my stomach, traveling higher to caress my shoulder. "I didn't hurt you, did I?"

I turn over, squirming to get closer. I cup his face, stroking his bristly cheek with my thumb, staring into his eyes, willing him to *feel* my love for him. "Nope. I think you put me back together."

CHAPTER FIFTY-NINE

Rooster

I'm up early the next morning, searching the clubhouse for Ice. I find him in his office, staring at the computer.

My knock seems to startle him. He blinks and lifts his gaze.

"Hey, Prez. Do you have time to chat?"

"Yeah. Come on in."

"Heard there was some excitement over at the house yesterday. Is Anya okay?"

"She's fine." He lifts his chin. "She's upstairs."

"That's good. She's safe here." I really don't have time for small talk and slowly getting to the point. "So I have to ask. . .This is going to sound weird, but I need to borrow a few cameras. Just for the day."

"This ought to be good." He cracks a smile.

I explain Shelby's situation and what I'm planning to do.

He's not laughing by the time I finish. He sits back in his chair with a thump. "That's fucked up, Rooster."

"Since I disconnected the camera in my room..." I smirk at him, "... do you mind if I borrow it? And a few others?"

He frowns at me. "What are you talking about?"

I point to the corner of the room over his right shoulder where there's a camera pointed at us. "Focused on the bed. A little disappointing, to be honest, brother."

Without a hint of shame or remorse, he laughs. "Where'd Shonda put you?"

"Second floor, right hallway."

"Fuck. That's not where we usually stick brothers. Sorry about that."

"I'm relieved you weren't hoping to secretly tape me whacking off, but what the fuck *are* they there for?"

A cold smile curves his lips. "Insurance."

I slap my hand on his desk and stand. "On second thought, I don't even want to know."

"Probably safer that way."

"So, you mind if I borrow some electronics? She has the next two nights off, so I'll get my own gear—"

He slashes his hand through the air, cutting me off. "Don't bother with that. I've got a few things that will work much better to help you catch this sick fucker."

ANOTHER DAY COOPED UP IN A CAGE. IN THE SUMMER. PERFECT riding weather too. But there was no way to haul all this equipment to the arena on my bike. I'm grateful Ice doesn't mind loaning out his truck, along with the thousands of dollars in cameras and computers.

Shelby twists and stares at the boxes of goodies in the back seat. We shot her sunrise salutation video in the clubhouse's backyard against the mountain backdrop. For a quick job, it came out nice. She said a few words to her fans, blew them a kiss, and we called it a wrap.

I have a screen to play it on, three cameras for surveillance, a giant black viewing booth, a tablet, and a laptop.

"I don't even want to know what the giant black box was used for," Shelby says. "Magician porn? Vampire porn?"

"The possibilities are endless, chickadee. I didn't ask too many questions."

I park near her van again, and Jigsaw slides up on my side.

"Logan, wait." Shelby rests her hand on my thigh.

"What's wrong?" I flip the middle console out of our way and pull her closer.

She stares up at me with wide, glassy eyes. "Thank you. For all of... for everything you're doing. You don't have to. It means a lot," she finishes on a whisper.

I cup her cheek, rubbing my thumb over her bottom lip. "You trust me?"

"I do." Her answer comes without hesitation and it socks me in the gut.

I can't let her down.

"Come on. Big day today." I force more enthusiasm than I'm feeling into my voice. If it were up to me, I'd keep her locked up at the clubhouse where no one could get near her. "Sold-out show. Then two days off."

"I'm *so* looking forward to two whole days with you."

"Same. How's your throat feel?" My gaze slides over her face and neck as she hums and works her jaw from side to side.

"Hurts a little."

"We're gonna have to rest your voice the next two days."

Jigsaw raps his knuckles against the glass. "Feelin' a little left out here, guys!" he shouts through the window.

"Jackass," I grumble.

Shelby pokes a finger in my side. "Be nice."

There's no sign of Greg yet. Shelby sends a text to let him know we're here. I want to set up my "viewing booth" as early as possible but I need to know which part of her merchandise table I can monopolize. For now, Jiggy and I drop off everything in her dressing room.

Trent leans against the doorframe. "Morning. Greg's down at security, checking out tapes from yesterday."

At least he's being useful.

A few minutes later, Greg stumbles into the room with a book tucked under his arm. Dark shadows under his eyes, wrinkled pants— doesn't look like anything good kept him up all night.

"Morning, Shelby. You ready for tonight?" His forced, upbeat tone fires up my danger radar.

"I will be."

"Logan, can I talk to you out here for a sec?" Greg motions me into the hallway. Jigsaw follows. Trent stays behind with Shelby.

Greg pulls a black envelope out of the book he's carrying.

I swear under my breath. "How? When?"

"Trent found it on the van's windshield this morning," he says in a low voice.

"At the *hotel*?"

His grave expression doesn't change. "Yes."

"Bro, this is bad." Jigsaw elbows me. "Thank fuck you brought her to the clubhouse last night."

"I have to agree." Greg's gaze drops to the envelope. "He's escalating."

I snap the envelope out of his hand and open it carefully.

Dearest Shelby,

Your voice is such a lovely gift. It's a crime to share it with a world that does not appreciate you. Up close, you remind me of a soft, tiny rabbit. Cautious, yet unaware of the dangers that surround vulnerable creatures in need of the safety of a cage.

You seem awfully cozy with that big, bearded man. A man that crude can't possibly provide the discipline you require. Or supply you with the proper intellectual stimulation you have been lacking.

Worry not—I am capable of providing for you and our children. You won't need to pursue anything else. Your heart will be content where you belong. You were built to properly care for your husband and children. I will lavish you with all the attention you require. In case you misunderstood my other letters— you belong to me, Shelby.

Very soon.

M

Fear—something I haven't felt in a long time—snakes through my insides, followed by mind-melting *rage*. I'm going to gut this motherfucker and hang him from a fucking tree as a warning to every other sicko.

"Bro, what the ever-loving fuck?" Jigsaw's low, disbelieving voice is almost as disturbing as the letter itself. Not much shocks him. "This dude's fifty kinds of twisted."

"It's bad," Greg agrees. "I've never seen anything quite that... unsettling before."

"You've had other clients deal with stalkers?"

"Obsessed fans that get carried away." He stops and seems to consider the question carefully. "No one that seemed to mean actual harm. *This* guy is several Fruit Loops short of a cereal box." He slips the letter out of my fingers and tucks it back inside the book. "Dawson sweet-talked the hotel manager into letting us go through the security footage. It's hard to tell from the angle of the camera and where we were parked, but it looks like it was this guy."

He turns his phone my way and a grainy picture fills the screen. From the width and set of the shoulders, it's almost certainly a man. He's average height, judging him against the vehicles in the background. On the heavier side. Wearing a windbreaker with the hood obscuring his face. The image is one fucking notch above useless.

"It's not great." Greg echoes my thoughts. "I have a copy of the video, and I'll send it to you to compare against the ones from tonight."

"Thank you."

"Local PD won't do anything. I think they figure we're rolling out of their jurisdiction tomorrow, so it's not their problem."

"Big surprise."

"I have an FBI contact but until there's more of an overt threat, they won't get involved either."

"That's just fucking great." Jigsaw smacks my arm. "We've got this, bro."

"You got some space for me up front?" I ask Greg.

"It's all set up. The girls working the table know you're installing a booth but they don't know about any of this. Just that it's for the fans. Anyone is allowed to stop in and check it out."

"Good." This is better than I'd hoped for. I'd fully expected Greg to dick me around all morning. Guess *this* letter finally woke his ass up.

"Listen, I don't want to tell Shelby about this now." Greg lowers his voice. "Not before her show."

Fuck. I don't want to keep stuff from her, but I'm not sure what good it will do to terrify her when she needs to start shifting her mindset to going onstage. "I'll bring her up to speed tonight."

Behind us, the door opens and I quickly stand back, hoping Shelby didn't overhear us. But it's Trent. He lifts his chin my way. "She's looking for you."

Is that a note of sadness or disappointment in his voice? I've always wondered if he and Shelby were ever more than bandmates or if he has feelings for her. What better way to have her jump in his lap than by scaring the shit out of her while she's away from home and everything familiar—except him?

"You're the one who found the letter this morning, Trent?" My mind's spinning in a hundred different directions. Gut instinct says it's *not* Trent but I can't help asking the question.

He widens his stance and places his hands on his hips. "Yeah, why? Kenny and Eric were with me."

The whole band could be in on it. Maybe they resent being no-name touring musicians. Shelby doesn't interact with anyone besides Trent that much. What if they decided to fuck with her?

"Everyone's concerned about this, Logan," Greg says, clearly reading my thoughts. "We all need Shelby to succeed."

"How long you known Shelby, Trent?" I ask.

"Years. Why?"

"She got any psycho ex-boyfriends? Maybe one who's jealous she's gaining some fame?"

"Shoot." He rubs his hand over his jaw. "Uh, she's dated a lot of assholes. Like, a *lot*. Swear the girl's an asshole magnet."

"All right," I growl. "Get to the point."

"I wasn't exactly privy to details and such. We don't discuss our love lives unless we're writing a song about it, ya know?" He scratches at his chin again. "Cheaters, cheapskates, fuckboys, but none of 'em stick out as psycho enough to write those disturbing letters."

I chew on that information for a few seconds.

Jigsaw taps my arm. "It's gotta be an older dude. No one her age writes *letters*. Fuck, half of 'em don't even know how to handwrite anymore."

"Okay, Grandpa," Trent mutters.

Jigsaw turns his scary eyes Trent's way. "Your guardian angel must day drink."

Trent, wisely, backs up.

"All right," Greg cuts in. "Logan, let's get you set up."

AN HOUR AND A HALF LATER, MY VIEWING BOTH LOOKS PRETTY damn good for something thrown together in less than twenty-four hours.

"What's up with you?" Jigsaw asks on the way back to Shelby's dressing room. "You think Trent's got a thing for her?"

"Don't know. His explanation of her dating history sure shed some light on her trust issues, though."

He stops walking and slaps his arm against my chest. "Trust. Issues. Where the *fuck* did you even hear a phrase like that?"

"Shut up."

"So you've had the relationship 'talk?' You're all committed and shit now?"

"No, I'm down here spending my morning cobbling together an *Inspector Gadget* spy booth for funsies. What the fuck do you think?"

"You never talked about her past?"

"You met her last boyfriend. The one who let her fall in the river and laughed about it."

"Riiiight. Shelby in her wet dress was a lovely sight." He closes his eyes and grins like a puppy laying in the sunshine.

"Knock it off." I slam my fist into his shoulder.

He scowls at me and rubs his arm. "She wasn't your girlfriend then. I can maintain that image in my whack album."

"I'm gonna whack *every* image out of your head if you don't knock it the fuck off."

"Fine. Fine."

We continue moving through the arena. The doors haven't opened yet, so the only people we pass are employees in their black and yellow shirts.

Shelby's sitting cross-legged on her yoga mat with her eyes closed when we enter her dressing room.

I close the door quietly behind us.

"Is she trying to float?" Jigsaw whispers loud enough to shake leaves off a tree.

"No, Jiggy." Shelby opens her eyes and smiles at us. "Just getting myself centered. How'd it go?"

"Good. I'm gonna have you come back out with me, and we'll film a few short videos to post online to let people know about it." I set the laptop Ice loaned us on the table and check that the video feed is working. "I sent Ice the video Greg had. He's going to monitor tonight's feed from his location while you're onstage to see if he notices anyone familiar."

"Really?" Shelby stretches and stands, bending over to roll up her mat.

"Eyes over here, fuckface," I growl at Jigsaw.

"Jiggy's just trying to inject some humor into our tense day, right?" Shelby tiptoes over to me and leans up for a kiss.

"No." I wrap my arms around her and tug her against me. "He's begging me to invert his fucking ribcage."

She tilts her head, peering at him over her shoulder. "You're a good friend for trying to take Rooster's mind off things."

"Suuure, you busted me." Jigsaw holds up his hands. "That's exactly what I was doing. It had nothing at all to do with those shorts tattooed to your perfect—"

"Do you *want* me to skin you alive?" I reach past Shelby and smack his shoulder.

He grins at me.

"If we get anything promising, I'm sending it to Z," I say, ignoring Jigsaw. "He has...access to a few databases."

"I don't want to know, do I?" Shelby asks.

"Probably not." The less details she has, the better.

Because as soon as I find this fucker, he's dead.

CHAPTER SIXTY

Rooster

Laptop is all set in her dressing room. I'm bummed that I'll have to watch *it* instead of Shelby's performance tonight. Jigsaw's at the table, already fiddling with the tablet he'll use to keep track of things.

"I'm sorry I'm gonna miss your show." I hug Shelby around her waist and lean down to kiss her forehead.

"You'll be able to hear me." She lowers her voice. "There's no one else I trust more to help me end this."

"I'm gonna try my damnedest. I can't guarantee he'll show up. But if he does—"

"I'm gonna boil his fucking teeth for scaring you, girl," Jigsaw promises, not even glancing away from his screen.

"That's...macabre." Shelby wrinkles her nose. "But thank you."

The doors to the arena opened an hour ago. I've been studying footage of fans popping in to view the video ever since. The camera's motion-activated and only records for a short time. But it's enough to get what I think we need.

We capture a lot of kids and teenagers. Mostly girls. I delete those clips right away. Our stalker has to be a guy, so any male eighteen to sixty-five who sticks his head in that booth is getting added to our files. The rest don't matter.

It's time for her to go.

"Stick with Bane after the show," I remind her. "I'll tear down the booth and meet you back here, okay?"

"All right."

I curl my hand around her neck, guide her head up, and slide my mouth over hers, tasting her and torturing myself in the process.

By the time she pulls away, I'm hard enough to pound nails through concrete. I lean down and brush my lips against her ear. "We skipped your pre-show orgasm. Tonight, I'll owe you double."

She slicks her tongue over her bottom lip. "I can't wait to collect."

I hate letting her go, but I release her with one final kiss on her cheek. "You'll be awesome tonight. I know it."

"Thank you."

"Kick ass, Shelby." Jigsaw barely glances up.

She throws us one last "thank you" before slipping out the door.

Feels like my heart went along with her, leaving me behind.

"Did I miss anything good?"

Jigsaw studies his screen. "Bro, there are a *lot* of hot moms here. I never suspected this would be such a—"

Here I am thinking he's taking this seriously. "Focus, please."

We're both quiet after that. The roar of the crowd and echo of music along with Shelby's muffled voice filters down to us, and my lips twitch.

"You want to go watch her? I can keep an eye on this," Jigsaw offers.

"Not tonight. Once we work out a system, I'll feel more comfortable."

"Shit, Rooster. I hope this isn't gonna go on much longer. She can't deal with that stress on top of the pressure of the tour and performing every night."

Maybe I shouldn't have threatened to skin him earlier. "I know."

THIRTY-FIVE MINUTES LATER, I'M SERIOUSLY DOUBTING THIS "genius" idea of mine. Kids. Parents. Teenagers. College kids. A bunch of frat-boy-looking types who whoop it up, high-five each other and make jerk-off hand motions about Shelby's yoga video. Clearly, the yoga was a terrible idea. How did I not see *that* coming? Makeup tutorials and music sessions, it is from now on. Thank fuck there's no sound, or I'd probably be out there on a murder spree.

A sweaty, older man pops onto the screen. Finally, the demographic I've been looking for all night. The hair on the back of my neck prickles.

"Jiggy, come here."

He stands behind my chair, leaning over to see better.

"Bring up the other video." Without taking my eyes off the screen, I tap my phone, sitting on the table next to the computer.

He pulls up the video Greg sent me earlier and examines it for a few seconds before studying my screen. "Could be."

I trace the image of the guy on my screen with my finger. "Height's about right. Set and size of his shoulders. I wish I had set this up to capture people walking away."

"What's he doing?" Jigsaw taps the screen. "Is that an envelope he's taking out of that...bag? What is that? Is he leaving a fucking letter right now?"

"No," I mutter, concentrating on the images. The lighting isn't the best. It's dark around the edges and the booth itself is black so I can't tell if it's one of those black envelopes in his hand or something less sinister.

The guy finally leaves, and a twenty-something couple takes his place.

"She's almost done. Let's get up there and break it down." I stand and close the laptop just in case any of the venue staff come into the room. We never asked the arena's permission. The camera will continue recording clips and storing them online.

"What if he visits the booth during Dawson's set?"

While I considered that, I also want to get Shelby out of here as soon as possible. Going forward, Jiggy or I should probably monitor things until the end of the show.

The asshole probably has front-row seats and ran straight for them when the doors opened. With Trent's help, we secured a small camera to Shelby's mic stand. I'll be able to get some video of her audience but it's not like she can swing the damn thing around, David Lee Roth style. I'll look over that once we're at the clubhouse.

We stalk through the mostly empty corridors. A few of Dawson's people nod as we walk by. I pull the pass around my neck out so it's clearly visible and check to make sure Jiggy has his. Last thing I need is some rent-a-bouncer giving me shit. I'm so worked up, I'm liable to knock a motherfucker out.

I hit the bar across the door that opens into the left side of the arena. The sound triples in intensity. I glance toward the front of the room, catching a glimpse of Shelby. So tiny on that wide stage. So powerful the way she has the audience's full attention tonight.

Pride and love curl together in my chest.

I scan the crowd from where we're standing, the rows and rows of packed seats. There are fans on their feet, hands over their heads. Little girls sitting on their father's shoulders waving glitter-heart-sprinkled signs bearing Shelby's name.

Determination to protect my girl fuels me.

Anger burns through every other emotion. Someone out there wants to ruin all of this for Shelby.

"Like looking for salt in a pickle jar!" Jigsaw shouts.

"What? Never mind. Come on."

The merchandise area is busier than I expected. As usual, Dawson's table has the most activity. The stacks of T-shirts at Shelby's station are much lower than they were a few hours ago, though. That's a good sign.

I nod to the girls behind the table before we start dismantling the booth.

Jigsaw secures the screen and other equipment in a cushioned crate while I break down the three-sided box and fold the black curtain.

"We should Lysol this all down." Jigsaw lifts his chin at the box he's carrying. "Probably crawling with germs now."

"Great observation. Add Clorox wipes to the list of improvements for next time, ya fuck nugget." I jerk my head toward the corridor leading backstage. "Can we get moving now?"

I want to make it to her dressing room before she does, and the last notes of Shelby's final song are already floating through the air.

"Hey! You two. Stop right there."

The command rubs against my awareness but they can't possibly be talking to us, so I keep moving.

Something heavy slams into my back, shoving me into the wall. Everything I'm carrying clatters to the floor.

"What the fuck!" My shout ends up muffled as my face is smooshed against the cold, filthy, white, cinderblock wall.

"You better start praying to your gods, motherfucker!" Jigsaw snarls as he gets the same face-into-the-wall treatment.

The need to get to my girl, to protect her, crawls down my spine.

The timing of this can't be an accident.

CHAPTER SIXTY-ONE

Shelby

Backstage is packed tight after my set. Bane's waiting for me and tucks me under his arm. Trent flanks my other side.

"Did Rooster catch anyone?" I ask Bane.

"Don't know."

"Is Greg with him too?"

"I think he's with Dawson," Bane answers.

Trent elbows me. "CMA nominations are supposed to be announced tomorrow. Are you excited?"

A lick of fear twisted with excitement and doubt coils in my stomach. "Maybe."

We keep walking. The din from the crowd drowns out most of the conversations around us. The pain in my throat prevents me from keeping up my end of the conversation.

Is it too much to hope that they find this creep tonight so we can stop this silliness? My heart pitter-patters. Rooster's going to join me on tour. I want to spend as much time as possible with him. Not force him to monitor boring videos every night.

Bane opens my dressing room door and waits for me to go inside.

Trent quickly searches the space behind the couch. He frowns at an orange handcart in the corner. "Want me to load your trunk now?"

"Not yet." I glance down at my dress. I need to change and pull out some clothes for the next two days.

"Don't go anywhere." He lifts his chin toward the makeup table. "Drink some water. You're soundin' a little raspy."

I rub my fingertips under my chin. "I'm glad we have the next two nights off. My throat's killing me," I whisper.

His mouth turns down. "You're so good about taking care of your voice. Maybe the tour is too much?"

I lift my shoulders. "It'll get better as I get used to it. Just muscles I gotta condition, right?" I force a smile, but tonight, even that hurts.

"We can talk about it another time. Rest your throat." He flashes a quick smile. "I'll be back for your trunk, so keep it decent when Rooster gets here."

I mouth "*shut up*" and push him toward the door.

After he's gone, I grab the bottle of water on my dresser and twist off the cap, sucking down almost half of it in deep, greedy swallows.

A salty tang coats my tongue and I stare at the bottle for a second before setting it down. Have to remember to ask for a different brand from now on.

I open the door and nod to Bane. "Have you seen Rooster?"

He shakes his head.

"I'm going to..." I mime taking off my dress and stepping into a pair of pants. He gives me a half-smile and reassuring nod.

"Thanks."

I grab my phone and send Rooster a quick text.

Me: Where are you?

No response.

Me: I'll be in bathroom changing. Can you grab a bottle of water or Sprite on your way back? Stuff in room is nasty.

I stare at the phone for a few minutes, waiting for an answer.

Still nothing.

Odd.

Maybe they actually caught Mr. Creepy Letters.

I hurry into the bathroom to change. Inside, it's stuffy as hell. I glance up to the bathroom window. It's wide open, letting in all the evening heat. I slam it shut but unless I stand on the toilet, I can't latch it.

"Shelby?" Bane calls out.

"Yeah?"

"I gotta run down to Dawson's. I'm locking the door. Don't open it for anyone except me or Rooster, okay? I'll be right back."

"Okay." The outer door clicks closed. I scurry to check that it's actually locked.

I send Rooster another text.

Me: Door locked. Knock three times.

I close and lock the bathroom door behind me.

A wave of dizziness washes over me and I stagger to the sink, bracing myself against the cool porcelain, setting my phone on the edge.

Can't breathe.

Get dress off. I'll feel better once it's off.

I work the zipper as far as I can and squirm-wiggle my way out of the rest of it, allowing the dress to pool at my feet.

That's better.

Beads of sweat roll from my temple, down my cheeks. I flip on the faucet and lean over to splash water on my face.

Mistake. Now I've made a mess of all my stupid stage makeup. Where's my remover? Out in the other room?

Fuzziness clouds my mind.

I splash another handful of water on my face and snag a paper towel to blot my skin.

Get dressed.

I yank off my boots, almost falling on my ass.

What the hell's wrong with me?

First, pants. One leg. Then the other. I wobble and bump my butt against the wall, leaning back to fasten my jeans.

My T-shirt seems to have sprouted three armholes. I jam my fist through the neck, then have to take it off and try again. Finally, the long, loose cotton flows down to my hips. I scoop the ends, attempting to tie a knot but my fingers don't seem to want to work.

Whatever. It looks fine.

I stuff my feet back into my boots and stagger forward. My palms land on the slippery sink and slide.

Bang.

My forehead smacks against the mirror.

"Ouch."

I rub the spot.

Is this heat exhaustion? Dehydration?

Behind me, there's a soft screech. The shower curtain rustles.

My heart thunders, trying to gallop out of my chest.

A man steps out.

Holy fuck, I'm in a horror movie!

The fleeting thought that I wish I had a weapon—gun, taser, pepper spray, or heck, even Heidi's ball peen hammer would be a relief. But I've got nothing except the cowgirl boots on my feet. Unfortunately, my legs are encased in concrete. Too weak to even knee this guy in the balls.

A scream sticks in my throat.

Dim recognition tickles the back of my mind.

He's wearing the same black and yellow polo shirts the other employees of the arena wear. But that's not it.

The fan. He gave me a fan at one of the shows.

"Shh." He places one finger against his lips and rushes forward. Malicious insanity burns in his eyes.

Terror steals my breath.

My palms hit his chest and I push. "Get. Away," I slur.

He staggers back a step, eyebrows lifting all the way to his hairline.

"Easy, little rabbit. I'm here to take care of you. It's time for us to be together."

Warnings explode in my head like fire alarms, piercing the fog clouding my brain.

Mr. Creepy Letters is in my bathroom!

I need to get away. Yell for Bane. Grab my cell phone.

"Rooster!" I scream.

"Oh, is that the big, bearded man's name?" He flashes a sinister smile that stings my guts. "He's indisposed at the moment."

What does that mean? Did he hurt Rooster?

Fear that somehow I contributed to the man I love getting hurt rips through my chest.

I'm backed into a corner. The door seems so far away. I reach for my phone, but the man shoves it off the sink. It flies in the air, landing on the floor, cracking my pretty mint green and flamingo print case.

Get out! I try to shove past him, but my arms are two limp strands of spaghetti.

Air wheezes through my lungs.

"It's okay, Shelby. We're going to be so happy together. I've always wanted the perfect wife to give me a large family." He licks his lips and drops his gaze to my stomach.

Oh, hell no.

He smiles wide. Rows and rows of shiny shark teeth.

Huh?

I shake my head. My vision blurs and now there are four shark-toothed people standing in front of me.

Something hard clamps around my wrist.

I jerk and twist. Fear burns through the cloudiness in my head. A scream tears out of me, like shards of glass shattering against my throat.

"The time has come. I can't have you cavorting around with these men any longer. It's not good for us."

Inside, I'm madder than a mule chewing on wasps. But my body can't seem to will the anger into action.

"Shh." He presses his finger to my lips. "Stay right here."

He guides me to the toilet and sits me down on the closed lid. My body slumps against the wall.

Do something. The bathroom door's wide open.

My gaze swings wildly around the bathroom, searching for a weapon.

Plunger.

Eww.

Better than a toilet brush.

I wrap my cotton ball fingers around the wooden handle, willing some strength into my limbs.

There's rustling, a bang, and a scraping sound. Mr. Creepy Letters appears in the doorway dragging my trunk behind him.

"You're going to have to be a good girl and get in there for me so we can leave without any questions."

Like hell. I'm not claustrophobic but who wants to take a ride in their luggage?

"How'd ya reckon we're meant to be together if ya gotta drug me and stuff me in a trunk?" The words seep out of my mouth slowly.

"I need to get you away from all of this and deprogram you. Then you'll understand."

Deprogram. I don't even want to guess what that means.

"You didn't finish this." He holds out the water bottle to me. "Here."

"Hell fuckin' no!" I smack the bottle out of his hold but use my hand holding the plunger. My burst of energy fizzles fast. I end up grazing his cheek with the rubber end, knocking the bottle onto the floor. The plunger goes flying into the shower stall.

I stare at my empty hand.

Well, that was about as effective as using a dishtowel to swat at a wasp's nest.

He lunges, grabbing my wrists and yanking me to my feet. My noodle legs refuse to cooperate, and I sag toward the floor. He uses my weakness, turning us toward the trunk and letting gravity do the work.

My ass lands in the trunk so hard tears prick my eyes. The backs of my thighs hit the metal edge and I yelp from the pain. My elbow burns from hitting something in the fall.

The man leans over, grabbing my ankles, attempting to fold me neatly inside like a damn tablecloth. I scrabble for the opposite edge, curling my fingers around the lip of the trunk.

With a grunt, he slams the lid. It bounces off my head. Good thing or he probably would've broken my fingers. In a daze, I stare at my hand. I need my fingers.

The blow to my head finishes the job the drug-laced water bottle started. My ears are muffled, like I've been plunged into a lake.

Rooster, please save me!

Slowly, I slump into the trunk, silently screaming at the darkness coming to claim me.

CHAPTER SIXTY-TWO

Rooster

"Sir, someone reported that you're carrying a gun. We need to search both of you for weapons," the asshole at my back informs me.

"Are you fucking kidding?"

"Do you give consent to search you?"

"You can see my fucking pass." I fumble for the lanyard around my neck and fling it backwards. "Shelby Morgan's my girlfriend."

He snorts. "Sure, buddy."

"Listen, you stupid fuck. She's got some creep stalking her. I need to be there when she gets offstage."

"She's got security. You can wait here a second."

"*I'm* her security, motherfucker."

"Sooner we can search you, the faster you can go."

"Knock yourself out." My need to get to Shelby blazes hotter than my need to kill this stupid prick.

I have no doubt who's responsible for this.

Terror melts my brain. Shelby's in danger and I have no way to warn her. "Hurry it up."

"Just hold your horses."

"Sir! Sir! What are you doing!? That's Shelby Morgan's boyfriend," a high-pitched female voice I don't recognize screams.

Thank fuck.

"I'm filming all of this, Logan!"

Cindy.

"Cindy, get Greg. Or anyone. Make sure someone's with Shelby," I shout. Something about this fucking reeks.

"For fuck's sake," Jigsaw growls "Let's fuck them up and go."

I twist my head and count. Five bouncers surround us now. But it's not the uneven number stopping me. Jigsaw and I could still easily take them. It's the pile of bullshit it will cause, delaying us even longer, that holds me back.

"They're clean," one of the guards announces.

I push away from the wall, barely restraining myself from punching the closest motherfucker.

Cindy—bless her soul—is still standing behind us, filming everything.

"You better pray I don't find you later," I swear at the guard who stopped us.

"We had a report. I had to—"

I don't even bother listening. My feet are already flying over the floor. The metal door slams into the concrete wall with a *clang* and bounces back. It clanks a second time. Jigsaw's heavy boots thunder behind me.

It's intermission. Shelby's offstage. People swarm into the aisles, blocking our way. I'm forced to slow to a maddening walk-push pace.

Bang!

I crash through the second door leading backstage. So many damn people in the way now. Crew are breaking down Shelby's set and setting up Thundersmoke's equipment. I blow past all of them.

"Logan! What's wrong?"

Trent's nothing more than a blur. I don't stop to answer. Jiggy and I pick up speed as we move past the activity near the entrance to the stage.

My gaze lasers in on Shelby's dressing room door. Slightly ajar. No Bane. No one in the immediate area at all.

Above us, the ceiling rumbles with sounds from Thundersmoke's show. Fine, everyone's probably up there watching, but Bane should still be here.

"Thought he was still watching her?" Jigsaw says.

"He should be."

I slam the door all the way open. The knob smashes into the drywall. A small part of my brain yells "take it easy" but the rest of my body disagrees. If something has happened to Shelby, I can't waste a precious second.

"Shelby?"

I rush into the room, my mind cataloging small details.

Piles of clothes dumped on the couch. More clothes scattered by the bedroom.

My fist hits the cheap wood door. "Shelby!"

No answer.

I shove the door open.

My gaze pings around the small room. My brain processes the scene too slowly.

Open window.

Water bottle on the floor.

Shelby's smashed phone.

The dress she wore onstage crumpled in a heap.

No Shelby.

My instincts scream at me to *run.*

Find her.

"Shelby!" I shout.

She's gone.

Rooster and Shelby's story concludes in
Lyrics on the Wind.

LOST KINGS MC WORLD

The Lost Kings MC® World

by Autumn Jones Lake

Sometimes I'm asked where the spin-off books fit into the series. If you wanted to read all the Lost Kings MC world books in chronological order, it would look something like this.

1. Kickstart My Heart (Hollywood Demons #1)

2. Blow My Fuse (Hollywood Demons #2)

3. Wheels of Fire (Hollywood Demons #3)

4. Cards of Love: Knight of Swords (Standalone in the Lost Kings MC world)

5. Slow Burn (Lost Kings MC #1)

6. Corrupting Cinderella (Lost Kings MC #2)

7. Three Kings, One Night (Lost Kings MC #2.5)

8. Strength From Loyalty (Lost Kings MC #3)

9. Tattered on My Sleeve (Lost Kings MC #4)

10. White Heat (Lost Kings MC #5)

11. Between Embers (Lost Kings MC #5.5) 1

2. Bullets & Bonfires (Standalone in the Lost Kings MC world)

13. More Than Miles (Lost Kings MC #6)

14. Warnings & Wildfires (Standalone in the Lost Kings MC world)

15. White Knuckles (Lost Kings MC #7)

16. Beyond Reckless (Lost Kings MC #8)

17. Beyond Reason (Lost Kings MC #9)

18. One Empire Night (Lost Kings MC #9.5)

19. After Burn (Lost Kings MC #10)

20. After Glow (Lost Kings MC #11)

21. Zero Hour (Lost Kings MC #11.5)

ABOUT THE AUTHOR

Autumn Jones Lake is the *USA Today* and *Wall Street Journal* bestselling author of over twenty novels, including the popular Lost Kings MC series. She believes true love stories never end.

Her past lives include baking cookies, bagging groceries, selling cheap shoes, and practicing law. Playing with her imaginary friends all day is by far her favorite job yet!

Autumn lives in upstate New York with her own alpha hero.

www.autumnjoneslake.com

f   facebook.com/autumnjoneslake
g   goodreads.com/autumnjoneslake
p   pinterest.com/autumnjoneslake